Welcome to the Lowcountry
of South Carolina

Where the summers are long,
The nights are sweaty,
And the swamps have a funny way
of hiding not just the past,
but the dead . . .
And the dying .

. . . that's been trapped down there for decades, maybe centuries . . . and makes you wonder if there ain't something really dark and shameful down there decaying in the bottom of the swamp—like festering corpses of unrighteous relatives or somethin'—trying to bubble to the surface to scare the hell out of you.

The secrets in the swamps are calling . . .
Down in the Lowcountry

Lowcountry Rising

It's been called "insightful, scintillating, heart-warming, witty, and eloquent." It's been declared "raw, penetrating, powerful, romantic, and *knuckle-biting suspenseful*."

It's a book about the past . . . that's ahead of it's time . . .

And it just might change your life.

Lowcountry Rising, a novel by Samuel Othello Barlow, will take you places you never knew existed. Down low. To the bottom of the bottom—where light seldom reaches.

The secrets in the swamps are calling . . .

"*Lowcountry Rising* is a masterpiece—a fast-paced and action-packed, yet cerebral, novel. Far ahead of its time, this first-person narrative submerses its readers right into the psyche of the main character. From all my years of reviewing the world's best literature, it's my opinion that *Lowcountry Rising* will be an instant classic. It's a suspenseful, psychological drama that left me deeply moved, deeply satisfied, and yet still wanting more -- a book readers will not want to put down. This novel has something for lovers of every genre: romance, action, literature, crime, and mystery. A must-read for anyone not afraid to examine themselves and the world."

Anthony Willis, M.A., University of Akron

"A riveting, sensational novel that will keep you coming back for more! Filled with plots and sub plots, you may find it challenging to keep up - at times your emotions may take you for a wild ride. I would recommend this book to anyone who wants to gain a deeper understanding of the human experience."

M. Beech, Ohio

"*Lowcountry Rising* is a 3-D read! My senses were totally engaged by the vivid descriptions of the characters and the scenes, my mind was caught in the grip of suspense of what's next and my heart was touched by the sensitive issues of life experiences in the story. I literally could not put Lowcountry down until I finished. The pearls of wisdom have stayed with me leaving me wanting more from Samuel Othello Barlow. Well done"   *O. Wilkes, Virginia*

"The Lowcountry is rising . . .   Ride alongside Sticker on his journey to tomorrow, hang on tight and don't dare look back . . . Tomorrow's hope might just depend on you."

Lorna J. Miller, author of Ink

Lowcountry Rising

A novel by

Samuel Othello Barlow

Perigree Publishing

© 2015 by Samuel Othello Barlow
All rights reserved.
Cover design by Samuel Othello Barlow © 2014
Printed in U.S.A.
Reproduction or translation of any part of this work beyond that permitted by Section 107 or 108 of the 1976 United States Copyright Act without permission of the copyright owner is unlawful. Requests for permission to copy or further information should be addressed to Perigree Publishing, 1130 E. Main St., #183, Ashland, OH, 44805

Barlow, Samuel Othello
    Lowcountry Rising by Barlow, Samuel Othello

p.cm.
LCCN: 2011906022
ISBN: 978-0-9835636-0-0

Perigree, 1130 E. Main St., #183, Ashland, OH, 44805

Lyrics to *Refugee* by Tom Petty used by permission.
Thanks to Anthony Willis, M.A., University of Akron, for his editing, input, and encouragement.

News articles cited:
1. Crary, David, Nation News, Record Number of Americans in Prison, Associated Press, 2-28-2008.
2. Vicini, James. U.S. Imprisons more people than any other nation. *Reuters*, Dec. 9, 2006 and U.S. Justice Department report, November 30, 2006.
3. Jason, et al. (Lazarou et al), Incidence of Adverse Drug Reactions in Hospitalized Patients, *Journal of the American Medical Association (JAMA)*, Vol. 279. April 15, 1998, pp. 1200-05.
4. Bates, David W., Drugs and Adverse Drug Reactions: How Worried Should We Be? *JAMA*, Vol. 279. April 15, 1998, pp. 1216-17.

Notices:

This story contains strong language and some content is controversial and may be offensive to some audiences. This book should not be read by anyone under the age of eighteen or those unable to reconcile the need to examine the darkness to understand the light. Reader discretion is advised.

READER BEWARE!
(Don't say I didn't warn you.)

The psychological discussions in this story are based in part on the pioneering work in pain management by John E. Sarno, M.D. Prominent people such as John Stossel (ABC News), Howard Stern (national radio personality) Anne Bancroft (actress), and Senator Tom Harkin have experienced success with healing various health problems with Dr. Sarno's methods.
For more, go to: http://www.tmswiki.org/ppd/John_E._Sarno,_MD
Scroll down and watch the interviews. We wish you the best for a happy, pain free life.

This book is a work of fiction. Names, characters, places, and incidents are products of the author's imagination or are used fictitiously. Any resemblance to actual events or locales or persons, living or dead, is entirely coincidental.

Dedication

To those who have struggled, to those who will overcome.

www.LowcountryRising.com

Part One

And all those questions boil down to the single
biggest question a body can ever have: Why . . .

Chapter One

. . . and I swear to God, if he doesn't show again this morning, that's it. We're done. Finished. That would make three times he's stood me up, and as I always say, three strikes and you're out. After all, saving someone's life has to count for something. If I hadn't gotten to him when I did down on the docks that night, that bullet sure as hell would have.

I open my eyes and push myself off the damp sheets. I make it to the front door, turn the knob, and push the door open. A bead of sweat drops off my forehead and plops on the wooden stair as I take a step down. I grab the back of my flimsy old lawn chair, pull it out from under the overhang, and sit my sorry-ass down.

When the bullfrogs are finally sleepin' and there's no cars on the highway and it's dark and clear and still, I sit in my lawn chair and look up. Most people, when they look at the night sky, will gaze at the stars. Me? I look at the black in between 'em.

All that black—so dark, so receptive, so inviting. I've been fighting like hell to keep from gettin' sucked into it. Fighting like hell.

My name is Sticker . . . and I'm a son of a bitch. I first noticed this when I was seven, when the kid across the street pushed a metal gate open too fast and right into my mouth. My mother was talking to a neighbor over the fence, and when she saw the gate hit me, she let out a quick little laugh. Of course, when she saw half my front tooth lying on the sidewalk, she acted all concerned. Took me to a dentist and got what little tooth left filed down and later capped, so I guess I shouldn't complain. Still, that joy in her eyes . . . well . . . you don't get much past me.

Thirty-three years later, that's the kind of shit that goes through your mind while you're sittin' in your lawn chair in the middle of the night trying to escape the heat. Damn summer came too fast this year—it's already August and it's only June. But the bull frogs are finally sleepin' and there's no cars on the highway, so I sit and look and think.

Eventually, the black fades into gray and then yellow and the birds start singing, so I get up and stretch. He's supposed to be here just past sunrise. Yeah, that'll be the day. And even if he shows, he probably didn't get all the stuff I need anyway. But, I'm done beggin'. Like I say, three strikes and you're out.

I climb the three steps into my single-wide and come back outside with a half-dozen eggs and a quart-size Mason jar. I put the eggs and jar on the card table that's standing under the patio overhang I just built over the front door. I crack the eggs into the jar, replace the shells into the paperboard egg carton, give the jar a shake, and gulp those slimy suckers down. Breakfast of champions, I think.

There's a week-old newspaper lying on the card table, so I thumb through it while I let the eggs settle. I'm in bare feet, cutoff blue jeans, and an old T-shirt with the album cover to the Beatle's *Magical Mystery Tour* silk-screened on it—a gift from Amy, an old friend. She'd dance around me and poke me in the gut while improvising one of the songs from the album: "You are the egg-man. You are the egg-man. You are the walrus. Coo-coo ca-choo . . . Coo-coo . . . Coo-coo . . ." She thought it was hilarious.

Yeah, he's late. I knew it. I wonder what his excuse is this time. Another party? Another girl? Was it just booze this time, or is he back to using?

I take my shirt off and leave it on the table, go out onto the lawn, and start my routine: push-ups, sit-ups, lunges, and jumping jacks. Then I practice the moves: the punches, kicks, spins, and blocks.

After I work up a hot sweat and my heart is pounding good and hard, I go over to the side of my trailer, turn my back as I take off my shorts, and step into the large, galvanized steel washbasin. I grab the hose hangin' off the spigot, hold it over my head and turn the faucet. "Aauuuggghhh! Son of a bitch!"

A cold shower ain't exactly the sort of thing a normal person does first thing in the morning. But livin' alone like I do, I usually need it, and in more ways than one. I lather up with a bar of soap, rinse the suds away, and step out of the washbasin. I grab a towel that's hanging off a screw, towel off, put my shorts and shirt back on, and look down the driveway.

Maybe he got his new truck by working harder. Maybe he finally built that second garage he always wanted by building another house or two. He's not dumb enough to be dealing again, is he?

You see, my cousin Tom's supposed to drop off the roofing materials I need to finish this overhang, and over the past few months he's been buying too many toys and been one cocky prick. Hell, we grew up like brothers and did everything together—hunt and fish, play ball, tease girls. As we got older, if nothin' else, we'd sit out in front of my trailer, drink a beer or two, and talk. But not lately. Having him do me this one favor was like pulling teeth, and I never would have asked but for the fact that he builds houses for a living and can get the stuff for half price. Is that too much to ask of a cousin and lifelong buddy to boot? I don't think so. So I sit back down in my lawn chair and wait. God, I hate it when I have to wait.

Tom owns the three acres my trailer sits on along with a house that sits in between my trailer and the road. His ex-wife still lives in the house with her nine-year-old daughter who wanders back here all too frequently, especially now that their TV's broke. The girl is cute and smart and charming, I'll admit, but she knows for sure the world owes her all sorts of things, and she makes sure you hear about it, especially when things don't go her way. I used to tell her and Tom that life is mostly learning to do without and the world don't owe you a damn thing except what you work for and even then you're lucky just to hang onto it. But they don't care, so I don't do that anymore, even though it's the sort of thing a son of a bitch does. Besides, Tom ain't even around much on account of the divorce. It's just his ex—her name is Candace—and her daughter, Sunny, in the house in front; and me, Sticker, the SOB, in the trailer out back.

So while I'm sitting here in my lawn chair in my front yard outside my trailer waitin' on Tom, little Sunny with her bouncy blond curls comes out the back door. Hard to watch morning cartoons when there's no TV, I reckon. She wanders towards me across the lawn in her sheepish and shy way that I know won't stay sheepish and shy very long.

"What'cha doing, Stick?" she asks.

"Sittin' here."

"Why you sittin' there?"

I'm not in the mood for some long conversation, so I take the lazy way out and say, "'Cuz I feel like it."

"That's all you ever say, Stick, *"'Cuz I feel like it."* she mocks.

I don't say nothin'.

"Why's that all you ever say?"

"Because it's the truth."

"Why's it the truth?"

"Because it is. I'm sittin' here because I feel like it."

"That's dumb," she says as she steps over to the card table and picks up the old newspaper, glances at it absentmindedly, and then puts it back down. Then she turns to me again and asks, "Why you ain't got a job, Stick?"

I give no answer.

"My momma's got a job and goes to work every day. Why you ain't got a job?"

"Because I don't."

"Why?"

"Because I don't feel like it."

She looks at a butterfly lighting on a dandelion. "My momma says it's because you're *too damn lazy*, Stick."

"Lazy! I've been working on this dad-gum overhang all week."

"Yeah, well Momma says it sure took you long enough and you shoulda done it five years ago!"

"Yeah. Well, that's the way it goes."

"Sticker," she says after she thinks a second. "I know what *lazy* means."

I don't say nothin'.

"It means you can do something but you don't 'cuz you don't feel like it!" she giggles, obviously proud of herself.

"That sounds about right," I reply dryly.

"Yeah. So you lazy, Stick? You lazy?"

"I reckon so."

"That don't sound good, Stick. People ought not be lazy. That's what my momma says."

"Well, your momma sounds real smart."

Sunny runs after the butterfly as it skips over the dandelions. She picks ten or so of the flowers and skips back.

"Stick, why are dandelions yellow?"

I don't say nothin'.

"Why, Stick? Why they yellow?"

Finally, I say, "Because they are."

"Why they yellow, Stick? Why ain't they blue or purple or red?"

"You ask a lot of questions."

"Well, why, Stick? Why they yellow?"

I sigh, and then say, "Because they give off yellow."

"They give off yellow?"

"Yeah. They keep all the other colors to themselves and they give off yellow."

"So they don't like yellow?"

"No," I say impatiently but softly. "They love yellow."

"So why they give it away?"

"Because."

"Why, Stick?"

"Because. Because they want you to have it. They like you so much they want you to have their favorite color. All right?"

"They do? That's nice, Stick."

She puts one of the dandelions behind her ear and another through a button on her shirt.

"I like dandelions, Stick. They're pretty."

"Real pretty. Your mother's callin' you."

"No she ain't. And you say they like me?"

"Yeah, they do. They like you just fine."

"That's why they're yellow?"

"Yes! That's why they're yellow!"

"I know something else that's yellow."

I don't say nothin'.

"You wanna know?"

"Not really."

She sniffs at the bouquet of dandelions she holds in her hands.

"Guess."

"I don't know."

"Guess, Stick. What else is yellow?"

"I don't know."

"Well, take a guess! Take a guess!"

"Okay! Okay! I guess that your Sunday dress is yellow."

"No, Stick!" she giggles. "My Sunday dress is pink! Guess again."

"How about your toes. Your toes are yellow."

"No, silly! Nobody's toes are yellow! Guess again!"

"Your goldfish is yellow."

"No, Stick! That's dumb!" she giggles again. "Guppy the Goldfish is *gold!*" She slaps me on my leg. "I'll tell you what's yellow! I'm standing under it right now!" She spins around with her arms outstretched then stops and looks me in the face and smiles. "It's the sun, Stick! The sun is yellow! Just like the dandelions—the sun is yellow, too!" She laughs and pushes the dandelions in my face.

"Smell them, Stick! Smell the dandelions. Don't they smell good?"

I push them away, but not meanly. She brings them back under my nose. I smell the dandelions with a long whiff. "Yes, they smell good. Now go away."

"What do they smell like, Stick?"

I don't say nothin'.

She takes one and pushes it to my lips.

"Taste one. Taste one and tell me what it tastes like."

"No."

"Yes."

"No."

"Yes. Taste one for me and tell me what it tastes like."

I don't say nothin'. Then I open my eyes real wide and my mouth real wide and lunge forward and bite the dandelion off its stalk and chew it real obvious-like, looking at her with my eyes buggin' out. Sunny pulls back in surprise. Then I stop chewing and shut my eyes, grab my throat like I'm choking and gasp for air. I let my head fall over and my body go slack and let out a moan and pretend that I'm dead.

She doesn't say anything for a few seconds. Then I open just one of my eyelids, and let a thin smile come to my lips.

"Oh, Stick! You're not dead! You're just foolin' me!" She slaps me on the leg. "You tried to fool me!" I open both my eyes and keep smiling. "I don't like you, Stick! You're mean! You're mean and I'm gonna tell Momma!"

She slaps my arm, throws the dandelions at me, and runs back to the house, the other dandelions still in her shirt and behind her ear. She opens the screen door and darts inside, and I hear the screen door slam shut behind her. I sit there with the dandelions scattered across my chest and in my lap as I begin to sweat. I hear an engine off in the distance tearing up the road.

Chapter Two

I get my tool belt and steel-toed boots out of my trailer as Tom pulls into my driveway. He's driving his new, gold Ford F-150 pickup with his company's name and logo stenciled on the door in red and black letters. Who the hell rides around in a gold pickup?

"Hey, Tom," I say as he climbs down from the cab. "How's it going?"

Tom's about five-ten, an inch shorter than me, decent looking with brown hair cut just below his ears, similar to mine, and a mustache, which I couldn't stand to have on my face. He's slightly thinner than me and doesn't have the definition I do since he doesn't work out, and his eyes are brown, not green like mine.

It used to be, when you'd look at him, he'd look content for the most part. But over the past few years, he's looked dejected or angry most the time, and recently, almost sinister—as if his eyes are getting closer together and his eyebrows are becoming permanently furrowed. Something's changed about Tom. And something's still changing. And you wonder *if* he's using again? Are you a fool? I sit down and start putting on my boots.

"Hey, Stick," he says with a shit-eatin' grin. Then, as if he's showing off some great work of art, he points down and says, "Check 'em out! Brand new *Frye* boots! Got 'em yesterday in Savannah!"

I don't look up to him or his fancy boots. "Yeah. Good for you."

"Sorry I'm late. Got lucky last night, if you know what I mean. Didn't get home till . . . till . . . Well hell! Didn't get home at all!"

"Yeah. Not surprised."

"Hey, what can I say? There's something about a pickup man—especially when it's gold!"

I know I shouldn't say what I'm thinking, because I'm bitter and maybe a little jealous, but it comes out anyway. . . "Remind me to run out and buy one for myself."

"Hey!" he snaps. "Don't give me that shit! I'm doing you the favor here, remember? Christ almighty!"

"Yeah, right," I say, almost sincerely. "Sorry. Appreciate it."

We each grab a roll of roofing off the truck and toss them on the ground. "So who's the girl?" I ask.

"Ahh . . ." his mood instantly changes. "A little fox from Savannah. Parents own a shipping company and are loaded with a capital L!"

"Uh-huh."

"Yeah, we partied all night. And *ooo-eee*, she's got a pair of headlights like you wouldn't believe! Goddamn, I almost got smothered!"

"Is that so? Sounds like potential."

"Hell, Stick! Are you kiddin'?" he says as he spits on the ground. "It'll be a long time before someone ties *me* down again. It's 1986, for Christ's sake! Who needs marriage anymore? But the rich parents—now they might be too hard to resist!"

We swing buckets of tar off the truck, grab the boxes of nails, and carry them over to the card table. "All right," I say as we walk back to the truck. "Thanks again, Tommy boy. And let me know if I can repay the favor."

"You got that right!" he says, sounding all too serious. He climbs in the truck, starts it with a roar, and revs it a couple of times to make sure I notice. "Gotta go, brother," he says as he puts the truck in gear. "Skippin' work and goin' fishin' with the boys. Don't work too hard!" He spins the tires and tears up the driveway, turns onto the road, and disappears around the bend.

"Yeah," I mutter. "Fishin' with the boys. Who am I? One of the girls?"

I put a roll of roofing on my shoulder, climb the ladder leaning against the overhang, and hoist the roofing on top. I climb up and pull the roll to the highest part of the roof, and as I brace the roofing with my knee to keep it from unrolling, I hear a buzz and feel something land on my thigh. A horse fly the size of a 747 jumbo jet starts sinking his spear into my skin to suck my blood, and I slap at it as quick as I can. But it's too late. "Owwww!"

My leg jerks up from the sting, and my hand recoils from the slap, and the back of my hand smacks me right in the forehead. "Ugghh!"

With my knee off the roll, it's free to unroll down the roof like a roll of toilet paper, which, of course, it does. On its way to the ground, it knocks over the ladder. "Figures," I grumble as I rub the welt that's already swelling up on my knee. "Play it again, Sam."

So now I have to slide over the edge of the roof to get down, and as I do, my chest scrapes along the edge of the plywood, tearing my shirt and burning my chest. I drop to the ground before I'm really ready to, and land kinda awkward-like and twist my ankle. "Ow!"

I hop over to the roofing, reroll it, reposition the ladder, hoist the roll up, and finally get it up onto the roof. It's gonna take four rows of the three-foot-wide roofing to finish the overhang. I get the first row down without any more drama, and I'm starting to feel right proud of myself. I measure, cut, and position the roofing for the second row. Now I need to overlap it and seal it with tar, so I open the can and scoop some out with a trowel. Some of that black gooey stuff drips onto the head of the hammer, and you would think it would make the hammer stick better to the nail head, but no. When I start sinking nails, the head of the hammer slides off the head of the first nail I hammer and right onto my thumb. "Owwwww! Ow . . . ow . . . ow . . . ow . . ."

I drop the hammer, which lands on the arch of my foot right near my sprained ankle, which causes my foot to jerk up and knock over the can of tar. And it, of course, rolls down and off the roof. "You're a freakin' joke."

Finally, after three more hours of messing things up without really trying and having to repeat them *with* really trying, I finish. I throw the tools and empty cans and rags to the ground and climb down. I take off my shirt that's now torn and wringing wet with sweat, take off my boots, and am about to sit down and rest when I remember one more thing left to do.

I go into my trailer and return with a roll of the *Super-Duper, Super-Sticky, Super-Large, Super-Flypaper* I got from Tom a few months ago as a birthday present. What a gift, huh? He said he saw it at a flea market in Beaufort (pronounced Bū-fert, if you please), and said it made him think of me. "Here, Stick," he said when he handed me half a dozen rolls of the stuff in a brown paper bag, "Maybe this stuff is as sticky as you." I think I was supposed to laugh.

But this flypaper is something like you've never seen. It's six-inches wide and two-and-a-half feet long when it's uncoiled and hanging, and it could snag and hold a bald eagle if it had to. I move the ladder and hammer and bend a nail smack-dab in the middle of the center stud on the underside of the overhang. I hold the roll of flypaper in one hand and pull the red tag to unfurl it with the other, and reach up to hook it to the nail. But as I do, a puff of breeze pushes the paper against one of my forearms where it sticks to my hair.

I'm determined to avoid any more calamities, so I carefully climb down the ladder making sure to hold the flypaper away from me. But I stumble a little on my sore ankle, and another part of the paper brushes against my chest and sticks like super glue right to my nipple. Of fucking course. I yank at it hard, like ripping a Band-Aid off as fast as you can, which doesn't feel too good, either.

Now the damn paper is stuck to the fingers of my left hand and my right arm and nipple is red and stinging like a son of a gun and my thumb is throbbing and my knee is stinging from the horse fly biting me and my ankle is sore and my forehead hurts from smacking myself in the head and my foot aches and my chest is burning and my favorite shirt is torn. "Damn it!"

I pull at the paper again, which only serves to rip it right down its middle. And wouldn't you know it, but two of its ends come together, like they're joining hands in holy matrimony or somethin', and form one long piece of super-sticky frustration that sticks to me in like two-hundred places.

Furious now, I yank at the flypaper blindly and fight with it like I'm trying to get out of a straitjacket. My bare toe slams into one of the legs of the card table, causing me to hop and stumble all over the place. And during one of my pirouettes, I hit the side of the trailer with my shoulder and the washbasin with my foot, and I fall ass-first directly into the tub.

Dirty, slimy water and suds explode all over me and up onto my face. I wipe my eyes and blow through my pursed lips, too exasperated to even swear.

I hear a giggle and turn to see Sunny standing just beyond the overhang with her long yellow-golden hair shining in the sun. She's pointing at me with one hand and covering her mouth with the other as she laughs.

I glare at her. "It's not funny," I finally say.

Sunny keeps giggling. And the worst part is, the flypaper's still stuck to me in like a hundred places. Her eyes wander a little to see the old newspaper lying on the card table and without a word, she skips over to it, brings the paper over to me, and unfolds it. She puts her little hand under the paper, reaches out, and grabs the flypaper.

"You're so dumb, Sticker!" she giggles. "You're so dumb!" She pulls section by section of the flypaper off me, giggling and calling me dumb all the while. Finally the sticky mess is crumpled within the newspaper, and I'm free.

I don't say nothin'.

"There now," she says. "All better."

She backs up a step and looks me in the eye and smiles. "See ya later!" she calls out as she turns and skips away across the lawn. She goes around the left corner of the house to where the trash cans are beside the driveway. I hear a garbage can lid slam down with a resounding thud. She skips back around and waves at me with a proud smile and then opens the back door and goes inside.

"That's just great, Sticker," I mumble. "Outsmarted by a nine-year-old."

I get out of the chair and scrub off any black tar and what's left of the stickiness from the flypaper with an old rag and turpentine. Then I turn the water on and wash it all away. I go back over to my lawn chair and collapse into it, causing one of the plastic straps to snap, sending my butt six inches closer to the ground so it's sticking out the bottom of the chair.

Just goes to show I never should have gotten out of my lawn chair this morning. And the weekend is still a day away. Not like it matters, I think. I sit here and pout in the midmorning sun.

Chapter Three

As you sit there in the light of day, sooner or later, you notice it again—*that* thing that haunts you. *That* pain in your back that hurts every time you get out of bed; or *that* memory of loss due to someone else's stupidity or just dumb luck; or *that* feeling of betrayal by someone you trusted; or *that* addiction to an addiction you just can't beat. Whatever *that* is, it never leaves. As much as you try to fight it, ignore it, or distract yourself with something else—as much as you try to feel anything other than *that*—it's still there, sticking to you like a piece of flypaper. If you try to pull it off, it sticks tightly to your fingers. And if you try again with the other hand, you just end up passing *that* back and forth from one hand to the other.

You may go to a doctor to get *that* off. You may go to a lawyer or shrink or the Gypsy lady across town for help. But as convincing as they sound, as well intentioned and expensive as they might be, they can't get *that* off you either. Most of the time they just make matters worse.

Thats in the body are tough, but can often be mended and you tend not to take them too personal. *Thats* in the mind are also bad, but there's usually help and understanding for them too. The worst kinds of *that*—the kinds that are stickiest of all—are *thats* of the heart.

A *that* of the heart is like a toothache in the middle of your chest that never quite goes away. You can think about it, analyze it, pray on it, or just try to forget it all together—but it's still there. It throbs in pain with every beat of your heart and radiates into every part of you, and the only way to change it is to change what caused it in the first place, which means changing the past, which ain't very likely. So you can't help thinking sometimes that you'd rather be like the fly that gets stuck on that flypaper and don't fly anymore or move anymore or breathe anymore. At least then, you wouldn't have to feel. At least then, you wouldn't have to feel . . . *that*.

I get up and pull the lawn chair into the shade under the overhang and sit back down. I look up and see the nail that's waiting for the flypaper, so I get up and get another roll from inside my trailer. This time, I hook it to the nail first, then pull the tag down and unfurl it as I step down the ladder. "Not brain surgery now, is it?" I get off the ladder, sit back down, and look up at it. "Can't do nothin' right the first time, can you?"

I pull my eyes away and look at the house and remember Sunny running into the back door all proud of herself for freeing me. But she'll be back—this evening or tomorrow morning—asking me questions again, with me, trying not to answer them.

The yard around my trailer is flat and sandy with some grass scattered in amongst the weeds. Flat goes on in all directions for miles 'round here and sand is everywhere because the sea is a few miles away and where I'm sittin' used to be a beach and the bottom of the sea before that. Now there's swamps every time you turn around with weeds up to your waist and oaks and cypress and sycamores and Tupelo gums with Spanish moss hangin' off them.

Yeah, you can't swing a cat without hitting a swamp 'round here. Sometimes it seems like there's more swamps than land, especially after a hurricane blows through and dumps a ton of rain. There's Calfpen Swamp, Great Swamp, Bluehorse Swamp, Fuller Swamp, and my personal favorite, Suggedy Swamp. There's no lack of swamps and therefore no lack of stagnant water and muck trapped down in their bottoms. Old stagnant water and muck that's been trapped down there for decades, maybe centuries, and'll suck you down if you happen to fall in. Old stagnant water and muck that smells like stale beer, rotten eggs, and piss and makes you wonder if there ain't something really dark and shameful down there decaying in the bottom of the swamp—like festering corpses of unrighteous relatives or somethin'—trying to bubble to the surface to scare the hell out of you.

The nearest swamp to Candy's place is down the road about a mile or so. Usually, you don't smell it, but if the breeze is right or the air is heavy and still—like on a hot summer's night—that stink will make its way up here. I could live without it, but you learn to live with it. Sometimes you don't even realize you're smelling it.

Then there's the damn piss ants. They're small and red and'll bite you any chance they get. When they do, it feels like you've been lighted on fire, so they call 'em fire ants. They're the nastiest, meanest creatures you'll ever run across and God must have invented them in Hell. Now they live here, in the Lowcountry.

You have to pour gasoline on their nest and wait a while and let it soak in and then pour more on it and light it on fire and hope you burn all them up including the queen, because if you don't, the hill will just come back with more of those agents of Hell than before. You see, the best way to get rid of fire ants precisely is to use fire against them. Water or freezing or happy thoughts and trying to make friends with them don't help one damn bit. In fact, it just encourages them. You need to let them die of their own agent of aggravation: fire.

So if you burn off all the fire ants—and you'd better, because if you give them half a chance they're gonna swarm on you and bite the hell out of you without blinking an eye; and what's more, somehow they signal each other and bite you all at once like it's a conspiracy or something— then you can walk around the yard freely in your bare feet.

When you do, you can feel the cool dew on the blades of grass early in the morning. You can feel the bottoms of your feet spread out like pancakes on the ground and your toes spread out like webbed feet. You might get grass seeds or pollen or gnats or pieces of Spanish moss stuck on your ankles and calves way up to your knees. You'll get grains of sand up between your toes so you have to brush them out with your thumb before you climb into bed at night. And those toes: you can scrunch them up to pull the ground closer—pull it up—like you're grabbing it and holding on. Or you can flatten those toes out to push the ground away—push it down—like you're pushing off and moving on down the road.

I make a point of burning up all the fire ants in my cousin's yard whenever they appear. I keep it free 'cuz I hate them ants, and then Sunny can run around barefoot and not have to worry about it. I think she likes that.

My cousin Tom, when he lived here, didn't like me doing that. He didn't like me lighting his precious lawn on fire. But since he left it's been okay since Candace doesn't really care. She's too preoccupied with all her other "important" things.

Now Sunny's mother, she's a piece of work. Maybe circumstances made her the way she is or maybe she was just born that way. Maybe she just *wants* to be that way. I figure it's a mixture of the three. But whatever the reason, she became what she is today, and I say, it's an adventure just to behold. I could say she's a lot like me, a son of a bitch, but that wouldn't be right. She's not a son of a bitch. No. She's a daughter of a bastard, and most of the time, it shows. She goes by the name Candy, but there's only one time when she's sweet, and I'll leave it to your imagination to figure out when that might be.

She's attractive with her streaky, dirty blond hair, cut in the latest poofed and curled-out style the famous actresses wear these days. Sometimes I see dark roots in it, so I know she colors it. Her face is pretty, but not stunning, and she has shallow-set brown eyes that look like they're longing for something or waiting for something or trying to figure something out. It's a look that makes you wonder if there's much of anything behind it; a look that hints that she couldn't tell you even if there were.

A few years ago, before the stress of her divorce, turning thirty, and raising Sunny on her own, she was considered a knockout. And it seems like all the men who knew her then must have had that image burned in their brains because they still chase after her all the time. When she tries hard and uses all her makeup and dress-up tricks, she can still look downright gorgeous. She's pretty well endowed, too, but not burdeningly so—just enough to have a little overhang of her own. And with the style of bras and blouses she wears, she can make those assets appear perky, young, and more than sufficient.

So I'm sitting here sweating when Candy comes out the back door with a laundry basket full of clothes to hang on the old rusty clothes line. She sees me sitting here, but she doesn't say anything. She never says anything first. It's annoying as hell to always have to be the one to start the conversation, but it's even more annoying not to have one. Finally, I say, "Hey, Candy."

"Hey," she replies.

"How ya doing?"

"Ohhhh . . ." she pauses a couple seconds, and then, as usual, she lets loose—

"That child, she's gonna drive me crazy! Now she wants me to drive her over to Becky's house this afternoon. I don't know why she can't have Becky's mom come over here and pick her up. I'm always having to drive them two all over creation! For all the money I spend on gas, I swear, I could buy a new house, or at least some new carpeting! And then she won't even clean her room. It looks like a hurricane just blew through it. Clothes and toys and crayons all over the floor. You can't even walk in it!"

"Yeah, " I mumble, but I doubt she hears me.

"And will that bum help me out? He hasn't sent child support for almost a year! How am I supposed to raise her without it? It takes money to raise a child! I can't do it on one measly salary! He should buy her clothes or give her money or take care of *me!* But what does he do? Nothin'! They're all alike. They make all these promises, get your hopes up that you're gonna have a better life and more money and nicer things and a new car and new carpeting, and then they just leave you flat! Just lyin', lazy, dumb slobs—every one of them!"

I wonder if she realizes that she's talking to one of *them.* She hangs up the last shirt, picks up the basket, and goes back into the house without saying another word.

Now Sunny's real name is Susan; but everyone calls her Sunny since she was a baby on account of her yellow baby hair. But my cousin Tom, he's not Sunny's real pa. No. I just said that before offhandedly. Tom married Candy about six years ago, and like I told you, they already split. But he's letting Candy and Sunny live in his old double-wide and charging her just a hundred bucks a month since he doesn't owe any money on it. But like Candy said, he stopped giving her any money for Sunny about a year ago—right around the time he started getting pricky and buying himself more toys. The more you have, the more you think you need, I reckon.

Sunny's real pa, his name is Wayne. He took off and abandoned the two of them when Sunny was two years old. He had a few beers one night and went out for cigarettes and just never came back. Candy didn't hear from him for a couple months, and then it was only by way of one of her girlfriends. Turns out Wayne found a new girl and got her pregnant, too. In fact, he's had two more kids with her and they all live together down past Hardeeville a-ways. He doesn't get drunk any more either. Go figure. Maybe he was just practicing on Candy. He doesn't send Candy any money for Sunny either.

So Candy got stuck with Sunny, or that's how she makes it sound. Must run in the family, though, 'cuz Candy herself was raised by her aunt after her mama left her on her aunt's back porch and took off for Oklahoma. Her daddy never took care of her neither, and for that, he was, is, and always will be, a bastard. He drove a dump truck on and off to earn a few bucks and keep a roof over his head, never married, and never had another kid. Candy used to go see him once a month or so, and when she went, she always ended up cleaning up his single-wide. She'd bitch about it though 'cuz she said that no sooner did she clean it but in a few days it'd be a total mess again. "What's the use?" she would shrug.

She used to give him a few bucks every now and then so he could stay on his medicine, so she said. I never saw him sick, though. Saw him drunk a few times, but never sick. Even with all that, I could tell Candy loved him. Being dad just about trumps everything, don't it? So take all that into consideration and poor little Candy, who can be a real bitch, is a daughter of a bastard. And me, Samuel Othello Barlow, who can sure be a bastard, is a son of a bitch.

One thing for sure with Candy, though—you never have to guess what's churning around inside her pretty little head since she invariably lets you know all about it: how her kid is breaking her, her boss is raking her, and her house is grating her. But on the other hand, when it comes to guys and relationships, she's as tight-lipped as a little neck clam. Although she makes a point of telling you when she thinks a guy is *cute*, you can never really tell if she likes or loves him. And the guy can't figure it out either.

She acts all sweet and secretive at the same time, and the guys must feel like they're searching for *Good & Plenty* candy in a pitch-dark cave somewhere. They can sense it, they can smell it, sometimes they can even feel it. But they can't ever really taste it. Maybe that's what keeps them coming back: "*Next* time, I'm gonna taste it!" they think. "For sure, I'm gonna get it *next* time! And when I do, oh, how sweet it will be!"

Is she playing head games? Perhaps. But then again, maybe she never defines herself simply because she can't, and that confusion comes across as a tease. How can anyone figure out someone who doesn't know why to love?

Chapter Four

Sunny comes out of the back door and sits at the picnic table on the porch and starts to color, the dandelions gone from her shirt and behind her ear.

The back of the house is long and straight with three windows in the middle and one door on the right side. Outside that door to the right corner of the house is a porch with an overhang under which the picnic table sits. Behind the left side of the house the ground used to slope away from the house just a couple feet, which was all right by Tom. But when Candy moved in, she just *had* to have a swimming pool. So Tom got one of his buddies to come over with a bulldozer and make that depression a hole, and they plopped a big-ass above-ground pool right there. The top edge of the pool is about the same height as the bottom of the house, so it looks almost like a built-in pool. Me and Tom built a deck around half the pool up to the house all the way across from the back door to the left edge of the house. Then we put in a few steps down the deck to the driveway. Doesn't look too bad, if I say so myself.

I said before that Candy lives in a double-wide. Well, that's not exactly true either, but I call it that for convenience. The house is actually the kind that they build in a factory and truck on out on a tractor-trailer, one-half at a time. So it's quite a bit bigger than a double-wide. You put the two halves next to each other, bolt them together, and there you have it—instant house. All that's left to do is to hook up your plumbing and electric, cart in your furniture, hang your pictures, and you're in business.

Her house—well really, Tom's house—is about twice as long as my trailer with tan siding and brown shutters. Tom bought it used just before they got married, and it was only supposed to be a temporary place to live while they built a real house behind it. But that never happened and was part of the reason Candy divorced him. The house looks okay, I reckon, but it still reminds me of a double-wide, which reminds me of squalor, which makes me think of rednecks—of which in these parts there are plenty to go around. People not from around here—like the snowbirds who migrate down south every fall to avoid winter up north—think these rednecks are cute and novel, especially the way they talk with their Southern drawl and all. But there's really nothing cute or novel about 'em. They're just regular old rednecks with a regular, limited way of looking at life.

But they don't just live here in the Lowcountry. You find them in the mountains, backwoods, suburbs, and cities too. Somewhere else they might dress a little different or sound a little different and drive a fancy car instead of a pickup or go to a night club instead of a saloon and drink beer that comes from some exotic country that you put a slice of lime in the bottle or somethin'. But that's all just window dressing, you see. It's like trying to dress up a double-wide with fancy drapes and carpeting and shrubs and a swimming pool. But any way you dress it, a double-wide is still a double-wide, and there's really no way to hide it. The only way to change it is to come in with the bulldozer and dump truck, knock that double-wide down, and truck off the scrap to a landfill. Then you can smooth over the land, start from scratch, and build you a real house.

But not many folks are willing to tear down what they're accustomed to and most folks don't want to work in the hot sun and use the best materials they can afford so they have a really fine and extra-comfortable place to live. Most folks just want to get off work, come home, sit on the back porch, and drink their beer and worry about what kind of boots they wear or what kind of truck they drive. And that, my friend, is a redneck.

As I was saying, Sunny comes out and sits at the picnic table under the overhang and starts to color. I can tell she's still a little sore at me about the dandelion thing 'cuz she doesn't look my way. About a minute goes by and then Candy yells from inside, "Sunny, come in here and pick up your room."

Sunny keeps coloring.

"Sunny! Get in here right now and pick up your room!"

Sunny keeps coloring as if she doesn't hear a thing.

"Sunny! Don't make me have to come out there! Come in here and pick up your room!"

Sunny still doesn't move.

Candy stands in the doorway—I can just barely see her through the screen—and pushes the screen door open a crack. But she changes her mind and turns and leaves. Sunny keeps on coloring as a little smile runs across her lips.

So Sunny sits there coloring, and I sit here sweating in my lawn chair under the overhang outside my front door. I hear the buzz of a fly overhead and glance at the flypaper just in time to see a big black one run right into the sticky paper. The buzzing sputters for a few seconds and then stops completely. Then I see Tom's truck come down the road and into Candy's driveway. What's he doing back? "Done fishin' with 'the boys'?" I mutter.

He gets out of the truck carrying a brown paper bag and he doesn't come around back, but goes straight to the front door, which is on the side of the house I can't see. Musta picked up some groceries or something for Candy, I think. I look at Sunny once more, and then my eyes slowly close . . .

"Now sit down and be still," she said as she pushed me onto the chair. I sat there for about thirty seconds, and then jumped down and ran around the room like a five-year-old will.

"Come back here!" she snapped. She pushed me into the chair and slapped me quickly across the face. It didn't really hurt, but I turned beet red with shame. We sat near the corner of the room, and although most of the chairs had cloth padding, mine was nothing but plastic. "Now stay put and don't move again, or mark my words, I'll take you over my knee right here!"

We sat there a long time. She didn't say anything else to me, but talked to a couple near by and remarked how cute and well-behaved their little boy was. Then the nurse behind the counter called, "Mrs. Barlow. The doctor will see you now."

She stood and looked down at me and raised her finger and shook it as she said, "Now stay put, I'll be back in just a few minutes."

"Mommy, I have to pee."

"Just hold it, for Christ's sake. I'll be right back!"

I sat there, being good and not getting up like I wanted to. A nurse was behind the desk, busy reading and writing. What's wrong with my sister? Why is Mommy taking so long? When can we go home? I'm hungry. When can I eat? I have to pee!

The nurse looked my way and started to come over. Good! Now I'll find out! She stopped a couple of chairs before mine and spoke to the man and woman my mom did earlier. They were holding each other's hand with their boy, who was a little bigger than me, sitting on his father's lap. "Yes, nurse . . . Please . . . Is she all right?" the lady asked.

"Oh yes! Your daughter's doing just fine. She's going to be A-okay! The doctor says she's going to grow out of it and will be just like any other little girl!"

"Oh, Thank God! George! Did you hear that? She's going to be okay!" The lady started to cry. She hugged the man and kissed the boy and they were all smiling and hugging each other. "Can we go see her?" the man asked.

"Yes, of course. Come right this way. Bring your son too. I'm sure he wants to see his brave little sister!"

They got up and walked to the desk and then down the hall. The boy scampered along between his parents holding one hand of each, his arms stretched up like unfurled wings, as they walked down the hallway together.

The nurse returned to her desk and didn't look my way again. I squeezed my legs together hard—I'm supposed to stay put in this chair! Where's Mama? Where's Daddy? Why didn't he come with us? Why are they making me wait on this cold hard plastic chair? Why won't anyone tell me what's going on? I'm hungry! I have to pee! No! I have to hold it! Someone will come soon. Mama will come soon. She's got to come. She said she would. I close my eyes . . .

"I'm sorry Mommy! I thought I could hold it! I don't mean to make more work for you! I'm sorry! Please, Mommy, don't send me into the closet again. Ow! I said I was sorry. No, I don't want to get locked in the closet. I promise, I won't do it again! I'll never, ever wet my pants again!"

I open my eyes. "Okay . . . I'll just . . . hold it. I can hold . . . it!"

Then the seat was wet and I heard tinkle dripping onto the floor. I put my hands between my legs and squeezed hard trying to stop it but the tinkle kept coming. The nurse looked at the floor and then me and frowned. She picked up the phone and called someone. I sat there in my puddle and looked at the floor. Then a man with a mustache came with rags and bucket and told me to stand up. He cleaned up my wee-wee and told me it was okay.

A different nurse came and the other one left. The phone rang and the new nurse picked it up. "Yes. A little boy? Why yes, he's still here," she said. "Yes. Okay, I guess. He wet his pants. What time did you . . . ? Oh my! Oh yes. I'll be here. I get off at two. Okay. Bye."

The new nurse came to me and said, "Your mother just called. She's coming back to get you. She took your sister home. Here . . ." She reached under the counter and gave me an apple. "Now go back to your chair and sit down and wait."

I sat in the plastic chair holding the apple, my stomach aching. Maybe if I was sick like her, they would love me too. I wrapped my arms around my chest and rocked myself back and forth.

"Sticker! Sticker!" Sunny's shaking me and pulling on my arm. "Come quick!" she cries. "Tom's here and he's acting mean! He's inside and acting mean to Mama!"

I jump up out of my lawn chair, take hold of Sunny for just a second and tell her, "Stay here. I'll take care of it. Just stay here. If you see Tom come out of the house, run through the back field to Mrs. Wegman's house, okay?"

She nods her head. I run across the grass in my bare feet and cutoffs and pull the screen door open, and it doesn't squeak, since I greased it just last month, and I quickly enter the house as quiet as I can. I stand in the laundry room a few seconds listening over my pounding heart. I need to be careful because Tom has guns—a couple of handguns and a shotgun he keeps in a rack in his pickup. He says he needs the long ones for huntin' and the short ones for runnin'. "And I don't mean runnin' marathons," he'd snicker.

Tom was running a while back, right before Candy kicked him out after she discovered the white stuff in one of her baby-powder bottles wasn't really baby powder. She threw all his clothes out onto the road and then marched right back around the house as he was begging and pleading with her and poured the baby-powder bottle into the swimming pool as if she was adding pool chemicals or somethin'. It was truly a sight to behold. That Candy doesn't back down for nobody.

I'm just starting to peek through the entranceway into the kitchen when there's a crash against the wall beside me—the wall between the laundry room and Candy's bedroom. There's no scream. No moan. Just a crash.

I tear through the doorway and around the corner and kick open the flimsy, hollow bedroom door that's open just a crack, busting a hole in it. Candy's sitting on the floor against the wall, her shirt torn open and blood on her forearms. Her arms are up around her head, trying to protect herself from what she knows is coming next.

Tom hovers over her—a whiskey bottle, half out of a paper bag, its last drops dripping onto the floor at his feet. His hands are reaching out toward her neck and there's blood on his forearms coming from long red scratches. He turns and looks up as the door bangs against the wall and sees me coming through the threshold. But his eyes never make it all the way up to meet mine 'cuz as his head is still turning, I clock him good right in the jaw with a right foot front-kick. I feel his jawbone crunch against the instep of my bare foot and his head snaps back and sideways as he topples to the floor. He moans as he hits the floor and starts trying to push himself up. But I get over him and hit him hard with a right jab right upside his head. He drops to the floor like a sack of flour, out colder than he would have been had he snorted everything out of that baby-powder bottle.

Candy's still on the floor curled up, her arms around her knees, and she's looking over at Tom. I kneel down and put one hand on her shoulder and with the other, I brush her hair away from her eyes. "Oh God," she says in a hoarse half-whisper. After a long pause, she asks "Where's Sunny?"

"She's out back at my trailer. She's okay," I say as I brush more hair away. She relaxes a little and stretches her legs out straight. She looks at me just as I glance at her arms. "Are you all right? How bad is it?"

Her chest heaves a few times as she gasps for air, and she drops her arms by her sides. Then she starts sobbing so quietly I can hardly hear her. I pull her head to my chest and let her cry. She doesn't move to hold me. She doesn't move to be held. She stays there on the floor, not even holding herself, sobbing. Finally, she pushes me away and moves to get up. "Here," I say as I reach to help her.

"Okay . . . I'm okay . . ." she says and pushes herself up. We both step over to the bed and sit down, a space between us and Tom lying on the floor a few feet in front of us. I raise my arm to put it around her, but let it drop behind her onto the bed. Finally, after a couple long minutes, in a strained and contracted whisper that can barely be heard, she says, "All right."

"Now go out back to my trailer," I say as I get up and walk into the bathroom. I get a towel and wet it. "Here," I hand her the towel. She takes it and starts to clean blood off her arms. "Go out back and stay with Sunny until the police come." I move to the nightstand past Tom lying there unconscious and pick up the receiver. "I'll take care of . . ."

"No," she blurts out. "No police."

"But he was about to strangle you!"

"No police. He was drunk and high and . . ."

"I don't care if he was . . ."

"He gets like that. I can stop him. I can always stop him."

"If you're afraid he's gonna retaliate, we can get a restraining order."

"Like that would stop him."

"Well, you need to stop him somehow! If he does it to you, he does it to others."

"He does not!" she snaps back, fire in her eyes.

"Yeah, right." I say as she goes into the bathroom and starts patting down her face. "Well, something needs to be done, and if you don't do it, I will." I start to dial the operator, but before I can finish, she sprints out of the bathroom, grabs the receiver out of my hand, and tears the phone cord right out of the wall. I stand there dumbstruck.

"Don't!" she hisses. "Leave me alone! Get out of here! Get out of my house!"

I look her in the eye. But Sticker doesn't back down from nobody either. And I find myself starting to have the inclination to slap her upside the head myself. For Christ's sake, I think. I just saved her damn life! And this is the thanks I get? What the hell?

I stare back at her and her glance falls down to the floor and she backs up a step. I figure I should just take care of getting Tom out of here and let things settle down. "Go back to your daughter and take her over to her friend's house. That's what she was supposed to do today, wasn't it?"

"Yeah," she says meekly. "But what's gonna happen to Tom? You can't call the police. Don't call . . ."

"Okay! Okay! No police! I won't call the police, all right? Just get out of here and I'll take care of it." She just looks at me, still holding the towel. "Now go! Get out. Go get Sunny."

"But he's still unconscious."

"Don't worry about it. Just get out of here before he wakes up. Now get!"

She throws the bloodstained towel into the bathtub and grabs a new one off the towel rack and walks out of the room. She stops abruptly when she sees the hole in the door and says, "Oh great. Now I have a hole in my door."

"Shut up!" I hiss. "I just saved your Goddamn life! Get out of here before I change my mind!"

She doesn't turn around or glance my way, but walks into the laundry room and then out the back door. I hear it bang shut. I bend over and find Tom's wrist and feel for his pulse. It's still going, so at least I haven't killed him. I roll him over onto his back and squat down near his head. I hook my arms under his shoulders, lift him up, and drag him out of the bedroom, through the kitchen, into the laundry room to the back door. I look out the screen and see Candy and Sunny walking back around the pool to the driveway. I drop Tom, and as they get around the corner, I step outside the door and stand on the deck to watch them leave.

Candy's climbing in the driver's side and Sunny's walking around the front of the car, about to get to the passenger side door, when she turns her head quickly, as if it were pulled by a string, back my way. She stops abruptly and pauses just a second. And then she's off.

She bolts like a racehorse out of the gate, back around the front of the car, across the driveway, up the steps, onto the deck and across those warped and faded boards. I drop to my knees as she runs toward me, and she flies right into my outstretched arms. She wraps her arms around my neck and holds me tight, like she's afraid of falling. I hug her back.

Several seconds go by as we hold onto each other. Without seeing anything, she knows what I've done. I open my mouth to tell her it's okay . . .

"Sunny!" Candy calls out. "Come on now! We need to get going! I have things to do!"

She stays in my arms and squeezes me even tighter. I hug her back.

"Sunny!" Candy shouts louder. "Let's go! Get over here now!"

Finally, she lets go. So I let go.

She looks at me for just an instant, flashing those clear blue eyes down at me, piercing through the fear and confusion of the morning and almost erasing the drama—like she's pushed a reset button on the day. My chest decompresses and my shoulders relax.

My hands slip off her waist as she turns and runs back to the car, her steps the same speed but noticeably lighter. She opens the car door and climbs in. Candy puts the car in gear and backs it onto the grass to swing around Tom's truck. She turns the car onto the road, and without looking back, speeds away.

Chapter Five

Tom's keys are still in the ignition of his truck, so I start the truck and drive it over the grass behind the house to the porch. I go back into my trailer and put on a dark blue T-shirt and my old sneakers. Then I walk to the shed behind my trailer and bring back a wheelbarrow and a plank.

Once I get the truck and wheelbarrow over to the house, I open the tailgate on the truck and suspend the plank off it to make a ramp. I pull Tom into the barrow and push him up the plank and dump him onto the flatbed. His limp body rolls over so his face presses against the floor. I slam the tailgate shut, get in and drive around to the driveway and out onto the road. I notice the knuckles of my right hand are sore and red, but I don't see any blood.

It's about a ten-minute ride to Tom's house, up Highway 17 to his house on Parkers Ferry Road. Highway 17 is a state-run highway so it's well maintained and smooth and for the first five minutes everything is quiet. I'm hoping to get him back without him waking up.

Just as I'm thinking this, I hear a rumbling behind me. I glance in the rearview mirror and see Tom rise to his knees and crawl up the truck bed to the back of the cab. I can see he's still groggy and trying to make sense of the situation he's found himself in. I step on the gas hard and he falls back, halfway down the truck bed.

"Hey!" he yells. "What the hell ya doing?"

He gets to his feet and starts forward again. This time I hit the brakes, and he slides and stumbles and bangs hard into the cab and grabs the sidewall to stop himself from flying out of the truck. "You son of a bitch, Sticker!" he yells. "You almost threw me out! You could have killed me! Slow down! Slow the hell down!"

He starts pounding on the roof of the cab. I step hard on the gas again and he slides back down the truck bed, this time all the way to the tailgate. He starts back forward, and I hit the brakes again. He stumbles forward, but steadies himself on the sidewall and only gently bangs into the cab this time.

I knew what was coming next, but I'm too late. By the time I find the button for the electric window, his hand is inside the cab, swinging at me. I lean over the passenger's seat, trying to avoid it as the window rolls up and pins his arm on the ceiling of the cab. I try to bat his hand away with my left arm as I hold onto the steering wheel with my right. I would have hit the brakes again, but if I had, Tom would have surely flown off the truck and I might really have killed him. So I keep swatting his arm away as he keeps flailing at me and hollerin'.

This goes on for right near a full three or four minutes, which doesn't sound like long, but believe me, when you're in the middle of it, it sure as hell is. All the time I'm weaving all over the road for being so distracted and busy swatting at his hand like there's a swarm of hornets around my head. Finally, we come to his driveway and I turn onto it and gas the car again, but not so hard, and feel Tom stumble back a step. His arm stops flailing and clamps up to the underside of the top of the cab. Then I hit the window button, which lowers the window, freeing his arm. After all, as much as an SOB as I am, I really don't want to kill him. And what I'm fixin' to do, just might.

I hit the brakes hard and the wheels lock and the truck skids right into Tom's new double-garage door, busting a hole in it with the front bumper and hood of the truck. Tom gets thrown forward hard, bouncing off the back corner of the cab, his arm free but still in the truck, which causes him to spin around over and around the cab and fly head first through the air right into the garage door. He sticks there for a second, like a wet sponge hitting a wall, and then slides down moaning until he ends up on the asphalt, piled up like dog shit. I climb out of the truck and stand over the pile of shit there in the driveway as he continues to moan. "You'll make it," I say. "Unfortunately."

He starts to raise his head to look at me, but can only make it far enough to look at my feet with their dirty old sneakers. "Tom," I say matter of fact-like, "I know you're kin, and you might be on drugs or booze or fairy dust for all I know, but there's no excuse for what you did. I'm givin' you warnin' right here and right now. Next time you cause trouble with Candy or her kid, it'll be your last."

His nose is bleeding and his face is scraped and there's a big gash diagonally down the left side of his forehead. He keeps trying to turn his head up to look at me, but can't do it.

"You understand?" I ask firmly. I take a step towards him and put my foot on his shoulder and push. He rolls over onto his back. "You understand?" I demand.

"Uhhh . . ." he moans.

"So here . . ." I take the keys out of the ignition and jingle them as I stand over him again. "I know you like to hunt, Tom, so here," I hold the keys under his nose. "Knock yourself out." I rear back and throw his keychain up over the garage as far as I can so they'll land in the field somewhere behind it. He'll be crawling around looking for hours, I figure. I turn and walk back down the driveway and out to the road. I walk away without glancing back.

A few steps down the road I feel it: the rubber-legs. My knees almost buckle; my arms turn to jelly; my head becomes dangerously light. I know I should sit down, but there's no way I'm going to let him see.

I hate the rubber-legs. After feeling so tough and potent during the fight, after it, you're as weak as a little girl. The last time I was in a fight the same thing happened. That was four years ago, just after I had gotten my brown belt. I was walking down Main Street in Charleston one evening just past sundown, minding my own business and taking in the scenery. I walked past this diner—one of those old 1950s-style silver aluminum siding kind that serves burgers and fries and milk shakes and has young teenybopper waitresses in pressed white button shirts, plaid skirts down to their knees, white bobby socks, and bright red lipstick, cruising the aisles and waiting on tables and then giggling to each other in the back near the kitchen. That kind of diner.

As I walked past, I glanced in the window to see what I might see, and saw a couple guys sitting in a booth right inside the window. I could tell by their leather jackets and slicked-back hair that they thought they were tough. More like thugs, I figured. I looked at them, they looked at me for just a second or two, and then I looked back to see where I was walking. Nothing unusual, I assure you.

So I turned the corner and walked down a side street looking in the windows of the closed shops when all of a sudden, I found myself sprawled out on the sidewalk on my hands and knees. One of the tough guys had kicked me from behind and had sent me flying and darn near knocked the wind right out of me. I got up off the concrete and turned to see the one tough guy glaring at me and the other reaching into his pocket; and I knew it wasn't to give me change for a dollar.

"What the hell you doin'?" I snapped, glaring back at them as I brushed my hands from the fall.

The first tough guy looked at me with his beady, sneaky little eyes, and said, "I didn't like your look back there."

"*Look*? What *look*?"

"That cocky-ass look. You think you're better than us?"

"Who cares if I do," I replied casually wiping my palms on my pants. "And if you think I'm gonna fight, you can forget it. I'm not an idiot."

That must have surprised them 'cuz neither of them moved or said anything. I turned to leave, and after a couple steps, the hair on the back of my neck stood up. Without thinking, I spun around blindly with my arm opening up and my hand open and flat and hard, thinking I would hit whoever was charging me. Instead, I chopped nothing but air. The thug was indeed coming at me, but I had turned too soon and was a second too early. I lost my balance and ended up spinning right into the sidewalk. He lunged at me again, but this time I was looking straight at him, and with my hand on the ground, I swept my leg out and cut his feet right out from under him. He fell hard right onto his shoulder and let out a high-pitched, girlish, yelp. His buddy didn't move. Instead, he started snickering.

"Ah . . . . shat up!" the wounded thug muttered, still lying on the ground. I stood there for a couple seconds in my fighting crouch to make sure we were done, the one thug still snickering at the other. I resumed my window-shopping, trying to stay strong and not let them see my rubber-legs.

Those rubber-legs. All from a little run-in with a couple of thugs or a fight with my cousin. Makes me wonder how I'd feel if I were in a real battle. Bullets screaming overhead, bombs going off all around, gunpowder choking you, buddies having their limbs blown off. And hand-to-hand combat? Come on. Makes my little run-ins seem like trips to Disneyland.

But my fight with those thugs was then and this is now and now I'm walking down a country road, not a city street, in the hot afternoon sun, sweating, and looking down at the sandy shoulder of the road trying to stay strong. The rubber-legs can last a while. So I keep looking down and every now and then a car passes by but I don't look up but just keep on walking.

I think back to Candy and Sunny and them driving off after I knocked out Tom and Sunny running to me and hugging me and squeezing me tight. So tight. I feel it again deep down in my bones. A lump forms in my throat and I have to blink hard to keep seeing straight.

But she's not mine. And I'll never know what it's like to have one. You see, for me, my life is more a story like *The Sun Also Rises*. Me and Jake—we're like *this*. Maybe that's why feeling her hug me, well . . . forget it . . . just forget it.

Candy will tell you that having kids—in her case, just one—sucks. They're too expensive, take up too much time, and wear you out. That may be, but I guarantee she'd have a hole in her the size of the Grand Canyon if she didn't have Sunny. What's more, years from now, as she watches the sun set on her life, that hole would grow even wider and deeper and suck her right down into itself.

But Candy will let on that Sunny "interrupted" her life and squashed her dreams. Yeah, she was gonna be a famous clothes designer or romance novel writer or something. But then she got pregnant by a guy she didn't love in a place she wouldn't have chosen and had Sunny. And without ever considering that she could have still at least tried to pursue her dreams, even with having Sunny, she used having a kid as a reason for giving up on them. When your dreams become excuses—it's happened. It's called resignation—"The Big R." And The Big R sucks.

And me? I've resigned myself to raising other kinds of frustrations. Although they can't hug me, I create them anyway. After all, I have to create *something*. You see, I'm hoping that when me, Sticker, is watching that final sunset with nobody to carry on the Sticker legacy, maybe I won't get sucked into my abyss. Maybe. But somehow, I doubt it.

The sun's directly overhead now as I walk along Parkers Ferry Road back towards the highway. A stray cat sees me and darts into the weeds. A car hasn't passed me in a while, and I've gotten into a sort of a rhythm with my steps and my diaphragm is rising and falling in beat with my feet rising and falling and my mind calms from the rhythm and sameness and consistency. The adrenaline is gone now, burned up and breathed out, and I feel a bit stronger. For a bunch of minutes, I don't thing about nothin'.

Then a brown delivery van passes me and honks his horn and its wake blows sand and dust on me and my mind kicks back in and I start thinking again. But I don't want to start thinking again. I didn't even know I wasn't thinking until I started thinking again, and when I did, I realized I liked it better when I wasn't.

But once you start thinking, to get to not thinking again is like trying to put a cat in a bag. That animal will fight and claw at you to stay out and you'll knock yourself silly and get all scratched up trying to get him in. So you've got to trick it, and that's a whole 'nother adventure in itself.

The easiest way is to shoot that cat up with drugs. Then there's spiking his water dish. Then there's sending him off to camp somewhere where he wanders around in the wilderness trying to find himself while communing with other cats trying to do the same thing; all of who pay some head-honcho cat all their money to show them how. All the while the head-honcho cat is holed-up in his cat-house with all his feline admirers who are so smitten with his head-honchoism that they stretch and purr and rub up against his leg every time he so much as looks their way or walks into the room.

This head-honcho cat—he tells you it's all your own doing, that you control your own destiny. He makes you feel all-powerful, because, he tells you, all you have to do is follow his teachings—the holy and ancient *Catnip Chronicles*—and you'll be saved. But on the other hand, you get to feeling all shameful and small, because, although he never comes right out and says it, since you *are* the one with the power, it's your own damn fault your life is so out of the bag and has so many holes in it. So a cat who listens to him gets his or her mind pulled one way and then the other with this power/shame contrast and gets all balled up and confused.

Sometimes a cat will think, "I'm the one in control! I'm such a cool cat! Ain't I wonderful? Purr . . . purr." And other times, the cat will think, "I can't do nothin' right and I'm nothing but a clump of used-up kitty-litter and such a shameful idiot for failing so! Hiss . . . hiss."

So all these cats, they keep trying to reconcile this confusion which just creates even more confusion since the whole premise is confusing in the first place and that makes the head-honcho cat even more in demand for his patronizing advice and syrupy ways and he becomes even more revered by his growing legion of feline admirers. And these confused and vulnerable cats end up agreeing with anything the head-honcho cat tells them. After all, he seems so nice and as far removed from being an SOB as you're gonna find. So these strays listen and follow and eventually forget that there's even so much as a bag altogether. And it's not just cats who do this kind of thing: There's foxes and squirrels and coyotes and pigs.

Since pigs are certain their *Swine Scriptures* are the only ways to wallow forever, and squirrels are positive their *Nut Novenas* are the only way to crack into heaven, and coyotes think their *Howling at the Moon* disciplines are direct from the *Great Howler in the Sky,* and the foxes think their *Sly Little Antics* are the way to get to Grandmother's house (true heaven), there's a lot of friction between them all. It can make for a real mess, you know?

But that's okay in the long run because they'll all just end up scratching and clawing and biting each other to extinction as they try proving they're the chosen ones. So I don't worry too much about it. The challenge is just staying out of their way.

Maybe I'll start my own discipline—*The Doctrine of the Fallen Apple,* I'll call it. If you simply believe that an apple falls from a tree, you'll be right on the money. There's no room for disagreements or misinterpretation. Initiation into the discipline would consist of a single question: "Do you believe that an apple falls from the tree?"

"Yes," the adept would reply.

"Congratulations. You are now a brother/sister of the *Doctrine of the Fallen Apple.* There are no other lessons. No dogmas to defend. Since you believe in the provable, you are perfect. Now go shake a tree, and don't look up." It would be a very boring Ashram. And since the guru wouldn't really be needed, he'd be homeless. Or maybe he'd live in a trailer.

So I'm walking down this road and my old white sneakers are scuffed and dirty and my hair is brown and tousled, and for a few steps, I close my eyes and see the black underside of my eyelids with the faint white specs, like grains of sand, that I see but really don't see and which never go away. As I walk along the sandy shoulder of the road, I force myself not to think, but to feel. I feel the sun beating down on my head and the air fanning through my fingers as my arms swing forward and backwards with my steps. I open my eyes and see the gray road ahead and the trees besides the road and the bushes and tall green weeds and the telephone poles with wires stretching into the future. I hear the birds in the trees chirping and the sound of my sneakers crunching on the hot sand as I walk. I smell the musky Spanish moss hanging from the trees and the stagnant water in puddles back in the swamp. I feel the spit in my mouth and my tongue on the roof of my mouth.

My mind settles into the present moment, the present feeling, and my body lets go. And I realize that this—what I'm experiencing right now—is nothing that I never didn't have or ever need to strive for. It is now—no rules, no threats, and nothing to follow other than where it directs me to go. And it doesn't cost a dime.

Chapter Six

I come to the highway and turn right, and there's a dashed yellow line down the middle and a solid white line down the side and cars driving by in both directions right regular-like. I start paying more attention and stay farther away from the road on the far side of the shoulder so I won't get mowed over by a truck or drunk driver or somethin'. I keep feeling the heat and the air and listening and watching.

After a mile or so, I hear a car slow down behind me and pull onto the shoulder. As I turn, I hear a gentle toot-toot of the horn. I see a vintage candy-apple red 1965 Mustang convertible with the top down and two young women in it. They look so similar in their general features they could be mistaken as sisters. I recognize the one driving: she's the daughter of the man I used to work for at my last job at the local newspaper seven years ago.

She was halfway through high school then, and now she's all grown up—in a couple of ways at least—with her long brunette hair falling well past her shoulders. She used to come into the office a few times a week after school to do some typing and filing for her pa, and we kinda flirted, despite our big age difference. Oh, the boys would swarm around her like hummingbirds to sugar-water to look at her blossoming emerald eyes and full, luscious lips that turn up at the corners, like a dolphin's, so she looks like she's smiling all the time even when she's just sitting there doing nothing fun at all.

And of course, even though she was just seventeen at the time, my mind would race, like any of those younger schoolboys did, at the idea of going back into the storeroom or out behind the garage with her and having a not so innocent time with such a sweet and innocent thing as she. All consensual, of course. That's what makes it such a turn on. That beautiful, pure vision would actually *want* me. And the other thing that made it equally intriguing, and a fantasy instead of a dream, was that I knew it could never happen. I'm sure her pa wouldn't have appreciated me thinking about his little angel that way. Maybe he read my mind and that's why he fired me.

"Sticker!" she calls out. "Is that you? Is that really you?"

I don't say nothin'.

"What'cha doing out here all alone, so far from home, Stick?" she asks in her playful, pouty way. A way that would make any man—especially an older man—feel something he'd given up on long ago: that all the holes in his life are suddenly filled and he all of a sudden became whole himself and that life is really worth living and maybe there's something even worth dying for. He starts believing he's superman and can do anything—anything at all—simply because this beautiful young woman smiled at him some and played with him some because she saw a man in him some.

"You lost, you poor thing?" she continues. "You lost and need someone to help you find your way?"

I fight back a smile, but I'm not too successful. "Hey, Kaitlin," I say. "Long time."

"Long time my ass! More like eternity!" she says. "Though it looks like eternity hasn't hurt you none." She smiles with those lips even more turned up and I see a twinkle jump from her pearly whites. A tingle shoots up my spine and explodes over my scalp like a starburst.

"You don't need to be walking on this God forsaken highway on a scorchin' hot day like this, now do you? And you can't duck into a store or alley out here on this highway to hide from me. So hop in. I'll give you a ride."

A car passes by. I stand there a second. You see, ever since I got fired, I've tried to avoid her. But I find myself walking over to the driver's side of the car and I watch as my hands place themselves on the top edge of the car door as if they know what they're going to do next.

"Come on, Stick. Climb in!" she says while whipping her head and glancing over her shoulder. I push myself up and swing my legs and body over the car door into the back seat. If I had a tail, it woulda been waggin'.

"Sticker!" she calls back as she puts the car in gear and starts pulling back onto the highway. "This is Kathy, my bestest friend ever in the whole wide world!" They both giggle. "Kaitlin and Kathy," she chimes, "the *Ditto-Amigos* they call us!" They giggle again.

I nod to Kathy and she looks at me and then looks back at Kaitlin as Kait gets the car into second gear.

"And this is Sticker, Kat. You remember, I told you abo. . ."

"I remember, Kait! For God's sake, I remember! You've told me about him enough so I'll remember him 'till moss swallows up my gravestone, for cryin' out loud!"

I can't see Kaitlin's face for sitting behind her, but by the silence that follows, I suspect she might-a been blushing. And if she had looked back at me, she might have seen me blushing too. Finally, she slaps Kathy's arm and says, "Kat! What're you talkin' about? You hush now. You know I haven't said all that much, just about when he used to work for my pa."

"Oh right! I must have *forgotten!*" Kathy says as she rolls her eyes.

Kaitlin says quickly, "Me and Kathy work over at Conways now." I inch over to the middle of the seat so I won't get whipped by her hair being blown back. "Both of us started the same week and both of us worked our way up to the front office. Makin' right good money now, too." She turns her head to look my way and says under her breath all secret-like, "Ten dollars an hour!"

She and Kathy exchange glances and giggle like girls who just got caught doing something naughty. "I still work for my pa too. I'm his 'investigative reporter' when there's a hot story or something. It's a blast."

"Sounds good," I say.

"So what'cha doing out here all alone, Sticker? Where you headed? What'cha been up to?"

"Just headin' home." I reply. "Had something to take care of and now I'm just headed home."

"Home!" Kaitlin exclaims. "You still livin' out in that trailer behind Tommy Simpson's house?"

"Yeah. Still livin' there."

"I heard he and Candy split a while back. That so?"

"Yeah. About two years."

"So Candy's livin' out there all alone?"

"Isn't she the one," Kathy jumps in, "You said . . ."

"No, Kat," Kaitlin cuts her off. "That was someone else. Candy has a little girl. What's her name again, Stick?"

"Sunny."

"Yeah. That's right. Sunny. How's she been doing?"

"Okay, I reckon. She's doing okay."

"Yeah, that's good. You should see her, Kat. The cutest baby-girl you ever saw. I remember when I worked at the skatin' rink way back when, Candy and Tom brought her by when she was about four years old. Cutest thing you ever saw out on that rink trying not to fall and holding onto her mama's and daddy's hand. Her blond hair was in pigtails and she had on this little pink jump suit. You just wanted to hug her and eat her all up, she was so darn cute! Some folks stopped their skatin' just to watch. Makes you want to run out and buy one for yourself!"

"Yeah, she's doing all right," I say. "She just turned nine a couple months ago."

"Nine! Well I'll be! Yeah, I guess so. That was right near five years ago. Feels like forever, though, don't it?"

She pauses and almost becomes reflective, but then stops herself and starts talking again, "So Stick, What you been up to? Got a job?"

"No. Don't got a job."

"What else . . ." She tries to make it seem like she's searching for something else to say, but can't help herself from being direct: "Still out in that trailer with no job. So you got a girl?"

"What'd you say?" I had heard her but asked her anyway.

"Got a girl, Stick?"

"No. Don't have a girlfriend neither."

"Oh," Kaitlin says softly, half relieved and half disappointed. "Not seein' Amy any more?"

"No. No more Amy. That was a long time ago, Kait."

"Yeah, I know, I know." She pauses a second and then says, "Hey listen, Stick. Me and Kathy took the day off and are going down to River-hole. Got our bathing suits and some wine coolers in the trunk. Wanna come?"

"Kait!" Kathy exclaims. "Can you *be* any more forward?"

"Oh hush," Kait replies. "He's just an old friend and it's a hot day and he's probably got nothin' better to do. That right, Stick?"

I don't say nothin'.

"Well, Sticker? What'd ya say? Come on down to The Hole with us and have some fun. You probably don't have no fun livin' out in that trailer all by yourself."

I can't argue with that. Most the time SOBs don't have much fun considering what they are and all. But you have to keep in mind that there are two kinds of SOBs.

The vast majority of SOBs have their fun by being mean to people. They enjoy seeing other people in pain—because they're constantly in it themselves. So to handle the pain, these SOBs flip it upside-down in their heads to trick themselves that it's really not pain at all, and even fun, because nobody alive can handle being in pain all the time. They don't even realize they're doing it, this emotion flipping; it's all unconscious, you see.

So when one of this kind of SOB actually does have fun and there's no pain involved, they flip it upside-down too, since that's what their mind automatically does. They're not satisfied with just having fun for fun's sake because fun ain't fun to them. They actually see it as kinda painful. They make it a problem so it seems like fun to them, and then they try to make it *your* problem too, since misery loves company. That's why these people are never satisfied and are a royal pain in the ass. That's one kind of SOB.

As for me, I'm the other kind of SOB. The kind of person that can take life and break it down into understandable parts and at the same time see the forest for the trees and get to the truth of the matter. But more times than not, the truth ain't very pleasant. Top that off with being successful doing your own thing, and people (especially if they're the first kind of SOB) find it very hard to forgive you. The bottom line is that both kinds of SOBs make people uncomfortable, and they both end up being hated and alone.

So now I have what you might call a dilemma: My loins want to go to River-hole with these beautiful young women, and my brain and SOBism wants to be sensible and maybe a bit of a martyr. Most the time my brain wins. This time it doesn't.

"So how about it?" Kaitlin continues. "Come on down!" she laughs, looking at Kathy, who laughs too.

I inch up closer to the front seat and yell, "Come on down!" I fall back into the rear seat, fling my hands into the air, and let out a "YEEEEE HAAAAA!"

The girls laugh again, look back my way, and thrust their fists in the air and yell, "YEE HA! We're going to The Hole! YEE HA!"

It's good to hear someone laugh. My chest relaxes as a sigh escapes my lips. Kat turns up the radio and we speed along the highway; the wind in our hair and the sun keeping us warm.

"Hey, Sticker," Kaitlin calls back. "We need to go by Kathy's house for a second, do you mind? She lives up 303 a-ways. It shouldn't take more than fifteen minutes."

"That's fine with me," I say, content to sit back and be driven. We get to Kathy's house and she ducks in and sprints back out with her purse, calling out over her shoulder, "We're going to River-hole, Mom. See you later!" and then we're back on the highway again.

We take a few turns and get on State Road 26 to the river, and after a while, Kaitlin slows down to get through what's known in these parts as *Wetman's Curve*. It's a stretch of pavement that bends left about ninety degrees to meander through part of a swamp. It got its name from the fact that if you go too fast around it while driving south and you're in the right hand lane, which you should be since 26 is just two-lanes, you'll skid right off the pavement and end up waist-deep in the swamp. So instead of dying, you just get wet. But you'd also have to thumb a ride back into town and get a tow truck to come and pull your car out.

We get through the curve and go a few more miles and there on the left, right before the sandy-dirt road to River-hole, is the remains of the old *Hallelujah God* church and cemetery. This church is kinda famous 'round here. Or maybe I should say infamous, considering its history and the legend about it.

You see, this church was built a couple decades before the start of the Civil War by a white man who wanted to do a good deed for all the negro slaves who worked on the plantations 'round here. So he up and built it and negroes started coming and they had their own preacher and they started burying their dead in the yard out back. The Civil War came and the white man who built the church and the negro preacher who preached there decided they should help move negro slaves up north where they would be free, so the church became part of the Underground Railroad, as it was called. They were right successful helping the slaves too. But there was one incident concerning a teenage slave-girl that was kinda spooky and which started the legend that was named after her—The Legend of the Martha Chimes.

We make the left onto the sandy dirt road that goes down to River-hole and drive slowly along side the churchyard. Behind the ruins of the church there's a few old melted-down gravestones leaning over showing above the grass, and just beyond them, there's a row of cypress trees with Spanish moss hanging off of them. That must be a real comforting sight on a foggy, moon-lit night.

Kaitlin stops the car and puts it in neutral and opens the door. "What are you doin'? Kathy asks.

Without a word, Kaitlin gets out of the car and starts picking some of the yellow and purple wildflowers growing on the side of the road. She gathers a couple dozen and ties them together with a long piece of grass and then jogs over to the stone steps at the front of where the church used to be. She props the little bouquet on the steps and jogs back to the car.

"Thought I'd leave old Martha a little present," she says as she climbs back in the car. "Let her know that someone's thinkin' 'bout her."

"You believe in all that legend stuff?" Kathy asks.

"Who knows?" Kaitlin replies. "It might be true, it might not be. I sure as heck don't know enough about those sorts of things to say one way or another. Won't do anyone any harm, I reckon. I know I wouldn't mind if it was my spirit stuck out here."

That's Kaitlin for you.

"Yeah," Kathy says. "Why not."

Kaitlin puts the car in gear and we start rolling down the dirt road again. Kathy and I look at the flowers on the steps, their colors showing brightly against the gray steps.

So as I was saying, this girl Martha Chimes was one of the slaves being moved along the Underground Railroad in June of 1862. She was from the Wentworth Plantation just east of Atlanta and she was born into slavery and never lived a day without being a slave. She worked in the cotton fields on the plantation picking that white puffy stuff that grows only up to your knees so you have to stoop over to pick it so you end up getting a bad back after years of doing it; and you carry it in big-ass baskets on top of your head to dump it into a wagon on the way to being cleaned, which doesn't do your neck much good either.

In the winter when the fields were bare she'd haul water up from the creek in buckets strung on the ends of a pole so she could carry two of 'em at a time across her shoulders. She'd haul the water to the plantation house for the white folks to take baths in and she would haul wood to burn in their fireplaces and stoves and to heat the water for their baths and she'd sweep the floors and beat the rugs and wash the clothes and windows and tend to the chickens and even the horses sometimes and this was all she knew ever since she was a child.

But Martha wasn't a child for long, because when she was just five-years-old, her mama died giving birth to her brother, and she learned real quick-like how to cook and sweep and do chores for her daddy and kin, like her mama woulda done. She never learned how to read or write, so she was dependent on what other people told her as to what the truth was and all. And her brother, he was in the same situation as far as learning went. So when some Confederate soldiers came by on their way to the war and wanted a boy to carry their guns and knapsacks, they told him how great and glorious war was and what a hero he'd be if he helped them win it, which, they said, they were certain to do. So even though his daddy knew better and told him so, the boy listened to one of the rough-necked white soldiers and snuck off one night to carry his stuff. Strangers are believed better than kin sometimes, you know. Turns out the young wog made it all the way up to Tennessee, but was shot and killed just a couple months later in the Battle of Shiloh while loading the white man's musket. He was just eleven years old.

So Martha and her daddy came down from Atlanta towards the sea, taking roughly the same route General William T. Sherman and his troops would later take when they raped and pillaged the South at the end of the war. Of course, taking that route wasn't hard to do, since Sherman and his troops burned a path about forty miles wide as they taught the South a lesson. I guess they thought the South needed to learn a lesson considerin' it had the nerve to question the Federal government and condoned slavery and all. And the South? Well they thought they were fighting the second coming of the original Revolutionary War. In fact, Jefferson Davis, the President of the Confederate States of America, had portraits of George Washington hanging on the walls of the Confederate White House in Richmond, Virginia, to pay homage to him and what the original Declaration of Independence and Constitution stood for.

You never know what the truth really is because those who win any war get to write its history and they make themselves out to be saints or somethin', as they did with Lincoln and the Union Army. And something they left out was that slavery wasn't at first the real main issue—the Civil War was more about free trade and the rights of the individual States; and one of those rights was the right to secede from the Union.

You see, the Federal government was forcing the South to sell its cotton and other raw materials only to factories in the north, rather than letting them sell them to whomever they wanted to, such as other countries. This was essentially the same thing as the *taxation without representation* Great Britain forced on the thirteen Colonies, which, we all know, was the main reason for the Revolutionary War. Heck, most southerners didn't even own slaves or plantations. Most of them were small family farmers fighting to live the way they wanted to without the United States Government dictating how they should behave or who they could do business with.

Slavery didn't become a major issue until after the Battle of Antietam—two years into the war—when Lincoln issued the Emancipation Proclamation on January 1, 1863. Little do people realize that this proclamation freed the slaves only in the Confederate States that were taking part in the rebellion, not those who weren't. Says something, don't you think?

So by the North winning, the Federal government got a lot more power. Some say too much. Some say that when this one nation-wide government usurped the individual States as the major governing body, everyone, both black and white, were on their way of becoming different kinds of slaves—of one omnipotent centralized oligarchy. In this case, it wasn't a king, but an institution. Isn't that just what the Founding Fathers were trying to get away from with a loosely bound union of sovereign states? I ain't for slavery in any form; and surely not the kind where I become one.

I figure that maintaining a government is much like maintaining a sidewalk—you'd better pull out the weeds that start growing in its cracks, or before you know it, those weeds will take over and swallow it up and after a while it'll be hard to tell there was even so much as a sidewalk there to begin with.

Anyway, Martha and her daddy finally made it to Savannah, and then started up towards Charleston where some white folks were helping the negroes make their way north along the Railroad.

Martha and her daddy were holed-up in the church for the night that long summer's day with a handful of other slaves, when finally that evening, her daddy decided to tell her what being free meant and all, since *his* daddy told him what it was like when he was a young'un back in Africa. At first, she didn't understand and just asked question after question. Her daddy was getting kinda exasperated trying to get her to catch on, when finally, the thought came to him to explain it a different way. Their conversation went something like this:

"You remember the parrot that Lady Wentworth had?" he asked Martha.

"Yes, daddy, I do."

"She kept that parrot in a cage, didn' she?"

"Yes, daddy, she shur did."

"Do you 'member when you were a little girl and you asked Lady Wentworth why she kept the parrot in the cage?"

Martha thought a second, "No, not really daddy."

"Well, you were real little, so that's not surprisin'. But you asked her just the same and she told you she kept it in his cage for to protect it. That if the bird got out it might fly off somewhere it wasn't familiar with and get hurt or killed."

"That's what she said?"

"Yes, child. That's what she said. But Martha, dear, now you're old enough to learn that she told you a lie."

"A lie? But I liked Lady Wentworth. She was a fine lady."

"Yes, child, I liked her too. An' she was awright as far as a master's wife went—kept us fed and didn't have us beat. But she was lyin' when she told you about the parrot. You see, she kept the parrot because the parrot pleased her. She liked having someone talk at her when her husband was gone all day. So she kept the parrot just to make herself happy. And that parrot, well, that parrot woulda rather been out of that cage flying anywhere he wanted to."

"But he woulda gotten hurt or killed if he flew away!"

"Well, maybe he woulda, Martha. Maybe. But do you 'member the couple times the parrot got out of his cage?"

"Oooeee! I shur do! We had to chase him 'round the house all day long to catch him!"

"An why do you think it kept flyin' and hidin' on y'all? I'll tell you, child. Because he didn' wanna go back in that cage. He wanted to fly around on his own, even if it might be a little dangerous."

Martha thought on this a little. Then her daddy said, "An' being slaves like we were was the same as being in a cage and doin' things jus' to make somebody else happy. No livin' thing naturally wants to be stuck in a cage. But when you're free, darlin', you'll be able to fly anywhere you want to, and nobody can tell you different."

Martha's eyes lit up. She liked that. She thought of herself flying up to heaven. "That's nice, Daddy," she said, and they both laid down on the floor beneath the pews to sleep. But she really and truly didn't fully understand yet. She did like the thought of flying though, and it helped her to sleep.

The light finally did dawn on her in a dream that night, and she finally got it in her heart and not just her head what being free really and truly meant. So she got up off that floor from under the pew and started pulling on the church-bell rope at three in the morning—said she just had to hear some music, she was so happy to be getting freed. She wanted to make music like the birds that can fly.

The bell started chiming and woke everybody up and some bounty-hunters who were camping down near River-hole wondered what the bell-ringing was about. So they rode their horses back to the church with their muskets and pistols and found Martha Chimes out back singing a gospel song right near the gravestones of old dead slaves . . .

Amazing grace. How sweet the sound
That saved a wretch like me!
I once was lost, but now am found,
Was blind, but now I see.

'Twas grace that taught my heart to fear,
And grace my fears relieved.
How precious did that grace appear
The hour I first believed . . .

When the bounty hunters rode up to Martha, she stood there tall and proud and just kept singing. But when they drew their pistols, Martha lost her head and made a break for it yelling, "Nobody's gonna cage me!" and got shot in the back.

Upon further investigation, the bounty hunters found the other slaves hiding under the pews in the church. A few of them tried to run too, but they were either shot right there or lynched a couple days later after they got tracked down in the swamps by hunting dogs.

Martha's daddy didn't get shot, but mighta wished he had considering his wife died in childbirth, his eleven-year-old son got killed in the war, and his daughter got shot just days away from freedom. Later, he thought to himself that he should have just kept his mouth shut and told Martha the truth after they had gotten all the way up north and out of harms way. But he wanted to do better than he had with his son as far as truth was concerned. Poor guy just couldn't win.

Martha and the others were buried in shallow graves out behind the church without any gravestones for markers, just branches tied into crosses. Their bodies weren't in coffins, but white linen sacks; the white man and negro preacher just couldn't stand burying them with nothin'. Then, the very next year on exactly the same day as the massacre, it rained so fierce the river overflowed its banks and flooded for a mile in both directions.

I'm sure you've heard stories or seen pictures about churches or statues of Mary or Christ or a saint being the only thing left standing after an earthquake or hurricane or tornado or somethin'. Makes you kinda believe in divine intervention, you know.

But it happened exactly the opposite 'round here, 'cuz even though a number of towns and farms were flooded because of the river overflowing, the only place that got destroyed was the *Hallelujah God* church on the side of the road down to River-hole. The river reached out and swatted that church down as if were angry and didn't know how to take out it's frustration—so it just took it's frustration out on one of its own. And not just that, but that river reached down into the earth and brought up out of it the remains of Martha Chimes.

You see, some say Christ wasn't the only one to rise from the dead. Martha Chimes did too and floated down to the river in her white linen sack. And some say that it wasn't the water that swatted the church down and lifted up Martha, but the spirit of Martha herself who did it. Some say that even to this day, on the same night every year, when the clock strikes three, you can hear that old church bell ring. I never have. But then again, I'm never 'round here at three in the morning.

Now they tried to rebuild that church three or four times. But each time, the next year on the anniversary of the massacre, a flood would up and wipe it out again. The last time they tried to rebuild it was just after the turn of the century. Now all that's left are the broken-up stones of the foundation and chimney and, of course, the old gravestones of former slaves. And as for Martha, well, people say she must have some unfinished business and keeps hangin' around. And there's all sorts of theories as to what that unfinished business might be. Makes for some hair-raising stories around the campfire when you're a kid, you know. All I can say is maybe there's a lesson or two we can learn from what happened to her and the church and all. Maybe if we did, that would help ease old Martha's pains. Who knows? Wouldn't do her no harm, I reckon.

A few turns and a mile down the dusty dirt and sandy one lane road later, we arrive at River-hole. It's a sharp elbow—almost an oxbow lake—in the Edisto River about three hundred yards wide where the water's deep enough to never feel the bottom and cool enough to want to swim in even in the hottest summer. Back in the day, anybody, even if they were nobody, would go down to The Hole several times a week and swing off the rope or float around in tubes and drink and smoke and even cook burgers and hot dogs and beans. The same kids went down there so often it became like its own little community with initiation rites (you had to swing off the rope butt-naked in front of everybody and do a spread-eagle into the water), unspoken protocols (if you mentioned any carryin'-ons to an adult, you were banned for the rest of the summer) and unspoken pecking orders (the coolest guys got to pick any girl they wanted and the nerdy smart kids swam in their own little area downstream).

Then summer would end and we'd all be back in school and we never let ourselves realize that those glory days were actually gonna end and be over. It never crossed our minds that when we got old, like forty, we'd look back on those days and wish we had paid closer attention to 'em and appreciated them more and lived them more because we'd finally realize that those days are gone and ain't ever comin' back—ever.

We should have slapped ourselves upside the head to wake ourselves up and grab that one day—*that one day*—and use it up so completely that we'd never have any regrets and it'd be impossible to forget. We'd use it up and make a point of remembering it so clearly—*so clearly*—that years later, we could close our eyes and just about be there again and just about live it again. But you never realize how good you have it until long after. It takes hindsight to realize that. It's called hindsight not so much because you're lookin' backwards, but because you're an ass for not realizing how good you had it at the time.

But then one spring there was a big fish-kill in the river upstream on account of the chemicals the new paper mill let leak into the river so they wouldn't have to pay to have them dumped the right way, and kids stayed away for a few summers and The Hole just never got popular again. These days, a lot of kids have swimming pools in their back yard with chemicals the parents put in them to keep 'em nice and sanitized and which would probably kill some fish on their own. Friends come over and hang out and maybe play pool-volley ball or something and watch TV or play these new video games they just came out with and get bored and anxious and then start looking for someplace else to go.

River-hole *was* the someplace else to go where all the kids went and played and irritated each other enough to not get bored. Every now and then a tough guy would argue with another tough guy trying to be tougher and a fight would break out which usually consisted of a shoving match until one of 'em got shoved into the river. Then they would yell back and forth a couple more times and call each other names and their girlfriends would stop them from fightin' and that would be that.

And in the evening on the way home we'd take the long way back because everyone thought it was cool to do and made it so you had to go through *Wetman's Curve* to get back to town. Two guys at a time would have it out on the highway racing their sooped-up cars or simple old jalopies down the mile-long straightaway on State Road 26 and into *Wetman's Curve*, with lookouts ahead who would signal 'em by flashing their high-beams when no cars coming the other way were in sight and it was safe to let 'er rip for all she was worth.

Most the time, each guy had his girl riding shotgun and having the panties scared off her enough so maybe the guy would get lucky later that night. And after the straightaway, after you got your car to 80 or 90 or even 100 sometimes, you'd come up on *Wetman's Curve*. If you were doing anything over 45 when you went through the curve on the right hand side of the pavement where the crown tilts the wrong way (the engineers musta been drunk when they designed it), you'd skid off the road and end up waist deep in the swamp.

The trick was to get in the left hand lane so you could bank into the curve where the crown was good, or slow down under 45, which took some doing without going into a skid and falling off the road anyway.

It was truly a hair-raising ride 'cuz you had to go as fast as you could, and whomever was in the lead by the time you got to the yellow warning sign that said *Dangerous Curve Ahead, 25 MPH*, got the honor of heading into *Wetman's Curve* in the left hand lane. The loser had to brake and down-shift hard and get into the right hand lane—the lane with the bad crown—as a punishment for losin'. Then the curve would be there and you'd hit the brakes even harder and the guy in the left hand lane only had to worry if the lookouts had done their job, and the guy in the right hand lane had to slow it down under 45 or skid off the crown into the swamp.

Some nights there'd be three or four cars ending up in the swamp. It was funny to watch and really pretty harmless. No one ever got so much as a scratch, except for the one time Johnny Fuller and his girlfriend Louise Taylor rolled their car before hitting the swamp. They each got bumped and bruised and a few cuts because we didn't have seat belts back then, and they fell on the window on Louise's side and shattered it and got cut. Nothing serious; we didn't even call an ambulance. But usually, all that would happen would be that the car would skid and go up on two wheels sometimes and smack into the cattails and stinky water.

The girls hated having to walk out of the swamp since it got in their shoes and socks and what-have-you, and they'd yell at their boyfriend for getting beat. But they wouldn't have missed riding with him for nothin'. Skidding into the swamp might have been a pain in the ass, but not getting to ride at all was a hell of a lot worse.

My best friend Steve, a six foot tall, blond haired Adonis-type, had the fastest ride in the county, and one time especially I remember 'cuz the next day after winning his race with his girlfriend at his side (and putting his rival into the swamp), Stevie looked at me with his eyes still glazed over, and said, "They love speed, Sticker! Girls sure love that speed! Something about all that power revin' up underneath 'em I reckon. It gets their motor racin' too! I tell you Sticker, those girls sure love that speed!" I didn't have to ask what had happened after the race that night. But he was the best driver around, and the only one ever to get through *Wetman's Curve* going over 45 in the right hand lane. That boy just had a way with driving.

Stevie ended up enlisting in the Air Force and got all the way up to flying F-16s. One day while testing a plane with a wing modification, he was banking into a turn, and the damn flap on the wing stuck. There was nothing he could do but eject, but he kept working it thinking he could hold the plane in the turn before spinning out and crashing.

"Get out now!" the radio control guy yelled.

"I can hold it!" Steve called back into his headset. "I can hold it!"

"Get out now! Eject! EJECT!"

"I can hold it! Damn it! I CAN HOLD IT!"

Those were the last words he spoke. The tip of the wing caught a tree on the side of a cliff and the plane spun and buried, not into a swamp, but right into the side of a mountain. And now anytime I look up in the sky and see one of those trails from a jets' engines, I think of Steve. Maybe all that speed used him up faster than normal. Sometimes I think I should start racing again.

River-hole is deserted today even though it's a scorching hot day in June. Kaitlin and Kathy change into their bathing suits behind the open trunk door and get the cooler and a big blanket and lay it out on some grass under the old oak tree where we see there ain't any ants. They sit on the blanket and twist open their coolers and Kathy hands one to me and they both take a couple sips. I take one sip too, and then put my cooler down and take off my shirt and sneakers. There's the rope, still hanging from that same hundred-year-old oak that's been hit by lightening so many times it's a wonder it's still standing and not washed down to the sea by now.

"Sticker," Kaitlin says. "Come on and set for a while. We've got catchin' up to do."

"Aw right," I say as I start down the bank and step into the water. "That's just what I had in mind."

"Stick!" she pouts. "What'cha doin'? I'm not hot enough yet to swim."

I swim out and reach up and grab the rope and swim it back to shore. The water's cool and almost clear since it hasn't rained in a while and the mud feels slippery and gooey as it squishes between my toes. I pull the rope up onto the bank and turn and look at Kaitlin and taunt her, "Catch me if you can!" and I sprint with the rope towards the river. As I swing out over the water, I look back over my shoulder to see that Kaitlin is already up off the blanket. By the time I let go, she's at the edge of the bank yelling and laughing and waving her arms,

"Sticker! You're crazy!"

I wrap my arms around my knees and hit the water as a cannonball, causing a concussion in my ears as I go under. I stay submerged and swim slowly away from shore, opening my eyes to watch for sticks and snakes and turtles. Gators don't usually come out during the day; they feed at night where there's a lot of plants in the water. There hasn't been a gator problem here at the Hole that I've ever heard of. But just to be safe, nobody ever splashes too much when we're here since a gator might take too much ruckus kinda personal. After half a minute I surface, spouting water out of my mouth like a great white whale blowin' out of his blowhole, and look back. There she is, holding the rope with both hands while searching to see where I had gone. Finally she sees me, and calls out again,

"Sticker! Don't *do* that! Don't *do* that!"

I raise my arm and wave and yell back, "Shark! Shark! It's a giant river-shark! Oh my God, a shark has my leg!"

"Sticker!" she pouts again. "Don't *do* that!"

Then she rears back and runs down the bank as fast as she can. I stop dead in the water, watching her as closely as I can, and see her virtually in slow-motion, frame by frame:

She grasps the rope high above her head, stretching her nubile body to its full length as her feet leave the ground; she pulls her knees up to her chest as she reaches the bottom of her arc—her toes just kissing the surface as they swoop, making the smallest of ripples on the smooth, glistening water below; her white bikini highlights the bronze tan on her tight and smooth skin, and her brunette shoulder-length hair trails behind her like the mane on a horse galloping across an open range; her eyes look down towards the water and then at me, and at the apex of her arc, she lets go of the rope and looks right at me and pinches her nose with her fingers; her body lengthens gracefully and her pointed toes break the surface as she plunges straight down into the water; her hair, the last to go under, disappears into the water like evaporating wisps of fog; and a compact splash claps straight up and then out, expanding into the sunshine like the wings of an angle taking flight; the drops hang there for a moment, and then fall and follow her into the river.

I close my eyes and replay in my mind's eye the miracle I just witnessed. Ain't no way I'm gonna forget it.

Remember . . . that *one day*.

As she surfaces, I swim straight towards her, fill my mouth with water, and do my best impression of a water fountain. The stream falls way short, as I knew it would, and she just gives me one of her perfect dolphin smiles as she treads water. I dive under and reach out as I kick full speed ahead. I find her waist and start to tickle. Instead of trying to get away, she pushes my head down all the way to her knees, finds the top of my shoulders with her feet, and pushes me even deeper. Then another concussion, and Kathy's in the water too. As I surface, the two women are both gunning for me spouting water out of their mouths and splashing at me some. So I return fire with some spray of my own.

Kaitlin dives underwater as me and Kathy shoot it out, and a few seconds later she surfaces downstream. She backstrokes towards the pier that's a couple hundred yards away with her arms rising and falling and drops of water flying up and falling and glistening in the sunlight. Kathy and I follow, and soon we're up on the pier sitting with our legs dangling in the water. Me in between two beautiful young women in bikinis. I must be doing something right, I think.

"So Sticker," Kathy says. "When was the last time you were down here with two hot babes?" Kaitlin laughs.

"Uh . . ." I say dryly pretending to think. "Like how about never."

They both laugh. "So Kathy," I counter. "When was the last time you were down here and actually wore a bathing suit?"

"What?" she squeals.

"Well," I say, "I hear you have a habit of getting a little wild and crazy when you drink a cooler or two." I had never really heard that, but I think it would be good for a laugh.

Kathy slaps me on the shoulder, "You did not! Sticker! I swear! Where did you hear that? I've never taken my bathing suit off around here."

I turn to Kaitlin, "Notice how she says *'round here!*"

"Oh stop it!" Kathy laughs.

"So if you don't skinny dip *'round here*, where do you, Kathy?"

"What? Skinny dip? I don't!"

"Yeah, right!"

"Really, Sticker. I'm not that kind of girl!"

"Oh," I reply. "Stop it yourself. I'm sure you've skinny dipped somewhere, sometime."

Kathy's face flushes beet red. Me and Kaitlin look at each other with raised eyebrows.

"Really?" Kaitlin asks. "You've really never been skinny dipping?"

Kathy's head drops in shame. She mumbles and squirms and squeaks out, "Well, I came close once at camp in tenth grade. But the counselors broke it up. Only the boys had a chance."

"Oh my *God!*" I exclaim.

"Oh my *God's* God!" Kaitlin laughs along.

"So your friend here," I turn to Kaitlin, "has never been skinny dipping!"

"Ain't that something!" she says trying to be serious.

"Yeah, really something."

Kathy squirms in her seat, blushing again.

"That's just not right," I continue.

"Not right at all," Kaitlin adds.

"It's a shame," I say

"Yes, a shameful shame," Kaitlin agrees.

"A crime against nature."

"A terrible, terrible crime."

"In fact, I think it's actually illegal in some states."

"Illegal as hell," Kaitlin says.

"I dare say, it's downright un-American."

"Very, very un-American."

"And I think we need to rectify this unfortunate and highly illegal situation." We both turn to Kathy with sinister grins.

Kathy jumps up and starts backing up the pier away from us as we scramble to grab her. "You guys!" she protests as Kaitlin catches her. "You guys! Don't! It's the middle of the day! Someone might see!"

Kaitlin wraps her arms around Kathy's shoulders and holds her still as I reach around and grab the strap of her bikini. "Awwww . . . Y'all!" she pleads with a hint of panic. "Please, *don't!*"

I look at Kaitlin and she looks at me and we feel Kathy's panic so we let her go.

"You know," I say to Kaitlin. "I think our friend Kathy here might need a little encouragement."

"Sure looks like it," Kaitlin replies. "Encouragement."

"Encouragement and an example to follow."

I gaze at her expectantly.

Kaitlin's eyes light up and her mouth opens in surprise and now *she* starts backing up away from me and Kathy. Now *she* protests, "Aw, now Sticker! Not me! I've been skinny dipping plenty of times. I already know how! I don't need to learn!"

Now Kathy and me are going after Kaitlin as she slowly backs up to the end of the pier. "You-all! She says amongst yelps of laughter. "I don't need any practice! Really, I don't!"

Kathy finally reaches her and for a moment, it looks like they're both gonna fall off the pier and just a nudge from me would be all it would take. But instead of satisfying my urge, I sense something better is coming if I wait. So I say, "Okay, you two. I think you both need some educatin'."

I turn my back to them and drop my shorts and throw the soggy jeans at them over my shoulder and dive head first into the water. When I come up, I look back and see them both doubled up in laughter pointing at me.

"You're just a couple of chickens!" I taunt. "Cluck, cluck, cluck! It looks to me like I'm the only one with any balls around here!"

"That may be," Kaitlin says, "but you can't play catch without a mitt!" She turns around quickly, glances to the car to see if anyone else has come without us realizing it, and then pushes the shoulder straps of her bikini off, sliding it all the way down to her waist. I tread water and watch and see her bare back with the tan line.

Kathy exclaims, "Kaitlin! What are you doing?"

Kaitlin looks over her shoulder at me and says, "Turn around and don't look!"

"What are you kidding?" I reply. "This is the highlight of my career!"

She smiles, but protests again, "Turn around, Stick, or I won't do it!"

"Do what? You mean there's more?"

"Just turn around!"

"Oh, all right," I say dejectedly, but I just keep treading water and looking right at her.

"Oh . . ." Kaitlin mumbles. "What the hell!"

She pushes both the top and bottom of her bikini down to her feet, steps out of them, turns quickly, and dives off the pier just off to my side. I see her naked body stretch out and plunge into the water and I feel a few drops of the splash fall onto my face.

"Oh my God!" Kathy blurts as Kaitlin surfaces. "Oh my God, Kaitlin! Are you crazy? It's broad daylight!"

Kaitlin just grins like a happy dolphin at home in the water and makes her way over to me and stays there, treading water a couple arms lengths away. I can't help but laugh. "Well, I'll be!" I say. "You did that just like a professional!"

She splashes me and I splash her back, and as we're there splashing and spitting water at each other, I see Kathy turn her back to us. "Hold on, Kaitlin!" I call out. "I think we have another volunteer!"

Kathy looks over her shoulder as she raises her hand to unhook her bikini. "I don't know, you guys . . . I've never done this before!"

"Oh, baby!" I call out. She turns back around and lets her hand fall to her side.

"Oh baby!" I say again. "Take it off! Take it *all* off!"

Kathy looks at me sternly, but still with a smile. "Well, now you can forget it!" she says.

"Take it all off!" I yell again and slap the water.

"Oh, come on!" Kaitlin says. "It's no big deal, Kathy! Really. The world ain't gonna stop turning 'cuz you show your little fanny and boobies! You're almost there! And it *feels so good!*"

Kathy turns back around and mumbles to us, "Promise y'all won't tell anybody!"

"Of course!" Kaitlin says.

"Of course," I say, and then lower my voice to almost a whisper, "not!"

"Oh, all right," Kathy mumbles, and in less than five seconds, she unhooks her bikini top, lets it fall, and pushes off her bikini bottom. She holds one arm across her breasts and the other hand over her crotch (or mitt, as Kaitlin would say), and jumps off the pier. But just as her feet leave the boards, she flings her arms and legs out as if to prove to herself she's a wild and crazy gal, and does a spread eagle into the water.

"Yaaayyy! All right!" Kaitlin and I scream. "Way to go Kathy!"

She paddles over to us and dips her head backwards into the water to let the water pull her hair off her face, looks at us, and grins.

"Kathy," I say all serious-like. "You're one of us now."

She laughs and splashes me and I splash her and Kaitlin splashes and we all splash each other and laugh. Then the splashing fizzles out and I turn and float on my back to rest. But the girls are afraid to do that on account of their boobies floating up and poking through the water, so they just doggy-paddle around and sidestroke in circles.

"Doesn't it feel good?" Kaitlin asks Kathy. "It feels *so good*. So smooth and silky and . . . *free.*"

"Yeah . . ." Kathy says shyly. "I guess so."

"Oh come on!" I jeer. "You may as well admit it Kathy—you enjoy it! Now that you're no longer a 'skinny-dipping virgin,' you really *do* enjoy it!"

"Hummph!" she grunts but smiles and turns and swims to the pier. "Even if I did," she calls out over her shoulder, "I'd never admit it!"

She grabs hers and Kaitlin's bathing suits and my shorts and swims back over to us. We all take our time and swim back to the rope and old oak tree, the girls in front, and me lagging behind. I get to the muddy bank under the tree and crawl out of the river and turn to see Kait and Kat splashing one more time at each other amongst playful catcalls and laughter.

For those all too brief four hours at River-hole that afternoon, I was seventeen again. We swung off the rope—alone, in pairs, and all together—sometimes laughing so hard as we dropped into the water with our arms and legs and torsos so tangled up that we could barely make it to the surface in time to suck air into our bursting lungs and laugh even harder.

We sat on the bank on the blanket and watched the lazy water pass us by with water bugs lighting on it and fish surfacing to peck at the bugs and an occasional stick or leaf floating down and then disappearing around the bend. We drank the coolers and told jokes and kidded each other about how ugly we were and how dumb we were and how rich we were and how rich would be rich enough. And the women brushed their hair and spread suntan lotion on their arms and legs and then on each other's backs and on my back too and we laid there and looked up at the underside of that towering old oak and the blue sky beyond it without a cloud to be seen.

We swam again and drank again and even nodded off as the late afternoon sun headed for the horizon. And I realized that this girl turned woman, who I hadn't been near in years, had cast a spell on me years ago and probably even before that. A spell that I'd never break. And I knew she suspected the truth about me and yet she didn't want to admit it 'cuz she tried to get around it in her sweet and innocent mind.

"Sticker," Kaitlin says softly as we lay there on our backs—both of us half dozing—as Kathy's clearly sleeping. We're both quite happy from the drink and the day.

"Yes, Kait."

"Why did God to this to us?"

I feel my throat swell. It takes me a long time to answer, and all I can manage to say is, "I don't know."

"It's not fair," she slides her hand along the blanket and takes a hold of mine. "It's just years. Just some time . . . a few years," she says.

Again, I can't answer. Finally, I say, "It's more than that, Kait. You know it's more than that."

"I know," she says even more softly. "But what they say or think doesn't matter to me. You know that, don't you Stick?"

"I do. And what they say or think doesn't matter to me neither. But still, you know it's more than that."

I look up at the branches on the tree overhead and follow one down to the trunk. "You see, Kait," I say trying to keep my voice from cracking, "you have a future waiting." I take her hand and raise it up and work her fingers so her forefinger points at the open sky.

"You see that?" I ask.

"See what?"

"What you're pointing at . . . the sky. Do you see the sky?"

"Yes," she says patiently.

"Tell me what you see," I say.

"I see a clear blue sky."

"Yes. It's a clear blue sky. What's beyond the clear blue sky?"

"Beyond?"

"Yes, beyond."

"Outer space, I reckon."

"Yes, space. And what's there in space?"

"You mean stars?"

"Yeah, stars. The same things you see at night when it's dark, are still there during the day. We just can't see them on account of the light."

She's quiet. I continue, "Your future is there, Kait. Like the stars in the sky are there. You just can't see it. But you know it . . . you feel it." I feel her fingers squeeze my hand. And then I say something that shows what a son of a bitch I truly am: "There's a star up there in your future, Kait, that I just can't give you."

Tears well up in my eyes and roll down across my temples and ears and down my neck. I feel her grip tighten even more as she rolls on her side towards me. She buries her head on my chest and silently weeps. I feel her tears on my sun-baked skin.

I hate you, I think to myself, of myself, of life, and of whatever there is of God. I really hate you.

We lay on the blanket and hug and sigh and love every second and hate every second and don't say nothin'. She puts her ear on my chest and listens to my heart as I lay my hand on her neck and feel her pulse. Two hearts beating together . . . Two hearts . . .

As Kathy stirs, Kaitlin pushes her head up and opens her eyes and searches for mine and finds them. And our eyes meet, our black pupils looking deeply into each other's. For several moments, there is nothing except the blackness of her eyes . . . the blackness of our eyes . . . the blackness . . .

Then they merge. They merge and a universe is born. Light explodes from the center of the darkness; space and time no longer exist; my mind and soul, the past and future, all swirl together into one all-consuming sensation. It's so intense, I don't think a thing.

We hang there for several moments, swimming together in each other's universe—totally naked, totally vulnerable, and finally, totally free. For those brief but everlasting moments, we are one. And that one is everything there ever was, and everything you could ever hope for.

And it feels *so good*.

Kathy stands and puts on her shirt and shorts and Kait and I do the same and we load up the car with the blanket and cooler and empty bottles and no one says much on account of the after-effects of the wine and being cold from the sunburn. But it's agreed that we're hungry and needing food and drink and as soon as humanly possible and that means stopping at the Dairy-Barn on the outskirts of town.

We order at the window and get a booth in the back corner and sit down. I don't care about the burgers or sodas or anything else. But I eat and drink and talk and continue living because that's all I can do—that's all there is to do.

It seems like the seconds and minutes keep coming at you—ruthlessly and relentlessly coming at you—pushing you into something you didn't want to do and to a place you didn't want to get to. Like you're going off to war and leaving the only ones who matter behind to face the worst thing ever created and you see it happening and you're right in the middle of it and you want to stop it and rewind it and get off that boat or battlefield or plane and go back to the picnic by the river on that sunny hot day in June.

But the seconds and minutes just keep coming at you and there ain't a damn thing you can do to stop them and even if you stop and do nothing yourself, the seconds and minutes turn that nothing into something and you feel like you can't hang on any longer and at the same time you can't let go either.

Then Candy and Sunny come walking into the Dairy-Barn.

Chapter Seven

Neither of them sees us, and they go up to the order window and look at the menu with faded pictures of the food and deserts that are hanging on the greasy wall. "What do you want?" Candy asks Sunny bluntly.

"Uh . . ." Sunny's bouncing up and down with excitement, her hair bouncing up and down along with her.

"Do you want a cheeseburger or hot dog or roast beef?"

"I want a strawberry sundae!" Sunny blurts out.

"No, Sunny. You have to eat some food. You can't just live on ice cream."

"Strawberry sundae," she calls out louder.

"Now, Sunny. You can have an ice cream cone after we eat. Cheeseburgers are good. Have a cheeseburger."

"Strawberry sundae! Strawberry sundae! I want a strawberry sundae!"

Sunny can sure be stubborn. Takes after her mom on that. Candy sees she's loosing the battle and is starting to worry about making a scene. "Sunny," she pleads. "don't you want some real food? Some good hot food that will . . ."

"It's too hot for food!" Sunny counters. "I want a strawberry sundae!"

Candy looks at the young woman behind the counter and I see the white flag of surrender go up. "Okay!" she barks back at Sunny without looking at her. "I'll have a cheeseburger with no onions and she'll have the strawberry sundae."

Sunny bounces a couple times and claps her hands and skips over to the first booth closest to the order window and sits down with her back to us and slides in so I can't see her anymore. Candy comes and sits across from her and opens her purse and rummages round in it and takes the money up to the window and pays the young woman and sits back down. She scans the dining room and sees me sitting next to Kaitlin and a dart comes out of her eyes, but she catches herself and pretends she hadn't seen me, even though we both know she had.

Me and Kait and Kathy finish eating and sit here a few minutes as they gossip about the young woman behind the counter who apparently had an abortion a few months ago. The guy wanted to marry her and start a family but she didn't want to 'cuz she wanted to go to college. Her grandmother was on her death-bed and was going to leave the girl a nice little inheritance, but she overheard a couple of nurses talking about the abortion one night and wrote the girl out of her Will right before she kicked the bucket. So now the girl doesn't have the money to go to college and she's stuck here working at the Dairy-Barn and will probably never get out of town like she wanted to. Now she's got this scarlet letter on her and is having a tough time finding another man 'cuz the first one left her when she had his baby sucked out of her.

The young woman behind the counter calls Candy when the food and ice cream are ready and tries to smile but doesn't do a very good job of it but instead glances longingly at Sunny sitting in the booth. Candy brings it all back to the table in a couple trips and sits down in the booth without looking my way again.

Me and the Ditto-Amigos get up and I leave a ten dollar bill on the table and we walk to the door. Kait and Kat are busy chattering away and I think for a second that they won't notice Candy in the booth, but they hear Sunny's voice, the voice of a young girl, and turn to look and see Candy and Sunny sitting there eating. Kaitlin stops and stares for a second and recognizes Candy and says, "Candy! Is that you?"

"Hey," Candy replies, not all that excitedly.

"And is that Sunny? Yes it is! Oh my goodness! Look at you! My have you grown! And still as cute as ever! Look at those pretty blond curls! And you're so much taller! Oh, you're going to be such a pretty young woman!"

Sunny stops slurping on her sundae and a big wide smile breaks out across her face and she bounces in her seat and she lights up like she just won the national spelling bee or somethin'. Kathy and me just stand there in the background and Sunny sees me but is so overwhelmed by all the attention Kaitlin is giving her that she doesn't say anything and I don't say anything to her or Candy either.

Kaitlin introduces Kathy to Candy and Candy to Kathy and doesn't mention me 'cuz she knows we know each other and all three of them start cackling away like hens in a hen-house catching up on each other and the rest of town. Sunny gets kinda mesmerized by all the talking and laughing and the occasional attention the Ditto-Amigos throw her way that she never looks my way again.

So I just slip out the door since nobody cares and walk around the parking lot some as the sun is sinking below the tree line. The air is cooling off, but it's still hot, and I can tell that it won't get that cool tonight even though it's still only June. I think that maybe I'll just sleep outside if it's too hot in my trailer. After about five minutes, I notice I have to pee, so I go back behind the Dairy-Barn to the toilet and pull on the door that says "Bulls," but it won't open. I notice a note on the ground that obviously fell off saying *Out of Order*, and a combination lock on the latch holding the door shut.

I can hold it, I think, as I fiddle with the lock absentmindedly. I'll just wait till I get home. I look at the lock and notice it's just like the locks we used in high school gym class to keep all our smelly socks and shorts safe from plunder. Some of us even wore jock straps to keep the family jewels from flapping in the breeze as you ran and offered some protection against getting wacked in the balls.

If you've ever been wacked in the balls, you know what a pain it can be. I've had my fair share of wacks growing up, so I even took to wearing a 'cup'—a hard plastic piece that looks like an oxygen mask that slips into your jock strap and rubs against your pubic hair and pushes on your bones and is supposed to stop all unwelcome advances to your Johnson & Company. I wore it when I played baseball on the high school team. I played second base and was darn good too, especially fielding grounders. I would suck those ground balls up from all directions just like a Kirby. In fact, that's what some of the guys called me—'Kirby the Suckmaster'. But that's not exactly the name you want the girls to know you by, and it never really stuck 'cuz it's just too long and complicated and everyone knew my as Sticker anyway.

But one day during practice, I was out suckin' up those grounders and one of 'em took a crazy, wild hop and went under my glove and yet up into my crotch and caught me right under the bottom part of the cup and squarely on my testicles. That ball must have flown like the bullet that went through JFK's throat and then the governor of Texas' shoulder (I forget his name—might have been Connolly), took a left turn, stopped in mid air and took a right turn, or something like that, to go through both men in a single trip, which, the left wing radicals said, was impossible.

Maybe in my case, there wasn't a second bullet from a gunman behind the fence on the grassy knoll, but a second grounder that came from behind me from the right fielder who was jealous of me because I was so handsome and talented and could have saved the ball club given half a chance. But really, that didn't happen and it was that grounder that caught me right under the cup and right on the bottom of my balls and made me fall to the ground holding my crotch and got me thinking while I was curled up on the ground and whining like a little girl with my face pressed into the infield dirt ('cuz getting hit in the nuts changes your voice), that there's nothin' I can do to stop it. I'm gonna get clocked in the nuts no matter what I do, no matter how hard I try to protect myself. When things like that happen, it makes you feel totally powerless. It makes you believe in destiny—and not in the good way.

I push the lock away and walk back around to the parking lot just as the Ditto-Amigos are coming out the door.

"Hey, Sticker!" Kaitlin smiles. "Had some catchin' up to do, you know. Hadn't seen Candy and Sunny for a few years. Hope you don't mind."

She turns to Kathy and says, "Didn't I tell you? Ain't Sunny just adorable?"

"You can say that again," Kathy replies. "Gonna be a real heartbreaker, I'll say."

"So we all ready to go?" Kait says while opening the car door.

I need to end this right now 'cuz I can see where it's heading. Sometimes it's better just to tear off the Band-Aid and get the pain over with. "Kait," I say softly. Kathy's already in the back seat, expecting me to sit up front again. "I might as well wait and catch a ride with Candy."

I try to look her in the eye, but I'm afraid to. Instead, I look through her hair at the trees behind her. Then a much bigger fear rips through me as I realize I can't not dignify her—for to disrespect her would be as big a lie as there's ever been told. So I hurry to catch up, but it's too late. By the time my focus changes, her eyes are already starting to look away, and our glances pass by each other's as if we were just strangers passing on the sidewalk. It felt like hell.

"Oh . . ." she says suddenly crestfallen and defensive.

"Kait . . ." I whisper, longing in my voice. "Kait . . ."

"Oh . . ." she interrupts. "Okay. Sure . . ." Her head sinks and her smile leaves and those dolphin lips are barely curling up and you could say were even curling down and actually looked unhappy for once. Instead of my scalp tingling when our eyes had met before, my gut clamps down like a vice around that greasy hamburger I just ate. And it wouldn't of taken much more to throw it up onto the parking lot.

"Kait . . ." I try again, but just a hoarse whisper comes out of my mouth. I try harder, "Kait, if . . . if . . . maybe we can do this again sometime." Oh, how lame. How cliché. How best to ruin everything.

"Yeah, right," she mumbles sarcastically.

I put the back of my fingers on her cheek and softly brush it a couple times. She takes my hand, pauses for a couple seconds, and then kisses it. I touch her chin and raise it up until she finally looks at me. Our eyes meet again and I can see she's sad and dejected, but at the same time knows deep down that it's what has to be done, and is thankful I'm man enough to do it. She climbs in the car and Kathy climbs into the front seat and Kaitlin starts the car and backs out, looking at me one last time. She waves once and utters a weak "Bye," and drives off. I watch as she turns out of the parking lot onto Main Street and speeds away. If there was a wall nearby, I woulda punched it.

Alone in the parking lot, I find Candy's white Chevy and lean against it with my arms folded on my chest and look down at the pavement. My gut slowly relaxes and I try to think of something other than how being lucky enough to find a woman like her who I would be happy with gets turned into sheer agony for having to do the right thing and push her away for her own sake. "You can't win for losin'," my dad's whiny voice whispers in my head.

"Shut up!" I mumble. "Don't get started on me. Go away, where you always were anyway."

"Who ya talkin' to, Stick? Yourself again?" Sunny says skipping towards the car.

I raise my head and smile weakly. "I'm talkin' to the little elf down here right next to my feet."

"Little elf!" she smiles. "Elves are make-believe, Stick. You should know that!"

"Oh no, little girl. The elf was right here, but jumped into the bushes because he said he can't be seen by those who don't believe. But before he left, he told me that you need a spankin' for being such a bad little girl."

"He did not!" she giggles as she gets into the back seat. "He did not because I'm a good girl!"

"That's not what he said." I climb into the passenger's seat and fasten my seat belt as Candy puts the car in drive. "And he's the head elf!

He said that little girls shouldn't have ice cream for dinner and if they do, they need a spankin'."

"Oh, he did not! You're fibbin'! Tell him Mama! Tell him to stop fibbin' and there's no such thing as elves!"

"There is too." I reply.

"Is not!"

"Is too!"

"Is not!"

Candy barks, "Would you both just shut up! I'm starting to get a headache and I can't stand your bickerin'!"

"Is too!" I whisper, turning to Sunny and sticking my tongue out.

"Is not!" Sunny whispers back and sticks her tongue out too.

Candy pulls out onto Main Street the opposite way that Kaitlin went, and drives a couple blocks and stops at the corner for a red light. There's a bank on one corner and a gas station on another and I think I should hop out and run into the gas station and relieve myself, but figure it won't be long before we're home, so I decide to tough it out and hold it.

"Oh, oh," Candy says. "There's Tony Caruso! It's the *last* thing I want to do is talk to *him!*"

Tony is a decent looking guy a couple years older than Candy and owns the *Wild Stallion Saloon* right off Main Street. He's walking across the street right in front of us when he notices it's Candy's car, so he hurries over to her window and bends down to look in and says, all enthusiastic, "Just who I was looking for! Candy Talbert! How ya doing?"

"Just fine," she says with a coy smile. Suddenly her reluctance is gone.

"Roll on over, I need to talk to you."

"*Where?*" she asks with a panicked urgency, as if there were a dozen cars behind her honking at her. The light's still red and there's no one behind us.

"Right there," Tony points to the bank's parking lot.

"Oh Jeez!" Candy blurts out. "Okay!"

Tony jogs over to the sidewalk and crosses the street to the parking lot and when the light changes, Candy drives across the street and into the parking lot and swings the car into the empty spot next to where Tony's waiting. Tony comes over and leans in close with his head almost inside the window. "So how ya been?" he asks Candy, and then looks at

Sunny. "Howdy, Sunny! Hey there cutie pie! What's up, Sticker?"

Me and Sunny look at him and say, "Hey."

He doesn't really notice as he focuses back on Candy. "So how ya been? Haven't seen you in a while. Was wonderin' how you been getting along."

"I've been okay," Candy says shyly, but obviously pleased with the attention. I've seen it all before—how she acts around men she doesn't know well enough but who want to get there. It's a childlike, almost infantile way that's receptive and teasing and vulnerable and gets a fella thinking she's like a bottle of beer that hasn't been opened yet. All you have to do is pop the top off and put it to your lips and the worries of the day and existence in general will fade away into a numbing afterthought.

"Well, you sure are looking okay!" Tony exclaims with a wide grin.

"Uh-huh," Candy says as a slight blush comes to her cheeks.

You'd think she'd be used to the compliments by now since the guys shower them on her often enough. But they appear to trip a switch in her that causes her eyes to glaze over—kinda like an alcoholic walking into a bar. I imagine it takes her monumental strength to fight the temptation to drop her drawers right then and there and take a long sip of that manly adulation.

"Listen," Tony keeps going, "we've got a new burger at the saloon now. It's the best dang burger you've ever tasted! It's giant size with tomatoes and cheese and pizza sauce and peppers. We call it the I-talian Stallion, and ummm, ummm, ummm, boy is it tasty! Makes my mouth water just thinkin' about it! Why don't you stop by sometime and give it a try. On the house of course! And we can catch up on things while we're at it!"

Candy smiles and looks at him and says, "Okay. That sounds good. Don't know when, but I'll stop over and give it a try."

"And bring Sunny along if you want. She can have the smaller one we make for kids, called the Bambino Burger, or anything her little heart desires. You know, y'all are always welcome."

Then he looks at me and says, "And you too, Sticker. Come on over sometime. But for you, you have to pay double!" He laughs and slaps the top of the car door and backs up a step. "So don't be a stranger, okay, Candy-bear? Come by and see me sometime!"

Candy bats her eyes and smiles even harder and says all coy-like, "Okay. All right. See you later." She puts the car in gear and pulls to the parking lot exit.

"Don't forget now!" Tony calls after her. "The I-talian Stallion! The best burger in the *en-tire* world!" He sounds like a car salesman on TV. "Ciao, baby!" he yells as we drive off. "Ciao!"

"Oh, *Gawd!*" Candy moans when we get to the next block. "He's been after me since we were in high school. He's still right cute too. But God, I don't know . . . *I don't know . . .*" she yaps, taking an imaginary sip of that masculine liquor. She waves her free hand excitedly as she drives with the other and keeps yapping . . .

"He just got divorced last month! Last *month!* And he wants to go out with me already! I don't know . . . *I don't know . . .* His wife was right pretty too. But she's put on some weight lately and I heard he just got tired of her layin' around the house all day while he was bustin' his butt in the saloon all by himself. He's a real worker all right, and he's got some money put away I hear. But I don't know. . . *I don't know!* But I could never get serious with Tony! He's not my type! Just not my *type!*"

We turn off Main Street onto our road. Just five more minutes and we'll be home and I'll finally be able to relieve myself. I'm straining hard to hold it now. I imagine my eyes getting bug-eyed and my cheeks blowing up to keep it in like you'd see the *Little Rascals* would do, but I keep myself from laughing since that might cause me to lose it.

"Oh . . ." Candy says to herself. "I don't know! He's just not my type! He's got money though. And he's I-talian. I've always had a thing for I-talians."

"Don't sound real Italian to me." I squeeze in.

"Oh, it was his great grandparents who came over and moved down here from Cleveland. I remember him tellin' me about it one night at the saloon last year when he was all sad 'bout his marriage falling apart. I always seem to be the one people want to talk to when they need a shoulder to cry on."

"Yeah, you're a regular Ann Landers."

She keeps on talking like I hadn't said a thing, "He's cute, but just not my type! Just not my *type!* Got money, though."

Suddenly a chipmunk darts out of the weeds right in front of us. Candy sees it and yelps and hits the brakes hard—way too hard for an iddy-biddy chipmunk. We all lunge forward as the brakes lock and the tires screech and we go into a skid for a good twenty yards and almost crash into the ditch.

"Ugghhh!" I groan as I'm thrown forward and the seat belt digs into my waist and my head almost hits the dashboard. The pressure of the belt on my tummy is too much for my tinkle-muscles to bear, and I feel pee squirt out into my shorts. And the shock and rush of adrenaline from the instinctive fear of crashing must have done something to weaken my muscles because even though I try to stop it, the pee just keeps on running out of me.

"Whoa . . ." Candy mutters after the car stops. She looks back at Sunny who had let out a little yelp of surprise herself but is okay on account of her wearing her seat belt too. "You okay?" Candy asks and sits there catching her composure for a few seconds. Then she decides that having the car stopped on the side of the road isn't the safest thing, so she starts pulling the car out from next to the ditch.

"Oh Jesus," I mutter. "Oh crap."

Candy glances down at my lap and sees my wet shorts. "What the hell is that? Did you just *pee?*"

I look at her puzzled and ashamed. "I . . . I . . . The seat belt grabbed me . . . and pushed my stomach in . . . and . . ."

"You peed in my car? You actually *peed* in my car?"

"I had to go but the toilet at the Dairy Barn was locked."

"You peed in my car? What is wrong with you? I just vacuumed and cleaned it and you go pee in my car! It's gonna smell like pee for weeks! I'll probably have to pay to get it cleaned! For cryin' out loud! What are you, like four years old?"

Suddenly I felt like it again, and this wasn't the first time Candy's said something to get me there.

"You peed in my car!" she yells again.

"Hey!" I finally snap back. "I'm sorry, all right? I'll clean it up, for Pete's sake! I'll clean it or pay for it or whatever!"

"You peed in my car! What are you like two years old?"

"Aw right! Aw right! If you had just run over the stinkin' little chipmunk instead of actin' like a dang elephant jumped out in front of us, this wouldn't have happened! I'm sorry! Okay? I'll clean it up!"

"I don't believe it!" she keeps at it as she gets the car back up to speed. "I just don't believe it! I just cleaned it too! Why me? Why me?" she shakes her head and mutters. "If it ain't one thing, it's another! He pees in my car!"

Now we're approaching her house and can see a car in her driveway. "Oh great!" Candy mutters. "Now my mom is here. What could *she* want?"

Candy drives into the driveway and then onto the grass besides her mom's green Ford. There's a towel on the fence between the driveway and the pool and as soon as Candy gets out of the car, she grabs it and throws it over the car at me and snaps, "Here! Put it on the seat!" Sunny gets out of the back seat and looks at me and isn't sure if she should laugh or not so she runs around the car and up the back steps and into the house.

"I'll take a shower and come back and clean this all up," I say as I put the towel on the seat. Candy just turns away and says over her shoulder, "Whatever!" and goes up the back steps and into the house too.

The woman inside the house who Candy calls mom isn't her real mom, but is actually her aunt Ruby who raised her when her real mom bolted for Oklahoma and left little Candy behind. Ruby had a couple kids of her own and Candy's real mom—her name is Dorothy and is Ruby's younger sister—figured one more young'un wouldn't make a difference, so she left sixteen-month-old Candy in an old bassinet on Ruby's back porch one morning. No warning, no note, no nothin'. No one heard from Dorothy for darn near a year, and when they did it was 'cuz she needed money. But now she's born again and claims she's got it all together and got remarried to a farmer in Oklahoma and even comes and visits once a year 'round Christmas and tells everyone how they need to read the Bible and get saved too.

Candy talks to her and they even go shopping and out to eat when Dorothy visits and Candy is surprisingly polite and accommodating. But later she'll bitch and moan to me about how she hates it when Dorothy tells her how to live and raise Sunny. Can't blame her on that. I never heard her call Dorothy mom. I don't know if she calls her Dorothy either. I've never heard her call her anything, come to think of it. But she calls Ruby mom every once in a while, and refers to her that way because she says she's her real mom because she raised her and was there for her even though she was quite the bitch herself.

Now Ruby is your typical grandmother-type: over sixty-five with short white hair puffed up in a perm, wire-rimmed glasses and a pasty-white drawn and wrinkled face. She walks with a limp due to arthritis in her hip and needs a hearing aid but refuses to get one. You have to say everything at twice the normal volume when you're talking to her, but if you ever turn up the volume too much, just to be sure she hears you or when you're repeating yourself after she's said "Hey?", she'll let you know you're shouting too loud by barking, "All right! I hear you! You don't have to scream!"

Most the time the nut doesn't fall far from the orphan tree.

Ruby was a depression baby when getting the bare necessities for survival was all a body needed or wanted to feel loved and cared for and you didn't expect anything more and didn't even realize anything more existed. She and her husband split a handful of years before Candy showed up, so she didn't have a man around to help her with Candy or her other two kids. So she was doing well to take Candy in and feed and cloth her and pick her up after swim team practice or life-guarding at the county pool in the summer and give her a place to call home.

I don't know what else she coulda done after finding a bundle on the back porch like she did. I guess she could have taken her to an orphanage or something. But she didn't, and Candy grew up in Ruby's circa-1920s two-storied clapboard house on the outskirts of town with a railroad track in the back yard until she graduated high school. Then as soon as Candy got her first job at the Dairy Barn (yeah, the same one), she left Ruby and moved into her first single-wide with a girl friend and she's been on her own ever since.

I go back to my trailer and take a shower inside, rinse my shorts out while I'm in there and hang them on the shower curtain rod to dry. I put on a fresh pair of cut-offs and shirt and go outside. I see the flypaper still hanging from the overhang since it's so big it's impossible to ignore, and I walk across the lawn to Candy's house to clean up my accident.

Sunny's already in the pool floating in an inner tube with a Daffy Duck head and kicking up a splash as she goes around in a circle. She sees me and waves but doesn't say anything—just keeps kicking. I climb the three steps to the back door and go into the laundry room and hear Ruby talking in the kitchen as I walk in.

"I'm telling you Candy! You need to make sure she eats some vegetables every day. Ice cream for dinner just won't do!" Ruby says.

"I know! I know!" Candy replies.

"And give her a teaspoon of cod liver oil too. Every day is best, but at least a couple times a week."

"I know, I know! You've told me that a hundred times!"

They both turn when I enter the room, but don't say anything to me.

"Would you just leave me alone!" Candy says to Ruby.

I wander into the living room towards the front of the house to wait out the storm. I hear what they're yelling but tune them out by looking at the nick-knacks and photos scattered around the room. Things I've looked at many times before.

There's several dolls on the top shelf of a darkly stained pine bookcase and a couple old tins and plates standing up on holders. An old encyclopedia set published in the 1940s and an assortment of hardcover and soft cover books and dime store novels are on the lower shelves with a lot of space in between 'em. On the wall in the dining area (that I've never seen anyone dine in) are color photos of Candy with her mom and Sunny standing in front of the house. A picture of Sunny diving into the pool and another of her playing in the snow with Becky. There's one of Candy on a stage receiving a plaque for winning the Best Worker of the Year award at her job, and one of her two girlfriends she never sees anymore: one moved away and the other got killed when she fell off her horse and cracked her head open.

Then on the shelf of a cupboard across from the front door are three old photos in gold-fringed frames. One is a black and white family shot of Dorothy's kin when Dorothy herself was about twelve years old. She, her sister Ruby, their brother Ed, and their mother and father—those being Candy's grandparents—are all standing in front of their Christmas tree. A handwritten note in the lower right hand corner says *The Talberts, Christmas 1937*. They're all smiling, but just barely, and there's a feeling of "do I really have to be here?" from the adults. The kids look happy with their presents, though.

Next to that photo is a color picture of Candy with her dad. Candy has her hand on her father's shoulder and is leaning towards him and smiling as she looks at the camera. He's sitting on a foldout chair at a table with a VFW banner on the paneled wall behind him. He looks thin and pasty and not all that healthy and is smiling too, but with hollow-looking eyes. The picture was taken over ten years ago when Candy was still single and without child and still had a flush of youth on her cheeks. A few years later, her dad was found dead in his trailer after suffering a stroke. Candy told me he was right proud of himself because he was down to just five cigarettes a day since he wrote about it in his diary.

The third photo is black and white and is of Candy alone when she was about sixteen-months-old, just before she was left on Ruby's back porch. It isn't a very good photo with scratches and blemishes on it and has the look and feel of a bygone era when wagon trains were headed out west and buffalo roamed the open plains—not of one taken just a few decades ago—and beckons you to smell the straw and manure in the barn or the freshly baked apple pie that's cooling on the kitchen windowsill.

Candy's sitting up on a wooden kitchen chair with her legs pointing straight out since they're not even long enough to fold under her and her little baby feet are covered by little baby boots that lace up to her ankles. She's wearing a little Sunday dress that falls down to her knees with little puffy sleeves that come down to just above her elbows. On her head is a little bonnet that's tied around her chin. Her hands are interlaced and sitting delicately on her lap. She looks not unlike one of the baby-dolls sitting on the bookshelf.

Her eyes are looking right at you and are innocent and trusting. Her lips are closed and yet curled up into her cheeks. It's not a big, open-mouthed smile she might have given had she been tickled. And it's not a joy-filled smile like she had just gotten her favorite treat. But it's a subtle, accepting, embracing smile that wraps around your heart and follows you and won't let you go when your eyes try to look away. Not unlike a Mona Lisa smile—but deeper and younger and innocent and more pronounced. It's a Mona Lisa smile plus . . . a Mona Lisa smile squared.

As I look at it, every time I look at it, I feel like somehow the secrets of the universe are held in confidence directly behind it and all that would need to happen would be for this little baby-girl Candace to smile just a little wider to give me a peek of the truth. Then, I too would understand. Then, I too, would be content.

That little baby girl sitting there with her chubby little legs and chubby little arms and little baby fingers and trusting, innocent eyes, and Mona Lisa smile squared makes you want to pick her up and hold her close and whisper the reassurance she needs to keep that innocence and trust and happiness and you let her poke you in the ear and tug at your nose and drool on your shirt and you let her fall asleep on your chest and you dare not move for being afraid of waking her because the sleep she goes to takes her back to heaven to visit the angels she left when she came into this world just a short time ago.

But instead, she gets wrapped in a dirty, tattered blanket and put in a broken bassinet and left on the back porch on a cold morning alone. Only her cries from confusion and fear brought the relief of a guardian who had more than enough on her mind already and really couldn't appreciate another little bundle of joy. So that innocence and trust and happiness turned into apprehension and sorrow and impatience and then spite when she realized—slowly and painfully realized—that she wasn't enough of what they needed to stay together or even raise her by either of themselves.

And she became like a butterfly, but in a sad way, jumping from flower to flower, trying to find the right one, taking a taste here and a taste there but never having that taste satisfy because it just doesn't feel right because it really isn't what she wants because she doesn't know what she wants because she can't find what she wants because there's nothing in her she wants because there's nothing in her that's good enough because that's what they made her believe.

Each thing within her is not good enough, so each thing without her won't be either. So she goes with one man who she discovers has this fault and another man who has that fault and the third one has a different fault and sometimes she'll go back to the first one thinking that "well, maybe I was mistaken about him" because her decisions are never good enough either and then after he disappoints her again she might go back to guy number two or three and try them again and then back to number one or four and all the time these guys are getting dizzy themselves because she's got them dancing like cats on a hot tin roof and they start getting frustrated because they can't pin her down—and that's what guys like to do in the first place is pin a girl down—but she can't let them pin her down because she needs a way to get away when the next man she thinks might be good enough comes around.

So her men, they start getting not just frustrated, but pissed without knowing why at first and then pissed at her, and that leads to them wanting to give her a smack upside the head.

She has to keep her guys from getting too close just in case she does find the man of her dreams, and almost as a contradiction, she still does have dreams—deep down inside and almost hidden from herself—she still has dreams, even though she'll never admit it and she really can't admit it because those dreams, like everything else inside of her, are not good enough.

Yet, in another way, she's stuck in those dreams because that's what little girls do—they dream. Candy does too because she's never gotten past a certain stage in her life because she was too busy looking for something good enough inside herself and she never stopped chasing it so could never stay on one thing long enough for it to take root and flower. She's like a seed caught in a wind that never quits.

So she has to have all her clothes and dishes and car just so because having them that way is the closest she can come to the way things should be—the way someone should have loved her. It's the closest she gets to being good enough, and yet, when that tragically shows itself, it simply can't be because that would contradict the truth she was taught. So instead of stopping her cleaning, she has to expand the scope and clean or organize other things. And there's always other things that aren't good enough. So she never goes without, and the vicious circle continues: She only feels fulfilled when she can't get fulfilled.

And since getting her things ordered and clean is the closest she can come, and since those unpleasable big people never let her know she was good enough and thus, never let her feel satisfied, she turns not to people for her satisfaction, but to things. *They* are the ones that can at least come close and answer her back with their cleanliness or orderliness or expensiveness. But people, not so much.

But she should know that really and truly she is not to blame for her parents' stupidities and weaknesses and callousnesses and she is and always has been more than enough and good enough (and that it was the big people who weren't good enough which is obvious by the way they treated her) and doesn't have to prove it by going out with every Tom, Dick, and Harry or being a superstar at work and keeping her house immaculate and shiny and hardly ever taking the time to rest and play even when there's no one there to impress. But how in the world is she ever gonna find that out?

"I know! I know!" Candy yells again.

"Well, I just don't understand how you expect her to grow up right if you don't give her some discipline," Ruby nags. "And givin' her a spankin' every now and then when she sasses you back ain't such a bad idea either!"

"Yeah, yeah, yeah," Candy mutters as Ruby heads for the front door. Candy doesn't follow.

"Okay, good bye," Ruby calls back.

"Bye," Candy says without any anger left in her voice.

I walk into the kitchen and Candy's standing at the sink washing dishes and putting them into the dish rack on the counter. "Give me some cleaning stuff," I say, "and I'll clean up my mess."

"No, I'll do it," she replies flatly.

"No you won't either. It's my mess and I'll clean it up.'"

"No, leave it alone. You'll just make it worse. I'll just have to do it over again. You're the worst cleaner I've ever seen."

"Look," I say, bordering on angry. "It's almost dark and I want to do it, so give me a bucket and some Pine-sol or something and I'll clean it so you'll never even know it happened."

"I said no! Get out of here! I'll get to it later! Just go back to your dirty old trailer. Go call Kaitlin or something! Go home!"

My eyebrows raise, "What? Candy . . . now . . ."

"I said get out!" she screams.

I look at her as she keeps wiping dishes and then I turn and walk out of the house. The knot in my gut returns, but for a totally different reason than when it cramped up with Kaitlin. This time, from anxiety and anger, not sorrow. Different reasons—same effect.

The woman just can't be pleased. I swear! If you don't offer to help her, you're inconsiderate. If you do or at least try to, it's never good enough.

I remember the spring before last when I took it upon myself to set up her new swimming pool filter because she was complaining so much about having to do it herself and how she didn't have a man around to do it for her. So I decided I should be the man. I carted it back from the store in my pickup, read all the directions, and set it up on the cinder blocks besides the pool. I hooked up all the hoses and valves and wires and stuff and turned it on and presto! It hummed and spit and bubbled just like it was supposed to. So I called Candy out to show her, 'cuz even though it ain't brain surgery, to tell you the truth, I was kinda proud of it. Candy came out of the house wiping her hands on a dishtowel, and came down the steps to take a look. Without batting an eye she says, "But I want it pointed this way—the way the old one pointed last year."

No "at-a-boy." No "thanks, but could you . . ." No "that's really sweet Sticker, that really helps me out, but . . ." You know, something someone *normal* would say.

"It makes no difference how it points," I said, my bubble burst. "It's fine the way it is."

But Candy started messing with it and twisting it and turning it and started taking it apart. So I finally gave in and helped get it turned the way she wanted. Half an hour later, I said. "There! Happy now?"

We climbed the steps to the deck as she kept complaining, "You should have just left it alone and let me do it."

"But it was working just fine the way it was. Who cares which the way it points? No one will even see it down there."

"I want it the way I want it. I should have just done it myself to begin with. I didn't ask you to help me anyway."

"It took me over an hour to set that stupid thing up. The least you can do is show a little gratitude." We stood there at the top of the steps on the deck beside the pool. The water was clear and cold since it came out of the well just a few days earlier.

"I don't care. I didn't ask you for help. You just make things harder."

"It would've taken you at least two hours to set . . ."

"I DON'T CARE! I've got enough work to do already! Besides, picking up after Sunny and the house and my job and the car . . ."

"That doesn't even make sense! That's exactly why I wanted to help you! All I want is a thank you."

"I don't care!"

She kept on complaining with no hint of appreciation. Bitch, bitch, bitch, that's all she did. It takes a lot to get me angry, but by then, I was. She was like an old record that skips when the needle gets stuck in a rut and just keeps repeating itself over and over. She needed to get out of that rut, and who better than an SOB to do it?

As we walked towards the back door across the deck—as she's still bitching and moaning about all the work she has to do and how unlucky her life is—I took her by the arm and shoulder, swung her over to the edge of the pool, shoved her hard in the waist and sent her flying into the fresh, cold water. Splash!

Ha! Take that! I thought. You daughter of a bastard you!

She landed on her feet, but they slipped on the slick plastic bottom of the pool and she toppled face first and went totally under water. She popped right up, spit out some water, and glared at me hard.

"Shut up!" I glared back at her. "Shut the hell up!"

She climbed up the ladder out of the pool and hissed, "Your ass is grass, mister! You've had it now. I want you out of here. You and your stupid trailer! I'm tellin' Tom, and he'll make you leave."

"Blah, blah, blah," I said. "I've heard it all before. He loves the rent money more than he loves you, so I've got nothin' to worry about."

Candy stood there, looking like a drenched mouse, dripping all over the deck with her hair matted down and her nipples hard and pointy and poking through her halter top. I was so angry I was hot, and I found myself wanting to push her down onto the deck and have my way with her right then and there. Suddenly, the line between anger and lust had been washed away.

See what a woman can do to you? They make no sense whatsoever and get you thinking crazy too—but somehow, you end up wanting them.

That's the way Candy is, and that's the way our relationship has been. She feels comfortable enough with me to be her real bitchy self, and I feel sorry enough for her to keep trying to help her and ease her pain. I hate it and she hates it, but it's been five years now and it's still happening. So the bottom line is, we must not hate it enough to change it.

I'm thinking this just as I make it back to my trailer. The sun's down, but there's a little light left, and I can faintly see my lawn chair and card table under the overhang. I'm tired from the arguing. I'm tired from all the walking I did today and the fight with Tom and the swimming with Kaitlin and the wine and burger and everything else. I'm tired of it all.

So I sit in my lawn chair and take off my sneakers and put my feet on the sand. It's still hot and the air is still and the crickets are chirping and the bullfrogs are croaking and I can hear a few cars out on Highway 17. In a few minutes, there's no light left and I can't even see any stars since I'm underneath the overhang. The blackness wraps around me and I feel smaller than a piece of dust. And sometimes, like tonight, when I stare at the black, I get the distinct feeling that it's staring right back into the black in me. It's poking me, prodding me, daring me to become one with it. The black out there, and the black in me: Black to black—like two sides of an Oreo cookie. Problem is, the creamy white filling—the part that tastes the best—ain't nowhere to be found. Instead, there's just empty space. And if I let the two blacknesses come closer to each other and actually touch, I fear that I may just blow up all over the Goddamn place. Little bits and pieces of Sticker raining down from the night sky. Like shooting stars falling to earth. Wouldn't that be a hoot?

As I sit here thinking about all this shit and trying to avoid falling into the darkness completely, all sorts of questions start bouncing around in my head like it's a friggin' pinball machine or somethin'. Questions about Candy and Kaitlin, my mom and dad, my pains and loneliness. Why did all of it happen? Why can't I undo it? Why did all these people do what they did? Why did I let them? Why was it them in the first place? Why do the same kinds of things keep happening? Why would I think I deserve all this pain and heartache? Why do I put up with it? Why can't I stop it? Why, why, why?

And all those questions boil down to the single biggest question a body can ever have: "Why me, God? Why fucking me?"

All those questions. You may think you come up with some answers sittin' by yourself in the middle of the night. You think you've finally figured some of it out. But then, when the morning comes and the day gets along, all those solutions that appeared so clear to you in the middle of the night suddenly don't count for nothin'. And the next evening, after another day of getting kicked around like a soccer ball, you go and sit in your chair and think about all your problems again and feel sorry for your sorry-ass self again because that's what you do. That's who you are. That's who you are when you're by yourself.

"Fuck it," I mumble. "Fuck them all."

I close my eyes, and in about thirty seconds, I'm asleep. . .

I was five years old and walking down a hallway. Its walls were plain and white and there were white doors alternating on each side for as far as I could see in both directions. Then I heard them—those hollow steps—and I started to run. The sound waves of those steps hit me, like waves on the beach hit you with the whole ocean behind them pushing them pushing you and your legs have to run faster just to keep yourself from falling on your face. Finally, on the left, an open door—an escape hatch. I ran to it, beads of sweat on my forehead, a knot in my stomach, the smell of scrambled eggs and bacon in the air. I couldn't see him, but I knew he was sitting at the breakfast table eating. He couldn't care about anything else.

I pushed the door and entered a room. Drawn curtains subdued the morning gloom that oozed through the window. I saw a bed just inside to the left, its bedspread neatly pulled and stretched over the two pillows at its head. "Under the bed? No! I don't fit anymore. Somewhere else. I have to hide somewhere else!"

Those hollow steps kept coming. Louder now. Closer. There! Double slatted doors into the closet. I pulled one of the doors open, went inside, and shut it behind me. Those steps, out in the hall, right around the corner! My breath quickened. The knot in my stomach tightened. "Maybe it'll keep on going. Maybe it'll miss me this time! The hallway door! It's still open! I forgot to close it! Oh no, Mommy! I forgot to close it! Now it'll know where to look!" I crouched down and tried to make myself small. I wanted to disappear . . . DISAPPEAR! I have to be gone. I never should have been here in the first place. I should have kept running down the hallway and found a better place, a better time . . . to come in."

THUD.

A step crossed the threshold. Dim light coming through the slats of the closet doors painted stripes on the walls and on me. Pungent moth balls in the thick, heavy air. So still. Sickeningly, deathly still. Except for my heart. It was beating through my chest. My breath was fast and hot and out of control. If I would have looked at my hands, I would have seen they were shaking. If I could have felt my lips, I would have noticed they were quivering. If I could have opened my mouth, I would have known I couldn't scream.

THUD.

The second step. I wrapped my arms around my knees. There was no place else I could go. Walls on all sides and the doors ahead. No where else to hide and no where to run. It knew where I was anyway. It always knows where I am. Make it go away. Make that *thing out there leave me alone!*

THUD.

The third step. I sensed that there was someone in its way: That hollow, empty man in front of the doors with an empty plate in his hands and a wistful look on his face asking, "Are you sure that's all there is? Can't I have some more?" If he had some substance and grit, he could have stopped her. Instead, that *thing passed right through him—as if he were nothing but fog on a gloomy day.*

The doors opened and dim, gray light oozed into the closet. A figure almost as big as the doorway hovered above me, angry and determined. There was just enough light for me to see it. It was wrapped around and around in strips of bandages; every inch covered in bandage, even the eyes. There weren't even eyes, just bandages sunken in the sockets where the eyes would have been. "Mummy!"

How could it know where I was? The mummy reached down, grabbed my hair, and yanked hard. The top of my head ripped off and at the same time, my crotch tore wide open. Like a pillow exploding at both ends, the feathers that were me blew out of my head and crotch with a loud roar—like a jet engine roaring during takeoff . . .

I jerk up in my lawn chair, awake. Heart beating hard, sweat on my forehead, roaring in my ears. The Mummy got me again.

This sound I know but can't place. Maybe just a memory of the dream. But no. It's real. I see the interior light in Candy's car is on and there she is, vacuuming the inside of the car. It's night. It's dark. I figure it's just around midnight. And she's vacuuming her car after cleaning up my mess.

I ease back in my lawn chair and catch my breath. No sense in trying to help her; I never do anything good enough anyway. The hum from the vacuum stops, and I notice a hint of swamp smell in the night air. I let my eyes close again . . .

I was three years old, looking up at my grandfather and laughing. He reached out for me, but instead of smiling, he started to growl. What? Why? I ran away, along the back of the house, but he ran after me, still growling. I turned the corner and kept running until I was blocked by the fence. No place to go except into the basement window well. I climbed over the metal and squatted down in the cool damp air of the well and wrapped my arms around my head. I wished I would disappear.

Then he was there, growling and hovering over me. I peeked between my arms and saw his big, black and sooty work boots on the edge of the well inches away. They were my grandfather's boots, but now, he was a monster. I looked up and saw him standing there, so tall it seemed like he stretched up to the sky. But he didn't grab me. He didn't even touch me. Instead, he leaned back with his hands on his hips and laughed. He laughed like a mean and crazy monster.

I climbed out of the well and ran back around the house to the rest of my family at the picnic table. I ran to my mom and buried my face in her side and cried. Grandfather returned, still laughing, and I clung to my mother even harder. She pushed me away and said, "Oh, stop crying Sam. Can't you see grandpa was only kidding? Don't be silly! He was only kidding."

I tried to hold her again, but she pushed me away again. I looked to my Grandma—maybe she would hold me—but she just sat there staring straight ahead. My dad was busy eating a piece of pie, like nothing had happened.

I forced myself to stop crying. How could I be so dumb? They started talking again. I put my thumb into my mouth and bit it, and put my other hand on the picnic bench. The wood was hard and cold. My sister called from inside the house and my mom answered her gaily. My sister opened the screen door holding a plate full of cookies and my mom jumped up from her seat and said, "Here, sweetheart. Let me help you." She helped my sister come through the door, and the door slammed shut behind her . . .

My eyes jerk open as Candy's back door slams shut. A few seconds later, she comes out of the back door and picks up the vacuum cleaner that's sitting on the deck and brings it inside. The screen door slams shut again. A few seconds go by, and the lights go out.

Suddenly it's pitch black. I hear a bullfrog croak and a car on the highway. I look up and can't see the stars for the overhang, but I can't see the overhang either 'cuz it's so dark. My head is throbbing and I'm thirsty but I'm so weary I don't move. I remember my dream and how it's the only memory I have of my grandfather. I close my eyes and try to remember something else about him but can only come up with how his clothes smelled in the closet at the top of the stairs where my grandmother kept them after he died.

It was a smell of the past, a smell of age, a smell of death.

A smell not unlike the smell from the swamp that's as strong as ever right now in this thick night air: the stench of stale beer, rotten eggs, and piss. "Festering corpses of unrighteous relatives," I mumble as my eyelids close. "Where do you come up with . . . this . . . stuff . . . ?"

Suddenly I'm sucked out of my lawn chair up through the overhang and into space. I'm shot up like a rocket with my face leading the way and my arms fast against my sides. I feel the air rush along my face as I soar up into the night sky.

Finally, I slow and hang there above the dark earth like a moon or a satellite in orbit. There's a giant dial turning in front of me counterclockwise, like the dial on a combination lock. It spins around fast—click, click, click. Then it slows—click . . . click . . . click . . . until it stops on number 21. I turn away and look down to earth. The moment I do, it all lights up.

I was hovering like a cloud above the roof of a brick building with a bench in front of it. Sitting on the bench was a young woman reading a newspaper. I zoomed in like a zoom lens on a camera to read the dateline—June 8th, 1941. The headline said, "Allies Invade Syria, Lebanon."

I zoomed out, back to my cloud. Another young woman came and sat on the bench next to the first woman who folded the newspaper and put it in her purse. The second woman handed the first a large heavy book, while patting it on the cover a few times. The two women smiled and talked for a minute and then the second woman got up, gave the first woman a loose and very brief hug, and walked away. The first woman opened the book and scanned the inside cover until she found a certain group of hand-written words. I zoomed in again, down to the words the woman was reading: "Dear Mitch, a soon-to-be great nurse! I don't care what the other gals say, you were never a bitch to me! Good luck! Jane Blakely."

Suddenly, I had total empathy with this woman—like I was attached to her by a cord. A bullet shot through her heart and shattered it like a pane of glass. "So that's really what they thought of me! That's really what they thought!"

A lump formed in her throat and tears welled up in her eyes, and she thought, "For as hard as I tried, for as many times I laughed at their stupid jokes and listened to their drivel about boys, that's what they really thought! Damn it! Just like high school! I thought I left that all behind in that dirty little town. But no . . ."

A tear rolled down her cheek. I was so close I could smell her. Her mind continued to race: "I can't help it. I just can't. As hard as I try, they still hate me and laugh at me behind my back! What is it I do? I'm nicer than Martha by far. I'm prettier than Jane. I'm smarter than Sarah. I gave better parties than any of them. What is it about me they find so repulsive?"

I was afraid to look at who it was. Other women can smell that way, can't they?

"I can't try any harder. I can't do any more. I'm just a failure. A miserable, scorned, embarrassing failure. Mitch the bitch! Mitch the bitch! MITCH THE BITCH!"

Instead of congratulating herself for accomplishing so much—getting out of that backward mining town, making her way in the big city and graduating nursing school—she believed she had failed. She didn't care all that much that the other gals didn't take to her, though it did hurt. What really did matter to her, more than anything in the world, was that no matter how much she achieved, no matter how good she was, no matter how hard and long she tried, he would always consider her a failure. The pain in her heart was almost unbearable, but there was nothing else she could do.

I had to force myself to look. I had to know for sure who she was. I started to turn my head towards her face.

"I'll just end it all," she thought. "It's just too hard. It's always been hard. It'll never change. Cursed. Just end it now." She thought about the Brooklyn Bridge not far away and she saw herself climb the handrail in her saddle-shoes and calf-length floral pattern cotton dress *and balance herself on that rail. She saw herself look down at the smooth, hard water below and felt the vice release from her chest as she leaned over and started to fall. She saw herself drop chest first towards the water with her arms along her sides and a smile on her lips. Relief was just seconds away.*

I had to know for sure who she was. I snapped my head towards her as another tear rolled down her cheek. "Oh my God!" I whispered. "It really is you. I had no idea . . ."

Then whoosh . . . I'm jerked up, like a fish on a line, up away from that woman who would five years later bear me. The dial appears again. Counterclockwise it spins. Backwards, slowing down and stopping on the number 10. I turn away from the black of space and look down to earth. The moment I do, again, it all lights up.

A girl with long blond hair walked alone down a gravel road on a sunny summer afternoon. I couldn't see her face since I was hovering above her, but this time, I knew right away who it was. She wore a faded red dress that had several patches on it, and black, buckle-up patent-leather shoes. The shoes were old and hand-me-downs, probably owned by several others over the years. Even so, I could tell they'd been recently buffed and shined to look as new as possible.

The girl clutched a quarter tightly in her hand as she walked. She had been given the important job only her brothers had done before, so she wanted to make sure she did exactly as her father had told her. She wanted to make him proud.

I saw it at the same instant she did—a silver flash in the gravel a few steps ahead. "What could that be?" she thought. Another step closer and it flashed again. Her heart quickened as she skipped the remaining several feet. She reached down and delicately pinched it between her thumb and forefinger. "Oh my!" she gasped under her breath. "A brand new silver dollar! It's a shiny brand-spanking-new silver dollar!" She looked at it closely and turned it over and looked at the other side. How pretty it is! All shiny and new and how it sparkled in the sun! She noticed the date:1930.

Quickly, she stuffed it in the one pocket on her dress as her eyes darted around. Good! No one saw. She started to skip, fantasizing about what kind of candy she was going to buy with it. Maybe a new dress too. "It's my lucky day!" she thought. "I found a silver dollar! A whole silver dollar! Yes, it's certainly my lucky day!"

She came to a driveway with a mailbox and skipped to the farmhouse at its end. She climbed the steps on the porch and knocked on the screen door. A man appeared, wearing a straw hat and overalls. "Yes?" he said. "What can I do for you?"

"Hello, sir," the girl replied most respectfully. "My name is Mandy. Mandy . . .

"Mandy Mitchinsky?" The man said.

"Mandy Mitchell," Mandy corrected him.

"Oh, yes. Of course." The man said with a smile. "Mandy Mitchell it is then. Come right in!" He opened the door for her. "I guess you've come instead of one of your brothers. You're getting all grown up now too, aren't you? Well, well, well. And you're a very pretty girl, now aren't you?"

Mandy held out her hand with the quarter in it, "Here, sir," she said. "Here's a quarter." The man put his hand below hers to catch it, but she didn't let go. All that money! She wanted to keep it for herself!

"Yeesss . . ." the man encouraged her. "A quarter . . ."

Still, she held on. It was like a spell had come over her. If she could keep it with her new silver dollar, she'd be rich! She could buy candy and anything else she wanted and show all of them and they would finally stop teasing her. Finally, the man took her hand and gently prodded her fingers and took the quarter.

"There you go," he said kindly. "I'll get your chicken, little Miss Mitchell!" The man talked over his shoulder as he walked into the kitchen, "A quarter gets you a live chicken with its head and feathers still on. But most folks pay me another dime to chop off its head and take off the feathers, you know. And that still comes to only thirty-five cents."

He disappeared for a few seconds. A thought of using her new silver dollar to pay him to do that came to Mandy's mind, but she quickly dismissed it. The man returned with the chicken, its feet and legs firmly bound with string, its beak wrapped shut, and a little hood over its head.

"I know money is tight these days, but remind your father when you get home, okay? I'm sure your mom has better things to do than undress a chicken!" He smiled and handed the chicken to Mandy.

"Yes, sir," she replied. "Thank you, sir."

She grabbed the string and pushed the screen door open and left. Down the driveway, down the country gravel road she walked, dutifully carrying the chicken bound in string and feeling very grown up. She *looked at it for a few seconds and thought how strange it was that she would be eating it soon. She pulled her eyes away so she wouldn't become fond of it. She turned onto a street just a couple of blocks from her house on the outskirts of that coal-dusted mining town.*

The chicken wasn't that heavy but it started to feel that way. She held it so its head pointed backwards, carrying it under one arm and then the other. It smelled bad, but she was used to it. Then she saw them: The older kids a grade or two above her. She used to play with some of them just last year, but now they were older and had decided she was more fun to tease than play with. They were playing Kick the Can in an empty lot, and she sped up, hoping to pass them unnoticed. Her stomach tightened. "But it's my lucky day," she whispered.

"Mandy!" the oldest and meanest boy called out. "What'cha got there?"

Mandy kept walking.

"What's wrong? Cat got your tongue, or are you just stupid?"

The other kids giggled.

"I got a chicken," Mandy finally said weakly. "My father sent me to buy a chicken."

The kids stopped their game and trotted to come up alongside her. The oldest boy continued, "Is that so? Well I'll be! I didn't know the Mitchell's could afford a chicken!"

The other kids laughed.

"I didn't know Pollacks even knew how to cook a chicken!"

The kids laughed louder.

"And look at that!" he sneered. "The dumb bird is still alive and has his feathers and head still on! What's wrong, Mandy pansy? Your father can't afford a dime?" He matched her stride for stride as the other kids followed in his wake. "Your dad, your Pollack dad, can't afford a dime to chop off the dumb chicken's head?"

Mandy kept walking as fast as she could as her lips began to quiver. A couple of the children ran ahead and turned, back-peddling in front of her, as they laughed and jeered.

"Mandy, pansy!" they called out. "Mandy pansy!"

The bully ringleader kept taunting, "Mandy the pansy. She sticks like cotton candy! She's a dumb poor Pollack and needs a lickin', and only eats dinner when the heads on the chicken!"

The other kids erupted with laughter and started howling at her. The bully chanted again, "Mandy the pansy. She sticks like cotton candy!

She's a dumb poor Pollack and needs a lickin', and only eats dinner when the heads on the chicken!"

The rhythm seemed to work the small mob into a frenzy and they started poking at her. Just lightly at first, but harder as they went. All the kids caught on to the taunt and badgered her together: "Mandy the pansy. She sticks like cotton candy! She's a dumb poor Pollack and needs a lickin', and only eats dinner when the heads on the chicken!"

The bully grabbed the arm Mandy held the chicken with, but her grip was strong and sure and she didn't let go. Then he grabbed at the bird itself, and when his finger caught under the string, he pulled harder.

Again, she held fast. But he kept on pulling and yanking at it and he grabbed it with both hands and tugged even harder. And as he pulled, he knocked Mandy out of her stride and she spun half way around until she and the bully were face-to-face, locked in a tug of war. Mandy saw his freckles and pimples and red hair and smelled his bad breath. Without thinking, she formed a wad with her tongue and spit it into his eye.

The bully recoiled as if he'd been shot. He released his hold and covered his eye with both hands and yelped. Mandy jerked away hard, spun, tripped on her leg and fell to the ground on her knees. Her hands flew out to catch herself, causing the bird to fall on its head and roll on the ground.

All the kids froze. Mandy's knees and palms were scraped and bleeding. She turned up from the ground to look at them, and as she did, I finally saw her face. I was taken aback by how cute she was. Another thing about her I didn't know.

Mandy got to her feet as the bully and mob were regrouping. She stumbled towards the chicken and reached for it, and as she did, she noticed out of the corner of her eye a flash of silver. Her silver dollar! It must have flown out of her pocket as she spun and fell. Everything happened so fast now: The bully yelled, "Get her!" and a couple of boys moved towards her. "Get the chicken!" he yelled. "Don't let her get away!"

Mandy was quick, but not quick enough. She grabbed the chicken and took one step towards the silver dollar just as one of the boys started for her. "Oh no!" she thought, as she saw the one boy and then another just an arm's length away. "I have to leave it!" shot through her mind as she turned to run, now with the chicken in her hands.

The first boy reached her and grabbed onto the pocket of her dress. As Mandy started to run, he held on and it started to tear away. Mandy kept pulling and trying to run, but couldn't break away. Then snap! The pocket finally tore completely off, and she was suddenly free.

"Get her! Get the chicken!"

No sooner had she taken another step, but another boy was upon her grabbing at the chicken. She was again locked in a tug of war. She kicked the boy in the shin, and he let go. As he stood there stunned, she kicked him right between the legs causing him to groan and fall to his knees. She would have kicked him there again, but he fell away from her as he squealed and covered up. "Take that, you bastard," shot through her innocent mind. She had never even thought a word as bad as that before.

The bully and the others watched in awe for a moment, but they didn't quit. As Mandy turned and ran with the now unconscious but still bound chicken firmly locked under her arm, they picked up pebbles and stones and threw them at her. One hit her in her back. Another in her leg. And one whizzed dangerously past her ear. But her legs did not fail her and she was quickly to the end of the block and around the corner.

As she turned the corner, she looked back at the mob one last time. And just before she ran past the corner of the house that would a second later obstruct her view, she saw that one of the boys, who she hadn't noticed but who had just thrown a stone, was her brother Francis!

She got home and brought the chicken to her father who was sitting in his chair in the parlor. She held it out to him as if she were making an offering to a lord.

"What's this?" he grumbled. "You call this a chicken? What happened to it?"

She couldn't tell him. She said, "I dropped it when I tripped on the curb."

"Dropped it! What is wrong with you?" he snapped. "It's all bruised and battered and has pebbles stuck in its skin! How do you expect us to eat this now?" She stood there ashamed and embarrassed and felt guilty even though she knew she had done nothing wrong. If her father had seen how hard she fought just to hang onto it, he would have been proud. But she couldn't let him know the others had teased her. Then, he would think even worse of her.

"See," her father continued, "I finally give you one simple task, and you fail. You fail me! How can I trust you when you fail me so?"

Mandy bit her lip. She wanted to stick her thumb in her mouth, but stopped herself. Her father stood up and unbuckled his belt. He pulled the long leather belt out of its pant-rings and sat back down. "You know what happens when you're a bad girl," he snarled. "Come here!"

Her eyes glazed over. Please, God, not the belt. Not that!

She went to her father just as Francis walked into the room. Francis reached into his pocket, and when their father wasn't looking, took out the silver dollar and flashed it at Mandy with a mean grin.

You bastard, Mandy thought as she looked at her brother. It was easier to think such a bad word the second time.

"Francis!" her father called out while wrapping the belt around his hand and pushing Mandy over his knee. "Now there's someone I can count on!"

Mandy thought of the silver dollar and her brother and how this wasn't over. Her lucky day had become a declaration of war. "You're gonna pay for this," she thought. "You're all gonna pay."

Her father raised the belt high above his head and pulled it down. It zipped through the air . . .

Whoosh! I'm pulled back up into space as the ground and everything around me goes dark. The dial appears again. Counterclockwise it spins, this time, longer. Finally, it stops on the number 9. Once again, I turn from the black of space and look down to earth. And once again, it all lights up . . .

Right from the start, I felt sick. I saw the ground and a farm below me, but was overcome by a sinking, wretched feeling that I'd never experienced before. Something was going to happen, here, on this farm of almost a century ago, that was beyond any of the most disgusting things I had ever imagined or seen. A crime against nature that would make war seem tolerable.

There was a mule and a horse tied to a rail outside the small wooden farmhouse, a wagon off to the side. A cracked and weathered sign hung off a pole besides the muddy road in front of the farmhouse. The sign read simply, "Cheucka." Below the name, in fresh paint, was printed "1898." (Wasn't Cheucka my grandmother's maiden name?)

An old woman stood outside and was talking to a boy. She spoke Polish, which I could suddenly understand. "Did you feed the chickens," the woman asked, "and fix the fence like I told you?"

"Yes, ma'am," the boy replied.

They continued talking, but I didn't listen. That sinking, wretched feeling had a power over me—like it wanted me to know it, feel it for myself. I felt like a cork being flushed down a toilet, fighting to stay up, but getting sucked down into the filth.

Finally, I couldn't fight it any longer. I let go and immediately zoomed past the woman and boy, over the farmhouse and into the barn behind it. To the back of the barn and into a horse stall I flew. There was hay on the floor, but otherwise, the stall was empty. I lingered there impatiently. The wretchedness was teasing me, torturing me with putrid anticipation. Seconds crept by. Minutes dragged. It felt like hours had lapsed while my feeling senses were being painted with vomit.

Finally, the door to the stall rattled. The latch raised and a nine-year-old girl entered, sucking her thumb. Her face was expressionless, her eyes cast down. A man entered behind her and talked in Polish. His voice was gravelly and gruff. "Now remember, Martina. If you ever say anything to anyone, God will punish you and I will beat you!"

She stood in the middle of the stall facing the outside wall. In front of her, up the wall, was a rectangular window opening with four wooden slats running up and down across its opening. It was cloudy and gray outside. She wished she could become a bird and fly away through the slats.

"Did you hear me?" the man demanded. She didn't answer. "Did you hear me?" he demanded again in an even angrier tone, but with his voice still low. Finally, she nodded her head, her thumb still in her mouth.

The man hadn't shaven in days and his hair was black and oily. His hands were covered with calluses and his breath smelled of stale tobacco and liquor. His clothes were brown and gray and dirty and torn in several places and the soles of his boots were worn through in a couple spots. He was thin and wiry and kept looking down at the ground, so I couldn't see his face. "Take off your boots!" he barked.

She reached down, untied the bootlaces, and pulled the black boots off to expose her thin and dirty white socks. She was still facing the wall and the window as he moved behind her. He skimmed his bony fingers down along the girl's sides barely touching her. A shiver went through her little body. I tried to close my eyes, but they wouldn't shut.

He raised the skirt of her long, gray dress and put his hands up under the dress and pulled them down. "Pick up your foot!" he commanded. She did as she was told.

"Now the other!" he said. And she did.

He took the worn undergarment and tossed it aside onto the hay. The girl didn't move, but sucked her thumb harder, biting down on her knuckle, making it hurt. Maybe, she thought, if she hurt somewhere else, she wouldn't feel it. And if she didn't feel it, maybe it didn't happen.

He was behind her looking at the ground as he unbuttoned his soiled pants and let them drop. He paused and listened one last time. All was still.

He raised her skirt above her waist, bent his knees slightly and leaned forward. He clamped his teeth on the hem of the dress to hold it up and out of his way. He grabbed her by the waist roughly with both hands. She felt his bony fingers dig deeply into her flesh. He picked her up off the ground. "Spread!" he whispered hoarsely. "Spread!"

She spread her legs, and as she hung there in midair, bit her thumb even harder. Tears came to her eyes and she winced in anticipation. "Please, God, not that!"

He tried to enter her, but she was dry so he bounced off. He thrust harder, and bounced off again. Then a drop and then another emerged from him and he pushed once again even harder into her fold. He quivered once as he entered her, and felt the warmth and peace and solitude and rapture and domination spread throughout his being. His breath quickened and his eyes glazed over. Now, he was in control. Now, he had the power. Now he could control it all. Now he was God!

The girl's eyes were glazed over too and barely open, and as her father pushed her forward to the wall after he entered her, right below the window opening, her eyes rolled up inside her head so only the whites were visible. She held one hand up to brace herself against the wall as she continued to suck the thumb of the other. She bit down harder and the skin tore around her knuckle and blood started to run out of the corner of her mouth. The skin tore down there too, and blood started to run down the inside of her legs as the man kept pounding and pounding into her as if he was nailing her to the barn wall.

Seconds went by. A minute. One thrust after the other. One sin after another. Each thrust starting another horror against life and humanity to unfold not just in her lifetime, but in years and generations to come. And finally, he did.

He exploded and every inch of his skin tingled, as if an electric charge had just passed through him. He held her still with clenched muscles, immovable as a rock, as he savored the sensations. Then his breath slowed and his muscles relaxed. It was finished . . . done.

The girl opened her eyes, took her thumb out of her mouth, and put her open palm against the wall, marking the bare wood with her blood. As he dropped her onto the hay-littered floor, her legs collapsed under her and she rolled to the floor, her hands barely breaking her fall. Sticky fluid oozed out of her and down her legs. Sticky, sickly fluid made runnier by her blood. It oozed down the inside of her legs and onto the dirt and hay.

The man pulled his pants up and fastened them. He turned away and found her undergarment, picked it up, and threw it at her as she laid there. "Clean yourself up!" he said in a more relaxed but still commanding tone. "Here . . ." he took a handkerchief out of his vest pocket and threw it at her. "Use this, and clean yourself up!"

Feeling started to return to the girl. She saw her thumb was bleeding and wiped the blood off her chin and lips. She picked up the handkerchief and pushed herself up onto her knees and tried to stand. But like a horse that just can't go on despite being whipped, she collapsed back down to the ground. Slowly, she started to wipe herself clean with the dirty rag.

"We will be eating dinner soon!" the man said. "So be quick. And leave the handkerchief under the hay in the corner. I will get it later."

I still couldn't see his face as he looked over the door and reached down to the latch. As he pulled the latch open, he turned and looked at the girl one last time. Then he glanced up at the slatted window opening as if to check the weather. I noticed that below the opening, scratched in the boards, barely legible, was Lev. 26.

As he looked up, finally, I could see his face. His brown and weathered skin was stretched tightly over his cheeks and his lips were curled into a maniacal, mindless grin. There was a mark—an old scar from his childhood, perhaps—that ran diagonally down and across the left side of his forehead. I saw the girl, still laying there on her side: her head turned with her cheek on the ground; her dress up above her waist; her legs sprawled out on the hay as if no longer attached and strewn there by chance; her feet still in those thin dirty white socks; the blood stained handkerchief dripping with her father's semen still in her limp and motionless hand. She did not whimper. The tears were gone. All was still. She closed her eyes. Everything inside her was black.

My eyes creak open. All is black. All is still. I lean over and feel the heave and taste the burger and wine come back up and hear it splatter on the ground. I heave and heave and heave for several painful minutes, even when there's nothing left inside of me. It didn't want to stop.

When the heaves are finally over, it doesn't matter that it's all out of me, I still feel sick. And I know that there's nothing I could take that would change it. I manage to stand and I drag the lawn chair away from the vomit and out from under the overhang. I sit back down and lean my head back and catch my breath. Finally, I look up to the sky.

Still no moon. Nothing but black. It must be late 'cuz the bullfrogs are quiet and I don't hear any cars on the highway. The dreams linger in my mind like the taste lingers in my mouth and I don't even get up for a drink of water because I want to remember it all so hopefully, someday, I can finally accept that it wasn't her fault or her fault either.

Eventually, my eyes close again, and finally, I sleep.

Chapter Eight

I wake to the sound of laughter. Sunny and her friend Becky are in the pool playing ring-toss. The sun is high in the sky and it's hot. My head is pounding and my throat is parched and raspy and I can't even swallow.

Candy comes out the back door and glances my way. I start to raise my hand to wave but let it drop when I see she won't see it. It's Friday, isn't it? What's Candy doing home? Doesn't anybody go to work anymore?

I push myself out of my lawn chair and walk slowly over to my trailer and turn on the spigot. I grab the end of the hose and hold it in front of my mouth and gulp at the water. Finally, I can swallow, and as I drink, relief starts to percolate into my flesh.

"Yippee!" Sunny shouts as she jumps into the pool. Candy stands and watches with no real expression on her face. Something in the flowerbed besides the deck catches her attention and she bends over, reaches out, grabs a weed, and pulls it out of the ground.

I pull the hose over to the vomit and point the stream at it to wash it away. The sand quickly sucks it up. I take my shirt off and raise the hose over my head and the water falls on my head and down my shoulders and body. The cold water shocks me but still feels good, and soon I start to revive. Friday, I think, as I turn off the spigot. One day shy of the summer solstice—the longest day of the year. Just what I need.

Candy looks my way again but glances away when she sees I notice her. It's irritating as hell when she does that. Why can't she just wave at me and say something like, "Hey Sticker! How ya doing today?" But no sir. She's gotta play her stupid little game. Either that, or she's so locked-up inside from getting whooped too much when she was little. Maybe like the dog I had a while back.

Now I'm no dog-lover or animal-lover, as you may have guessed. But a few years ago this dog that looked like a German shepherd, but not quite, showed up and started hanging around my trailer. It was the most docile and skittish dog you'll ever see. Most the time walked around with her tail between her legs. She started hanging around 'cuz it was summer and dry and the wash tin I left in the yard had some water in it. When I saw the poor mutt and how shoddy, skinny, and destitute she was, I felt sorry for her and filled the tin up every couple days with fresh water. So she kept hanging around. I really didn't care much about keeping the stray, so I never fed her. But I didn't want her to shrivel up and die of thirst neither. She must have gone off and hunted and ate squirrels and possums or something 'cuz she kept on hanging around and didn't get any skinnier. By and by, she let me pet her, with her tail hanging low and her butt dragging on the ground and her head slunk down all sheepish and shy and all. It was pitiful to see, really.

"Musta been beaten a ton when she was a pup," Tom said one day. "Sad to see such a nice dog behave so skittish and scared. You can't change it neither—she'll always have that scared in her, no matter what you do." That was one of Tom's more intelligent comments.

Anyway, Sunny and Candy took pity and started throwing table scraps out into the yard for her. That dog was just besides herself to see Sunny or Candy and even me, since I kept water in the basin. She would come to you all tentative-like with her ass dragging and head down and tail hanging low and quivering. Then when you finally did pet her and talk all sweet to her, she would pick up her head and tail and bounce around and play like a normal, well adjusted dog. We used to call her Shegone 'cuz we figured that after she was beaten a bunch and the owner finally figured out he didn't want her and dumped her on the side of the road out in the country 'round here, that he went home and told his wife, "Well, she's gone."

So Shegone would hang around the yard and play with Sunny some and chase some rabbits and probably still ate some of 'em and in the winter would hole-up under my trailer on a blanket I threw under it for her. Candy never let the dog into the house and I never let her into my trailer, so she toughed out the winters outside. She didn't seem worse for wear, neither. Must have been so happy to have a family of sorts, some minor inconveniences didn't bother her none.

Then one day when it was foggy out, Shegone got confused while sniffing around the roadside ditch and got hit by a pickup truck. The bumper clocked her right in the head, and she died right there on the spot. Poor Shegone. Just when she finally found a good, happy life, she got run over. Now she's gone for good.

But we loved her so much we just couldn't bear to see her *really* gone, so we had her stuffed and she's standing guard right now on Candy's front porch. I'm just kidding about that. But I did know a guy— Earl was his name—who lost his wife, and then soon after his little Dachshund named Pepper, and it must've been too much for him to take, so he had Pepper stuffed and stood him up on his front porch. Swear to God, it's true. I'd drive by his house all the time, and there'd be Pepper, just outside the front door, with his tail up in the air and a smile on his snout. Funny what a body will do when they get lonesome. I often wondered if his dead wife was propped up on the couch in his living room.

Anyway, Shegone was always shy and reluctant to come and greet you until she knew you really, really well, which took a darn long time to get to. And maybe Candy's shy too since she was abandoned and all. I don't think she was ever beaten, but maybe being ignored and left on your aunt's back porch as a baby has the same effect. Or maybe it's worse.

So I'm still pretty pissed about the way Candy acts about never saying hello and being so shy, and I beat those thoughts around in my head for a good five minutes and yell and scream and hate her in my mind until I just wear that out and tell myself, "Oh, the hell with it. Let her do what she wants. I can't change her anyway. I'm tired of worrying about it."

It's funny though, because I've noticed that as Candy is so negative and bitchy and shows it to me all the time, it seems to bring out the opposite in me. I find it a challenge to do things and act in a positive way in an attempt to get her to lighten up. It's almost like she's used up all the bitchy, and there's no more left to go around for me; or that whatever she is, I have to be different and the only other option is to be nice and accommodating. It's back-assward, I tell you.

On the other hand, it makes me think about this bank teller who used to work down at *Lowcountry Savings and Loan* who was so darn happy and perky and super syrupy-nice when I came up to her window, that it made me want to grab her by the throat and shake some reality into her. Of course she would ask me how my day was going in that syrupy-sweet voice that bordered on condescending, and I would reply all down-in-the-mouth like, "Yeah, all right I reckon."

"Oh, and isn't it just a glorious, glorious day?" she would chirp back. "Just a wonderful day! And the best part about it is I get to share it with wonderful customers like you!"

You'd think that would make me feel good. But it made me feel like putting a finger down my throat. Maybe it's just me, but I just don't trust really happy people. It turns out she was doing some work-at-home thing selling soap and toothpaste and make-up and stuff to people around town and she just kept at it and kept showing people and being her super-nice and happy self and selling a little here and a little there and then one of her customers started doing it in Charleston and sold a ton of stuff there and then it spread to Columbia and Greenville and Atlanta and she had people all over like five states selling the stuff. She got commissions on everything they sold because that's how the business worked and she made so much money she quit working at the bank and her husband quit his job too and started working with her (or really, *for* her) and they ended up buying a house right on the beach on Hilton Head island and traveling all over the country telling other people how to get successful and happy just like them. So I bet she's really, *really* happy now. And good for her. Just goes to show what I know.

I coil up the hose and hang it off the spigot and as I do I hear the pitter patter of little feet coming up behind me. I turn and see Sunny and Becky running at me barefoot soaking wet in their little girl bathing suits. Of course, they giggle as they run, and they hold their arms out like they're airplanes and bob and weave and make airplane sounds as they flitter across the yard . . .

"Vroom . . . Vroom . . ."

Giggle, giggle.

"Vroom . . . Vroom . . ."

Giggle, giggle.

They're breathing fast when they finally get to me.

"Sticker," Sunny says in between pants. "Mama wants to know if you want some homemade lemonade."

Well I'll be, I think. Just when you think there's no hope.

"That'd be all right," I tell her. "Yes, I do want some homemade lemonade. I do. I do!" I scrunch up my nose as I say it and cock my head sideways.

"Ha!" Sunny laughs. "You're dumb! We got our TV back this mornin', Stick. The repair man brought it while you were sleepin' in your lawn chair. Me and Becky are gonna go watch it. Wanna come?"

"Maybe later," I reply. "Right now I'm just gonna have that lemonade."

"Okay, Stick. Let's go Becky."

The two girls take off and fly around the yard on the way back to the house. "Vroom . . . Vroom . . ."

I put my shirt back on and walk across the yard in my bare feet. The sand and grass are hot. I sit on the picnic bench outside the back door, and Candy comes out carrying a tray with a pitcher filled with lemonade and ice and four glasses.

"Well look at that!" I say approvingly. "Doesn't that look good!"

"Sunny! Becky!" Candy calls out. "Here's your lemonade." She picks up the pitcher and pours the lemonade into the glasses and adds some ice to each one.

"I made it just he way you like it," she says glancing my way. "Real lemons and honey, not sugar, and a little bit of apple cider vinegar."

"Yeah. Ancient Chinese recipe," I say like Confucius. "I'm finally getting you trained."

"Yeah, right!" she sneers. "That'll be the day!" She goes over to the side of the deck and pulls a few more weeds. The girls come over and gulp some lemonade down and then go inside to watch TV.

"What time is it?" I ask.

"Almost eleven thirty," Candy replies. "I thought you were dead sitting there."

"Whoa." I say dryly. "I guess I was tired. Didn't sleep too well last night, what with you vacuumin' the car in the dead of the night."

"I was cleaning up your mess," she says, but not meanly, and she doesn't follow it up with a snide remark either. I'm not ready for that, so I keep my mouth shut. She sits down across the table from me. Then I say, "This lemonade is terrific. I think it's the best I ever had."

She doesn't smile, but her eyes sparkle some. I notice she has just a hint on mascara on, which is unusual for her just being home. And I feel something I've never felt from her before. I feel like . . . Could it be? I feel like . . . she's *wanting* me. What the hell is going on? We sit on the bench for several seconds in silence. Finally I say, "So'd ya get the car all spic 'n span?"

"Yeah. It wasn't easy, but it wasn't *that* bad. I had to use white vinegar on the seat to get the pee out."

"Clever. Sorry again. Kinda funny though if you stop and think about it."

"Yeah, real funny. Sunny's right. You're dumb."

Most people are kidding around when they say something like that, but not Candy. When she says it, she really means it. But today, at least, she doesn't say it meanly. And believe it or not, that's something I like about her. She may be abrupt, but at least she's honest and not trying to white-wash you.

But a lot of times people will kid you how dumb, silly, or whatever you are and it's supposed to make you laugh. And maybe it does. But for me, I've never been good at it. Whenever I do it, it comes out all awkward-like and it sounds like I really mean it, and that makes people think I'm an SOB for saying it. So now I don't even try to kid around like that hardly ever, and if I do, it's just with people I'm really, really comfortable with. Then I can pull it off.

That in itself is back-assward again because what I'm saying is that you have to really like the person and feel comfy with 'em to insult them in the way that's not insulting. So go figure. Maybe I just don't know enough people well enough.

Still, I think that people can get in the habit of kidding around so much they forget to do anything else and all they do is kid, kid, kid until it goes all the way around and back to what the words actually mean. Or maybe some people are like me and take things at face value, and that insult that's meant to be funny is understood for what the words actually mean. And maybe some of these people are kinda little and look up to the bigger people as gods and the purveyors of truth and when these gods kid them that they're dumb or silly, these little people actually believe them and accept it as truth, and, impressionable and trusting as they are, the joke gets sucked down into them so that they end up really not just thinking they're dumb or silly, but *believing* they are and making the world happen in such a way to make it keep being the truth. Maybe too much kidding isn't that good for your kids.

It's better to turn off the kidding-around spigot and turn on the you-do-a-good-job-and-I-appreciate-you spigot every once in a while. Even though it may not be cool and it's so much harder to do, the simple truth is sometimes simply true—and actually refreshing. And it might make your kids simply happier too.

So instead of coming back with a zinger of my own and starting a sparring contest, I just say, "Yeah, you've got that right." Although you have to sacrifice your ego to do that, saying it usually stops all the kidding dead in its tracks. Candy looks at me, and takes a sip of lemonade.

"You got to bed late last night then, didn't you?" I ask her.

"It wasn't *that* late, not even midnight. What'cha do, spend all night on your lawn chair again?"

"Yeah, I guess so."

"Why don't you just get a house like a normal person?"

Uh oh, I think. Here it comes . . .

"You have the money, and you have no wife or kids, so you can certainly afford it!"

I've heard this all before, but today there's something different. Her tone is not as harsh, not as bitter. It's almost like she's detached from the words and their meaning and just saying 'em because they're expected from her.

"Yeah, I know. But, I'm not normal," I say in a similarly detached tone.

"Back with Kaitlin, I see," she says not quite so indifferently.

"Never was with Kaitlin," I reply. "Reports of our togetherness are highly exaggerated," I try to joke, but Candy doesn't catch it.

"Yeah, right!" she sneers. "Everyone knows she was in love with you. And I can tell seeing you two together yesterday, she still is. Why don't you just up and marry her?" She's getting real close to sounding angry.

"Uh . . . That's just not possible."

"Oh! You bug me!" she bites back. Here it comes . . .

"I swear! Here you are, what are you now, forty for cryin' out loud? Still single and livin' in a trailer! You've got money from inheritance and from some crazy business you do that I never see you doing, and some beautiful young woman wants to have your baby and you don't do nothin' about it! What is *wrong* with you?"

Now she *is* angry. But as bitchy and selfish as Candy can be, she can also be dead on target. The only problem here is that if that was all there was to it, I *would* up and marry the girl. But now I'm starting to get angry too, 'cuz she hit a very raw nerve that's been exposed for a very long time.

"You don't know everything, Candy. You just don't know. And why do you care, anyway? What's all this interest all of a sudden?"

"Nothin'. No interest at all. I could care less except to get you and your dumb-ass trailer out of my back yard."

"Okay," I say. "That's so nice to hear. I love you too."

"Oh, shut up!"

It's not hard to get Candy angry. In fact, she can easily get there all by herself, as you are now witnessing. I'm about to get up and go back to my trailer since I'm not in the mood, but Candy beats me to it and gets up without another word and goes into the house. A few seconds later, I hear her washing dishes.

Sunny and Becky come back outside and come over to the table and finish the rest of their lemonade. "Okay, you two," I say. "Last one in is a rotten chipmunk!" I take off my shirt, run across the deck, and cannonball into the four-foot deep water. I hit the bottom hard. I come up for air and see Sunny and Beck jumping in after me. "I am the Creature from the Black Lagoon!" I growl at them with the Daffy Duck inner tube on my head and my arms up with fingers extended like claws. Both of them shriek and laugh and turn to get away. "I love to eat humans who fall into my lagoon!" I continue. "Especially little girls!"

I march towards Becky with my arms out like Frankenstein. She yells and laughs and runs away from me as fast as she can, which is not very fast at all because the water comes all the way up to her armpits. "I will not be satisfied until I eat you for dinner!" I growl. I step towards Becky, but then turn quickly towards Sunny who's sneaking up behind me. As I turn, I lunge at her, knowing full well I'll miss since she's still out of reach, and I say, "Or, I will eat one of her friends for dinner first, and save Becky for desert!"

I lunge at Sunny again, and this time, I reach her and brush her shoulders with my hands. She screams in delightful terror as I let my hands glance off her and slap the water. "Roooaaaarrrr!" I growl. "You have escaped me again! You think you are too quick for the Creature from the Black Lagoon? But you are wrong, little girl!"

I lunge at her again and miss on purpose again and she screams and trudges away from me through the water. Then I quickly turn back to Becky who is now the one sneaking up behind me, and I hurl myself at her and let out another war cry, "Aaaaauuuugggghhhh!" I catch her around her shoulders with one arm and get her in a very loose half-nelson as she hollers and giggles and flails her arms against me.

"Now you will pay!" I snicker. As I hold her with one arm I tickle her with my other hand under the water, right into her side near her ribs, and she laughs and wiggles to get away. Sunny won't be denied, however, and she quickly comes to her friend's rescue, trying to tear me away from Becky.

"Oh no!" I cry. "Not two of them! No, no, no! There's no way The Creature can defeat two little girls at the same time!" I let go of Becky and turn to Sunny, and tickle her too underwater so's to not have her feel left out. Then Becky jumps on my back. "What is this?" I ask bewildered. "Tag-team wrestlin'? That's not good for the Creature! I must retreat! I must save myself! The Creature is simply no match for two pretty girls!"

So I dunk under the water to get away and swim over to the side of the pool. I climb out of the water and the girls howl and raise their arms in victory. "You may have won the battle," I cry, "but I will win the war! Rooooaaaarrr!"

The girls keep laughing and splash at me. I run across the deck and turn to them as I descend the steps to the driveway. "The Creature is leaving now. But he will return to claim his victory! But when will that be? All little girls beware! The Creature may return at any time! Ehh. . . ehh . . . ehh . . ."

The girls shriek and laugh as I disappear below the steps and around the corner of the house. I walk down the driveway past Candy's car to the road, looking down at the ground to see if there's any agents of aggravation from hell around. Then along the roadside ditch across in front of the house to the edge of Candy's yard, where another driveway—that's really just beaten down grass—starts that leads back to my trailer where I park my pickup.

No ants to be seen. Maybe word has gotten out that if they cross the road or property lines they're gonna get burned to a crisp. I crisscross the front yard a few times, just to be sure, and seeing no encroachments, I walk around the other side of the house. I turn the corner to see Sunny and Becky in the back yard bending over and looking at the ground.

"You see, Becky," Sunny instructs, "dandelions are yellow because yellow is their favorite color and they like me so much that they keep all the other colors for themselves and give me their favorite one." Becky nods her head and reaches out and picks one of them. "Do you understand?" Sunny asks.

"Yeah," Becky replies. "I like dandelions too. They're pretty. Maybe we can make a bouquet like . . ."

"Like we're getting married!" Sunny blurts out. "Here! Here's another one! And another!"

I sit down on the bench and pour myself more lemonade as the girls flit around from flower to flower assembling their bouquet. I hear Candy put clothes in the washing machine just inside the back door and start the machine. She takes clothes out of the dryer and goes back into the kitchen. I notice the clothes she hung on the clothesline yesterday are gone. I feel like a guy with wife and kids just hanging out on a Sunday afternoon. All that's missing is the grill and steaks. The girls come over holding a dozen dandelions each and push them in front of me.

"Look, Sticker!" Sunny says. "Look at all the dandelions we have! We're gonna put them together and make a bouquet, just like if I was getting married! Here, Becky, give me yours." She turns and takes Becky's dandelions. "Mom!" she yells. "Mommy!" A few seconds go by and then Candy appears through the screen.

"What?" she says impatiently.

"Look, Mommy! Look at the bouquet me and Becky made!"

"That's nice," Candy replies. "You picked them out of the yard, didn't you? Just goes to show you what a high-class lawn I have. That's something my *husband* is supposed to take care of!"

"But how do we make this a real bouquet, Mommy? How do we keep all the flowers together so we can throw it when we get married?"

"Married! Candy snorts. "You don't ever want to get married. It's nothin' but more trouble and less money."

"Mommy! How do we make a bouquet?"

"Here," Candy opens the door. "Come on. I swear! You two are gonna drive me crazy!"

Sunny and Becky scamper into the house and the door slams shut behind them. Five minutes later, they all emerge with the dandelions bound with a red ribbon and bow. Candy puts a small vase on the picnic table and inserts the bouquet. The girls look at it approvingly for about two seconds, and then Sunny exclaims, "But Mommy, we want to pretend to be married and throw the bouquet! Let's throw the bouquet, Becky! Don't you want to do that?"

"Yeah!" Becky agrees. "Let's throw the bouquet and catch it to see who gets married next!"

Sunny snatches the flowers out of the vase, steps away from the table and directs us all: "Me first! Becky, you stand in front and Mama, you stand behind her, and Sticker, you pretend you're a girl waiting for the bouquet too and stand next to Mama. You're all bridesmaids and I'm the bride and just got married to Donny Osmond!" She turns around and then looks over her shoulder and says, "Y'all ready? You ready to catch it?"

"Yes!" Becky exclaims.

"Yes!" I squeak. "I'm ready too! Oh please, let it be me! Let it be me!"

Candy slaps me on the shoulder and says, "Right! I bet you'd look real cute in a dress!"

"Of course," I chirp. "With legs like these, who wouldn't?"

Sunny bounces up and down with excitement and says, "I now pronounce you husband and wife!" She tosses the bouquet up as hard as she can and it flies straight up and hits the underside of the overhang and ricochets straight back down and lands right smack dab on top of her head. It bounces off her head straight in front of her face and right back into her hands that are still outstretched from releasing the bouquet just a second earlier.

We all stand there dumbstruck, not sure if what we just saw really happened. Then Sunny turns back around with this wide-eyed surprised look and me and Becky howl with laughter and Candy laughs under her breath and then even lets out a genuine full-fledged laugh and when Sunny sees us laughing at her she holds the pose and even exaggerates the look on her face so she keeps us laughing. Candy says, "Sunny! What did you do? You caught your own bouquet!"

"What's that mean?" I ask. "You're gonna get married twice?"

Then Sunny turns around again and this time flings the flowers over her shoulder with just one hand and the bouquet flies straight at Candy and hits her right in the chest. She pins the flowers there with her arms and kinda swats them away to Becky, saying, "Oh no! Not me! I went down that road before and look where it got me! Here, Becky, be my guest!"

"Your turn, Becky!" Sunny calls out. "Now you be the bride and I'll try to catch it!"

So Becky turns around and flings the flowers over her head and of course, knowing Sunny's luck, they make a beeline right into her arms. She jumps up and down and exclaims, "Yippee! I caught the bouquet! I caught them the very first time! Did you see me Mama? Did you? Did you? I caught them and now I'm gonna marry Donny Osmond and live happily ever after!"

"Good for you," Candy says. "Now are we done here? I've got laundry to fold."

Sunny and Becky skip out onto the lawn and play the game again. I sit back down and take a sip of lemonade and watch Candy pull on the screen door. She glances over her shoulder and says, "My mom gave me some steaks yesterday from the cow she and her neighbor buy every year. You want one?"

"Yeah, sure," I say. Another first, I think.

"And we can get the grill out."

"You mean start a fire and cook them . . . now?"

"I don't know . . . I guess. I've got nothin' better to do. You probably don't want another hamburger tonight."

I feel like there's some hidden meaning there, but I let it go, and say, "You got that right. The grill's in the crawlspace under the house, right?"

"Yeah."

"And the charcoal and lighter fluid?"

"In the house. I'll get them."

"Okay. You've got a deal."

I crawl under the house and get the grill and set it up and Candy brings out a can of lighter fluid and a new bag of charcoal. I stack the bricketts and pour the fluid over them and let it soak in some and then light it with a match. I guess I didn't wait long enough for the stuff to soak in because the flames explode about three feet into the air, and it's a good thing I'm not leaning over it 'cuz I woulda got my eyebrows burnt off. But the fire calms down and starts to smolder and in about a half-hour will be ready to cook on.

The girls finally tire and go inside to take a nap. Candy stays in the kitchen as I stay outside and walk around the yard and pick at weeds and feel the heat of the day waning. Then I lay down on one of Candy's lawn-loungers on the deck and close my eyes. I reckon you can guess what's coming next . . .

I was young, of course. I ran through the side door of our house. "Mommy! Mommy!" I yelled. "Look what I got! Look what I got! Look!" I held up the paper. On the top of it was written in large red numbers, 98. "Look! I got the highest grade in the class!"

She glanced at it briefly as she wiped the table. "Well," she said flatly. "What happened to the other two points?"

I died right there. I couldn't say anything. I was about to cry, but was too ashamed.

"Oh," she said when she saw my reaction. "Don't be silly! Don't you know I was only kidding?" Then she said, "Maybe next time you can do better. Maybe next time, you can get it right. Now go outside and do your chores. If I catch you playing with Joey before you're through,

there'll be no dinner for you. Now go!"

I turned around. I'm such an idiot! I wanted to hit myself. I don't know nothin'! I never do nothin' right! I shuffled back out the door.

As I crossed the threshold, I was no longer a boy, but a man. Instead of ending up outside, I found myself passing through the large wooden doors of a church. Inside there were stained-glass windows, dark wooden pews, a crucifix at the front behind the alter. I walked slowly down the center aisle. Then the doors I had just come through opened again.

I turned to see brilliant light stream in on me, and the silhouette of a woman in a dress emerged from the middle of it. She looked like an angel emerging from the light, and she walked slowly towards me, getting larger and more distinct as she approached. It was a woman in a wedding dress, and she walked directly down the middle of the aisle right at me, holding her bouquet of flowers in front of her chest, her high heel shoes clicking loudly on the hardwood floor. The organ started playing, "Here comes the bride . . ."

She got closer still, and I looked up to see the smiling face behind the veil. Kaitlin! My heart skipped a beat . Was it really possible? Could I really be marrying my perfect woman? And for the first time in twenty years, I felt absolutely no pain anywhere in my body. I was free.

She kept coming towards me in her wedding march, right at me, almost to me now—she was too close! She was going to march right into me! Maybe she was going to kiss me! By instinct, I jumped aside and watched as she continued down the aisle. I saw her bare back and the train to her dress flowing behind her as she walked away from me towards the alter where a man in a tuxedo waited.

My heart clenched and the knot in my stomach returned. I turned to leave just as the groom lifted her veil, and as he did, she turned her head quickly and looked right at me. Just a quick glance that was hopeful and a little spiteful and yet, at the same time said, "It should have been you!" I couldn't bear it. I turned completely around and ran out of the church.

Another door in front of me—the side door to the house of my youth again—and I punched it with all my might. The pain shot from my fist up my arm to my shoulder. I hit the solid wooden door again, and again, and again. When that fist and arm and shoulder were broken and too weak to move, I punched the door with my other fist until it too, was broken and weak. I noticed that now my arms weren't solid anymore, but transparent. Like fog.

I kicked the door with my foot and knee until they were broken and fog. Then I kicked with the other foot and knee. Then my back and chest. Then I banged my forehead, side of my head, and the back of my head against the door over and over and over again until my whole head was nothing but fog. "You happy now?" I thought. "There. I saved you the trouble. And you still won't love me, will you?"

Now that I was nothing but fog, I passed through the door without needing to open it. I went into the kitchen. There was no one there. I heard talking and laughter in the hallway, and went to it. Still no one there. The hallway stretched in front of me seemingly forever, with doors alternating each side every few feet all the way down its length.

I walked with foggy legs down the hallway until I saw an open doorway on the right. I thought it was my old bedroom, but instead of entering those familiar surroundings, I entered the large and cluttered laboratory of a medieval castle. There were Bunsen burners under beakers that spewed steam and hoses and candles and spider webs and wires with electrical sparks zapping through the air. A woman approached with a lab coat on. Her name tag said Mary S. "I've been expecting you," she said. "Come . . ."

I followed her further into the lab. We stopped, and she swept her arm to lead my eyes to a large black marble slab with a body laying prostate on it. The body was mine. It wasn't fog, but solid, and almost every inch of it was black and blue and swollen. She fastened wires to my body's arms and legs and put a metal cap with wires coming out of it onto my head. She went to the wall and grabbed a large switch. I looked at the body laying there, so beat up, so tortured. Its fingers still curled into fists. You dumb shit, I thought. Look what you've done to yourself. Then out of nowhere, the thought came to me, "Even a monster needs love. But for a monster, what would that love be?"

I heard the scraping of the switch as it was being pulled, and I turned to look at the woman. But it was no longer a woman pulling the switch, but a mummy wrapped in bandages. "Oh my God!" shot through my mind. "Not that!"

The mummy pulled the switch all the way closed causing jagged arcs of electricity to rip along the wires as my consciousness that was floating in the transparent and unsubstantial fog that was me, condensed into a pink ball the size of my fist. Together, the current and the pink ball *crashed into that body laying on the slab; and as the current hit my head and arms and legs, the pink ball hit my solar plexus, and they all combined to jolt my body and soul into a rippling convulsion of bone-chilling . . . death!*

The body jerked and sat bolt-upright on the slab . . .

"Tee hee!" I hear as I bolt straight up in the lawn-lounger, dripping wet. Sunny and Becky scamper away, giggling, dropping the plastic bucket as they do.

"What the . . . ?" I mutter as I try to make sense of what just happened. I stand and wipe my face with my hands. I know they were only playing, but it's still a shock. I hold my tongue as I give my mind and senses time to recover. The mummy got me again.

"Sunny!" Candy calls as she comes out of the back door holding a plate with steaks on it. "Go in and get the salad and bowls." Candy holds the plate with the three steaks as I spear them with a fork and place them on the grill. I notice she's got even more makeup on now and is wearing a tight fitting shirt. Sunny doesn't balk at the command, and she and Becky bring out the salad and bowls and put them on the picnic table.

I bring the steaks to the table and Candy comes out with a string bean casserole. As I look at it, I can't help thinking about what happened last spring at Easter dinner when Candy served a similar string bean casserole. I call it *The String Bean Casserole Incident,* and I'll remember it until the day I die. It's something Candy would rather not talk about, and would kill me if she knew I told you, but I really can't help it—it's got to come out. So here it is . . .

It was Easter Sunday and Candy and Sunny had just gotten back from church accompanied by Ruby and one of Ruby's grandmother-widow friends. They were having glazed ham for dinner, and Candy had a new beau who went to church with them-all and she thought that he was the answer to her prayers. His name was Nick, and he was an okay guy as far as I could tell. They all came home all dressed up and fancy and Candy had on a nice white dress with a few red roses printed on it and Sunny had on her pink Sunday dress and Nick had on a suit and tie and Ruby and her friend were dressed up too. Candy invited me over for dinner since Sunny wanted me there so I put on some khaki pants and a dress shirt and went on over.

Well, it was a warm and sunny Easter Sunday so we sat outside on the picnic table with a table cloth on it and the ham came out and there were mashed potatoes and gravy and a string bean casserole. We all dug in and everything was fine and dandy, but I didn't eat the mashed potatoes, just the ham and string bean casserole. You see, I have this theory that when you eat meat and potatoes together, it gives you indigestion and gas, so I don't eat them at the same meal anymore. Sunny started asking me why I wasn't eating the potatoes, and I tried to ignore her since indigestion and gas ain't the kinds of things you talk about over Easter dinner. But she asked again and again and was kinda starting to make a scene, so finally I told her my theory. Everyone else listened and kinda nodded their heads and were too polite to say I was crazy or crude or anything. Everyone but Candy, that is.

She got on one of her rolls where she kinda forgets what she's saying and got on about how I was always coming up with these stupid ideas and that if it was true that meat and potatoes caused indigestion, everyone would be farting up a storm every time they ate! I just told her I feel better if I don't eat the two together and I was content to just have the ham with the string bean casserole, thank you very much.

Well, we all finished dinner and were just sittin' there chatting and enjoying the evening and Candy was doing her best to impress Nick by battin' her eyes and smiling at him and all. But then the strangest expression came on her face and her eyes widened and her face got a little flushed and she said, "Uh, please excuse me," really abruptly right in the middle of one of Nick's compliments about how pretty and feminine she looked in her new dress, and she put her hands on the picnic table to get up, but before she could get her legs out from under the table, there came from behind her a little squeak.

At first I thought there was a mouse or chipmunk or something behind us. Sunny was sittin' right next to her mother and she turned around and looked down at the ground thinkin' there was a mouse or something back there too. And then Candy kept standing up straighter and there it came again, but a little longer this time—"squeeeaaak."

Well, Sunny looked at me and I looked at Sunny and then Candy panicked and jumped up and finally got out from under the table and had just turned to run into the house, when all of a sudden, well, I guess you could say that those meat and potatoes wanted to make their presence known and she couldn't stop them from doin' so any longer . . .

"Pppppppppaaaaaaaaaarrrrrrrrrrrpppppppppp!"

I mean it was LOUD. And it was lonnnnngggg. It was like the tuba section of the high school marching band had just had a head on collision with bass drum section.

A second went by. We didn't say a word, everyone was so shocked and all. Then, apparently not to leave her symphony incomplete, she finished it off with a few staccato praap, praap, praaps!

Sunny didn't laugh or anything at first, she just looked up at Candy, who stood frozen on the steps into the house, and said matter-of-factly, "Mama, you farted."

Well, me and Sunny tried to stifle our snickers, but weren't too successful. Candy didn't say a thing and bolted into the house and straight into her bathroom and never came out again the entire evening. She locked the door and didn't answer us as we pleaded with her through the door and told her it was okay and that everybody farts now and then and that's it's a perfectly natural thing to do. But she wouldn't answer back or anything. So after an hour or so, Nick took off and me and Sunny played a board game and then I went back to my trailer. But before I went, I tapped on Candy's bathroom door and whispered loud enough for her to hear me—"Told you so!"

Since then, I've never seen Candy eat potatoes with meat again. But I keep my mouth shut about it. It's probably a good thing I do, too.

We eat the steaks and salad and string bean casserole and drink more lemonade as the afternoon turns into evening and the air cools and the birds quiet and the tension from the day releases. And as our stomachs are full, we relax and sit there and me and Candy listen to the girls chatter on about bouquets and weddings and dresses and flowers and how wonderful it's all gonna be.

I stand and stretch my arms up to the sky, about to make an excuse to go back to my trailer, when Candy stands and does the same. As I step away from the table, she does too, and follows me to the edge of the porch. Suddenly, I have a shadow. Again, I feel her wanting me.

"The steak was good," she says shyly. That's Candy-speak for "You did a good job cooking and thank you."

"Yeah," I say absentmindedly. I found it hard to believe I was about to say, and then I did, with a hint of a butterfly in my gut, "You wanna take a walk? Just down the road a-ways?"

And I'm sure she found it hard to believe it was her who was about to say, and then she did, "I don't care." That's Candy-speak for yes.

So we take a couple steps towards the driveway, and I can almost feel our hands reaching out for the other's and having it be just a natural reaction, like we'd done it many times before, when the phone rings.

"I'd better get that," she says and looks at me and smiles. And the smile she gives me isn't just any old smile. It isn't a smile she'll wear every once in a while when talking about boys or clothes or make-up. It's a different smile that's younger and deeper and more pronounced. It's a smile from long ago—a Mona Lisa smile squared. Those butterflies make another pass through my gut.

She goes inside and after a minute returns holding her purse. "That was Becky's mom," she says indifferently. "Says her car won't start and wants me to drive Becky home now." Candy's mood changes as she talks, "I swear! If it ain't one thing, it's another!" Now the spell is definitely broken. "I think she's lying. She has too many excuses and I'm always the one who has to drive those two." She glances my way briefly and starts walking across the deck to her car.

"Aw right," I say. "You want me to drive them?"

"No, I'll do it. It just pisses me off, I tell you!" She calls out to the girls who are playing in the yard, "Sunny! Get over here! It's time to go."

"Okay," I say. "I'll see you later then."

Candy walks across the deck towards the driveway as the girls trail behind her. She says over her shoulder, "Just put the dishes in the sink. I'll get to them later."

I hear the car door slam as I gather the dishes. That was weird, I think. But now Candy's back to bitching and the earth is once again spinning normally on its axis. Maybe it wasn't butterflies I felt in my stomach just a minute ago. Maybe I was just dizzy from the earth spinning the wrong way.

Chapter Nine

After I put the dishes in the sink, I take my time walking the fifty yards back to my trailer, pausing as I go, watching the sun get closer to the horizon. If you've never seen a summer sunset in the Lowcountry, I'll tell you, it can be a sight to behold. When the sky is clear and there ain't no wind to kick up the dust, the blue of the day sort of melts into a darker shade of blue that glows and seems to vibrate. And after the sun dips below the horizon, the sky just above it turns bright orange with red and pink and yellow mixed in and some of it pokes through the branches of the trees and the Spanish moss. Carolina blue on a layer of Georgia peach. And it's beautiful.

It's gonna be an hour or so before the light is totally gone, so I just stand there looking at the sky and the trees and grass and smelling the evening. Most people don't see sunsets anymore. They're usually inside watching the evening news or some dumb-ass game show. . .

"Is there a 'D'?" BUZZ. "Sorry, no, there's no 'D'. Take another spin."

The sunset of another day: another past that will never change. But as I stand here alone, with my shorts and shirt still damp, my attention goes down to . . . *that.*

There's no one around to distract me now—nothing to keep my mind away from it. And the aftertaste of the fun and laughter and painless innocence of the girls and the good food and drink and the smile that was granted me, makes *that* seem ever more poignant. I wonder again, for the seven thousandth plus day of pain, if I'll ever escape it, if it can ever be healed.

I think back to how it happened so long ago and how I think I would love to go back—make it so it never happened. Then the pain wouldn't be in my body or my mind right now. But I can't. I can't go back and change time. The thing that caused the *that* has happened and it's in the past and there's nothing I can do to make it so it never happened, just like there's nothing I can do to make this day in June I just lived not happen. So *that* is still here, and *that* will always be here, if nothing else, as a memory.

I realize it was so freakishly unlucky that it ever happened at all. If any one little thing from my whole past before *that* had been different, it never would have been. It's like a car accident. If we had just taken a second or two longer talking to Tony, the chipmunk would have run out into the road yards ahead of us and Candy never would have hit the brakes. I never would have been thrown into the seat belt and peed in the car and Candy wouldn't have been vacuuming in the middle of the night and so on and so on. Just a second, just a moment, can change everything.

Yet, as much as most of me wants *that* gone, another part of me wants it to stay, because now that it's here, to let it go would be an admission that it wasn't important enough to hold onto. And nothing that's ever happened to *me* is *not* important. After all, it is *me* we're talking about. Not you. I don't really care that much about you, simply because you ain't me. But me, when we're talking about *me*, now *that's* important.

Anything that's ever happened to me is important: the good times and achievements, and the bad times and injuries. All the *thats*. They're all important 'cuz they're all me. Doesn't make sense? Think about it. Being alive demands that we not be dead. To ensure we're not dead, the most important things in our lives has to be ourselves. The last thing our nature, or nature itself, wants us to be is dead. The first thing our nature wants us to do is survive. So if you or your progeny, which is really you in the future, are not the most important things in your life, you'd better slap yourself upside the head and wake up.

You see, helping others is all well and good and necessary and the second thing nature wants, but the only reason you do it is to feel good about yourself anyway, so it all comes back 'round to taking care of yourself.

Now, while I'm looking at the trees and the Spanish moss hanging off 'em and the calm of the evening falling down on me, as I'm standing here in my bare feet on Candy's sandy backyard lawn with dandelions almost outnumbering blades of grass and thinking so hard, I may as well keep going and see where it takes me, 'cuz if you haven't figured it out by now, I like to preach. In fact, Candy says I should have been a preacher. But there ain't many churches that want an SOB for a pastor, so this will have to do.

By now you're probably thinking, "How's Sticker's preaching gonna help *me*?" Well, I'm glad you're finally catching on.

What I'm addressing here is the *thats* in your life. I know the *thats* all occurred in the past, but what we have to do is get past 'em. You see, because they happened to *you*, all the *thats* are special to you. And even though they might rack you with pain, you really don't want to let them go. Why? Because letting them go would be admitting you were wrong. And your brain—your superego mostly and your ego partly—doesn't like that one damn bit. The superego and ego, more than anything else, need to be right. And to be right—and I mean all-the-time right—they make the unconscious twist things around to make it so. They do this so they don't have to face their arch enemy, which is guilt.

If we believe that everything we ever did was right, how can a *that* be wrong? When nothing we ever did was wrong, we don't feel guilty. But here's the kicker: In order to not feel guilty, we have to hold on to the *that*. And that, my friend, means holding onto the pain.

If you want to get past your *thats* and get out of pain, be it of the body, mind, or heart, you need to do a few things. First, you've got to stop making the *that* stronger. You do that by not resisting it. Resisting something only makes it stronger. Here's why: It's a law of physics, yes physics—and if you don't know what I'm talking about, go back and read your high school science books—that for every action there's an equal and opposite reaction. That's Sir Isaac Newton's Third Law, to be exact.

That's all well and good for matter—lifeless matter that is. But for life, it doesn't work like that. When something is alive, the law becomes—and I call this the First Law of Stickerdynamics: "For every action there's a *more than* equal and opposite reaction." You see, life goes beyond inanimate matter in so far as life creates more force when a force is exerted against it. It overcompensates, it overcomes. If life exerted just an equal force against the force or action against it, it would not be life at all—it would be just lifeless matter.

But life is more than that. Life is more powerful than inanimate death. So any time you resist something, any time you want to change something (which is just another way of saying you're resisting the way it currently is), you cause whatever it is to push back. If it's an inanimate object, it will push back just enough to maintain its own integrity. But if it is something alive—like a person, memory, feeling, thought, or state of being—it will push back even harder in accordance with the First Law of

Stickerdynamics. That something will have a more than equal (more powerful) and opposite reaction against your resistance, making it stronger. This is unavoidable: It is the very essence of living energy.

Want proof? To build muscle and make it stronger, you need to overexert it—you overload it. You put a lot of resistance against it by lifting weights or what have you. Doing so actually breaks down the muscle fibers which, when they recover, grow back bigger and stronger than before. Adding resistance doesn't weaken the muscle fibers—even though at first it may appear that way. It makes them stronger.

So if you want your *that* to get stronger and keep on plaguing you, go ahead and resist it. Resist thinking about it, resist facing it, resist talking about it. But you don't want a more powerful *that*, do you? I didn't think so. So what do you do? You invoke the Second Law of Stickerdynamics, which is what I call "Doing a 180."

If you want your kid to pick up her room, you go in there and mess it up. If you want your kid to quiet down, you insist he yell and scream even louder and that silence is forbidden. If you want your girlfriend to pay more attention, you ignore her—or better yet, show interest in another woman. If you want people to be more respectful to you, you act like they're beneath you. If you want them to be nicer to you, be more of an SOB. If you want people to pay more attention to something, make it a secret. If you want to have an uprising, you keep the people down. The only exception to the 180 rule is when it comes to food. If you want to be healthier, you eat healthy food.

So to handle your *that*, you can't be nice to it. If you are, it's just gonna take advantage of you and treat you worse. You've got to be disrespectful and mean and an SOB to it and beat the living snot out of it in your imagination—which is just as good as reality most the time—so it reacts more than equally and 180 degrees in the opposite direction. Which means, it's gonna stop nagging you and worrying you and holding on to you and it will leave you and your mind, body, and emotions alone.

Now let me make this real clear: I **do not** ever, ever, *ever* mean for you to beat the living snot out of anybody (unless they start it first or your life or the lives of your loved ones are in danger). You never beat your kids. You never beat your husband, wife, boyfriend, girlfriend. You never beat the dog or your neighbor. NEVER!

Well, you can beat up fire ants, but they're from hell, so that's okay.

You exaggerate your feelings in your mind's eye, your imagination, your senses. You beat up the *thats*. You beat the hell out of the cancer that's eating you, that cough that's nagging you, that headache that's pounding on you, that sleepless night or stupid-ass neighbor with the yappy-ass dog, that person in your life that made it a living hell—*that* pain that won't go away. You beat them up, torture them, throw them over a cliff, shoot them full of holes, knife them through and through, set them on fire and watch and feel them burn.

If it's jealously you feel, be super-jealous. If it's fear, be super-afraid. If it's doubt, be super-doubtful. Exaggerate to the nth degree whatever you're feeling about yourself, another person, thing, or event. Exaggerate it so you really feel it deep inside, like it's happening all over again.

You see, when you were little, you were trusting. You had to believe that whatever your parents or guardians did was right since your very survival depended on it. So if they did something wrong that hurt you, instead of realizing they were wrong, you did the only other thing you could do: you made your reaction—your feelings—to their abuse wrong. And in so doing, you blamed yourself. You probably never even realized you did it—your unconscious twisted it around so what you were going through made sense so you could continue to believe (and trust) that the gods in your life were right.

The first step in this unconscious process was to suppress your feelings. You pushed your feelings down inside of you instead of letting them be expressed outside of you. Then to keep them deep down inside so no one (even yourself) could see them, you covered them up with the muck of excuses, denial, rationalizations, and plain old forgetfulness.

Since suppression is a kind of resistance, those feelings you pushed down got stronger (due to the First Law of Stickerdynamics). They festered, fermented, and gained strength—down there in the bottom where light seldom reaches—and they started to stink. And so did you. And so did your life.

Those feelings, being buried so deeply down in your heart, are hard to perceive sometimes. After all, they've been covered with layer upon layer of muck over the years. So when you catch a whiff of one of them, maybe on a clear summer's night while you're sitting in your lawn chair trying to escape the heat, you need to go into that stinky old swamp and confront that sick feeling and expose it for what it truly is. You go down there and show it who's boss by being even more of an SOB to it than it is to you and give it a good old-fashioned ass-whoopin'. That way, it'll get dislodged from the muck and it'll bubble up to the surface and its stink will be released.

You do this with exaggeration. Exaggeration not only exposes and illuminates those self-sabotaging, suppressed feelings, but gives life a chance to exert its more than equal and opposite forces against it.

Try this out—if you're brave enough. But you might want to put your hip waders on. The swamps can get kinda deep at times.

When you go down to that feeling and start to unearth it with exaggeration, you may feel your face flush with anger or shame. You may feel your stomach knot up or your hands turn into fists of rage and start to sweat. You may feel smaller than a piece of dust and get scared to hell. Don't worry. That's just the stink bubbling up.

But life, I said *life,* will react against the exaggeration—your SOBism—to your *that* and overcompensate with the opposite of what you are exaggerating. It has to. It's the sprout pushing up through the dirt; the chick breaking through the egg; the fetus kicking out of the womb. It pushes harder against whatever is against it.

Now there's a lot of people who may be well intentioned who'll tell you that you have to turn the other cheek and love thy enemy as thyself and all that. But feeding and nurturing whatever is against you doesn't make sense to me. And for every part of the Bible that says stuff like that, there's another part that says an eye for an eye.

Once you subjugate your enemy, once you render your *that* impotent, then go on and love it all you want. But while it bothers you and you hate it and want it gone, admit the obvious and stop suppressing your true feelings. Loving something you really hate is just denial, confusion, and fear.

By exaggerating your *that,* and beating the living crap out of it in your imagination, you're no longer resisting what you really wanted to do in the first place anyway. You are no longer resisting the resistance— the *that* that's against you. And since the superego and ego want to believe that everything you ever do is right, then beating the crap out of your *that* will be seen as right too. Look Mom, no guilt!

It's helpful to understand that by suppressing whatever feelings you may have—from something that happened in the past to what's happening in the here and now to even what might happen in the future —is a sure-fired way for them to come back and haunt you even worse later. Like the festering corpses of unrighteous relatives, they might bubble up and cause all sorts of havoc at any time, and probably when you least expect it. And I know it's not socially acceptable to get pissed in public or cry or carry on whenever intense feelings arise. But pushing those feelings down does you (and others) harm in the long run. So let your feelings out as best you can without offending anyone too much. Go off to a room and punch some pillows. Ride around in your car and yell and scream and pound on the steering wheel. Then whatever junk is left over, you can handle later on in the way I'm showing you here. It's no surprise to me that research shows that people can handle more pain when they swear. They're letting those emotions out instead of pushing them down into the muck.

So now that I'm on a roll with my preaching, I'm gonna keep going and tell you the rest of Stickerodynamics so I can finally stop suppressing it and get it off my chest. In order to get all those *thats* up to the surface so they no longer stink up your life, there's a little more work to do.

Close your eyes. Imagine two open windows, one on the upper left and one on the upper right. In the one on the left is the person who wronged you. Look up to the left at the window they're in—actually move your eyeballs in your head to look and imagine him or her. Imagine them yelling at you, beating you, ignoring you, or whatever they did to you that was wrong. Now feel the initial feelings that come up when you experience that situation again. You may be angry or sad or scared—whatever. Really feel it again and remember how you felt at the time and the confusion that was going on in your mind and how you had to do what they wanted or else there'd be trouble. Let those feelings flow through you for a few seconds.

(You can do this with things too, like alcohol, drugs, cigarettes, money problems, shyness, or whatever it is that's an issue. Just visualize it in some way, and let it speak to you. Listen to what it says, and then talk back to it.)

Now imagine the second window on the upper right, and in it is the same person (or thing) doing the same exact thing. (Actually roll your eyeballs in your head to look at him or her.) But this time, you are not dependent on this person (or thing) in any way, shape, or form. Even though you may still be a kid in this scene, you are totally independent, strong, self-sufficient, and have the balls (or mitt, as Kaitlin would say) to stand up to this person (or thing).

Now feel how *that* would feel. Really feel your strength and power and independence. Since you're strong now, you don't need that person, and you don't need to obey them. You can do what you want without any fear of being yelled at, belittled, beaten, abandoned, or worse. Just shut the window! You can let the feelings you have (had) for them flow, without having to suppress them. You can tell that person off if you want. Yell up at them in that window to the right and give them a piece of your mind. (Actually talking or yelling out loud is helpful and very cathartic.) Slap them around some if you feel like it. Blow their head off even. Throw them over a cliff. Knife them through and through. (All in your imagination, of course.) Go ahead and release all that pent-up rage!

If you want, you can have your anger do all the dirty work for you. Just imagine the *anger* kicking them around as you simply watch and see that justice it done. It's the *anger,* and not the real you, that's lashing back and expressing what needs to be expressed. Understand that if someone harmed you (physically or emotionally), you didn't deserve it. Consider the imaginative therapy you're doing here as giving back what they gave to you—evening up the score so to speak. And you're harming no one.

Feel what it's like to be strong enough and self-sufficient enough to do this. Feel what it's like knowing you'll survive and thrive just fine and dandy leaving them behind.

Actually rolling your eyes upward to look at the windows (with your eyes closed) helps put you into an alpha brainwave state—one which is more relaxed, receptive, allowing, synchronized, and efficient. Kinda like a hypnotic state, but one where you're in control. This makes it easier to get through the muck and let all those festering feelings bubble up and be released.

After you feel that for a while, go back to the window on the upper left and see that person again doing the same exact thing, but this time, you are once again dependent on them and must do what they say.

Then go back to the window on the upper right and feel that you're totally independent and can do what you like with no fear.

Feel the difference? Can you feel what it's like to be a pawn in their game? Then, can you feel what it's like to be free?

Back and forth, back and forth. Feel powerless, feel powerful. Feel powerless, feel powerful. Dependent, independent. Left, right. Left, right.

All this time you're activating different parts of your brain and allowing it to synchronize. Instead of being all broken up, fragmented, and distorted, your brain is becoming whole, more harmonious and more powerful. In essence, you are coordinating the left (rational) side of the brain (the part you had to use to suppress those feelings to ensure your safety and survival) with the right (feeling) side of the brain (the side that operates through instinct).

As you do this, you'll find that you will naturally enjoy and want to feel what it's like to be powerful, independent, and free. After all, no living thing wants to be stuck in a cage.

Whatever feelings come up, no matter what they are, let them come and rise to the surface. You don't need to act on them, just allow them to bubble up. Once the bubbles get to the surface and become fully exposed, they will pop on their own.

Feelings are never wrong. They only become wrong when you suppress them and don't know how to handle them. That's when they start to fester and stink up your life. I'll say that again: Feelings—no matter what they are, no matter where they come from, no matter how many people will tell you to the contrary—are never wrong. How you handle them is the important thing.

Next, turn away from the windows all the way—180 degrees—so you're facing the opposite direction. There's another window there, upwards and in the center of your field of vision this time. As your eyes are closed, it'll feel like you're looking right at the bridge of your nose. That person or thing is in the window again. But this time, imagine he/she/it saying to you, "Please, forgive me."

Now here's the trick—do not try and forgive. If you try, you're going to kick up some resistance. After all, some things just can't be, and shouldn't be, forgiven. If you do forgive them, that's fine. If you don't, that's fine too. You're under no obligation to forgive or forget. But, what you want to realize is that this person (or thing) is *seeking your forgiveness*. That's the important thing. Feel what it's like for them to do that. You may notice somewhere along the way sadness or guilt start to bubble up from inside you. That's okay. If you feel like crying a river, go ahead and let it flow. Those tears will wash you clean.

Surprisingly, you'll find that the more emotional garbage you unload, the more logical and rational it will be for *you* to forgive *them*, even as *they* are seeking forgiveness from *you*. Forgiveness requires strength in self, and you're gaining strength in self by doing this exercise in your imagination and feeling the power of *not needing them*.

Forgiveness is getting unstuck and letting something go; getting unstuck from that nasty flypaper and taking it to the trash can and letting it fall out of your hand and into the garbage. It takes some effort. It takes some moxie. It takes being smart enough to put that newspaper under your hand and pluck that flypaper off you instead of passing it back and forth from one hand to the other and making a bigger mess. And sometimes—but not always—it takes the innocence of a child to show you how.

After you exaggerate in your imagination whatever your *that* is and you feel some relief in your mind, body, or emotions because the resistance is gone; and after you alternate what it's like to be dependent and then independent and your forgiveness is sought, the next thing you do is congratulate yourself: Give yourself a pat on the back: an at-a-boy or an at-a-girl. You do this in a language that taps into the more impressionable layers of your being and nurtures you at the same time.

Now I don't have the time here to get into all the science behind this 'cuz the sun's getting lower and it's a beautiful evening and I just want to enjoy some of it without a lot of chatter going on in my head, so I'm just gonna tell you the basics. So what you do is this:

After you beat the living snot out of your *that* with exaggeration and you feel some relief, and after you feel what it's like to be independent and forgiven and you've cried a river, you take your dominant hand, put the pads of your thumb and forefinger together like a 'okay' sign, put it on your tummy and rub it in a counter clockwise direction—the same way the moon goes around the earth and the earth goes around the sun and a horse races around the track—nice and slow, and you say to yourself out loud, "Thank you, that's a good little boy," or "Thank you, that's a good little girl."

Now I don't give a hoot if you're ninety years old, and I don't give a hoot if you feel like the biggest fool this side of the moon. You say this to get yourself on the same frequency you were when you were wide-eyed, trusting, and impressionable. You rub your tummy to comfort the center of your being—the area where most of the tension is held—which really was the center of your being while you were connected with the umbilical cord to your mother. You use your dominant hand because it's the hand (and especially the thumb and forefinger) that activates the largest areas of your brain, and you say it out loud because that activates other areas of your brain so what you're saying gets deep down into the core of your being so you really start to believe it.

You see, when you believe you're a good little boy or good little girl you feel and think well of yourself. Your superego and ego are satisfied, since being a good little boy or girl makes them right. Then there's no need to feel guilty, twist things around, and punish yourself.

You stop holding onto things—the *that*s that are tearing you apart—out of obligation, fear, or the need to avoid guilt.

Not only that, but you stop bringing things into your life that are on the same lousy and self-abusive frequencies and wavelengths that keep making those bad things happen. You start making better decisions. Your luck improves. You stop being a Calamity Jane. You no longer stink.

You can rub other places too if you want, like where the boo-boo is or cancer is or whatever is if it's a physical pain. Or rub your head if it's a mental problem, or your heart if it's an emotional pain. But do that in addition to rubbing your tummy. You can use your non-dominant hand sometimes or both hands at the same time. It's all very relaxing just on its own.

Also, instead of saying ". . . good little boy or girl," you can insert anything you think is appropriate, such as: "Thank you, you are a smart little boy." Or "Thank you, you are a deserving little girl." ". . . cared for little boy," ". . . pain free little girl." Or, "happy," "strong," "desirable," "healthy," "loved."

If your *that* doesn't go away all by itself right then and there, notice if something comes around that will kill that cancer or make it stop spreading; silence that cough or make your head stop pounding; get that neighbor to move away and take his yappy-ass dog with him; make peace with that person who hurt you. You've got to pay attention and sometimes follow the signs.

Now I can hear some of you wise-guys already. Some smart-ass will say, "Well, Sticker, why don't I just tell myself I'm a bad little boy or girl, and then the 'more than equal and opposite' law (the First Law of Stickerdynamics) will make me think I'm a good little boy or girl."

Well, Mr. or Ms. Wisenheimer, I'll tell you why you don't do that. To some degree, it would work. How many times have you heard of someone achieving something to prove someone else's opinion of them wrong? It is a motivator, but it can only take you so far. You're achieving to prove someone else wrong, not to prove yourself right, and this does nothing to satisfy your superego, which wants you to do everything properly. When you put your attention on someone else, you're no longer focused on you; and by proving that person wrong, you would be, in a sense, hurting them, which is not the socially correct thing the superego wants you to do. So even if you do achieve your goal and prove them wrong, you end up only feeling partially fulfilled and would likely feel somewhat guilty.

However, when you achieve out of gratitude (i.e. thank you), not only do you get the full feeling of accomplishment, but can accomplish more in the end. Meaning, you can take it to true completion. You see, gratitude is the emotion with the longest, most powerful wavelength. That's been proven scientifically. It means it's the most powerful thought and feeling there is. Even more powerful than love. So it supersedes all the shorter, less powerful thoughts and emotions and can actually cancel them out—kinda like a tidal wave making all the regular-sized waves seem puny. Gratitude acts directly on your mind in a straight-forward way, not some twisted, back-assward 'I'm gonna show you' kind of way some of the lower emotions use. A seed will push its way past the dirt, but can't grow to its full height without the light of the sun.

Feel thankful for what you have. Feel thankful for what you want. Feel thankful for having the courage to feel thankful. Just feel thankful.

Don't be thankful for what you hate. Don't be thankful for what you don't want. That's just more suppression. Those things are not in your life to teach you "lessons"—other than perhaps that you need to be more thankful. You don't need hardship to learn. People say that only because they themselves may have learned that way and they want to justify that it was worth it and then they can have other people think they're heroes for going through all that crap. As long as you're grateful, you don't need all that drama.

You've heard the saying, "In the beginning was the Word, and the Word was God?" My take on that is: "In the beginning was the Word, and that word was Thank you."

I figure the universe was born out of gratitude. God was so happy and grateful to be forever alive and well he/she threw a party for him/herself and created heaven and earth and all the creatures after their kind. And that party is the very act of creation itself, since the greatest joy comes from creating. And since God is always happy and thankful, he/she is continually having a party and continually creating (the universe is expanding, is it not?). More gratitude is constantly being created as God's party gets bigger, and since one must be alive to be grateful, life is forever being created. Therefore, it is never ending.

Since gratitude is the highest vibration there is and God is the most high and mighty, wouldn't God then *have to be* gratitude?

How can God be anything *but* grateful? Do you think he/she has all these unresolved issues and hurtful emotions buried deep down in the swamps of his/her heart that gets him/her all twisted up? I don't think so.

Do you think he/she went through hell to get to heaven? I doubt it.

Who said God is unfathomable? Who said man could never figure out God? It's simple:

God is gratitude.

So if God is never ending gratitude, and gratitude gives rise to the universe and life never ending, it can surely give rise to something you are grateful for. Being more grateful is being more Godlike.

If you're really brave and have a partner who's brave, you can do Stickerdynamics together and role play and yell at the other as if he or she were the SOB that hurt you and then have that person ask for your forgiveness and then rub your own belly and then have the other person rub your belly too and tell yourselves and each other you're a good little boy or girl. Heck, for a real fun time, you could even have a Stickerdynamics Rubbing Orgy (SRO for short, which rhymes with grow). Just imagine three or four or five people putting their hands on your tummy and rubbing it and thanking you and telling you you're a good little boy or girl. You would feel so good, you might just turn into a Stickerdynamics addict!

If you're worried you're gonna get all stuck-up and cocky when you and everyone thinks you're so such a good little boy or girl, don't worry. It won't happen. Have you ever seen an egomaniac who's grateful?

(I can imagine a day when SRO's will be banned. It'll be illegal to practice Stickerodynamics since it's so good for you and doesn't cost anything and therefore is harder to control. It wakes you up and helps you get healthy and when you get healthy, you think better; and those who do will see the insanity that life has become and move to change it. But those in power don't like this one bit because if life got rational, they would lose their power and have to face the fact that they are the first kind of SOB who wants you to be in as much pain as they are.

(So I can picture some people meeting in some dark back-alley somewhere, behind the dumpster, and one will say, "Hey, dudes, you the ones up for a SRO?" And the other people, who are dressed all dark and secretive-like will say, "Maybe, dude. What's the Second Law?" [Asking for the Second Law of Stickerdynamics will be like asking for a password.]. And the first guy will say, "Doing a 180." And the second ones will say, "Yeah, man, that's right. Let's go!"

(The second ones will direct the first ones to a deserted warehouse, with an old mattress lying on the floor, and it'll smell like old diesel engines or somethin', and they'll use candles since the electric is off and one of them will lie on the mattress and the others will place their hands on his or her stomach and start rubbing and telling him or her what a good little boy or girl he is.

(And sometimes when people did this, the cops would find out and bust in on them rubbing each other and the cops would have their guns drawn and be wearing black uniforms with big-ass yellow lettering on the backs that say SROT, which stands for Stickerdynamics Rubbing Orgy Terminators. They'll grab them and push them to the floor at gunpoint and handcuff them and take them away in a paddy wagon to some jail. That's my vision of the future, you see. So you'd better do your SROs now, while they're relatively unknown and still legal.)

There's gonna be a big contrast from your being an SOB to your *that* and being a nurturing nice guy to your tummy and yourself, and you may feel like you're being pushed and pulled and stretched and shook all over and you may feel a bit wiped out or spent and your shoulders might let go and your tummy unknot. That's all good. That means you're changing. That means your *that* is leaving you.

Now here's your first session. I want you to picture me as you imagine me—and I'm very handsome, so make sure you get that right. Next, summon up all the anger and venom you have for me, since now that I've woken you up some, I'm sure you are pissed at me because nobody wants to be woke from a sound sleep. I want you to feel that hate like you've never felt hate before and then, in your imagination, beat the living snot out of me. Shoot me or tear me apart or light me on fire or throw me off a building or all of the above because right now, I am your *that* that you want to get gone.

Go ahead. Take your time. Take your best shot. Beat me up. Destroy me. Make me hurt. It's all okay. Stop resisting. Don't suppress anything. Go ahead. Abuse me.

Now, after you feel done and I'm just a pile of shit on the driveway or whatever, stop and imagine two windows. In the one on the left, imagine me up there yelling down at you to wake the hell up. You don't really want to wake up, but I'm the boss. What's it feel like having to obey me?

In the window on the right, there I am again yelling down at you to wake the hell up. This time, you are totally independent and can tell me where to stick it. So go ahead. Tell me. "Ah, the hell with you, Sticker. If I want to stay asleep, that's what I'm gonna do. So screw you and go preach to some other bozo. I sure as hell don't need *you* telling me what to do!"

Then go back to the window on the left and feel stuck and dependent. Back to the window on the right and feel self-sufficient, strong, and independent.

Then turn around 180 degrees and imagine me there in the center window saying, "Please, forgive me."

Got it? Okay.

Now, put your dominant hand on your tummy with your thumb and forefinger together and rub it counter clockwise and say out loud, "Thank you, that's a good little boy," or "Thank you, that's a good little girl."

"Thank you, that's a good little boy."

"Thank you, that's a good little girl."

Do that a bunch of times.

Okay? How do you feel? Are you still mad at me? If you are, do it again. Do it until you just don't care about me one way or another. It may take a few sessions or a few days or a month or a year to get to that point with your *that*, but you keep doing it until you do.

When you get to that point—when you don't care about your *that* one way or another—that's when you're past it. That's when you're past your past. To be most effective, do this every day with one of your *that*s. You'll be picking them off like ducks in a shooting gallery at the amusement park. You'll have a blast.

Remember, you are under no obligation to anybody to stay in pain. You are not betraying anyone (your mother, father, grandparents, great grandparents, step-mother, step-father, husband, wife, lover, friend, sister, brother, cousin, society, the church) or anyone's memory when you stop caring what they think. If someone abused you or tried to convince you that there's a payback for pain, you don't owe them respect. You don't owe them the reverence we've been taught to feel for a parent or relative simply because they are a parent or relative. They may have provided for you in some ways, but they harmed you in others. It's like paying homage to the King even after he cuts off your arm simply because you live in his castle. There are better kingdoms to live in.

Now during the day, if you find your *that* comes up and gets in your head or body or emotions and you didn't suppress it the best you could at the time, now that you're addressing it during your sessions, you don't need to get anal about it. So I want you to ignore it, push it out of your mind and think of something else. Say to your *that*, "You're not worthy and I'm through with you," and go onto something else. Here's why:

Ignoring something or someone is the worst thing you can do. It's worse than hating them. Eventually you'll be able to ignore your *that* without any effort after you've beaten it up enough times. But before that happens, you need to pretend you're already there by ignoring it on purpose. It's like if you see someone across the street you don't want to talk to. Duck into a store or alley or hide behind a lamppost. Ignore the *that* now, and deal with it again later, under your terms in another session.

If it keeps really bugging you, then go off somewhere quiet and have yourself another Stickerdynamics session right then and there. If it ain't that critical, however, just ignore it the best you can and do that later.

A short-cut to a tummy-rubbing exercise is to just rub the pads of your thumb and forefinger together counter clockwise, and say to yourself, "Thank you. That's a good little boy or girl." You can do this anywhere, and no one will know. It's okay to do even without a reason. Just do it a few times during the day, and you'll feel better.

There's a Third Law of Stickerdynamics you need to know about, but I can't get into it now because I hear a car out front that's slowed down and stopped and is backing up and turning into my driveway. But just to give you a hint, here's the basic law: The Third Law of Stickerdynamics states that your mind and emotions are only as good as your body is sound. You can have Mario Andretti behind the wheel, but if he's driving a junker, he ain't gonna win the race. So you've got to get your body in shape.

But that's a whole 'nother story and that car's pulling up and I see it in my driveway and I can hardly believe my eyes. It's that vintage candy-apple red Mustang—today, with the top up—with Kaitlin behind the wheel. She's backing into my grass covered driveway and her head is turned to look backwards and she's not doing a very good job of it as the car veers right then left off the tracks a few feet and just before she backs right into my pick-up, she finally sees it and stops the car.

I stand there like a deer in headlights. Our eyes meet. Her's are a pleading forgiveness of anticipation and hope and reluctance all rolled into one. I'm trying to remember the moment, with her hair falling down on her shoulders and her smooth radiant young skin and those pleading eyes and dolphin lips and how she's here to try one last time to get the one thing in her life that keeps pushing her away. But the moment can't last forever, so I finally uproot myself and walk slowly over to the car.

"Hey, Kait," I say.

"Hey, Sticker," she replies.

Chapter Ten

That's all that needs be said. We both understand from there how this evening will turn out. But we keep talking anyway, hoping that by some small chance we're wrong. "How you doing today?" I ask as I put my hands on the roof of the car.

"Fine. Okay . . . I guess. How you doing yourself?"

"I'm okay. Just standin' here watching the sun go down. After tomorrow, the days get shorter you know."

"Yeah, it's pretty." She lowers her eyes and pinches some of her hair and fidgets with it. She doesn't smile, but her lips are turned up as they always are.

"What'cha doing all the way out here in the boondocks?" I almost smile.

"I don't know. You know, I was just driving around and then I noticed I was near your place so I figured I'd drive by and see it." She pauses. "So that's your trailer, huh?"

"Yeah, that's it. Come on and I'll show you around." I reach into the car and turn the key and the car shuts off. She smells so good. She puts the stick in neutral as I open the door for her. Just then, I hear another car drive by, but I don't pay it any attention until I hear it too, slow down in front of Candy's house and then turn into her driveway. I pause and listen and I hear a car door open and the warning buzzer buzz.

I tell Kaitlin, "Hold on a second, we've got company," and turn and take a step towards the house and see Candy coming up the side steps to the deck. When only half of her body is visible, she sees me and Kaitlin standing besides the Mustang and she stops abruptly, but just for a second, and then comes up onto the deck to the back door.

I remain silent, but watch her open the screen door and fumble with the key trying to put it in the lock we both know isn't locked and she calls out over her shoulder, "Forgot something!" Finally, she opens the door and disappears. I turn back to Kaitlin and I notice a look on her face I'd never seen before.

"Yeah, right!' she mutters.

"So as I was saying," I say as I take her arm and nudge her gently towards my trailer. "My estate is right this way."

We walk back to my trailer, and as we're standing there under the overhang, I say, "As you may have guessed, this is not just a simple trailer some crazy-ass, Lowcountry yokel lives in. No, Kaitlin. No, no, no. This particular trailer . . . yes, this one right here settin' before your very eyes . . . here . . . you want to touch it? Yes?" I take her hand and press it against the cold aluminum. "This very trailer was actually, believe it or not, a space ship that got stuck in a time-warp and got sucked back in time from the twenty-second century. It had to make an emergency landing here in the Lowcountry to save the passengers, who are really an Amish family who were the only one's left on earth after the Grand Reversal that plunged the earth into another ice age. They were chosen by the freezing and dying masses to be blasted into orbit to circle the earth—ironically frozen in suspended animation—for seven generations while the earth thawed out. And now this Amish family is living over near the Air Force base when they're in between assignments as double agents and country music recording stars." I don't think she bought it.

Meanwhile, Candy emerges from the house and doesn't close the door but lets the screen door slam shut and walks across the deck and looks back at us one last time as she goes down the stairs to the driveway. We hear her shut the car door and back out of the driveway and then squeal the tires as she guns it up the road the same way she came. I notice Sunny and Becky still in the back seat.

"I passed her on the road," Kaitlin broke the silence. "I had a feeling she'd come back and be nosey. I know jealous when I see it."

I motion her to the fold-out lawn chair near the card table and I sit in the other one, but she hesitates and says, "Why don't you show me inside? I always wondered what the inside of an Amish spaceship looks like."

"Ah, yes. Well, I wish I could, but they left laundry all over the place since they had to leave on a special mission. Let's just sit out here a spell and watch the sun go down."

She sits and fidgets with her hair again, and I would normally let her sweat and squirm, but for her, I know I have to be the nice guy now and start to stop her suffering.

"Kaitlin," I say sincerely. "You know this isn't easy for me either.

Ever since I met you, ever since I saw you, I've loved you. I think you know that. And I would do anything in the world to be with you." I look into her eyes and she looks back at me in confirmation, then glances down at the table. "And I've told you before, as I told you yesterday, that being with me . . . well . . . it just wouldn't work." She is quiet, relieved I'm getting things out in the open.

I continue, "You need someone younger, someone you have more in common with. Someone you'll grow together with instead of apart from." Old clichés, I know. But at least it's a way to break the ice.

Finally, she speaks, and speaks as one who hasn't yet had her dreams turn into excuses. "But Sticker, I've told you that age doesn't matter. What they think doesn't matter. All I care about is love."

My eyes float down to the ground as she talks, and notice movement on the sand. "Yes," I say slowly, obviously distracted. "In a rational world, that would be all that mattered . . ." my voice trails off as I keep looking down. There, in a line, are four or five fire ants marching to the spot I had washed away my vomit from earlier. Right in the middle of my bare-earthed porch under my overhang, a colony is starting. "Damn!" I swear under my breath.

"What?" she demands.

"Oh, nothing. I . . ." I look up quickly. She stands up abruptly, knocking the chair over backwards as she does.

"It's just the ants," I motion to them. "The ants are back. I keep the yard free of the ants so Sunny can run around barefoot, and there's some ants coming back."

"Is that so? Well, that's real nice of you Sticker, but here I am pouring my heart out and all you can think about is Sunny and some dumb old ants?"

I stand too, and put my hand on her shoulder and she swats it off. I bend down and pick up the chair and situate it behind her and touch her shoulder again to have her sit down. "Here," I say. "Here. I know. You're absolutely right. Here. Please sit back down and let me explain. I'll explain it all so you'll never wonder again why I'm the way I am with you."

She sits and I do too. She glares at me intensely, but is willing to listen. I move to the edge of the chair and put my elbows on the table with my fingers intertwined in front of me, and I look straight ahead at my truck and her car and the trees behind the road. "It all started years ago, before I met you."

And I tell her. I tell her everything. What happened to me and the pain I've been in and all about my *that* and how it just wouldn't be fair to her or me or the stars if we were together and how eventually she'd start thinking about it and worrying about it and feeling a little resentful about it and then a lot of resentful until she ended up hating me for it. I would end up hating her too because it would eventually get that every time I looked at her it would remind me of my failure, even though it really wasn't my failure at all, but just something passed on—the culmination, the end, of mistakes that came before me that just happened to reach their nadir in me and how that would trap me into believing again that it was all my fault when in fact, it wasn't. And it wasn't her fault or her fault either.

And how now I'm just getting to the point where I'm starting to understand and actually believe it wasn't my fault, and that now maybe I can go on with my life and just make the best of it and maybe, if I keep at it, the pain will somehow go away.

Finally, I look at her. Her eye's are filled with tears and are no longer angry but understanding and sympathetic. She gets up out of her chair and puts her arms around my shoulders as I sit here and hugs me tight for a long time. Then she takes my face in her hands and kisses me on the forehead. Then she leans over and kisses me on the lips.

And I kiss her back. Once, twice, three times. I kiss her as I've never kissed before. I kiss her with a passion—a raging, hot, all-consuming passion forged from defying a lifetime of loneliness and guilt.

I rise from the chair and our lips never part, our hands cupping each other's cheek and our fingers intertwining in each other's hair and our legs pushing up against each other's thighs. I smell and feel her hot, fragrant breath all the way down to my chest and I could not stop, I just could not stop touching her and holding her and kissing her and pulling her into my soul for this one time—this one and only time—to be one with her, even though that oneness could never be complete.

My hand goes to the small of her back and pulls her hips hard against mine and she puts her hand on the nape of my neck so gently, so delicately—like a magnolia blossom pedal had just fallen there—that the hair on my neck and all the way down my arms stands straight up and my skin tingles and my whole body quivers from her touch.

We kiss and kiss and kiss. Gentle kisses, hard kisses. Short kisses, long kisses. Soft kisses, deep kisses. Kisses that hold no secrets. Kisses that hold nothing back. Kisses that tell the truth. Kisses that open your heart, open your soul, open sequestered chambers so deep inside you, you never even knew they were there.

I feel her knees give and I pull her even closer to keep her from falling as I cup the back of her head in the palm of my hand and feel her soft hair press against my skin. Her breaths gets shorter and harder, and a whimper—a whimper that's just a little more than a sigh—escapes her lips as she wraps her arms around my neck and surrenders into her dream.

I hadn't heard Candy's car drive up the road and into her driveway or her car doors open and shut or her and Sunny walk up the steps and across the deck and open the screen door. All I hear is the screen door slam shut behind them with a loud and angry bang. It shatters me out of my trance. I stop kissing Kaitlin as her body, too, stiffens. I look down and feel a fire ant bite my big toe, but I don't move to stop it. She's still in my arms and I can feel her eyes looking at mine, searching for a reprieve, searching one last time for her fantasy. I feel ashamed. My impotence shows. I push her away.

She squeezes my shoulder as my arms fall to my sides and my head droops. I hear a single, soft sob escape her lips as she moves away. I hear her car door open and shut. She starts the engine and puts the car in gear and I hear the tires crunch slowly on the grass covered gravel of my driveway. Finally, I look up and see her in the car, her hands trembling on the steering wheel. She's just staring straight ahead, her eyes almost empty, almost blank, that sparkle almost extinguished. And she drives out onto the road and out of sight.

I reach down and squash the fire ant that had buried his head in my toe. "Damn," I mutter under my breath. "Damn."

The sun is just about to fall below the treetops as I stand here, at a loss for what to do next. It's that time thing again that just won't leave me alone. So I stand here. Just stand here and look to the west but not at the sun. I'm tired of the sun. There's been too much of it lately. I'm tired of the day too, and I think about how I woke up this morning in my lawn chair and how that seems so long ago and how I'm looking forward to laying in my bed and finally getting a good nights sleep. For as hard as it was to finally put any chance of Kaitlin and me to rest, it is, at the very least, a relief for all hope to be gone. Another corner turned, another bridge burned.

Just as I'm thinking my day is almost over and how it won't be long before I crawl into bed in my simple, old, trailer, I hear Candy's screen door slam once again. And there's no way in hell I could ever have imagined how wrong I was about how this day was going to end.

Chapter Eleven

Candy comes out with a laundry basket full of clothes and starts hanging them on the clothesline. "Oh brother!" she calls out, obviously wanting to be heard. "I don't believe it!"

Everything is such high drama. So once again, I play her passive aggressive game and walk on over. I've got nothing else to do anyway. "What's up?" I say. "What's the problem?"

"Oh, it's this dumb-ass clothesline. It gets stuck here when I try to turn it. I swear."

I look at it and see where it catches and get a pair of pliers from inside the laundry room. I take the pliers and squeeze the metal just a hair. "There. Now it'll turn."

She pushes it around and it turns like it should. "Oh. Okay." She says

I pick a shirt out of the basket and hold it out for her. She takes it and pins it to the wire with a clothespin. "So I guess *now* you're back with Kaitlin," she says.

I don't say nothin'.

"With your huggin' and kissin' and all. You should have just gotten a room! Sunny was embarrassed and mad. You know she thinks the world of you."

I pick a pair of jeans up and hand them to her. "Temporary insanity," I say. "That was the end. It's really over now, not that it ever really started."

'Blah, Blah, blah," she says without much energy.

"None-the-less," I say, "I don't want to argue about it and I don't want to hear your drivel. Just leave me alone, okay? Leave me alone." I turn away and say, "I'm going for a walk. See you around."

I take a couple steps towards the deck and Candy says, "Wait! Don't go. I'm . . . I'm . . . I didn't mean it."

"Yeah, right. Just leave me alone."

As I walk across the deck, I hear her open the screen door and call out to Sunny, "Sunny! Sunny!"

I keep walking down the stairs and onto the driveway, past her car and onto the road. Candy comes up behind me running. "She's in there watching TV. Her two favorite shows are on tonight. She'll be sitting there glued to the tube for over an hour at least, and she usually just falls asleep on the couch."

I don't say nothin'. I notice she's wearing her white running sneakers. Not that she ever goes running.

"Sticker," she says in an almost compassionate voice—a tone I've never heard from her before. We walk down the road towards the setting sun, which only a sliver of remains above the horizon. "I'm . . . I just don't get it. Why don't you just marry her and . . ."

"Enough!" I bark in a tone she's never heard from me before either. "I don't want to talk about it!" Shocked, she stops in her tracks. I keep walking without breaking stride.

A few seconds later, she catches up to me again. She babbles on for a minute or so about getting the TV back from the repair guy and how much it costs and how expensive everything is and I don't complain or respond in any way but just pretend she isn't even there.

Finally she stops talking and just keeps walking with me. We walk in silence around the bend, away from her house, in the opposite direction of the highway and towards the forest and swamp. The air is cooling and getting heavier and the sounds of the night are starting as the sun is now all the way down and the only light remaining is an iridescent glow. That Carolina blue on a layer of Georgia peach.

We swat at mosquitoes that light on us a couple times, but otherwise, there's nothing else going on. All I want to do is walk. I want to walk forever—to the end of the earth and then over its edge. I want to walk because it distracts me just enough and makes it easier to forget. Candy stays besides me, a half step back, just behind my right shoulder, pacing herself to keep up with me but never pulling even or overtaking me. She doesn't say a word.

And neither do I. So there's a quiet. A quiet that comes from a familiarity. A quiet that comes from being tired of complaining and no longer needing to patronize. And even without words, or really, because there are none, I feel her. I feel her there besides me and a little behind. With every step, I feel her more and more. And the heat of her body and the rhythm of our steps and the words that aren't spoken crumble a wall that's been around her to reveal something I've never felt from her before. A feeling of . . .

Compassion.

A compassion she can't put into words because no one showed her how. A compassion that's been forever there, locked inside the chambers of her heart because nobody ever used their own compassion to unlock it—to set it free. Oh, what a shame, what a pity, what a suppressed and buried jewel, I think.

As we keep walking, I keep ruminating on that seemingly sensible explanation, and after a while, I realize that it's something I just can't swallow. Yes, it is compassion I feel from her. And yes, she can't put it into words because no one showed her how. But . . .

She's not showing it now because of my own compassion. After all, I've been compassionate enough with her on countless occasions and if compassion was all that it took, it would have shown itself long ago. It isn't a 'you get what you give' sort of thing. No, it's not a reciprocation in kindness that's setting her compassion free, here, tonight, walking on this deserted road towards the swamp. It can't be. That's like expecting her to be fluent in a foreign language without ever learning it. Something else must be going on.

Finally, I get it. The something else is the same thing that set the combination on the lock on her heart in the first place. You see, in Candy's case, that something else is really nothing at all. That something else is: being left . . . alone.

The only way to anyone's heart is to give them what they're used to and what they think they deserve. In Candy's case, it's being abandoned. The baby girl can't think anything other than that the big people parents must be right, and right all the time, since they are the ones who spawned her and then met her initial needs. Who else could she pattern herself after? So if Candy's parents were right in abandoning her, she makes it feel right to be abandoned.

All those men who have done the normal things to get into a woman's heart like flowers and dates and holding hands, have eventually gotten frustrated because doing those things doesn't work on Candy. In fact, those things make her suspicious. But leaving her alone and even shunning her—*that* brings her closer. It's a paradox, I know: the closer you get to her, the more distant you are; and the farther away you stay, the more she loves you. And that's why I feel her compassion for the first time just now.

In another quarter mile, I feel that compassion in her change. It melts, or grows—I can't tell which, and maybe its both—into devotion. A devotion that's ragged and rough and raw and cold. A devotion that's as hard as a diamond and as resilient as hope.

As we walk into the fading light of the day, that devotion, as cold and raw as it might be, radiates out and lights my path in a way that makes me realize it no longer matters if it's dark. It's a light that's been hibernating, condensing, compounding inside of her, and is of such density now that it bursts into reality in a fear-melting brilliance. I can't help but let out a laugh—just a short and quiet chuckle. Candy hears me and laughs too, as if to agree that she didn't know she had it in her. But there it is. The cat's out of the bag, and there's no putting it back.

I turn my head and see her, her head hanging down, little expression on her face, as she peers down through the dim light to make sure of her steps. She notices I'm looking at her and she picks up her head and she smiles her Mona Lisa smile squared and I stop. I turn and face her.

The trees, with their Spanish moss hanging, block most of what little light remains, and I search through the darkness of the night to find the darkness of her eyes. She doesn't look away but keeps her eyes open and vulnerable. And as we look into each other's eyes, we each are able to feel something neither of us ever felt before. For the first time, we feel what it's like—to trust. To trust someone else.

At least I think that's what it is. But I never learned a foreign language either.

I have an overpowering urge to kiss her, and I can tell she wants to be kissed, so I bend down and put my lips to hers. Her lips—so soft and warm and tender and childish. And after the kiss, I linger a moment, suspended in time as our breaths mix. For several seconds, so much blood rushes through my veins with so much passion, I forget *that*. And I envision us being so swept away that we ease each other down to the ground and come together there on the pavement and make wild and passionate love.

Then I remember that's impossible. Then she pushes me away.

"Sticker," she says quietly as she pats me on the chest with both palms.

I don't say nothin'.

"Sticker," she whispers. "I think I might have left the stove on after making tea. We need to go back. I need to get back."

Well, I think. That was fun while it lasted.

"Yeah," I mutter. "Of course. Of course. Let's go."

Candy turns and starts back the way we came. I follow and catch up to her and walk alongside her. Within a couple paces, I take her hand and hold it as we walk.

"Oh, I hate it when I do that," she complains. "You'd think I'd pay more attention. I just hate it when I do that."

I try to think of something to say—something romantic or reassuring or even funny—but nothing comes. When our palms get sweaty I let go of her hand and we continue walking side-by-side, except occasionally Candy pulls out in front of me and I have to step on it to pull even again. Is she thinking about the stove or her house or another man? I know she's not thinking about me. And I wonder already if our being together is already over. But amongst my doubt and separation, I feel a strange familiarity and comfort. Not deja vú exactly, just something very familiar.

There's a sliver of moon now, and its faint light flashes like a strobe light through the trees and Spanish moss as we walk. The air is cooler and the smell of the distant swamp seems to grow stronger as we get farther away from it. A hoot-owl calls out in his undeniable cadence as a few crickets chirp weakly from both sides of the road. At times, in between the flashes of dim moonlight, the road is so dark and black that it seems like it disappears. As my feet drop down in front of me, it feels as if I'm about to fall off the edge of the earth.

It's hard to see Candy's features even though she's right besides me, and suddenly it feels like I'm not real, but she is. Eerie. Almost like a premonition.

Our pace is faster coming in, dictated by Candy, and we cover the distance in much less time than we did going out. The hurriedness and doubt cause my anxiety to grow with every step I take. Finally, when we're just at the bend before Candy's house would come into view, I can't take it any longer. I need some definition, some reassurance, some validation. So I jump in front of her and put my hands on her shoulders and stop her and turn her towards me. I look at her as she continues to look straight ahead and I say, "Candy, I want to . . ."

She glances at me in the briefest of moments—just long enough to keep her balance—and then looks forward again as I speak. Just as the words are leaving my lips, I see her crane her neck forward and squint, her eyes lighting on something through the trees.

"Oh my God!" she gasps under her breath.

Then she's off. Like a racehorse bolting out of the gate, she's gone from my hold and sprinting up the road towards her house. "Candy!" I call after her. "Come on now! Don't do this!" All I can think about is my own anxiety and apprehension. It never crosses my mind that she's running for any other reason but to leave me.

I turn to look towards her and the house. Just around the couple of trees that are still in the way, just barely visible through the branches and moss, there, barely illuminated from the faint light of the moon, I see a vehicle in her driveway. It's a truck. It's Tom's truck.

"Oh shit!" I mutter as I start to sprint. "Wait!" I yell. "Wait for me!" I don't want her to be alone with Tom. If only that was all there was to worry about.

Chapter Twelve

By the time I get to the driveway, Candy has already disappeared around the back of the house. I'll save some time and use the front door, I think, and I run straight to it over the front lawn. I yank open the screen door and turn the knob to the door. "Hell! The one time she locks it!"

I hear the back screen door slam. I break away from the door and consider diving through the dinning room window, but instead, sprint around the far corner of the house, around the side to the back, past the picnic table and the laundry basket full of clothes to the back door. Just as I grasp the handle of the screen door, I hear it: a blood-curdling shriek that could tear flesh off a bone. It's high-pitched, like a girl's, yet low, like a caged animal's, and it takes a moment for me to realize that it is, in fact, Candy's voice.

Two strides through the laundry room to the opening into the kitchen, and without looking, I practically dive into the kitchen until the kitchen table stops me. I look ahead, past the table and counter into the family room and I see Sunny laying on her back on the couch with her head turned too far sideways, almost backwards. Her shorts are off, exposing her underwear, and her shirt is yanked up to her armpits. One leg is draped up on the back of the couch and the other is hanging off the edge of the bottom cushion.

I see Tom, with his pants off but his underwear still on, crouching like a wrestler awaiting his foe. His face is contorted into a crazed and maniacal look and his eyes are glazed over and yet focused—even over-focused—on Candy, who's flying through the air with her arms outstretched and her fingers and nails clawing out in front of her like a tigress pouncing on her prey.

She lands on Tom, who tries to push her away, but she doesn't miss. The claws of one hand sink into his neck as the other one scrapes down the front of his face, over his eye, and down his cheek. Candy growls and Tom swears in pain. I quickly step sideways to get around the table, but slip on a loose rug on the linoleum floor. My feet fly out from under me and bang into the cabinet next to the stove as my arms fly out to break my fall. Then bam! My head bounces off the edge of a chair and I'm down on the floor.

Dazed, but not out, I hear the struggle continue as I push myself up with white specks of light dancing in front of my eyes. I make it up to my feet and steady myself on the table. I see a plastic sandwich bag laying there that has white powder spilling out of it and a glass half full of lemonade besides it.

I'm woozy and can hardly move. Candy has gotten away from Tom who's bleeding from his face and neck. She runs at him again, with her claws out, but not quite as high. As she pounces on him this time, he catches her and hurls her across the room like a sack of flour, down to the side, right at the television set. Candy's head hits the glass front of the TV and bounces off it as the tube shatters in every direction. Her head lands on the threadbare carpeting in front of the TV as pieces of glass sprinkle down on her. She's out.

Tom turns towards me. I brace myself on the table as the white specks still fly before me. He comes, step-by-step, slowly, realizing I'm already injured. Painful, frightening steps they are to me. Proud, blood-thirsty steps they are for him.

"This is gonna be fun," he sneers. "It's payback time you son of a bitch."

As he gets to the kitchen, he grabs a knife out of the knife holder on the wall besides the sink—an eight-inch meat-carving knife that flashes silver daggers under the fluorescent light above the sink. He holds it in his right fist, and raises it up above his head as he takes the final three steps towards me.

The specks are gone now. My head hurts but there's no more dizziness, no more wobbling. I think to lunge at him, but instead, don't move. Better to let him think I'll be easy.

He raises the knife higher, back behind his head, as he takes the final step. My hands are still on the table with my head hanging down and I can just barely see the knife in the fringe of my vision as my eyes stare straight ahead into the family room where Sunny and Candy lay.

Then everything slows down. The time it takes for the knife to fall down on me feels as long as the whole day before it. A handful of thoughts go through my mind—a clear progression of the moves I'll make to thwart the attack. Moves I've practiced successfully so many times before, but only practiced. And I realize that this time, it's for real.

This time, it's for my life. I wonder if this time, I'll never do good enough again.

At the same time, another part of my mind is thinking about Candy and Sunny laying there in the family room in front of me. What they are and the life they've had. How petty so much of it seems, and yet how meaningful it truly is, and how it's the only way it could ever have been.

Tom's arm comes down. The knife slices through the air. I fling my right arm up above my head so my wrist bangs into his as he pulls down. I push his fist with the knife to the side, and my wrist slides along his. I take a quick step to my left.

The knife whooshes past my ear and down along the side of my body, missing me by half a foot. But my head starts spinning again. As I sidestep and push Tom's arm aside, I should have then turned my wrist over his, grabbed his wrist and yanked his arm around his back to pin it there. What I actually did, was far from that.

Instead of grabbing his wrist, my hand slips and grabs nothing but air. Instead of pinning his hand behind his back, he's free to raise the knife again. The only thing I can do is push him with both hands as I duck behind him. I send him banging into the cabinets next to the refrigerator.

I'm still light headed, but I know that that can't stop me. I need time to regroup. I stumble backwards into the family room as Tom picks himself off the floor, still with knife in hand. I think of running outside to his truck and getting his rifle, but then I'd be leaving Candy and Sunny alone with him. Instead, I steady myself, get into my crouch, and wait for the next advance.

Sunny is laying on the couch, still. Candy is behind me, sprawled face down on the floor in front of the shattered TV. Tom comes around the table. He sees me wobble as my hand moves out for balance. He grins, knowing this time it'll be easier. He comes at me faster and holds the knife in front of him pointing straight at me, as if to run me through with a bayonet. Again, everything slows down. Again, my hands and body react out of instinct. Again, I almost succeed.

He lunges straight at my guts. My right hand goes up and then down as my left hand goes down and then up, and they meet in the middle on his wrist with a thud. My hand speed isn't fast enough though, and instead of knocking the knife out of his hand, I just manage to deflect it to my right, away from my guts and towards my hip. The blade slices through the fabric of my shorts and lances through the flesh over my hipbone. I hardly feel a thing—it's like a fly had landed on me.

Now, Tom's face is right next to mine, and I smell the stale liquor and smoke and see the gouges Candy gave him and the blood flowing freely out of them. I push him again, but this only serves to turn him around to face me more squarely. I back up a step as he raises the knife over his head again, this time, with both hands on the handle, and quickly and forcefully, he plunges it down.

Down towards my face it comes. I back up another step, not fully in balance, not fully ready for the thrust. But my arms don't fail me and they fly up as they should in a V, my wrists pressed together, and catch his arms coming down. I fall backwards, almost to the couch where Sunny lays, and crumble onto my knees. He keeps thrusting down, straight down at my face, right at my eyes. I push my wrists against his as hard as I can.

I'm on my knees, being bent backwards, with my feet under my butt and my body angled back over them and my arms above me pushing hard against his wrists, the knife just six inches away from my forehead. He keeps pushing and pushing it down at me. It feels like my back is going to snap.

We hang like that for several moments barely moving—the unstoppable force against the immovable object. But his weight and strength become too much, and the knife begins to slowly, but surely, get closer to my eyes. Fraction by fraction it comes down towards me. My arms are shaking, my breathing has stopped, my heart is thumping uncontrollably fast.

Three inches to go. Fractions closer it comes . . . two inches.

He's getting stronger and his leverage is improving. I'm getting weaker and bending horizontally with my back almost to the floor. In a few more seconds, the knife blade will puncture my eye.

And then I hear her. I hear Candy let out a slow, painful, and delirious moan. I begin to pant, my arms shaking violently to stop the knife. Out of the corner of my eye, I see Candy move. And it all flashes before me in a surreal distinctness what would happen if I weaken just an inch more: The blade plunging into my eye and Tom twisting it and pulling it out and plunging it into the other; him stabbing me in my chest over and over and over, even after I'm dead; Candy moaning again and Tom rolling her over and slitting her throat and then turning back to Sunny and finishing what he started; then slitting her throat too and lighting the house on fire and watching it burn as he cleans himself in the swimming pool.

It's like I'm the one to determine if that possibility of a future will actually occur. It's all up to me. Right here, right now, with no possibility of a second chance, and without stopping time.

I'm looking at Tom's face above me as we struggle with the knife and I see the fresh scar across the left side of his forehead, formed from getting thrown into the garage door yesterday. And for some strange reason, it looks familiar. Not familiar from yesterday, but familiar from last night.

Then I see a replay of part of the dream I had last night when that smelly, dirty, sick, and degenerate man finally raised his head to look out the window of the horse stall with the girl laying still on the ground. Now, as I look at Tom, I realize that I'm looking at the same exact face! And although I've looked at it for a lifetime, now is the first time I've really, truly seen it. It's just a different time, a different place, a different era. But the same person, the same being, the same spirit!

I keep the tip of the knife an inch away from my eye, but I sink another inch closer to the floor. Out of the corner of my eye, I see Sunny's foot hanging off the edge of the couch with a thin white sock on it. As I sink another fraction, her foot slips from the couch and brushes my cheek.

Instantly, another part of that same dream flashes through my inner vision: It's the same foot that was laying on the hay-littered floor of the barn! The same shape, the same attitude, the same sock! Their feet are actually one and the same—the young girl who was raped in the barn, and Sunny who's passed out on the couch! They've returned. It's all so similar. But now, I'm right in the middle of it and this ain't no damn dream!

Then it rips through my mind in the clearest, most poignant realization I could ever have, just who I'm really fighting for. I'm no longer fighting for me, you see. No longer fighting to get past the abuse and neglect I was born into and suffered through which caused me turn upon myself like a twisted up coil of flypaper. I no longer matter and never really have, you see, except to be here . . .

For them.

For if I'm to fail and die here, on this threadbare old carpet Candy has long dreamed of replacing, in this run down old double-wide that's the epitome of commonness, that something very uncommon would not be realized. And even though the events I'm revisiting in my dreams are all in the past and cannot be changed, changing this outcome from the one in that barn so long ago would be a retribution of sorts, a validation that the spirit of that little girl has risen appropriately to Sunny. And although that soul wasn't allowed to flower into true womanhood back then, it could be now. But the only way I'm going to save Sunny, and Candy too, from the certain carnage from this sick and psychotic spirit embodied as Tom, is to save myself first.

A bolt of electricity explodes from my heart and surges through every particle that is me. A wellspring of clarity and purpose gather instantly in my veins like blue sky emerging after a thunderstorm. "Not again, you bastard," I whisper through clenched teeth. "The buck . . . stops . . . here."

I feel my strength gather without effort or thought. My breathing returns in a smooth, strong rhythm. My heart beats full with pride and purpose. My arms stop shaking and become determined and sure. They push up harder, and harder, and harder still.

"The fuck . . . stops . . . here," I say louder in a clear, determined voice. The knife stops its slow descent. It hangs there for a moment . . . still . . . frozen. And then it reverses.

Upwards, back away from me, the knife and Tom with it go back up the same way they came down—slowly, inch by inch. As drops of Tom's blood drip on my neck and chest, his expression slowly morphs from a fiendish, maniacal grin, into a queer and twisted realization that grows more pronounce with every inch he looses.

I hear Candy moan again as I finally topple him over. Tom lets go of the knife with one hand to break his fall and twists away from me as he goes down. The hand with the knife gets turned back on him as I continue to push, and he falls to the floor right onto the knife. Both his hand and mine are still on the handle as the knifepoint breaks his skin and plunges deep into his abdomen.

A geyser of blood spurts right into my eyes. I blink hard to look through the blood and see Tom fall over onto his back as a gurgle-filled moan escapes his quivering lips. His body twitches several times and I feel his grip on the knife handle slacken—the blade still stuck in his gut and blood gushing out all around it.

His eyes are open in anguished disbelief and the scratches on his face and neck are still oozing blood. I reach over and take the knife out of his stomach and drop it on the floor. Instinctively, I try to cover the gash to stop the bleeding. But the blood keeps coming. Tom tries to talk, but the best he can do is another muffled gurgle mixed with blood.

I cover the hole in his side with both hands, trying to gather the skin together to close it. But it slips under my open palms and kneading fingers as the blood just keeps coming.

"Uuuggghhhh," he finally croaks. "I . . . I . . ."

I raise my head and look at him, his face streaked with blood and its gashes open and oozing. Blood is flowing like a river out of his guts, and it's obvious that nothing I could do would stop it.

Our eyes meet. A final look . . .

Into my cousin. The kid I grew up with. We played ball, skipped school, went fishing. We talked about getting out, laughed at the same jokes, thought the same girls were pretty. The cousin who was my best friend and the brother I never had. So similar in upbringing and appearance. So similar in trying to make sense out of a life that was far from ideal. But then, a fork in the road. It showed itself in the spring of our junior year. I went west, he went east, and we both tried to ignore we were headed in different directions. But the gulf between us widened, even though for several years you could hardly tell. And he did all right for a while—working hard with a wife and kid and living a normal American life: Barbeques with friends on the weekend, a trip to Disneyland with the family, church on Sunday to appease the wife. Then his first divorce. Then his marriage to Candy and helping her raise Sunny—for a while, at least. But when Candy found those drugs and kicked him out, something inside him snapped. He started hanging out after closing time with more of the wrong people and got further into drugs and got foolish and greedy and even more messed up and started selling them to cover his addiction. And then that night when I tailed him to Charleston and spied on him as his drug deal went bad. He was standing on the dock, bare to the world, trying to explain why he didn't have the money to Louie the Letch who was pointing a gun at him. It was a miracle I got to him in time—leaping out from behind a stack of pallets, sprinting the ten yards to where he stood and tackling him as the first shot was fired. Somehow we scampered over the railing and dove into the water below as bullets screamed over our heads. Yes, I saved his life back there on that chilly spring night. But now, that's not gonna happen. Now it's come down to this: Dying on the floor in his own house in a puddle of his own blood—getting stabbed to death by his cousin, the son of a bitch.

If you're expecting me to pick up his head and hold it in my hands and have some heartfelt moment with my dying cousin where he says he's sorry for his sins and I realize he's still human after all and just a victim of society—you know, something politically correct that you'd see in the movies or somethin'—you can forget it. Tom's beyond hope and about to die and if there was anything else I could do to prevent or even ease his death now, I wouldn't do it. You see, we're not talking about some Ubermenche here. I'm talking about some guy who had the same chances I did. But the difference is, he didn't fight. He didn't fight like hell. He didn't fight like hell to keep from getting sucked in. Instead, he lived to excess and lost balance. And instead of climbing back up on this balance beam called life and trying again, and again, and again if necessary, he just gave up and wallowed. It was comfortable for him down there. Zarathustra he ain't. Untermenche—subhuman—he became.

Some would say the drugs and alcohol did it, but that's just an excuse. He decided to get drunk and he decided to get high. His habits and addictions were just a reflection of what he was—what he had chosen to become. Habits don't make the man, the man makes his habits.

I stand up and wipe my hands briefly on my shorts and gather myself for a moment. I force myself to focus on the present moment instead of getting emotional about what just happened. "Focus," I mutter. "Focus." I remember my wound and look at it and realize it can wait, and then turn to Sunny laying on the couch. Tom gurgles again and lets out a feeble, pathetic, dying moan.

"I . . ." he says as he pushes his hands out. "I . . . wan . . ."

I glance his way as I put my fingers on Sunny's neck to feel for her pulse. "You're dying, Tom," I say. "You're dead already."

"I . . . wan . . ." he tries again.

"Whatever you say," I mumble as I keep searching Sunny's neck, unable to find the pulse, leaving smears of blood on her skin. Where is it? Where's the pulse? Come on! Where's the pulse?

I push my fingers into her neck harder and my face flushes as I realize that maybe, just maybe, the pulse isn't there! "Come on!" I plead. "Where are you?"

I feel around, all across her neck. Nothing. I notice her eyelids are closed only half-way, with only the whites of her eyes showing. "Just like . . ."

"Shut up!" I mumble. No time to wonder about that shit. Where's the pulse?

"Come on!" I plead again. "Come on, damn you! *Where are you?*"

Then Tom moans again, "I . . . wan . . . my . . . mama . . ." he finally croaks.

"Fuck you!" I mumble. I feel like taking the knife and cutting him to shreds. "Where you're going, Tom," I say coldly, "even she can't help you."

Tom shutters one last time and finally stops gurgling. His outstretched arms fall and bounce off his chest and onto the floor, his eyes still searching for a comforting bosom.

I gently lift Sunny off the couch and lay her on her back on the floor and start pressing on her chest with the heel of my hand with the other hand on it pushing too. Down-up, down-up, down-up . . .

"Come on, little one," I plead. "Come on!"

Down-up, down-up, down-up . . .

"It's not time for you to go."

Down-up, down-up, down-up . . .

"You can't go now, baby-girl. That would mean . . ."

Down-up, down-up, down-up . . .

"That would mean . . . if you die, Sunny, that would mean . . . darkness lives. If we lose you, little one, it means . . ."

Down-up, down-up, down-up . . .

". . . Aw hell, Sunny. I don't care what it means. It just don't matter. You can't go now, because . . . because . . ."

Down-up, down-up, down-up . . .

". . . *I need you.*"

I feel a movement, a flutter in the air around my head. Just for an instant, just a couple puffs right across my face.

"No! NO! Not yet! NOT YET!"

I tilt her head back, pinch her nose and open her mouth. I blow until her chest moves up and is full of air. Release. Exhale. Blow again. Still nothing.

Back to her chest. Down-up, down-up, down-up . . .

"Damn it! Damn it girl, wake up! Mother of God, wake up!"

I think to slap her across the face to shock her, but wait! Something better. I run to the refrigerator and open the door. I grab the pitcher of cold water Candy keeps and a couple trays of ice cubes from the freezer. I crack the cubes into the pitcher and go back to Sunny. I pump her chest again—down-up, down-up, down-up . . .

Two more breaths into her little mouth. Then I take the ice-cold water and splash it on her chest and face. I grab a couple ice cubes and rub them all over her neck and chest, and then push them hard into her skin right over her heart—down-up, down-up, down-up . . .

Another splash of ice water . . . Another icy rub down . . . Down-up, down-up, down-up . . . two more breaths . . .

I feel for her pulse again. Still nothing.

She's gone, shatters into my mind. No!

"Now, little one, come back. It's safe to come back. It's safe to be home. I won't let them hurt you again. Come home, Sunny! Come home *now!*"

I splash her again with cold water and ice.

Down-up, down-up, down-up . . .

Still nothing.

I watch as my hands leave her heart and slide down to her tummy. Without knowing why, they start rubbing it in a circle, and I start praying: "That's a good little girl, Sunny. Thank you, Sunny, that's a good little girl. It wasn't your fault. Tom beating your mother and your pa leaving you, it wasn't your fault. You're just a kid, for Christ's sake. It wasn't your fault!"

Circles on her tummy; mumbling into her heart; asking and praying and demanding and thanking all at the same time.

"Thank you, that's a good little girl . . . Thank you, that's a good little girl . . . Thank you, Sunny . . . come home *now!*"

Still no pulse.

I fall back on my heels, exhausted. It's too long, I think. It's too late now. Too late. What will I do now? What will I do . . . *without her?*

I see her little feet with those thin white socks still on. Not yet, damn it. I can't give up yet. I grab the pitcher and dump the rest of the water and ice on her chest. I lean back over her, put my hands on her chest again, and push.

Down-up, down-up, down-up . . .

Two more breaths into her little mouth. "Thank you Sunny. Thank you . . ."

Then . . . a twitch. Her shoulders twitch and her arms wiggle just a little, and I look at her face and her eyelids flutter open for just a second and then close completely, the whites no longer visible. I feel her neck and there it is! Bluh-thump. Bluh-thump. Bluh-thump.

It's weak, but it's there. Oh God. Oh God. Thank you God.

Candy moans again and rolls onto her side and opens her eyes. I pick Sunny up under her shoulders and knees, glance one time at Candy, and head for the back door. Damn the rubber-legs.

I kick open the screen door and burst into the cool night air. My head's still throbbing, but all traces of dizziness are gone, and I know I'll be okay as I carry Sunny across the deck, down the stairs and to Candy's car. I lay her on her back across the back seat and feel her neck again. Bluh-thump. Bluh-thump. Bluh-thump. I turn and head back into the house.

By the time I get into the kitchen again, Candy has risen to her knees, with her head hanging low and right over Tom's dead body. I rush to her side and pull Tom's body away, and then touch her arm and shoulder softly. She looks at the couch and sees Sunny isn't there, and it's easy to see she remembers what's happened. She tries to speak as she feels her head, but I save her the trouble.

"She's in the car. I put her in the car. I'm taking her to the hospital. Here," I pull her gently. "Sit on the couch." She rises slowly to her feet with my help.

"No. No couch," she mumbles.

I look in her eyes and inspect her skull. She's not bleeding but has a lump where she hit the TV.

"Let's go," she says. I know not to argue.

We start for the door, stepping around Tom's body and walking tentatively but as fast as we can. I see a towel near the kitchen sink, grab it, and escort Candy to the back door.

"Wait a second," I say, and go back into the kitchen and take an empty plastic milk carton from under the sink and half fill it with water. I grab another towel and more ice from the freezer. I notice the plastic bag with the drugs on the table, so I grab it and put it in my pocket. I grab Candy's purse too that's sittin' on the counter.

We get outside and walk to the car, she, leaning against me and holding onto my arm to steady herself. I open the passenger door for Candy to climb into the front seat, but she ignores it and opens the back door and climbs in with Sunny. She picks Sunny's head and shoulders up and slides under them, letting Sunny's head come to rest on her lap. I get in behind the wheel and give Candy the plastic jug and towels and ice. She starts wiping Sunny with the towel and strokes her forehead as I find the keys already in the ignition where she normally leaves them. I start the car and back up just a couple feet, and then bam! We hit Tom's truck, crashing into the crunched up front bumper.

"Shit," I mutter, finally looking back behind me. Candy's too preoccupied to comment. I put the car in drive and swing it off the driveway and across the yard, through the roadside swale and onto the road. In another few seconds, we're doing 70.

It's Friday night, but there's not another car in sight. When we get to the highway, I have to slow to almost a stop to make the turn onto the smooth pavement, and then once I'm on it, I put the pedal to the floor.

It feels like I'm racing again. And the thought comes to me that now I'm racing not so much to win, but to just not lose. And that not losing now would be the best win I could ever have.

"Careful," Candy says.

"Right," I reply.

Part Two

None of that matters.
I'm not going to run.
I'm not.
And you know why?
I'll tell you . . .

Chapter Thirteen

We get to the hospital in Beaufort in well under an hour. Didn't see a cop once. We burst into the emergency room, me carrying Sunny. I lay Sunny on a bed and the nurses get busy, calling the doctor, getting equipment, checking her blood pressure and temperature and using a pen flashlight to check her pupils. Nurses. Angels of mercy. Gotta love 'em.

I give the bag of drugs to one of the nurses, feeling totally helpless. The doctor wants us to go to another room while he tends to Sunny, but Candy won't have that, so we sit on the bed next to her's as they stick a tube down her throat and pump her stomach.

Then they put an IV into her little arm and check her blood pressure again. They wipe her down with a warm, moist towel and make sure she's comfortable. Then they tell us that's all they can do for now and we have to wait and see. The doctor says Sunny would probably make it. We didn't like the sound of probably. Even if she does, he said, she might end up with some brain or liver damage or she might just stay in a coma for a while. It all depends on what the drug was and what it was cut with, and we won't know that until they get the lab results back, which won't be until tomorrow.

A nurse cleans Candy up and the doctor checks out the bruises on her head and gives her a clean bill of health except to take it easy for a couple weeks. They clean me up too and put seven or eight stitches in my hip to secure the wound, and tell me I'll be okay too.

All the while I'm not saying much about what happened—just told them we were in a fight after we saw Sunny was drugged. Neither Candy or I feel much like talking about it, and we're both pretty darn tired at this point. The doctor says he wants to call the local police, but I tell him I'll do it myself. After a while, another doctor comes into the room, and he's holding a syringe with a long needle on it.

"What's that?" I ask as he goes to the side of the bed, holds the syringe up, and flicks it with his finger. A drop of yellow pus-looking liquid comes out of the needle.

"I'm doctor Nelson, Chief-of-Staff here," he says all haughty-like, like I'm some moron or something. "You're lucky I'm on duty tonight—usually not here at this hour. This shot is a vaccine that will keep her from coming down with an infection while she's recovering."

Suddenly I get this feeling—a feeling that something just ain't right. I don't know if it's the cockiness of the doctor or having Sunny get stuck with a needle and injected with puss, or what. But I just want to call a time out while I figure out what's really going on. "Now doc," I say as I take a step towards him. As I do, the room door opens. "I don't . . ."

I glance back at the door and see Candy coming through it, returning from the bathroom. She sees the doctor holding the syringe and swabbing Sunny's arm with an alcohol swab. Her eyes open wide, and the next thing I know, she bolts across the room and runs smack-dab into the doctor with both hands, hitting him in the chest just as he's about to stick the needle into Sunny's arm. She pushes him hard and he crashes into the wall behind the bed. He falls halfway to the floor, throwing out his hand to stop his fall, and the syringe flies out of his hand and the needle sticks right into the other doctor's leg! It sticks there, embedded in his calf muscle.

The doctor who just got stuck lets out a yelp and frantically grabs the syringe and yanks the needle out of his leg. He doesn't say a word, but limps to the door while holding his leg and stumbles out of the room. Dr. Nelson, the almighty Chief-of-Staff ass hole, tries to pick himself up off the floor, but slips on the alcohol swab and falls back down, crashing again against the wall.

Candy's hovering over him, with her finger raised, pointing right at his face. "What the hell you doin' tryin' to shoot-up my child? How dare you!"

The doctor mumbles as he slips down further against the wall, "It's just standard procedure, ma'am. Just a vaccine. It'll keep her from catching pneumonia while she's recovering."

"Pneumonia my ass," Candy scoffs. "Don't you *dare* touch my child without my permission! You hear me?"

The doctor cowers from Candy as his eyes widen all remorseful-like, like he had just been scolded by his third grade teacher or somethin'. I guess when someone has the balls (or in Candy's case, the mitt, as Kaitlin would say) to lay down the law with what's right, Mr. High and Mighty ain't so high and mighty anymore. And that Candy, I've never felt prouder. She may not have gone to college, but boy, she sure has gumption. Or maybe, I think, she's got that gumption because she never got so "educated."

Dr. Nelson doesn't say another word. Finally, he scrapes himself up off the floor, gathers himself by tugging his lab coat down to pull out the wrinkles, and scurries out the door.

"Jerk," Candy says. "Nobody's gonna shoot *my* child up with pus."

I don't say nothin'.

We go over to the chairs beside the bed and sit down and look at Sunny. "I didn't feel right about it either," I say, "but you beat me to it."

"What an ass," Candy says. "Where does he get off doing something to my daughter without my permission?"

"I don't know. Sometimes these doctors think they know everything."

"You got that right," she says as she gets up and picks the alcohol swab off the floor and throws it in the waste basket. "All I know is that my sister's son got retarded after one of those shots."

"Little Eli? I thought he was born like that."

"Hell no. He was fine until he was two years old. Then my sister took him in for his regular 'Baby Bright' check-up and they gave him his shots. A couple days later, he was screaming and hollering and crying like you can't imagine. Nancy called me to come help her, she was freaking out so bad. He was drooling all over himself and just staring out into space like he was totally stoned or something."

"Really? So you think it was the shots?"

"What else could it be? Nothing else changed. The kid was happy and smiled all the time before them. Was no trouble at all. He looked into your eyes when you looked at him and smiled and cooed like a baby should. Never sick a day in his life and used to sleep through the night like a champ. But since those shots, well, Nancy has had a terrible time. You know. You've seen her."

"Yeah," I say looking down to the floor. "That's tough."

"All the doctors said later was that Eli has some . . . what'd they call it . . . genet . . . ic pre . . . predisposition, I think they said. They said it wasn't the shots that did it, but they just speeded up something that was gonna happen anyway."

"Sounds fishy to me."

"Of course it is. Damn idiots. What do you expect when you inject crap into a little baby? It just doesn't make sense. This woman Karen in my office had something happen to her two-year-old girl after she got her shots, too. The girl got sick as a dog the very same day and now Karen says she's just not the same anymore."

"Really?"

"Yeah. Karen's husband started reading medical books and stuff and found this guy who works for some government agency in Atlanta. He said he finally got the guy to tell him what's actually in those shots since they try and keep it secret. Says there's aluminum, mercury, formaldehyde, I think it was, and they're grown on aborted baby tissues."

"You're kidding."

"That's what she said. She swears it's true. Now they're thinking of suing the doctor or something."

"Hard to believe."

"I don't know nothin' about aluminum and mercury, but aborted baby tissue?"

"That's awful."

"You can say that again. So I don't care what they say those shots are *supposed* to do. I've seen with my own eyes what those shots actually *do*. Nobody in my family was ever retarded. Not even close. We may not be a bunch of geniuses, but we sure as hell ain't retarded."

I don't say nothin'.

"Eli's six, almost seven now, and he can hardly say two words."

"Man."

"So no doctor's gonna stick my kid. Just ain't gonna happen."

Finally, when everything's settled down and Candy is sitting next to Sunny holding her hand and stroking her hair. I go to the nurse's desk and use their phone to call the police in our town. There's one deputy sheriff on duty, and I can tell I woke him up. I tell him there's been an incident at Candy's house and I'd rather discuss it in person. So we agree to meet in Candy's driveway in an hour. He presses me for details, but I just hang up.

There's nothing left for me to do as we wait for the morning and lab results. All that can be done at this point is make sure Sunny's hydrated and hope for the best. I squeeze Candy's shoulder and kiss her on the forehead and take off.

One of the things about being an SOB is that you make some enemies. I was about to find out that I had a couple on the sheriff's force. It's just after eleven o'clock as I drive up to Candy's house. The cops are already there, a sheriff's car in the driveway. I pull onto the grass and notice the front door is open. What the hell? Did they just barge on in? Wouldn't they need a warrant for that? Fuming, I walk through the threshold, and the moment I do, the two cops put down their coffee and donuts, jump off the couch, jump on me, and slam me to the floor. "What the f . . ."

One of them, name is Jackson, I know never liked me 'cuz of my being friendly with Kaitlin. He used to date her and even though I was never around or never even as much as saw Kaitlin while they were together, he heard she loved me. I reckon he could tell she always would, so he didn't have fond feelings for me.

The other cop's name is Andy Y. Why they call him Andy Y, I don't know since his last name is Purvis. Andy Y doesn't like me because I don't know why. Never even talked to the guy. But the few times he and me crossed paths, he was sure to be a prick. Maybe he just didn't like the way I looked, like those thugs in the diner. But whatever the reason, it's obvious that he's gonna take every opportunity to make my life hell.

They grab my hands and handcuff me and read me my rights as I'm laying there with my face in the carpet. I don't say nothin'.

Andy Y finally says, "Sam Barlow, you're charged with the murder of Tommy Simpson and with the possession and trafficking of illegal drugs."

Now I know some folks don't take kindly to me, but this is ridiculous. Of course, if I ever expected anything like this, I never would have called the police, at least not before I got an attorney or something. I realized later that I was the proverbial "babe in the woods." But now I felt like a cat backed into a corner. A pretty dumb cat at that.

Jackson goes into the kitchen and returns with the bloody knife in a plastic bag and a plastic sandwich bag half-full of white powder—identical to the one Tom had. He has latex gloves on, and before I can clench my hands into fists, he swings the baggie around my back and presses it against my fingers.

"That's a good boy, Sticker," he smiles sarcastically. "Now we have nothin' to worry about."

He and Andy Y laugh and push me to the door. As they push me towards the car, an ambulance pulls into the driveway and swings around onto the grass, its red and white lights whirling. "It's all yours," Jackson tells the driver. "The body's in the family room. You can't miss it." The driver looks at him with raised eyebrows.

"It's pretty gory in there," Jackson continues. "Lots of blood, so prepare yourself. But we have all the evidence and photos we need, so just take the body to the morgue. We'll be notifying the next of kin in the morning."

The driver and the other EMT, a woman, get out of the ambulance and walk to the back of the ambulance and start taking the gurney out. "What the hell happened?" the driver asks.

"This son of a bitch killed a good man, is what happened," Andy Y replies. "Caught him red handed trying to hide the drugs he had on him too. It's the most gruesome thing to happen in this county in a long, long time. Maybe ever."

"Sticker," the woman says. "Is that Sticker?"

I don't say nothin'. I don't recognize her, but apparently, my reputation precedes me.

"Yeah, that's him," Jackson says. "You know him?"

"Nah," she replies. "One of my girlfriends pointed him out to me once. Said he was kinda weird and lived in a trailer."

"Yeah, he did," Jackson snickers. "But not anymore. His new address is gonna be the State Pen, and that'll be a step up for him!"

They tighten their grip on my arms and Jackson shakes me. When the EMTs turn away to go into the house, Andy Y raps me on my lower back with his billy club. "Say hello to the electric chair, Sticker," he says and pushes me into the side of the cop car.

Andy Y pulls me away by the hair and yanks the door open and shoves me in. I have to duck my head down fast to keep it from banging into the top of the doorframe. Jackson and Andy Y get in, look at each other, laugh, and give each other a high-five slap of the hands. Jackson swings the car onto the road, and turns his head to talk to me through the wire mesh that separates the front and back seats.

"You've got perfect timing, Sticker. You just made our job a whole lot easier!" He looks at Andy Y and says, "What do you think JM's gonna think?" They both laugh.

"Dispatch," Andy Y finally says all serious and professional-like into the radio transmitter. "This is car two-o-two. We're en route back to you with . . ."

My mind shuts down as my ears tune him out. I sink into the seat, my hands and the handcuffs digging into my back. The car smells like coffee, cigarettes, and donuts. By the time they get me to jail, I had nodded off, and they have to wake me. A few slaps on the face will do that. They push me into the jail cell, take off the handcuffs, and turn out the lights. I grope around and feel the bunk, collapse on it, and pass out.

I wake up to see a plaster ceiling with bars coming down out of it. I turn my head and see that the bars go down into the floor and wrap around me. There's another cell next to mine and there's a guy on his back on the bunk reading a paperback book. There's a small toilet under a window that's streaming in light so I get up and piss. I turn the knob on the little sink faucet and suck in some water up out of the palm of my hand and splash some onto my face.

Jail. What the hell?

There's only two cells in the room, with a door with its top half in glass that opens to the office. I can barely see the room outside and the framed picture of the President Ronald Reagan on the far wall. A bare-bones, one-horse town jail.

I see someone walk by the door. Not a cop, but someone in brown clothes. The guy in the next cell glances my way but says nothing and keeps reading his book. He looks downright comfortable—like he's relaxing in a hammock under a tree on a lazy summer's afternoon.

Oh man . . . what the hell is happening? What day is it? Friday? No, Saturday. Yeah, Saturday. Retrace your steps. How did I get here? I replay some of yesterday. What do I need to do next? That's a good one. I pace the cell . . . one, two, three strides. About face. One, two, three. About face.

Candy and Sunny—in the hospital still? Do they know I'm in jail? Probably not. Should I call them? Don't know. I run through all the possible scenarios in my head. They're trying to frame me, that's obvious. They had more drugs, too, and are probably in on it with Tom. One, two, three. About face.

One less partner to cut in on the profits, so they weren't too sad to see him go. In fact, they were downright giddy their friend is dead. Drug money explains Tom's new garage and truck. Then it was almost like I heard a voice, "Don't put anything past them. They'll do anything for the money. Anything." One, two, three. About face.

Candy and Sunny were the only ones there when I killed Tom, and even though Candy didn't see me kill him, she could at least come close to showing that I did it out of self-defense. The only witness. "They would do anything," reverberates in my head. Would they kill her too? And Sunny? A chill goes through my body. One, two, three. About face.

Gotta call her. Get the guard. I want to use my phone call. Wait! If I call, they might trace the call or check the number or listen in on the conversation. Can't call her. Not yet. Hope she's still at the hospital. Gotta get out of here to get them, protect them, save them. Gotta get out.

The cell room door opens. Jackson and Andy Y come in and open my cell with the large metal jailhouse looking key. "Okay, slime," Andy Y says. "Turn around." He cuffs my hands again and grabs my arm and pulls me out of the cell. Jackson leads the way out and into the office and then into another room about the size of a walk-in closet. Andy Y shoves me into a hard wooden chair behind a table. Cut into the opposite wall is a large mirror.

"Okay, Stick," Jackson says. "Time to confess your sins. Why'd you kill Tommy?"

Andy Y sits in another chair and turns on a tape recorder. They look so official in their fancy cop uniforms, walkie-talkies, and pistols hanging from their belts. I bet they feel so important. I don't say nothin'.

Jackson asks me again and again and again, getting more hostile and belligerent each time. I don't say nothin'. I don't ask for an attorney or my phone call or a drink of water or nothin'. I look at the mirror and wonder who else is watching.

After a good five minutes of haranguing by Jackson, Andy Y pipes in, "Now Sticker, you're not making this any easier on yourself. Come on and do yourself a favor and tell us why you killed him. We'll make sure you get credit for cooperating with us. That always helps when the judge sentences you. Come on now. Maybe you won't get the death sentence. Maybe you'll just get life."

His voice is calm and compassionate. The good cop-bad cop routine? You've got to be kidding. I don't say nothin'.

Then Jackson says, "And Candy and her little girl—what's her name? Sunny, right?" My eyes flare.

"Did you kill them too? Take them out to cover your tracks? Not taking any chances now, are you? But it's smart. Very smart. I like your style, Sticker. But your mistake was coming back trying to pretend you're innocent. You just should have kept going."

He takes a couple steps towards the mirror, and then turns back towards me, "So where'd you take 'em? Candy's blood was on the carpet. We know you did it. Where are they? Where the hell are they?"

I form a wad in my mouth and lean back and spit at him. It lands on the front of his uniform, right near his badge. He raises his hand and slaps me across the face. "Bastard," I mutter. "You fucking bastard."

"You know," Andy Y says and then lights a cigarette, "that Candy—she ain't the little angel you think she is."

He walks around behind me. "Why do you think she put up with that dumb-ass cousin of yours? I'll tell you why—she was helpin' him make a fortune selling drugs."

I stare straight ahead at the mirror. He comes back around and stands in front of me and takes a long drag and blows smoke in my face. I hold my breath and close my eyes.

"Yeah," Jackson says joining in Andy Y's game. "She was in on it too. We were just about ready to bust the both of 'em and then you had to go kill Tommy on us."

I don't say nothin'.

"So here's what we can do," Andy Y says all consoling and helpful sounding. "You tell us where she is, and we'll give you a break. We'll call what you did to Tommy self-defense. We can get the judge to agree to that, since there was no one there to refute it. You get to go free, but Candy pays for her sins."

I have no intention of agreeing, but I pretend to look interested. "And what about Sunny?" I mumble.

"The little girl?" Andy Y asks. "Well, she'll have to go live with her next of kin. Don't know who that is, but I'm sure there's somebody."

My mind starts racing. Candy, dealing drugs with Tom? Come on. I know she hated being poor, but deal drugs? With Tom? Can these guys be trusted? Can *Candy* be trusted? Are they trying to bait me into something? Are they so hot to get Candy that they'd really let me go? If she was really in on it with Tom, then maybe they want her out of the way too. Maybe she'd end up having an "accident" so they wouldn't have to deal with her at all. And what about Sunny? If they get rid of Candy, would they do the same with Sunny?

My silence must have given them hope, because Andy Y says, "I hear Candy treats you like shit anyway. She's just a bitch and you know it. The world won't be any worse off with her locked behind bars. It's where she belongs anyway."

I feel blood rush to my face.

"So you see, Sticker, you've got nothing to lose. You just tell us where Candy is, and you're a free man."

"And what about Sunny?" I ask again.

"Tell you what," Jackson says. "You're so damn concerned about that little whippersnapper, here's what we'll do. Tell us where Candy is, and once we have her, we let you go. We'll even throw in some cash. You can use it for the little girl—give her everything her little heart desires. We'll arrange for you to keep little Blondie since we don't know where the next of kin is. One condition though—you and her leave the Lowcountry and never come back."

I just look down at the floor.

"How's ten grand sound?" Andy Y says. "That should last you two a while. Just tell us where Candy is and you'll get it in unmarked bills. We need to stop her from pushin' more drugs around here. The folks 'round here deserve better."

Candy pushing drugs? Send her to prison? Me and Sunny left to ourselves? Ten grand? Leave the Lowcountry and never come back?

What the hell? What the hell is going on? Candy . . . *What did you mean by that kiss?*

I don't say nothin' for a good two minutes. Both Andy Y and Jackson stand in front of me, waiting.

"Then it's a deal," Jackson says, sounding like it's done and settled. "I knew you weren't that stupid."

My head is hanging with my chin on my chest and finally I mumble into my shirt, "Eat shit."

"What's that?" Jackson asks.

I raise my head and look him in the eye. "I said, *eat shit you a-hole.*"

He shakes his head, turns away from me for just a second, and then turns back swinging and slaps me hard across the face. Andy Y whacks me in the ear. I start to get up out of the chair, and as I do, Jackson punches me right in the gut, knocking the wind out of me. I double over and bounce off the chair onto the floor. I can't breathe. They both kick me several times on the body and head. I can't cover up since I'm still cuffed, and each blow seems to get harder. I notice they try to avoid my face, but a few blows land there anyway. They grunt as they kick me and I grunt as I get kicked. It's like they're possessed, whipped into a frenzy as they exert their power.

The door opens. A deep voice bellows, "Enough, boys. That's enough."

The beating stops. I look under the table, through its legs and see fancy wing-tips, navy blue slacks, and above them, the dark brown hem of a robe. The legs walk out the door and it closes. A judge? JM? Judge

Mooney? So he's in on it too. Probably the brains behind the whole thing since these two morons are dumber than dirt.

They pick me up off the floor and take me back to the cell, uncuff me, and leave. The guy in the next cell looks up from his book and sees I've been beaten and shakes his head. "Welcome to the United States of America justice system," he says flatly and goes back to his reading.

About an hour later, Andy Y comes in with two trays of food. He slides one into each of the cell door slots without a word. The guy in the next cell finally gets out of his bunk and goes to the cell door and starts to eat. I do the same. The moment the baloney on white bread sandwich touches my lips, I realize just how hungry I am.

"So what'cha do?" The guy asks in between bites, looking at me through the bars. He doesn't have a Southern accent at all. I just keep eating.

"So what'cha do?" he asks again in exactly the same tone.

"Didn't do nothin'," I finally croak out. My stomach, ribs, back, legs, head—you name it—they're all sore. My whole body hurts. My whole being hurts.

"Yeah," he smiles knowingly. "Me neither."

He finishes his sandwich and grabs the apple and sinks his teeth into it. In a few seconds, I do the same. "So did you finally confess?" he asks.

"Ain't nothin' to confess to," I say indifferently.

"Yeah. I believe you." He bites into his apple. "What'd they *say* you do?"

I bite into my apple. "They say I murdered my cousin over drugs."

He doesn't say anything for a while as we're both finishing our apples. I go and lay down on the bunk. He keeps standing near the cell door. "Well, that'll put you away for a while. Or get you executed, more than likely. Can they prove it?"

I don't say nothin'.

"Doesn't much matter these days if they can prove something," he continues, "especially if there's drugs involved. All it takes is hearsay, you know, for them to put you away for twenty years just because somebody drops the dime on you. They get away with that by calling it 'conspiracy.' And if the cops say they saw you, you're toast."

He starts pacing back and forth in his cell. "The thing is, if they want you, they'll have you. You know the saying, 'even a ham sandwich can be indicted.'"

I see him go back and forth in the corner of my eye as I stare at the ceiling. Back and forth, back and forth, like wipers on a windshield. "You'd think this being the land of the brave and home of the free, they couldn't do that. You'd think they'd need some evidence. Used to be that way, you know. They used to need cold, hard evidence to get you—like you see on TV. But not now. Not for drugs. Murder, maybe, but not if there's drugs. And usually if they prove the drugs, a jury will agree to the murder with only circumstantial evidence."

He stops walking for a moment and I can feel him looking at me through the bars. "And it's not just drugs they don't need cold, hard evidence for. No sir. Like what I'm in her for—embezzlement." He pauses again, looks up to the ceiling and sighs. And then it's like a dam breaks . . .

"The boss man gave me the wrong numbers," he pleads. "He gave me the numbers he wanted reported to the stockholders and I put them on the balance sheets. Just like I've been doing for the past fifteen years. Fifteen fucking years I did the same thing. Just took the numbers he gave me and wrote them down. Well it turns out the bastard had been giving me the wrong numbers for the past three years and putting the difference in his pocket."

He leans towards me. "How was I to know? There was no way I could! So when the Feds finally caught him, they said I was in on it with him.

"What a load of crap! I even have documented proof I didn't know what he was doing. But the damn judge wouldn't let my evidence into court. Can you believe it? Only shows that they're all in on it together. But you don't see the corruption until you go through the process. Then you see how everything is stacked against you. What Ben Franklin said, "That it is better 100 guilty persons should escape than that one innocent person should suffer," has been turned on its head. Now it's more like: guilty until proven innocent, and proving your innocence is impossible!

"And when you get out, *if* you get out, and start telling people how bad it is, who's gonna believe you? You're a convicted criminal! Do you think anyone's gonna believe a convicted criminal? No sir. It's all a racket, I tell you." He pauses again and I can feel him staring at me through the bars.

"You know what I think?" he continues. "I think they're all out to put as many people behind bars as they can, whether they're guilty or not."

Now the guy's all lathered up. It's like a raw nerve's been exposed and it's dragging behind him over a floor with broken glass. He keeps passing back and forth as he rants. Swish, swish . . . Swish swish . . . Swish, swish. Like he's trying to wipe himself clean.

"And you know why? You know what for? So they can keep their cushy little jerk-off government jobs with their insurance plans and retirement benefits. Convictions get them brownie points and dumb-ass promotions! It's like the State Troopers having to give more speeding tickets out at the end of the month so they can meet their quotas." Swish, swish . . . Swish, swish . . . Swish, swish . . .

"I heard one prosecutor say—by the way, do you know what a prosecutor is besides a piddly little no-good piss-ant blood sucker? He's a piddly little no-good piss-ant blood sucker! Ha! Anyway, I heard one prosecutor tell my defense attorney—and do you know what a defense attorney is? The guy I paid 50 grand to keep me out of prison? He's a piddly little no-good piss-ant blood sucker too! Hell, the government's bad enough, you know they're out to get you. It's the lawyers who really screw you, pretending to help you and then making things worse on purpose so you need them more so you pay them more. They're the ones you have to watch more than anyone. What's the saying? 'Keep your eye on your enemies, but watch your friends even closer?' They were thinking of defense attorneys when they said it.

"Anyway, so this prosecutor tells my defense attorney when they thought I was still in the can taking a piss, he says, and I'm giving you a direct quote here because it's something that was branded on my brain with a red-hot poker . . . like you would use to brand cattle . . . hey . . . get the irony? Cattle. Ha!

"Anyway, it's something I'll never forget because now the whole world won't ever forget I've been branded as a felon. So this prosecutor, he slaps my attorney on the back and says, 'You know, John, convicting a guilty man is easy. Convicting an innocent man is a little harder—but just a little!'

"And they both laugh! Like they're sharing a joke down at the local bar or something. They slap each other on each other's back like good-old-boy buddies and laugh! It's all a big game to them! And the judges are in on it too and hand out years in prison like they're passing out jellybeans! I got six years. Six fucking years! I paid that bastard attorney 50 grand, and I swear, he got me convicted on purpose! Lost my job, lost my license, lost my career. Gonna lose six years of my life plus another five on probation.

"Looking back on things is always easy. But do you realize how long six years are? When you're counting every hour, every minute, sometimes every second—when you're X-ing out each day on that itsy-bitsy calendar that's hanging in your locker that can barely hold a change of clothes and pair of boots, hoping that the next day goes faster but knowing it won't. X-ing out those days as if they're something to get rid of, something to purge from your life, an enemy you want to kill.

"It's hard. These hours, these minutes, these seconds. No matter how you try to rationalize it or distract yourself, it's always hard. Waiting to be free again, out of the Big House and free. Home to your own house and your wife and kids and feel them in your arms again. Hear their laughter again. Watch them play again. It's hard, I tell you. Hard. Hard time. Any time behind bars is the hardest time you could ever spend."

He stops in his tracks and looks down, tears running down his cheeks. He sits down on his bunk and puts his head in his hands and sobs for several minutes. Then he clears his throat, blows his nose on the sleeve of his shirt, stands, and starts pacing back and forth again . . .

"They offered me a plea agreement, you know, where you plead guilty and get a lesser sentence. I would have gotten just two years. Two years? But I didn't do anything criminal! I may have written down the wrong numbers, but I was instructed to and I had no intention of breaking any laws. What's more, I could prove it with hard evidence. This is America, right? Innocent until proven guilty, right?

"Wrong. So I took it to trial. Paid another 15 grand for that. And you'd think the jury would look at the facts and be logical, right? Wrong again. They see some guy who the government says is bad and the government is there to protect the people, right? Then the judge doesn't let my evidence in and it's a slam-dunk for the prosecution. The government wins like 95 percent of their cases. You don't stand a chance."

The windshield wipers stop. I can tell he feels a little better. "And my wife and kids? How are they gonna make it without me? They can't even collect on my life insurance because I'm not dead. I'm worse than dead! I'm an expense. You would never know it, but being in prison is expensive. It's costing me almost a hundred bucks a month to be locked up. You need to buy extra food since the cafeteria food sucks; long distance phone calls at five times the going rate; clothes, toiletries, boots.

It adds up fast. It's only been two years now and I can tell my poor wife is at the end of her rope and may even be having an affair. She's a good woman, but God, who can blame her? She has needs, you know, and who wouldn't get lonely?

"And the kids, they're ten and twelve now. They need a dad. And they're all ashamed. I'm ashamed, too, even though I didn't do anything any other accountant wouldn't have done." He sits down on the bunk again and puts his head in his hands. I hear him sniffle a couple times. He raises his head and continues . . .

"Look, I understand there's criminals and bad people who lie and cheat and steal and push drugs . . . although, hey, I read an article that prescription drugs are actually more harmful than recreational drugs! Ha! So who are the real drug pushers? The doctors, that's who!

"Anyway, I know we need law enforcement and all, but when the system puts people behind bars just to make quotas and profits and secure jobs, something is definitely wrong."

He thumbs through his paperback book and pulls out a separate piece of paper. "Here," he says holding up a newspaper clipping. "Here's some statistics for you if you don't believe me. One thing about prison is you get to read a lot. Says here that the U.S. has the largest prison population and the highest rate of incarceration in the world. More than China, Russia or anywhere else. Are we more lawless than the Russians or Chinese? I don't think so.

"One out of every one-hundred adults in the U.S. is in prison. That's an average of seven times more than other Western industrial nations. One out of every thirty-two adults in the U.S. is either in prison, on probation, or on parole. The U.S. has five percent of the world's population, and twenty-five percent of the world's incarcerated population. We rank first in the world in locking up our fellow citizens and we now imprison more people for drug law violations than all of western Europe incarcerates for all offenses.

"And by the way, Americans are the most drugged people on earth. Not with street drugs, but prescription drugs. Ironic, don't you think?"

He puts the clipping back inside the book, looks up at me and says, "You wanna know my theory? Besides the prosecutors and judges earning their living on how many people they put behind bars? There's another reason, and it doesn't have to do with the lawyers this time, but the doctors.

"You see, the medical schools are financed mostly by the drug companies. So what do you think the drug companies are going to teach the aspiring young innocent wanna-be doctors? I'll tell you what. They're going to teach them how to prescribe drugs. That way, the drug companies make more money, right? The only way Mr. And Mrs. John Q Public can get these precious and life-saving, *cough,* drugs is to get a prescription from one of the drug companies pimps . . . uh . . . excuse me . . . doctors. But what if an independent-minded entrepreneur tries to sell drugs to people without a prescription? I already told you that recreational drugs are less dangerous than prescription drugs and sometimes more effective . . . like marijuana helps those with depression better and safer than antidepressants.

"You know, you probably never heard of antidepressants since there's not many people these days with that problem. But mark my words, in the years to come—maybe twenty-five, thirty years from now—you're gonna see people getting shot and killed by people who are taking these antidepressants. The media, which is also controlled by the large corporations, drug companies being one of them, will put the spin on these killings saying that the gunman went crazy because he had stopped taking his medication or was on the wrong kind, when in fact, that person actually went crazy and started shooting people because the drugs messed up his brain so badly that they turned him into a homicidal and sometimes suicidal monster. It's got to do with fluoride, the active ingredient—the same active ingredient in rat poison, by the way. Go look it up. You'll see. Fluoride makes you not only homicidal and suicidal sometimes, but submissive—and sterile. The Nazis used it in concentration camps trying to sterilize the Jews. Really.

"And since the authorities told them it was because the gunman *didn't* take his medicine, that's what people will believe. After all, the FDA is here to protect us, right? Think again. Most people who work there used to work for the drug companies and have obligations, you could say. Conflict of interest? Of course! But when there's billions of dollars to be made, you know what happens.

"It doesn't matter that doctors and the drugs they prescribe are the third leading cause of death in the U.S. Every year, over 100,000 people die because of the side effects of the drugs doctors prescribe! In all, about 250,000 people die a year from all medical mistakes. This was reported by the Institute of Medicine and published in the *Journal of the American Medical Association*—not some quack rag. I read it just last week in another prison's library. Like I said, you read a lot in prison."

He pauses a second in thought. Then he says, "I wonder how many people have died from smoking weed, you know? And here's a twist: They figured out that doctors are 9,000 times more likely to accidentally kill you than someone who owns a gun! A while back the doctors in San Francisco, I think it was, went on strike. And you know who protested the most? The undertakers! Swear to God! Ain't that a trip? You know why? Because death rates go down when doctors go on strike! What's that tell you?

"I swear, drugs are going to be the death of this country. But back to my first point. These drug companies don't want any competition, you see, so they buy off the law makers and politicians to pass laws that make selling drugs illegal as hell so that you're going to go away for a long, long time if you get caught selling them. The doctors get humanitarian awards for giving people drugs that cause shootings and the pusher gets a year in prison for each prescription pill he's caught with. A mere ten pills gets you a full ten years.

"So they all win. The drug companies keep their monopoly, the prosecutors and judges get raises for putting more people in jail, the bureaucrats have jobs to administrate the prisons, and the politicians get gifts, vacations, and money under the table for passing the laws. What's not to love, right? It's capitalism gone horribly wrong.

"Personally, I haven't had as much as an aspirin for over a year now. I've read enough in here to see that every drug there is has nasty side effects that'll mess you up one way or another. All you gotta do is read the damn advertisements! Hell, if it was up to me, I'd make them *all* illegal.

"Can you imagine? What would a doctor do if there were no drugs? He might actually have to study how God intended us to stay healthy— using common sense and nature. But that's not very cool. No, that's too simple. No fancy machines. No dangerous surgeries. No magic potions to drive the evil spirits out of your head. We need to make things complicated and difficult, and then swoop in with the solution. And in the end, that solution isn't a solution at all, but actually creates more problems. What's that saying, 'First, we kick up the dust and then complain we can't see?'"

He looks down at the floor again, runs his fingers through his hair, and lets out a long sigh. "So now they're transferring me to a different jail and jerking me around on the way. Diesel Therapy they call it 'cuz they diesel you around on all these busses. They send you all over, six, seven, eight different jails over months. The worst county and two bit jails with the worst food and conditions.

"They push you around like a piece of meat—worse than freakin' cattle. Why? Because maybe you ticked one of them off by standing up for your rights and they want to teach you a lesson. They want to make an example of you that if you resist the system, you get screwed even worse. Or they fuck with you simply because they can. It gets you angry and hostile and mean. If you ain't got a criminal mind going in, you sure as hell have a one by the time you get out. Some rehabilitation system, huh?"

He gets up and walks in a circle this time, like he's going around with the water inside a toilet bowl. "You know, buddy," he looks at me. I turn and look at him and our eyes meet. Suddenly I feel a sympathy, an empathy, a kinship, with this poor, spindly man wearing wire-rimmed glasses.

"You know," he says again. "I used to believe in America. I used to love America. And I still do. Deep down, I love America, her people, the land, the spirit and her brave and hearty souls. But Jefferson and Washington and loveable old Ben would puke their guts out and roll over in their graves if they saw what this once great nation has become: A land of lawsuits, convictions, and blood sucking piss-ants who hide behind three piece suits and robes and corrupt court decisions. And the sheep, like you and me, who let it all happen.

"I'll tell you," he comes over to the bars and lowers his voice to a whisper, "I really think it's all just a new form of slavery. They're trying to turn us all into felony slaves. Once you're a felon, you can't have a gun. You can't get public assistance. You can't travel like you want. Hell, Canada won't even let you visit for as long as you live. Once you're a convict, they make you scared as shit to never do anything against them 'cuz you'd go away for even longer the next time. They'll make you pay, one way or another.

"Once they have their hooks in you, you don't stand a chance. You see, it's all about money. Once they start an investigation, they're spending money, and they have to justify spending that money. If they don't get a conviction out of it, they've spent the money for nothing and it means they made a mistake. They can't admit they made a mistake because it wouldn't look good, and eventually, with enough mistakes, they might lose their job. So they make sure they get a conviction, even if you're innocent, so they can justify the money they spent and maybe even get a raise.

"And the defense attorneys? They make more money the more trouble you're in. So the whole deck is stacked against the accused—both legally and financially."

He goes and sits on the corner of his bunk and takes a deep breath. "But the solution to that is simple. Have every defense attorney work for the government, just as the prosecutors do. Then the two sides would be pitted against each other, instead of both sides profiting from the citizen getting convicted. The defense attorneys would get raises and promotions based on how many people they get off just as the prosecutors get raises and promotions for putting people away. And the citizen doesn't have to worry about paying outrageous legal bills and having things turn from bad to worse.

"Heck, if the government can pay prosecutors, they can pay defense attorneys too. The judges would have just as much chance of getting bribed by both sides! At least the corruption would be equal! Hah!

"So that's my idea of the next America: no drugs allowed; and equal protection not just under the law, but from the law."

The spindly man with wire-rimmed glasses lays down in his bunk and picks up his paperback again. "Wouldn't that be a trip?" he laughs quietly. "Wouldn't that be a trip?" he whispers to himself. He opens the book and starts to read.

It's quiet again. So quiet. I stare at the ceiling and try to remember all he said. As my body throbs from the beatings and my mind torques from the rising of my awareness, I suddenly realize the true gravity of the situation I'm in: That the corruption that's spread all the way to this little Lowcountry town could very well destroy me and the ones I love; and the only way to be sure that Candy and Sunny stay safe is to make sure of it myself. No lawyers, no cops, no deception.

My head is kinda spinning from all this crap, so I've got to settle down. Got to settle down. Calm down. You can't think straight when you're scared like this. You can't always act out of instinct. Use your brain. Use your brain!

I sit on the edge of the bunk and close my eyes. I listen to my heart. I feel it beating in my chest. I feel my feet on the ground. I concentrate on excluding everything else.

Then I allow myself to think. I've got to get out of jail somehow . . . without any help . . . without passing go. But how? I jump up and grab the bars on the window and tug as hard as I can. Solid as a rock. I inspect all the bars around my cell, the door, the bunk, the plumbing. Nothing. Maybe if I jump them the next time they let me out of the cell. It'll probably be my only chance to have just those two alone. I could kick one of them in the nuts and butt-head the other. After all, I do have a black belt. I should be able to handle two slime balls like them even with both hands tied behind my back. Then, I run. No shackles yet.

Time to make that phone call. But . . .

If I jump them before I make the call, I may never get another chance. So I'll jump them *after* I make the call. Maybe that way I can get some help from outside. If I knock them out, I can bolt and won't need anybody. If I fail, then maybe someone will come.

Okay. That's it. That's the battle plan. Now who can I call? Mom and Dad? They've been dead to me for years. Sister? Last time we talked was four years ago and she'd probably believe the police instead of me anyway. No other relatives since we were never close to any of 'em. Don't have an attorney, and now I don't want one.

Can't call Candy. I don't want to get Kaitlin involved. But my old buddy Jim, he might help me. Jim's a bricklayer and doubles as a *State Bureau Insurance* agent and he's been a fishing buddy for years. We don't get out much anymore, but I think he'd try to help me. Might as well try. There's nobody else. "Guard!" I shout as I grab the cell door bars. "Guard!" Nobody comes, though I can see them walking back and forth through the window of the cell room door. "Hey Jackson! Jackson!" I scream.

Finally, Jackson opens the door but he doesn't say a word. "I want to make my phone call." He looks at me briefly and closes the door. "Hey! I want to make my phone call!" I shake the bars and keep yelling. After about five minutes, Andy Y opens the door. I glance over and see the guy in the adjacent cell look up from his reading with a knowing little smile on his face. Like he's watching a kid on his way to learning a lesson.

Jackson and Andy Y open the cell door, put the cuffs on me—but with my hands in front of me this time—grab me hard by the arms and lead me into the same closet-interrogation room. There's a phone on the table.

"You're a royal pain in the ass, Sticker," Jackson says as he pushes me in. "But not for long." He shuts the door as they leave. I remember Jim's number, and dial it. After four rings, it gets answered. Hallelujah, I think. "Hey Jim!"

"Hello!"

"Jim!" I shout into the receiver.

"You have reached the home of Jim and Emily, Sandy and Marc."

"Jim!" I shout again. "Pick up!"

"We'd love to talk to you,"

"Jim!"

"So please leave . . ."

"Jim! It's me! Sticker!"

"A message at the sound . . ."

"Oh, man. Jim!"

". . . of the beep. Or call back 'cuz we're on vacation until next Friday. Beep!"

"Friday? It's only Saturday! Jim? Jim . . . ?" I drop the receiver and hang my head. I'm stunned. A thousand thoughts try to come out of my brain, but they all jam up at the exit. Like a crowd of people racing to get out of a burning building, they get stuck in the doorway and nobody can get through. So all these people get trapped inside and yell and scream and scratch and claw and trample each other to get out. But they can't. They just keep pushing forward and get bottled up and the pressure builds but can't be relieved and it starts to push the other way. And that's all a surprise and you're not ready for it and it starts to come out the other end.

Scared. Scared shitless. I never really understood what that meant. Now I do. I feel the pressure go down and right through my body and I have to clench my ass hard to keep from shitting on the floor right then and there. Looking back on it, I should have taken down my pants and shit on their floor. But I clench hard and push it back up, except for maybe a trickle. Then a bitter thought escapes my brain and it causes me to sweat.

I think that this is war. This is *my* war. And this is a real life-and-death battle. If I don't figure something out or get some help soon, I'm gonna be as dead as a soldier who got his head blown off by a howitzer. A real war or a war like mine. Both could scare the shit out of anybody.

I sit down in the chair and keep squeezing my ass. Remember, you had a plan. You had a plan! Wake up!

The door opens. Andy Y is laughing, "Have a nice chat?" he sneers knowingly as he walks towards me. Suddenly, my fear is replaced by anger, and I'm ready to fight.

Jackson is right behind him. "What? No answer? Get one of those damn answering machines? Too bad you wasted your call. What'cha gonna do now, ass wipe?"

I jump out of the chair and swing my leg straight up in a perfect front-kick and catch Andy Y right in the nuts. As he doubles over, I swing my other leg around and hit him in the gut with a roundhouse kick. He grunts and stumbles back and bumps into Jackson, who throws his arms out against the wall.

I've got 'em now, shoots through my mind. As Andy Y is gasping for air and holding his nuts, I charge Jackson head first. I throw the hairline of my head right at the bridge of his nose. I hit it dead solid perfect. Crunch!

His head snaps back and bangs hard against the wall. I see his eyes go blank and kinda roll up into his head as he drops to the floor.

Yes! I see the open door and lunge for it. I get through the threshold into the main office of the jail. I hear the spindly man with the wire-rimmed glasses yell at me from his cell, "You go, boy! You go!"

Seconds away from freedom now! Faster! Move faster! I get to the front door panting and shaking, grab the doorknob with both hands and turn it. I pull the door open as fast as I can.

As the door swings open, suddenly, I'm crumbling to the floor. Hard to believe that the last thing I remember before I black out is hearing a song in my head . . . "Turn out the lights, the party's over . . ."

He snapped to attention in his sharp looking uniform and gave the major a crisp salute. I felt proud, because I knew it was my dad's father—my grandfather, Sergeant Baraloni—even though I'd never met him. He looked important.

"Yes, sir!" he said in Italian. "Reporting for duty, sir!"

The major barked orders to him, also in Italian. "Take these dissidents to the holding cells. Lock them up with the rest of them! No food until tomorrow! If I catch you giving food again, we'll lock you up too!"

As my grandfather walked past the major to leave the room, the major slapped him across the back of his head. "You hear me?" he barked. "One more time! Just one more time!"

My grandfather recoiled from the blow but stood up straight, faced the major and snapped another salute. He turned and pushed the family out the door, across the roadside ditch and down the muddy road. A man and a woman, two boys and a girl, all frightened and confused. I was shocked. The pride I felt for him left. "We have done nothing!" the father pleaded. "We have done nothing! Let us go! Let us go!"

My grandfather kept pushing. He would rather let them go, but he was frightened too. He had a wife and children of his own and could not disobey. A corporal joined him and helped push the family down the road.

"Stinking terrorists!" the corporal sneered, expecting agreement from my grandfather, who did not give it. "The President said it would happen this way. First, the foreigners fly aeroplanes into our buildings. Then the war to punish the evil ones and to protect ourselves from their big weapons. Now, terrorism spreading into our very own people! They must be stopped! They must be eradicated! Isn't that so, Dominique? Aren't you proud to be part of 'the good fight?'" My grandfather just looked at the ground.

It was night, and the ship was about to sail. One long wooden plank still fettered it to the dock. "Quickly!" he called in a whisper. "Quiet now! Quickly!"

My grandmother held baby Leonardo, my father, to her breast and dashed for the plank. The other seven children followed her without question or pause, like a gaggle of chicks following mother hen, as my grandfather closed off the group and brought up the rear.

Up the plank, across the deck they scurried, down into a damp, dark storage room in the belly of the ship. They huddled there in the darkness. The sound of dripping water echoed in their ears. The smell of kerosene, sawdust, and rotting fish filled their nostrils. But the taste of freedom soon to come made them content.

My grandfather struck a match and lit a kerosene lamp. The dull yellow light revealed the family was all there. The trip would be long and uncomfortable, but safe. Off to another country—a freer country, he thought—where fascism is not allowed.

America.

He breathed a sigh of relief and wrapped his arms around his wife. "We're going to be all right, sweetheart," he whispered as he kissed her hair and rubbed his nose on her scalp. "We're going to be all right."

Chapter Fourteen

My eyes open. Although it's hot in the cell, I find my arms wrapped around myself, like I'm giving myself a bear hug. The back of my head is pounding like a son of a gun. Owww! Son of a bitch! What did they hit me with, an anvil? I turn my head and notice the guy in the next cell is gone. It's dark outside and I'm hungry.

At least they didn't shoot me. I wonder why? Andy Y must have recovered from getting nailed in the nuts faster than I thought he would. Or maybe the judge watched it all from behind the glass. Whatever. All I know is I'm still alive. But man, does it hurt!

I get out of the bunk and go to the bars and look out the glass of the cell room door to see if I can make anything out. The door isn't closed completely, and there's maybe a half-inch of gap between the door and the jam. Not like it matters, I think. But it won't be long until I learn that it does.

I notice a tray of food on the floor just inside the cell door—an ice cream scoop of some Spanish-style ground beef, a slice of bread, another apple, and a small container of skim milk. Wonderful.

Soon after I'm done eating, I hear the outside door open, and open quickly, because the air pressure it creates makes the door into the cell room area creak open another inch wider. I can hear the footsteps of the person who just came in the jail on the linoleum covered concrete floor.

Click-clack . . . Click-clack . . . Click-clack . . .

What's this? It sounds like high heels! And even though my head is sore as hell and the rest of my body is throbbing, when I hear her voice, then and there, and most unbelievably, I feel that tingle of electricity shoot up and explode over my scalp again. "Hey, Jack," Kaitlin says.

Suddenly, nothing else matters except my jealousy. Jealous to hear her say those words in the most seductive voice ever, and say them not to me.

"What're you doing here?" Jackson barks, obviously still sulking from when she dumped him months ago.

"Well . . . You know . . . I heard," Kaitlin continues, still all sexy-like, "you were workin' late."

"Yeah, that's right," he says, but in just a slightly softer tone. "Got some phone calls to make. Got your old pal Sticker in there, too."

"So I hear."

There's a pause. I imagine he's looking at Kait. If she's wearing high heels and a dress or skirt to go with them, it'd be downright impossible for any man not to stare.

"Yeah," he finally says, obviously distracted. "Can't talk about it though. It's all con-fi-dent-ial. So if you're trying to find something out for that stupid newspaper of yours, you can forget it."

"That's cool," Kaitlin says quick and friendly-like, not the least bit put off. "I didn't come here about that. Well, not that exactly."

I hear her step closer to the door. I still can't see her, but I can smell just a hint of her perfume coming through the crack in the door. Sweet magnolias.

"So what'd ya come here for then?" Jackson asks, *exactly.*"

"Oh dear," Kaitlin says. "What happened to your nose?"

"Nothin'. Nothin'," Jackson replies. "Just had a little run-in with your friend in there trying to break out."

"Is that so? So did you show him who's boss?"

"Of course. Now what're you here for, before I lose my temper."

"Well," she says, and I can hear her still walking around—walking away from him now so he can see that sweet little fanny of hers. "I heard about how brave you were and how you got Sticker down and handcuffed him and all." She pauses. Her steps come closer. "You know, Jack. Like a true, blue, hero and all."

My heartbeat picks up and a flush spreads across my face. I imagine she's probably running her fingers across his cheek by now.

"You did?" he asks sheepishly. He's a gonner already, I think.

"Yes, I did." Another pause. Another stroke of the cheek. "And I'm thinking that maybe, just maybe, I made a mistake."

"What kind of mistake?"

"This kind of mistake . . ." Kaitlin says in her most seductive voice yet. I hear papers rustle and a couple sighs from those dolphin-like lips. Kaitlin! What the hell are you doing? I feel like tearing through the bars and pouncing on the two of 'em and ripping his guts out and running and hiding from the heartbreak all at the same time. But I bite my tongue and stay quiet. My shoulders slump and my chin drops down to my chest.

"Oh, Jack!" she exclaims as all the stuff on the desk hits the floor. "Have you ever done it in a *police station* before?"

"Not exactly," he snickers. Okay. That's kinda funny, I have to admit.

"Well, now's your chance," she says.

I hear them wrestle around for a few seconds. His belt hits the floor and all the keys jingle as it does. There's more fidgeting and then Kaitlin says, "Jack . . . oh . . . that tickles! Tee hee! Jack . . . JACK! Wait! One second!" The rustling slows, but doesn't stop completely.

"Jack, I brought something that will make this night even more special. It's in the car. You know, it's your favorite. I've got some cans of Coke and a nice big bottle of good ole Jack." The rustling stops completely.

Kaitlin continues, "Remember what you used to say? 'Jack and Coke for this Jack and poke—cowpoke that is!'"

"Yeah?" he asks longingly. "You've got Jack Daniels?"

"That's right, cowpoke. Out in the trunk of my car."

"But I'm on duty. I can't."

"Oh, silly! It's late and there's no one else around and they won't be here till mornin' right? And you were such a hero yesterday that even if they do catch you—which they won't, trust me—they would certainly forgive you for having a little celebration for saving us all from a murderer with your fee-aun-say."

Another pause. "What?" he finally blurts out. "What did you say? Are you saying yes? Kaitlin, are you really saying yes?"

"Of course I am, you big, strong, cowpoke, you!"

"Oh boy!" Jackson says. "Oh butter-boy!"

What a fool. I sit on the floor.

"Oh yeah!" he exclaims. "Oh! The ring! It's home in my mom's cookie jar. I'll get it tomorrow! Wow! Kaitlin!"

"Here's the key," Kaitlin says. "I had to borrow Kathy's car tonight 'cuz mine had a flat. Now go outside and get those delicious libations so we can celebrate!"

Oh, she sounds so Southern—and so sexy. But I still can't believe my ears! How could you, Kait? I thought I knew you! And Jackson? Really? My head is spinning. Just goes to show—you can't open up to nobody. The very next day after I bare my soul to the one woman I've ever loved, here she is saying yes to a total douchebag.

"Hand me my pants," Jackson says.

And it's more than her saying yes to a jerk and knowing I'll never have her. It's the fact that her love for me was my ace-in-the-hole: the rock that I clung to when things got really dark. Believing that Kaitlin truly loved me and only me, gave me comfort, confidence, swagger. It vindicated everything. And now it's all gone.

Nauseating heartache envelops me. Mind numbing heartache worming its way down into the core of my being . . . again . . . and laughing at me as it goes,

You sap! You fool! Ha ha! Thought you had something to live for? Thought she was different? Thought you were special? You should know better by now, you fool! Ha ha! You fool! Fool!!!

"Oh, silly," Kaitlin replies quickly. "That'll just slow things down. There's nobody out in this one-horse town this time of night anyway. So be a naughty little boy and hurry up and get that Jack and Coke, you bad-ass cowpoke you!"

Sick to my stomach. Oh Kaitlin! How could I be so wrong about us. How could I be so wrong about *you!*

"Okay! You're right! Ha, ha! Don't you run off now, you naughty little cowgirl."

"You bet I won't!" she says. "Now giddy-up!"

I hear Jackson scurry to the front door and open it quickly. The door into the cell area opens another inch due to the air pressure and I feel a little coolness across my sweating forehead. I think to call out to Kaitlin, but what's the use? Instead, I find myself thinking about how to tie a bed sheet to the window bars and . . .

I hear a couple steps out in the office. The cell-room door swings open abruptly. I raise my head . . .

And see Kaitlin bursting through the door and coming right at me!

She rushes to my cell door, her high heels clicking fast and loud and her perfume filling my nostrils. She's not even looking at me but her eyes are focused on the cell door lock. She has Jackson's pants in her hands and is fumbling with his belt and the ring with all the keys hanging off it.

"Kaitlin!" I exclaim in hushed surprise, my stomach doing cart-wheels all over the place. "Kaitlin!" I say again as she fumbles to find the right key.

She's wearing a short black skirt and a tight blue top with a loose outer shirt; and I can just see the garters below the hem of her skirt that hold up the nylons she's wearing. I'm dizzy and disoriented.

"Which one?" she demands. *"Which one?"*

This can't be happening! What's she doing? I reach through the bars and, with my finger shaking, point to one of the keys. "Try that one!" She grabs it and rattles it into the key hole and turns it and pulls on the door. It doesn't budge.

"Damn!" she gasps.

"The other way!" I say. She turns it the other way and we hear a click, and the door opens. I push it half-open, as she backs up a step.

"No!" she snaps almost angrily. "Not yet!" Her eyes look up and finally reach mine. I see their emeraldness and then blackness and almost fall into them right then and there.

"I'll have him passed out drunk in half an hour. Just stay put and wait." She raises her finger to her lips like she's telling a child to hush, then reaches down and slips off her patent-leather high-heel pump and takes out a small folded piece of paper.

"Here," she says as she hands it to me through the bars and pushes the bars so the cell door closes but doesn't lock. "Here's the key to my car. It's parked on Elm Street, near the middle of the block. And the note—read it later." She smiles briefly, almost embarrassingly so, as she puts the paper in my hand. I take the paper with the lump in it and then take hold of her moist and trembling hand. She lets me hold it for just a second, then pulls it back through the bars and darts for the door. Just as she gets there, the outside door opens. Shit!

I stuff the paper and key into my pocket. Kaitlin hurries through the door and pulls it behind her, but not all the way shut, while she holds Jackson's pants, belt, and keys behind her back with one hand.

"Hey!" Jackson barks. "What'ya doing back there?"

"Oh my!" Kaitlin exclaims quickly. She points and shifts her gaze to the window besides the outside door of the jail. "Is that Andy?" she asks. She whips the pants around her legs and coughs as she tosses them so they quietly skid across the floor to the desk where they were laying before. It works.

"What? Where?" Jackson asks belligerently. "No. There's nobody there. What the hell you doing back there?" he says as he comes to the half-window door where Kaitlin still stands. I dive for the bunk and lay on my stomach and close my eyes.

"Oh, silly goose!" Kaitlin says without missing a beat. "He's fast asleep."

Jackson burst through the door and into the cell area. I hold my breath to stop my panting so it looks like I'm sleeping. I hear the cell door rattle just slightly as he grabs it. Five seconds . . . ten seconds . . . my lungs are about to explode. Say something Kait! Say something!

"I just never saw a murderer before," she says as I hear her high-heels click closer. "You know, Jack baby. I just wanted to see what a real murderer looks like. You think you know somebody! But boy-oh-boy, was I wrong about him! And now I know who my true love really is . . . a big, strong, super-sheriff who can protect me from scoundrels like him."

"I ain't a sheriff, Kait, just a deputy," he says as I hear him let go of the bars as the door rattles just a little more.

"Not yet, big boy," she whispers. "But someday soon, I'm sure."

They step slowly to the cell room door and I can hear them go out into the office. Phewwwww. I exhale and gulp air into my lungs. Kait's whimpering all sweet on his shoulder as she pulls the door behind her, once again leaving it slightly a jar.

"Here," she says when they get back to the desk. "Let's play a game. It's a new one I read about in a girly magazine. It's supposed to get your man really, really hot!"

I sit up with a more-than satisfied grin on my face. Maybe it's gonna be all right after all.

"What kind of game?" Jackson asks.

"It's called Strip-shooting," I hear her pull down the blinds to the front windows.

"Strip-shootin'?"

"Yeah, baby. I dance, and for every piece of clothing I take off for you, you take a shot of Jack Daniels for me!"

"Oh, yeah? Anything with strippin' and drinkin' in it sounds good to me!"

"So let's forget the Cokes for now, and show me what a bad-boy you really are! Here . . . Here's a shot glass."

They start the game with Kaitlin taking off her headband. I can see her through the crack in the door.

"Awww . . ." Jackson whines. "Head bands don't count!"

"Oh yes they do. Now you take a shot."

"Oh, aw right!"

I hear the tinkle of glass, then the glass slam on the desk, and Jackson lets out a loud and annoying "Ahhhhh . . ."

Kaitlin dances again and reaches up to her ears.

"Now your earrings?" he complains again. "Those don't count

Kaitlin!"

"Oh yes they do. That's what the girly magazine said."

"Oh, aw right . . ."

Tinkle, slam, "Ahhh . . ."

"So J," Kaitlin says all syrupy-like. "How's your new business going?" She hums the striptease tune like she's at a burlesque show, "Dum, da dum . . . Da dum, dum, dum . . ."

Kaitlin takes off her outer shirt.

"Yeah!" Jackson says. "That's better. What'd you say?"

"How's your new business going? You know, the one you make all that extra money with?"

"Oh yeah. It's goin' just fine."

"Now it's your turn, baby," Kaitlin says. "Another shot for you."

Tinkle, slam, "Ahhhh . . ."

"That's a good boy. Now J, babe, are you really making all the money I hear the other girls talkin' about? And now that we're engaged, will you buy me nice pretty things?"

"You know I will baby! Yeah . . . that's nice. Do that again!"

"It'll cost you, big boy!"

Tinkle, slam, "Aahhhh . . ."

"Good boy, Jackson. You are soooo cool. So who-all are your partners? In this new business I mean."

"Hey! Take it off!" he yaps. Then he says, "Really can't say."

"Oh, come on now J. It makes no difference, really, and I'll probably forget by mornin' considerin' how drunk I'm gonna get with you tonight."

"Ohhh! That feels gooood!"

"So let me in on the secret, J-bone. Who's your partners in this big-time money-machine business of yours?"

"Oh . . . jus Andy. Yeah baby! Another shot? Aw right."

Tinkle, slam, "Ahhh . . ."

"And JM. Tom's gone now, so it's just the three of us."

"Oh really! That means more money for you and more money for *me!*"

"That's right, baby. Now your skirt! Let me see those panties!"

"Oh, not yet, big boy. Your turn."

Tinkle, slam, "Aaahhhhh . . ."

"And when's the next time you're gonna conduct this money-machine business . . . if you know what I mean."

"Oh, I don' know," he's slurring badly now. "Maybe tamorroooow. Maybe toni . . . Hell! What day ish it?"

"Saturday night, dear. Sunday morning."

"Shaterdaaay? Er . . . Shundaaay mornin'? Well hell'sh fire! Then itssh tonight! Itssh tonight Goddamnit! Tonight at two-thirty. Ohhhh . . . I have to stop drinkin'. That's jus one, twooo, tree . . . twoo . . . eah . . . two hours from now!"

"Now J baby. We're not finished here yet, and we had a deal. I would strip for you and you would get happy for me. And once that's finished and I'm all naked and . . . horny . . . and . . . hot . . . and . . . well, you know . . . I'm gonna do you like you've never been done before!"

Whoa, Kaithlin! I think. You don't have to go overboard now!

"Yeah?" Jackson perks up. "Yeah?" Then he kinda mutters under his breath, "Weell isssst's aboout tiiiime."

"That's all right, J-bone." Kaitlin says. "It'll be worth the wait. Now my stocking . . ."

"Oh . . . I love stockin's an garter beltssss, an . . . an . . . pannnties!"

"Your turn, J."

Tinkle, slam, "Aaaahhhhh . . ."

"And now my other stocking."

"Ohhh . . . baby!"

Tinkle, slam "Aaaaaaahhhhh . . ."

"And I'll even do that other thing you always wanted. You know, kissey, kissey down there. I'll even do that!"

"Reeeeally? A BJ? Thash's my fa-vo-ite! Forrr reeeaaallll?"

"If that's what they're callin' it these days. Yeah, even that."

"Wowwww! Kaaaitlin! This sur is my luc . . . hiccup . . . day!"

"Your turn again, sweetheart."

Tinkle, slam, "Aaaaaahhhhhhh . . ."

"So where do you go at two-thirty, to do your business, I mean. Where do you go?"

"Ohhh, I don know. I can' reeeeemember. Ohhh . . ."

"Come now. Where do you have to be at two-thirty, just in case, so I can make sure you get there in time. You know, so you . . . uh . . . *we* can get all that money."

"Oh! Gooooo ideeeaa K. Yeahhh . . . Gooooo ideeeaaa! River-hole. Ya know, at the rope. That lill dock off to the shide. Yeah baby! Tha's where the new sshhipment comesss in. Now the skirt! The skirt!"

Tinkle, slam, "Aaaaaahhhhhh. Come 'ere, baby."

"First, one more for your hot, horny fiancé. One more drink, J."

Tinkle, slam, "Aaaahhhhh. . ."

"Come . . . come . . . er . . . K . . ."

His voice breaks off in mid-sentence and I hear his fat head fall on the desk. Thud. I hear clothes rustle, and in a few seconds Kaitlin comes through the door fully clothed (unfortunately) and says, "Give me five minutes and then skidattle."

She looks at the cell door as I open it and walk through. "I guess I could have waited till now to unlock it!" she smiles. I step towards her and reach my arms out to her but she holds out a hand to stop me. As brave as she's been, she's shaking.

"No," she says weakly. "Sticker, I need to go. Andy might come back. There's no time. I can't . . . I can't . . ."

I recoil at first, and then reach out again and take her shoulders in my hands and gently but firmly pull her to me. "No," she trembles.

"I know," I say. "Just for a second. Just one second . . ."

She collapses onto me and her whole body quivers. I pull her to my chest and stroke her hair gently. "You done good," I whisper. "You done real good, Kait."

She's there, in my arms, and we hold each other like we'd never hold another again. A minute goes by, our hearts pounding together. "You've got Kathy's car?"

"Yeah."

"Good. She'll understand," I say. "Go straight to my trailer and look under the big throw-rug in the living room. There's about five thousand dollars spread out under it. Gather up about half of it and take it with you. Can you remember that?"

She nods her head.

"Where's the money?"

"Under the rug . . . living room."

"Right. Then drive straight to Charleston. Don't stop for nobody or nothin'. Don't tell Kathy or your dad or nobody. Got it?"

"Yes."

"Go get a room at the Holiday Inn near the causeway. The round one. You know it?"

"Yeah."

"Stay there until I come for you. Don't use your real name and don't open the door for anyone. Use your middle name, Sarah, and the last name Wilson. When I come for you I'll leave a message that I'm in the lobby with my Sunday bonnet on." She exhales a tense little laugh. "You'll never forget that, now, will you?"

She shakes her head.

"I need some time to clear this up. If I don't they'll just bring me back here or kill me trying. If they get me, they'll forget you. If I win, you'll be safe too. But that may take some time. If I don't come for you in two days, call your dad. He'll know what to do. So stay away. Got that? No more private eye stuff, okay?"

She smiles that dolphin smile and we hug each other tighter and kiss briefly—as if I was the husband leaving for work in the morning. "Now go. I'll be right behind you."

We let go, and she walks to the front door, her high heel shoes clicking on the linoleum covered cement floor. She takes hold of the doorknob and turns it as I say, "And Kaitlin . . ."

She pauses, not turning her head.

"Just don't go and spend all that money on shoes or somethin'," I smile.

She turns her head quickly and looks at me with a glance that's hopeful and a little spiteful and yet, at the same time says, "It should have been you!" A spark shoots up my spine.

"Don't worry, Sam," she says as our eyes linger on each other's. "I'd rather go barefoot."

She forces herself to open the door as her eyes never leave mine. She steps through the threshold and pulls the door shut behind her.

I stand there a couple seconds. Then I look at Jackson passed out with his head on the desk. I think to move him back into the cell and lock the door and throw away the key, but that might mess up their plans to get the drugs tonight. At least I'll know where they'll be. I hear the car outside start and drive away.

I go back into the cell and put the pillow under the blanket to make it look like someone's sleeping there. It's not very convincing, but maybe it'll buy me some time. I remember Kaitlin's note and reach into my pocket and take out the paper. I open it as I stand just inside the cell.

Inside the paper is a silver keychain with one key on it and a small, thin silver locket—the kind you put a picture of your sweetheart in— about the size of my thumbnail. I find the tiny clasp and pop the locket open, wondering if there's anything inside—maybe a message or picture or something. There's a tiny little frame to hold a picture, but there's no picture within it; just empty space. I pause a second and take a deep breath, then flatten the quarter-sheet of paper and read the handwritten note:

> *Dearest Sam,*   *6-21-1986*
> *I know you would never murder anyone or do anyone harm on purpose. And what's the saying, "No good deed goes unpunished?" Knowing you, you were trying to help someone - Candy probably. Maybe saving her from another beating from that dumb-ass Tom.*
> *I pray you're going to be all right. I'm going to try to help you. You'll know how when you see me (if you see me!). And if you get to read this note, then I was probably successful (Hooray for me!).*
> *And don't fret, because my daddy has a lot of friends in high places, and as you know, I'm Daddy's little girl, so he always gets me what I want.*
> *So be brave. You always are, my love. It'll all turn out all right. I promise I will always be there for you, even after what you told me last night.*
> *Loving friends (I hope) forever,*
> *Kaitlin*
> *P.S. There's food in a bag in the back seat, and a flashlight and baseball bat in the trunk.*
> *P.P.S. I just filled up the tank, too! I'm so thoughtful!*

A short chuckle escapes my lips. But then it hits me. Like a tornado hitting a house and ripping the roof off and sucking out all the furniture and clothes and everything else, it hits me, and without warning, I break down. I stumble to the bunk as tears fill my eyes. I sit down and put my head in my hands.

I can't stand it when I see men cry. It's just not natural. But I can't help it. I just can't. The tears gush out and down my cheeks and drip onto the cold concrete floor. How can it be so hard? How can it be so cruel? How can things get so twisted and why won't they let you go? Why does it all hurt *so damn much?*

And it's not just the pain that sticks in your head and your heart, but as a total contradiction in logic, it's the holes that get blown through you too. I feel like someone just blew a hole in my heart the size of the Grand Canyon, and all my hopes and dreams are gushing out of that hole onto this concrete floor—leaving me totally empty, totally barren, totally alone.

You don't want to go on. You'd rather just sit there and never move again because you know that anything you do will eventually make something happen that will just hurt even more.

But you have to. Time doesn't stop. You have to go on or something else will happen that'll just make it worse. And the only way to keep going is to suck it up somehow, harden your heart with the same concrete you use to patch the holes with, pick up your foot, and take another step. Probably right into another trap—another disappointment that blows another hole in you—but forward at least. Maybe the best you can hope for is that all the concrete you use to patch the holes and harden your heart will make you harder, tougher, stronger. What doesn't kill me makes me stronger, right? *Right?*

After a good five minutes of blubbering and feeling sorry for myself, I get up and walk out of the jail cell, out the front door, and into the thick night air. "Fuck you, you whiny-ass cry baby," I find myself saying. "Sunny and Candy need you. Shut the fuck up and do your job!"

I walk down the block, staying close to the store windows trying to stay out of the light and at the same time not look too awkward and obvious either. About halfway to the corner, I see the door to *Dee-Dee's All-Night Corner Cafe* open and two men come out. I duck behind a big blue mailbox, the diner just a hundred feet away. One of the men is wearing a cop uniform.

I look out across the street and see around the corner the front half of a sheriff's car, right under a street light. "So it's all set," the cop says in a voice I'm now all too familiar with. It's Andy Y. "It's still on judge. It's going down at two-thirty at The Hole. You got the money on you, right?"

There's a pause and then JM replies, his words contradicting his deep, confident voice, "I don't know, there Andy. This . . . I . . ."

"Now, judge. If you're worried about that SOB Sticker, forget it. We're framin' him good, with his prints on the murder weapon and a bag of drugs. All we gotta say is that he and Tom were fightin' over who was gonna be the kingpin 'round here, so he killed him.

"Everybody always believes the police, you know. It's perfect, judge, just perfect. We get him for murder and drugs, so that helps cover our tracks for the last year or so and puts everyone at ease that we found the culprit. It makes us look like heroes, and he's on death row before you know it."

"But what about witnesses?" the judge asks. "That girl Candy and her daughter?"

"We don't know yet . . . can't tell for sure. There's no tellin' what Tom might have told Candy. You know how he liked to brag when he was stoned. Plus, she might be the only one who would testify that Sticker killed him in self defense. Best we take care of her. Can't risk it. Just can't risk it."

The judge puts his hands in his pants pockets, looks down and shuffles his feet.

Andy Y continues, "We tried to get Sticker to tell us where they ran off to, but he clammed up. We told him he'd be free once we got Candy and even told him we'd throw in ten G's so he could take care of the little girl, so long as they left the county. But the son of a bitch said no. But Jack's in the station right now makin' calls to track the girls down. We'll find 'em all right, and it won't take long. There's no way we're gonna let either of them stand in the way of our fortune, now or ever—if you get my drift."

There's a pause. The judge sniffs loudly and says, "I'm not an idiot."

"And," Andy Y continues, "this is the last time we'll need you anyway. Once we get all the stuff tonight from our friends to set up the lab, we won't need you or your money any more."

"Yeah, that lab. What's the name of that new drug you're gonna be making?"

"Meth, judge. Methamphetamine. It's the new thing, you know. We went through this all before, remember? It's all the rage up in New York, Chicago, and DC. It makes weed seem like soda pop and it's ten times as addictive. We'll be the only lab down here anywhere—anywhere in five fuckin' states! All you gotta do is bankroll us getting started, and you'll make ten percent for the rest of your life. We're talkin' millions, judge. Millions! This is as big as it gets. It's between just you, me, and Jackson now.

"And we would never rat on you judge, you know that. You're our man, and we know that if anything ever happens, you can keep us out of the pen. So it's win-win for everyone."

"Yeah. I know, I know. But there's the election coming . . ."

"Oh screw the election judge. You'll be set for life. You'll be able to go fishin' and huntin' every damn day. And that Sticker—he's behind bars already and ain't never gettin' out. Nobody likes him anyway. Hell, he didn't even have anyone to call. You think a jury's gonna believe some hermit who lives in a trailer and's got nobody?"

"Yeah, yeah. It's not really that."

"You afraid of what's gonna happen to the girl and her daughter? Gettin' mushy on me judge?"

"Shut your mouth. It's just that . . ."

"Listen. We're gonna find the bitch and her daughter soon, probably tonight. We have the knife Sticker used to kill Tom with his fingerprints all over it and it's already under lock and key. We'll just use the same kind of knife on the girls, so the knife marks will match. We'll bury 'em behind Sticker's trailer. Some huntin' dogs'll nose 'em up soon enough.

"It's perfect, judge. Just perfect. You'll be takin' home half a mill a year for life, judge. All tax free. All for doing absolutely nothin'."

There's another pause. Oh my God. Oh my God. This can't be happening. I feel a bead of sweat roll down my forehead. The two of them stand there on the corner, looking nonchalant, like they're talking about the high school football team or somethin'.

"Okay, Andy. Okay. But this is it. This is the last twenty-five G's you're gonna get." the judge sounds more confident now.

"That's fine, judge."

"And you're sure you can take care of the girls?"

"Absolutely. They can run, but they can't hide. Jack's a master at findin' people."

"All right. Just one more thing."

"You name it judge."

"I want to be there for the drop tonight. I want to see all the equipment and chemicals and sheets telling how to make it." He unbuttons his suit, flashes Andy Y an envelope, and quickly rebuttons his suit. "So I'll be bringing this with me."

"Of course. Of course. Sounds perfect, JM. You know how to get there?"

"Yeah."

"That'll work out just right. Drive the van. That way, me and Jack can ride in the cruiser. Always good to keep up the image."

"Right."

"Oh, and judge. We're getting our usual shipment of blow tonight too. Me and Jack got that covered. So we'll give you a bag as a token of our appreciation for all your help getting us started."

"Yeah. Okay."

"So be ready to party, JM, 'cuz our ship just came in!"

The judge grunts and walks around the corner and out of sight. Andy Y gets in the cop car and lights a cigarette. He sits there a minute, then finally starts the car, pulls out onto Main Street, and turns towards me. The headlights swing across the mailbox and sidewalk below my feet. I stay still and watch as he slows down and stops in front of the police station. I'm hoping that he just rolls on by, but he doesn't. The blinds! I think. He must see that the blinds are drawn!

He parks in front of the station and gets out of the car. He pauses as he puts his hand on the front door knob as if he's still deciding whether to go in or not, takes one last drag on his cigarette, and flicks it away. He opens the door and disappears inside.

That's all I need to see. I take off around the corner and run as fast as I can to Elm Street, then down the block until I find the red Mustang. The door isn't locked and I put the key Kaitlin gave me into the ignition, the silver locket dangling off the chain. My nostrils fill with her scent.

I swing around and head out of town driving as fast as I can without squealing the tires, get to the highway and put the pedal to the floor. I figure it's gonna take a few minutes for Andy Y to wake up Jackson and discover I'm gone. I'm hoping it gives me enough time to get far enough ahead of them.

With all the blood on the carpet and the TV shattered, it wouldn't take a genius to figure that Candy or Sunny might have needed to go to a hospital, and the closest ones are Walterboro and Beaufort. That's not many to have to check, so I probably don't have much time to get them out of harms way.

My stomach growls. I reach back and grope around and find the shopping bag with sandwiches, pretzels, and celery sticks. There's a bottle of water on the floor. I grab a sandwich and start eating as I speed down the road.

I try to come up with a plan. How am I going to clear my name and protect Candy and Sunny? I toss around all sorts of ideas, but not one of them makes much sense. The only sure-fired way to stay out of jail, and the electric chair, is to run. Or to prove that Andy Y, Jackson, and the judge are running drugs, and Tom was part of it and drugged Sunny.

But how? By the time I find and convince another cop to come with me to watch the drop, it'll be over and done. They'd probably put me behind bars before I get to explain anyway. All I know is I have to get

Candy and Sunny to a safe place. Then I'll just take it one step at a time, try to watch the signs, and see what happens.

I turn the radio on to try and stop thinking. It's just past 12:30 a.m. and Tom Petty & the Heartbreakers are singing. . .

. . . it don't really matter to me baby,
You believe what you want to believe.
You see you don't have to live like a refugee.

Somewhere, somehow, somebody
Must have kicked you around some.
Who knows why you wanna lay there
And revel in your abandon.

It don't make no difference to me baby,
Everybody's got to fight to be free.
You see you don't have to live like a refugee . . .

Somewhere, somehow, somebody
Must have kicked you around some.
Who knows, maybe you were kidnapped,
Tied up, taken away and held for ransom.

It don't make no difference to me,
Everybody's got to fight to be free.
You see you don't have to live like a refugee.
I said you don't have to live like a refugee . . .

Yeah, I think. Easy for you to say. Screw you, Tom Petty. I turn the radio off.

Watch the signs and see what happens. Sounds too simple. I try to think of something more sophisticated, more complicated, more cool to do. Something I could point to later as an epiphany, a stroke of genius, a realization only I could have thought of.

But . . .

But the smell of Kaitlin's perfume distracts me and I can't stop feeling the steering wheel she holds when she drives and I can't stop myself from remembering her just minutes ago in the jail and how she put herself on the line for me and truly came to my rescue. I can't help myself from thinking about how much I yearn for her and how I always will—since we first discovered each other at her father's newspaper, I've loved her.

She was really not much more than a child when we first met, and her bob haircut made her look even younger than her seventeen years and she looked so darn cute, and on the way to being beautiful, I found it hard not to stare. And most the time, I didn't stop myself.

I didn't stare just because she was such a beautiful blossoming young woman and as beautiful as any model in a fashion magazine. I stared because she was, and still is, a work of art. A wonder of nature that nature could form such a wonder—proportioned, symmetric, refined. That something so sublime could be created out of nothing but water and dust.

Across the room, across from me she sat at her desk in profile to me, with her smallish, perky nose, slender brunette eyebrows, roundish face with high cheekbones. She would hunt and peck at the typewriter and mumble to herself and laugh at herself when she made mistakes. She'd glance my way every now and then and catch me staring; and she wasn't angry or uncomfortable when she did, but treated it more like a game of "catch you if I can." And when she did, she would flash an embarrassed, but flirty, smile and quickly turn back to her work.

Then I started borrowing her stapler and tape and paper clips and she full-well knew that I had all of those myself and was just coming over to be closer to her and talk to her and breathe her sweet magnolianess. I flirted with her fearlessly, mostly because I knew there was no chance of us ever getting together. And because I wasn't trying to impress her, but just trying to have some fun, she saw me for who I really am, or really, who I hope I am.

That was so different from all the boys who were starting to swarm around her and bribe her with flowers and gifts and dates to the movies. She preferred me and my cocky, 'I don't give a darn let's just have fun' playfulness.

If she was older or I was younger and didn't have my *that*, there might have been a chance of a we. But then I probably would have been just another one of those average guys who gawked at her. But not then. Not that summer, seven years ago. We even started bumping into each other at the Mini-Mart or Dairy-Barn, all by coincidence, of course. And we'd sit in a booth and drink a milk shake or eat a sundae and I'd tease her and she'd tease me back and all the while we both weren't teasing at all but very much wanting it to be serious. She would laugh at my bad jokes and even ask for more and it seemed like we could laugh at just about anything—the guy behind the counter's nerdy uniform or the look on the five-year-old's face as the cherry on top of his sundae rolled down his ice cream right into his lap or how the menu called mac and cheese a vegetable. Oh, how we'd laugh. And since I couldn't take her anywhere for real, I would talk to her about places she liked and dreamed about and would get her thinking about all her favorite things to the point that they were almost better than for real. Sometimes she would take me with her on her imaginary vacations to the mountains or beach and we would feel the cool mountain air near a swift running stream, or build sand castles and then watch them wash away with the tide. We would taste the gourmet dinner we were eating at the finest restaurant on the boardwalk and sit on a bench with my arm around her shoulder and her hand on my thigh while gazing at the moon as it came up over the ocean. We would have a time. Yes, we would imagine a time. And yet, when we were together, there was no such thing as time.

People started talking about how unnatural it was to see a man my age carrying on with a girl almost half my age and how I was almost old enough to be her daddy and blah, blah, blah—all the old clichés. I thought at the time, well, maybe it would take a man so old and wise to truly appreciate such a treasure. And maybe that's true.

But her pa didn't see it that way and he didn't like the rumors and he most certainly did appreciate his creation, and after all, he had a newspaper to run and an image to uphold. So he called me into his office one morning and told me he didn't need me no more. No excuses. He didn't say he was downsizing or couldn't afford paying me. We both knew what was going on. He just said, "Sam, I won't be needing you any longer. You can work another week, and then I'd like you to clear out."

Blunt, yes. Cowardly, no. If I had a daughter, I'd do the same thing. And he didn't have to say it because I knew what he meant—that being—"and stay away from my daughter!"

But that didn't change what I think about her. I've surrendered to the fact that she is the pure, innocent, embodiment of the grand order. For if a beautiful woman isn't the crowning glory of the universe, what is?

I know she's dated other guys and talked to them and laughed with them and kissed them and let them stroke her hair and kiss her earlobes and whisper sweet nothings that they hoped were sweet somethings to try and convince her that they were the one for her. I also know that she has stopped them—every one of them—because she knew that each of them wasn't the one and if she couldn't have the one, she, in her little girl, dolphin lips, idealistic patient stubbornness, didn't need them. And since she didn't need them, she didn't want them.

It wouldn't be until her bubble of hope was burst by the one she had been hoping for that she finally realized that it's not going to happen and all her hoping and praying and longing couldn't change it. Then she could pick herself up and leave those dreams drying on the floor, go on, and live a life that might not be perfect, but could be tolerable and even good. But never great. And that's what I did to her yesterday evening while sitting in front of my trailer on the lawn chairs under the overhang with the flypaper hanging there above us that had the one dead fly on it.

Some would say that those kinds of unfortunate things happen to everyone and living the life of your dreams doesn't happen for nobody. But they say that because those kinds of unfortunate things happened to them, and they have to console themselves that they are just like everyone else who are just like them.

But good things do happen to some people and some people actually do live wonderful lives—just like some people live horrible lives. It's simply a matter of probability. You see, most people live okay, tolerable lives. But on the two ends of the spectrum are those less fortunate and those more fortunate. Just like a population bell-curve: There's short people and tall people, but most people are average. There's dumb people and smart people, but most people are average. There's the unfortunate and then there's the fortunate, and most are somewhere in the middle. And sooner or later, if you pay attention, you realize how fortunate or unfortunate you are—you figure out what part of the 'fortunation bell-curve' you're on. It isn't a Wheel of Fortune, you see, but a Curve of Fortune. And your position on that curve is pretty much set.

Sure, you can change your position on the curve some if you try real hard—like by using Stickerdynamics and making a superhuman effort. But can you make yourself two inches taller? Can you increase your IQ 30 percent? Can you go from a scorned loner to an adored celebrity? Maybe. But most the time, I doubt it.

I know I possess inside of me everything a person needs to have a wonderful life. All the ingredients are there. There's one problem though: I'm on the wrong part of the curve. I could have had that wonderful life with Kaitlin where we each would have lived our dream life. It wouldn't have matter if we were rich or poor or lived in a mansion or double-wide or we had superstar kids or average kids or even below average kids because the life we would have been living would have been the fulfillment of each of our dreams because that dream was simply to be with each other and become part of each other. And each night, when we crawled into bed and nestled up close to each other like two spoons, you couldn't tell if you were rich or poor anyway because you couldn't tell what was there or wasn't there because it was too dark to see in your bedroom at night and all you could do is hear the other making pillow talk and feel the other's thighs against the back of your legs and you try to find a comfortable way to put your arm so it doesn't fall asleep while you're holding the other. You smell dinner in the other's hair and maybe fall asleep holding them in your arms or move to the other side of the bed before falling asleep but knowing that the other is right next to you, sleeping through the night, feeling their warm body and knowing their heart is only a foot away from yours. And each night you grow together more, like vines intertwining up a trellis and getting so tangled up in each other it's hard to tell where one ends and the other begins.

It's natural that it happens. It happens because of a thing called resonance. Like one vibrating tuning fork causing another one to vibrate too, even though it was never struck with the hammer. Like all the women in the office eventually getting on the same cycle. You live together, close by each other, eating and sleeping together, and you start vibrating together. Your hearts start beating together. They start beating as one. And that's the way it's supposed to be.

I don't care if most couples these days have problems and split. That doesn't matter because even after everything I've gone through, I still, God help me, believe that that kind of life is possible. It should be possible, not just for someone else, but for me, too, because if you look at my life and how I treat others and because it's supposed to be a law that what goes around comes around, I should be living a wonderful life with the woman of my dreams. Even though I may be a little rough around the edges, I still have good intentions and generally do the right thing. So where's the karma, huh? Where is the justice?

But just like Candy not being able to find something she wants because there's nothing inside her she wants because it was all shown to her to be not good enough, I'm also suffering from what someone made me believe: that I never did anything well enough so I have to do it over. Instead of having a child, which is me made over, I have to *do* everything over. And having a child is what really scares me because what if I don't do *that* right? What if I do to them what I had done to me? Then someone else, some innocent soul, suffers.

I've made plenty sure to ruin good things that come my way and it's been that way ever since I was a kid. Even when something amazing is handed to me on a silver platter, I find a way to mess it up. I remember when I was just ten-years-old, there was this cute girl in my class, Diane Harper, who lived down the street and who thought I was the cutest thing she ever saw. She lusted for me in her little ten-year-old way, and wanted to kiss me. So she got some of the boys in the neighborhood (who thought *she* was the cutest thing *they* ever saw) to wrestle me down so she could give me a kiss.

So I'm on the ground squirming to get loose with four guys holding me down, and here comes Diane—her face floating down from the sky like a little angel's, right toward my lips. It would have been my first kiss, from the cutest girl in school, and I didn't even have to try and get it. In fact, it was being forced on me! Talk about good fortune! But what did I do? I ruined it of course. I spit in her face. Literally, spit in her face.

I used to think I did that because I felt trapped like a cat in a corner and was doing the natural thing fighting back. But now I know different. I did it because she was giving me exactly what I wanted. You see, I figure that how you treat others is the same way you treat yourself. If you spit in someone's face when they give you what you want, then you spit in your own face when you give yourself what you want. If you want a pretty girl, and things start going well, you're gonna screw it up. If you want a lot of money or a fast car or a nice family or simply some peace and quiet, and you actually get it, then you're gonna find a way to lose that too.

Those guardians, they were so big and smart and you were so little and unsmart, so you respected them and believed them. So if everything you did growing up wasn't good enough, how can you respect yourself? And when you don't respect yourself, you don't trust yourself. You may love yourself until the cows come home, but if you don't respect and trust yourself, you ain't got nothin'.

Love is easy. Love is blood and family: no thought needed there. Love is lust: no thought needed there, either. But respect is harder and deeper than love. Respect takes more than just some knee-jerk instinct. And when you respect someone, you can finally get to the deepest— which is trust. And with trust, comes gratitude.

Those who have good lives are the one's who respect and trust themselves enough to allow someone to trust them. They can accept it when something good comes out of the sky, like an angel, and not spit in her face. Instead, he'll let that angel kiss him, and even wrap his arms around her and tell himself he's a good little boy for allowing that angel into his live. That's what brings success. That's what *is* success.

But what happened to me? I got nailed in the nuts. Not as I was squirming on the ground trying to avoid Diane Harper, but ten years later when I was getting more than a kiss. Then I found a surgeon to make it even worse. Funny how I'm so good at doing that sort of thing. Twenty years later, it still hurts.

All because of a mummy and a ghost who wouldn't stop her.

Yes, I blame them. Even though I said it wasn't her fault or her fault either, I still blame them for stamping into my psyche the pattern, as if from a dye. A pattern of 'accidents' and 'trying' too hard to fix them. I blame them because somehow they should have known better than to bolster their egos by belittling mine and making me believe *that* is what I deserve. You see, it's simple:

They should have tried harder.

And Kaitlin makes it even harder to face because when I see her I think of how wonderful she is and how wonderful my life could have been had it not been for my *that* and I end up hating myself more and hating the people who took their pain and passed it along—like a baton it went—from him to her to her to me. And now, maybe, from me to Kaitlin.

I realize that yesterday evening was the first time Kaitlin had experienced that kind of pain—a *that*—shortly after I had told her about my *that*. I saw it in her eyes as she drove out of the driveway: the confused emptiness from having to deal with something unfathomable. Her bubble was burst. Her assumed, patient, loyal joy for what was to come ripped away. Now she has to invent a whole new way of looking at life and the future. And it will be a shaky way—unstable because in the back of her mind, she will wonder if that perspective will also someday be torn apart.

That instability will make her vulnerable to settling for something and someone less than her dream. Some other fella who'll probably be a descent guy (since her daddy was) will woo her and marry her and take her away on their honeymoon. She'll fight and maybe succeed a little pushing me out of her mind wishing it was me above her doing what she had been holding out for me to do for so long. She'll learn how to turn her dream into an excuse and resign herself to a life that may be good, but never great. That ugly R word again.

And the thought crosses my mind that I could resign too. I could give up fighting city hall and injustice and stop trying to be the hero nobody wanted in the first place. I could go back to my trailer, get the rest of my money, and take off in Kaitlin's car—maybe to Oklahoma (I hear it sucks, but at least it's flat)—and change my name and grow a beard and start all over. I'd just mix up a fresh batch of concrete and plug the newest set of holes that were just blown through me and harden my heart one more time. After all, everyone has to live with the Big R sometimes, in some sort of way, don't they?

It dawns on me that I can go anywhere, fly anywhere I want—like a bird who's still free. I could go back to my trailer and get the rest of my money and run. I could even call the cops and tell them where Candy is and meet them somewhere in public and get Sunny and take their money and bolt. I can do anything I want. After all, this is Candy's ordeal, not mine. If she was running with Tom, then she'd be getting what she deserves. If she wasn't, well, at least Sunny would be safe and nobody would get killed. As for me and Candy, I was just a guy she put up with all these years. No blood between us—no holy bond. I could call her at the hospital and tell her I'm running and give her the head's up so she and Sunny could run from the cops too. Then it would be up to her, not me.

The choices are here. There are no rules, no guidelines. I could do it. I could. And who in the world would care but just a few people? In the end, would it matter to the universe and the stars and the black of night if me, Sticker Barlow, just runs away?

No. No it wouldn't.

But you know what? I don't care. I don't care if there's no blood between us or no holy bond or nothin'. I don't care if Candy was runnin' with Tom or not. I just don't care. None of that matters. I'm not going to run. I'm not. And you know why?

I'll tell you . . .

I'm not going to run for one simple reason: I'm the anchorman. I'm taking my place—*embracing* my place—on that fucking Curve of Fortune and hoping that even though I always seem to get nailed, I can at least make it so somebody else doesn't. After all, Christ got nailed too. Not in his nuts like me, but through his hands and feet. He did it to stop a world of batons from being passed along. I'm doing it now to stop one or two. So I'm holding onto that baton as tight as I can and I ain't passing it on to nobody, no way. You see, it's simple:

I'm trying harder.

I get to the hospital and take the stairs, and half way up the first flight, it hits me: What if Candy and Sunny aren't here? What if *they* left *you*? Maybe Andy Y or Jackson has already called the Beaufort sheriff and he's already gotten to Candy and *she's* cut a deal with *them!* Never thought of that, did you? Can you really count on Candy? Wouldn't she be safe, and be able to keep Sunny safe, if she played a game of her own? She could just agree with them that I did it—that I was dealing drugs with Tom and killed him on purpose. Then I would be history and she and Sunny could live happily ever after. It wouldn't be a bad move on her part. Couldn't really blame her. So what will you do if she's done it? What will you do *then*, you pontificating ass?

I stand still in front of the door to the hospital room, unable to move. Suddenly I'm light-headed with the harsh realization that knowing Candy and how our relationship has been, it's not just possible she'd turn on me, but likely. I could just hear her at my sentencing: "But you threw me in the swimming pool, you ass-hole! I never forgot it, and I'll never forgive you! So go and rot in jail for the rest of your life! You're just like the rest of 'em—lyin', cheatin', lazy slobs!"

Yeah, that's Candy, all right. But . . .

Maybe deep down she's all right. I've always kinda felt that way, I reckon. Why would I put up with her if I didn't? Her rough edges are just side-effects of her childhood—just like me. And besides, we had something special, didn't we? That kiss under the trees in the moonlight on the road leading to the swamp. We turned it around, didn't we? We finally understand each other, don't we? We're two of a kind, right?

Right?

They say that years of trust can be destroyed with just one act of deceit. But can years of buttin' heads be forgiven with just one kiss? Oh God, what should I do? Oh God, what's behind this door?

Maybe the Beaufort sheriff is in there right now waiting for me. Maybe this is the last thing I'll do as a free man. Maybe Oklahoma wouldn't be so bad after all. Maybe I should run now before anyone else has a chance to hurt me.

Not so sure of all your convictions when you're right in the middle of it, now are you, you son of a bitch? What the hell should I do?

I inhale deeply. My right hand goes up and presses against the door. It pushes the door open, and . . .

I see Candy slumped over in a chair besides the bed where Sunny lays in a hospital gown, her eyes closed. I pause a second, step into the room, and let the door close behind me.

I shake her gently. Her eyes flutter open. "What happened to you?" she gasps. "Are you hurt? Where have you been?"

"Later. We gotta get out of here.'

"But Sunny's still asleep. The doctor can't tell when she'll wake up. I . . . I . . ." she buries her head in my chest and starts to cry.

"Okay. Okay, Candy, I know. But we've got to go—*now!*"

"No! I don't care. I can't leave her."

"No. We *all* have to get out of here. They're coming for both of you, *all* of us."

"What? What are you talking about?"

"The police. The sheriffs—Jackson, Andy Y, and the judge. They're all in on it with Tom. I'll explain in the car. We've gotta go *now!*"

"But she's still sick."

"I know. I know. But she'll only have a chance to pull through if we get out now. If not, we're all gonna die." She looks up at me and starts to freeze. I get busy before she freezes solid.

"Here, help me. Let's see. We've gotta do this somehow. We need more IV stuff. Have you noticed where they keep it?" She points to a cabinet besides the bedside table. I open it.

"Here," I take out a half dozen of the plastic IV bags and hand them to her. "You got a bag somewhere? Like a shopping bag?" We scan the room.

"Here." She takes the plastic bag that's lining the trashcan near the window, pulls it up and dumps a few old cups and napkins into the empty can. We put the IV bags and a couple extra tubes and needles into the bag along with Sunny's shorts and shirt.

"Where's the nurse?" I ask.

"I don't know."

"Go look." She goes out into the hallway as I disconnect the tube from the needle going into Sunny's arm and turn off the drip. I take the bag and tube and put them in the plastic bag. Candy returns and says, "She's down the hall in another room."

"Good. Let's go."

I tell her to carry the bag and lead the way. I pick Sunny up under her shoulders and knees and we go out the room and down the stairs. We get to the lobby, pause to make sure no one is watching, and walk out the door and make it to the car. I lay Sunny down in the back seat. Candy and I climb in, and we drive out of the parking lot. After a couple of blocks, I pull over, get out, and me and Candy work to suspend the IV bag off the clothes hook above the back seat window and hook up the IV to Sunny. Candy sits in the back seat and puts Sunny's head on her lap under Kaitlin's blanket. I pull the car back onto the street.

Everything's going smooth. Almost too smooth. I feel like we're on a roll and that this smooth passage might be an omen for good things to come. But not so much in the back of my mind, in fact, right smack dab in the front row of it, I'm scared. I'm scared that because it's going so well, it's gonna turn bad. Just like everything else in my life.

"You just can't stand prosperity, can you?" his whiny voice whispers in my head.

"Shut up," I mumble

"What?" Candy asks.

"Nothin'."

I think I should do something to keep the good fortune coming—maybe knock on wood, cross my fingers, throw salt over my shoulder, say a prayer, or simply ask for guidance. I should hope and pray for something, someone, to watch over us. Yeah, I should.

But something . . . *"Can't stand . . ."* snaps . . . *"prosperity . . ."* in my head . . . *"can you?"* and I'm suddenly totally and mercilessly pissed.

"Oh, yeah?" I hiss as I pound on the steering wheel with both hands. "Damn you! Damn you, and fuck that!"

Out of the corner of my eye in the rear view mirror I see Candy lift her head in surprise. "Can't stand prosperity?" I growl. "We're gonna see about that! You hear me? WE'RE GONNA GODDAMN SEE ABOUT *THAT!*"

I push the gas pedal down hard. The acceleration pushes us back in our seats as we tear down a city street. "Not here," I say in quiet resolve. "Not tonight. Not on my watch. *Not on my damn watch!*"

The wind blows into my half-open window. It smells like honeysuckle. "Oh jeez," I mumble.

Chapter Fifteen

After several blocks, I calm down. But then an overwhelming feeling of discomfort hits me. Something starts gnawing at me. I know we should be speeding off somewhere to make something happen, but I just can't do it right now. I turn onto a side street and pull over next to the curb. I hit the lights and shut off the engine.

"What are you doing?" Candy asks.

"I don't know. I have to think. I need some time to think."

We sit there for a few minutes as I try to get my mind in gear. Nothing comes.

Then out of the silence, Candy says softly, "This is how it happened."

"What? How what happened?" I ask.

"This is how he died."

"What? How who died?"

There's a long silence. Then she says, "My . . . my dad. It's how he died too."

"Your dad? He died of a stroke."

"No . . . no, he didn't. We just told people that. He died of an overdose."

Oh God, I think. "An overdose?"

"Yeah. They did an autopsy and found a bunch of pills in him. He took a handful of pills. *Tylenol*, of all things. That's what killed him."

It's like a fist just punched me in the gut. "Oh, Candy," I say as I hear her start to sob. "Candy . . . I'm sorry. I'm so sorry."

"He knew what he was doing," she says between sniffles. "The bastard knew what he was doing."

I don't say nothin'. I turn my head and look at her over the front seat. She's looking through her tears down at Sunny. I know what she's thinking.

"Maybe it was an accident. Maybe he was drinking and made a mistake."

"No mistake. He knew."

What can I say? How can I make this right? "Candy . . ."

"He couldn't stand it anymore," she sniffles. "He couldn't stand . . . me . . . any . . ."

"That's not true."

"Yes. . . Yes, it is."

"No it's not. I could tell the way he looked at you—he loved you."

"No, he didn't," she whimpers dejectedly.

"Yes, he did. He just wasn't strong enough . . . strong enough to show you. Strong enough to tell you."

"But why? Why would he do *that?*" She pounds the door with her fist. "Why would he . . . he . . . *leave me?*"

"He was just a little weak. He probably had a tough life too."

Tears are streaming down her cheeks. A few of them fall onto Sunny's face below her. She takes her hand and wipes them away.

"It's like a curse," she says softly. "The men in my family—it's a curse."

"What do you mean?"

"A curse. They can't take it. Neither could my grandfather."

"Your grandfather? I never heard you talk about him."

"I never met him. He killed himself too. Ruby says he drank himself to death by the time he was thirty."

My guts are all knotted up. Oh, Candy. I look out the window at the cars parked on the curb on the other side of the street. Maybe the three of us should just take off for Oklahoma. Maybe we will.

Finally, I say, "Your dad, he was just confused."

"No, he wasn't," her voice still spiteful. "I told you, he knew what he was doing when he took all those pills."

"I don't mean confused in that way. He was just confused. Confused about life. Confused about *his* life. When someone gets like that, Candy, they get scared. Sometimes so scared that all they can think about is how to end the confusion and all the suffering that goes with it."

She doesn't say anything for a while. We just sit there in the car, me looking out the window and her looking down at Sunny. Then she says, "You think? You think that's what it was?"

"Yeah. Of course. He was confused, Candy. Maybe about how his dad died so young. Maybe about how he didn't know how to show you he cared. Maybe he just couldn't figure it out. That doesn't mean he didn't love you."

"Oh, Sam," she whimpers and then bursts into tears. "He wasn't perfect, but do you think he really loved me?"

"Yes, Candy, I do. I know he loved you. I know he did."

How could he not? Baby-girl Candace.

Tears come to my eyes and I hear Candy weep louder. But her tears are no longer tears of spite, but tears of relief. ". . . just confused," she says softly. I turn and see her gently brushing Sunny's hair, with a glint of pride in her eyes and a tight, trembling smile on her lips. It's as if now that she understands, she knows she'll be able to show it to Sunny.

". . . just confused," Candy whispers, almost like a lullaby.

A minute goes by. I start the car and put it in gear. I pull out into the street and drive on side streets as long as I can until we get to the edge of town. I see a bank's time and temperature sign a block away and take a one-lane alley to pull up next to the bank. Time: 1:43 Temperature: 82°. I glance over my shoulder and see that Candy's head is down and she's sleeping; Sunny's head cradled softly in Kaitlin's blanket on her lap.

Now I can think. My biggest worry is that Andy Y will wake up Jackson and discover I'm gone. If they do, which I know they will, what would be the sensible thing to do next? If I was them, what would I do?

I'd think that I'd be either running away, or trying to protect Candy and Sunny. They know a son of a bitch like me wouldn't run, so that leaves the other option. If Candy or Sunny weren't hurt in any way, then we could be running away somewhere, and where that would be would be anybody's guess. So the only chance they have of finding us tonight would be to assume somebody got hurt and needed a hospital.

Time: 1:44 Temperature: 82 °.

The drug drop tonight is at 2:30. That's 45 minutes from now. It takes 45 minutes to get from the police station to the hospital in Beaufort. If they're going to get to the drop on time, they would have had to have been here by now. What's more important to them, finding us, or getting the drugs? Probably the drugs. But for all I know, they may have just called the hospital, discovered that Candy and Sunny weren't there, and left for the drop.

The only way out of Beaufort going north towards River-hole and home is Highway 21 to 17—the way I came and the way they would come. If we were to take Route 170 southwest towards Hardeeville and Savannah, we could circle back north, but we wouldn't be able to make it to the drop in time. But, if we go back up 21, we'd get to the drop in time and I'd be able to spy and see if I could turn the tables on 'em. If nothing presents itself, then me and Candy and Sunny will run. We'll go see Kaitlin at the Holiday Inn, get some money, and split for points north, I reckon. We'll have enough to last a while. On the other hand, if we run now, we may be safer for a while, but we'd be living on the run and might never find a way to get out of this mess. The only chance to do something or learn something that could free us all, will be tonight— starting now.

Time: 1:46   Temperature: 82 °.

I open the bag Kaitlin packed for me, and grab a pretzel-stick. I'm hungry as hell. I pull the car out on onto Highway 21 and turn north. I just hope, for my sake and theirs, I'm guessing right.

I put a pretzel in my mouth and suck the salt off it, bite it in half, and crunch it into smaller chunks. But instead of chewing the chunks up completely, I just swallow them. I feel the chunks make their way down my throat. I try to focus on the road, but I can't help it—my mind starts racing again . . .

As I swallow, I realize that my whole life has been just like eating these pretzels—a bite here and a chunk there; always taking whatever it is only so far and then pushing it down and moving on. Never finishing it off.

Losing a girlfriend or a business deal because you can't go all the way is one thing, but losing your life or the lives of your loved ones is another. I had Tom dead to right twice in our fight. I had turned the advantage to mine, and yet, I let him slip out of it. I couldn't finish him off. It was only a sudden burst of strength that saved the day. And that wasn't even my strength—it was from Sunny or Candy or somewhere else. Something rushed into me when I heard Candy moan and felt Sunny's foot brush against my cheek.

The lit-up reflectors on the side of the highway whiz by me like bullets that have just barely missed their mark. My mind keeps going . . .

If anything could have pushed me to completion, you would think it would be the knife being pushed at my eyes. But I didn't feel the extra strength from worrying about what could happen to me. It came when I worried about what might happen to *them*.

Not me—them. *They* were the catalyst. *They* were the key. Their key into my lock. And when the key fits, as it did back there and as it might for anyone, it will turn all by itself and wonderful and seemingly supernatural things can happen. These things may be super and they may be natural, but they are not beyond this world. They are this world—the way it *can* be. And even if the lock and key doesn't fit forever, it's still worth a turn. And the only way you can ever know if it's the right key for your lock, is by watching what happens: noticing if you can do things you never thought you could and if you want to do things you never thought you'd want to. Since going to completion—where getting unlocked can take you—is something different, if you're not doing something different, you're not getting there.

I round a bend in the highway so fast I almost lose control, and I just miss slamming into a reflector. The white, bright reflectors come shooting at me now, and they whiz by me almost before I can focus on them. Steady, I tell myself. Focus. Stay in the moment. Stay in the present. Stay completely in the present. You've got time.

Time.

By the time I see the reflectors now, they're gone—gone behind me. I can't keep up. I turn my head to look out of the side window to see if I can follow one or two completely as they whiz past, but I can't. Instead, my eye is drawn from the reflectors to the stars I can see through the windshield—other points of light way off in the distance, far, far away. Millions of miles away.

It takes over four years for light from the closest star to get to earth. That's a long time. And since light travels so fast, it's also a long way. But what about the reflectors? They're away from me too, just not as far. The time it takes for light to travel from the reflector to my eyes may not be years, but it's still something. Just a fraction of a second, perhaps, but that's still time. So just as I'm looking at the past when I look at a star, I'm looking at the past when I look at one of those reflectors, or anything else for that matter. Then it takes even more time for the impulses to travel from my retina to my brain and then for my brain to figure out it's a reflector. So everything I see, everything I hear, touch, taste, or smell— it's all the past. As I observe my environment, or even myself, I'm observing something that's already happened. Which means . . .

I already happened!

Oh my God! I've already happened! My mind, my senses, are just catching up, observing something—myself—that has already occurred!

All this stuff you hear about staying in the moment to get the most out of whatever it is you're doing—like driving a car without wrecking— is not exactly true. If you're paying attention to what you're seeing, you're actually paying attention to the past. So how can you be in the present if you're always in the past? It's that time thing again—you can't stop it. It's always coming at you, and yet, it's always behind you. Everything is always in the past.

If everything you're observing in the present is really already in the past, then how can you get to the present? There's only one way: You have to go to the future.

I'm going to make that the Forth Law of Stickerdynamcs: "To be in the present you have to go to the future."

You see, maybe it's best not to just take one step *at* a time. Maybe it's best to take one step *ahead* of time. Maybe I'm supposed to anticipate the moment, and if I do it right, it'll put me in the present . . . and *that's* when the magic happens. But how?

Maybe I'll figure that one out later, because right now I see the flashing lights of a cop car coming towards me in the oncoming lane. "Oh shit," I mutter. I guess they wanted us bad after all.

I'm going about 70, and the cop car must be going 90, so it doesn't take long for it to whiz right by me just four feet to my left on this two-lane highway. I have the high-beams on and it's dark, so I'm sure it's just about impossible for them to tell it's Kaitlin's car that just passed them, let alone that it's me behind the wheel. I look in the rearview mirror and see the car disappear around a bend. Thank God, I think.

Then, about a minute later, I see flashing lights behind me. Damn! Jackson must have noticed it was Kaitlin's car, or maybe he smelled her as we drove by. Whatever and however, they're on to us.

So what do I do now? Pull over and let us all get killed, or go for it? Not much of a choice. Thank goodness Kaitlin likes a fast car. Thank goodness her daddy gets her anything she wants. I put the pedal to the floor.

The highway we're on is fairly straight. I get up to about 90 and see the cop car isn't gaining any longer. But it's still there, about a quarter mile back. I've got three-quarters of a tank of gas. It's almost two in the morning. What are we gonna do, ride like this all night?

I start thinking ahead. I gotta shake them somehow. Turn off into the woods on a dirt road? This car isn't made for off-road since it's so low to the ground, so that won't work. Out race them? Even though this Mustang has a 289 V-8 with a 4-barrel carburetor (Kaitlin told me all about it while we were lying on the blanket), those cop cars are pretty sooped up too.

I know. I'll do the old First One Home Loses. We used to play it in high school coming back from The Hole or the beach. Whoever got home first, lost, you see. So you had to find places to hide on the side of the road to get the other guy to pass you and get ahead. If he noticed you, he'd try and hide on you. If not, he'd get home first and end up losing.

There's a little town of Greenpond coming up here in a couple miles. I know the perfect spot, right behind a billboard before you get to Main Street. We start passing houses on the outskirts of town and the speed limit drops to 45, and then 35. I'm still going 80. The road bends right before Main Street, and I take it going 50. The cop car's lights are gone—they're still far enough behind me to risk it.

There's the billboard. I hit the brakes hard but don't let the car go into a skid. Still, it throws us forward in our seats, causing Candy to wake up.

"Whaaaa. . ." she gasps.

"Hold on. We've got company."

My timing is perfect. We slow down just soon enough to turn into the short little grassy driveway behind the old billboard. I slip it into neutral, cut the lights, and tell Candy, "It's Andy Y and Jackson. They're after us."

As the words are leaving my lips, they drive past us going about 45. There's a building to my left, so I can't see if they've slowed down or just kept on going. I jump out of the car and run towards the road the few steps to see around the building. I can see the one stop light in the middle of town a hundred yards away, and the cop car is stopped right in front of it. They're obeying a stop light? Immediately I know why. Their backup lights go on.

"Shit!" I run back to the car, hop in, and put it in reverse. The tires spin on the grass a little and then catch, and we dart rear-end first into the road as I turn the wheel hard to the left. Our rear end turns towards town as the car gets into the street, and I hear the screech of tires as the cop car goes into a skid backing up right at us. It bangs right into our rear end. Our heads snap back from the impact and hit the back of the seats. I put the car in first, and let out the clutch. The transmission catches and I feel the rear wheels turn, but we go nowhere—the tires just squeal on the pavement. The bumpers are hung-up and now we're locked together with the cop car! I turn the wheel and gun it again. Still, nothing but burnt rubber! Damn!

I glance in the rearview mirror and see the driver's door of the cop car open. Andy Y emerges, his hand on his hip. Candy's leaning all the way over the length of the seat, covering Sunny as much as she can. What am I gonna do? What am I gonna *do*?

I'm gonna have to get out and fight them now, I think, and now is when I'm gonna die.

My left hand goes to the door latch, pulls it, and pushes the door open. My left leg swings up out of the car and my foot lands on the pavement. Somehow, I think, I've got to scramble around the car and jump on Andy Y before he starts shooting. I have no idea how, but I have to try and do *something!*

I turn quickly in the seat to jump out of the car, and as I do, my right hand brushes against the silver locket that's dangling off the keychain. Instantly, a message shoots into me—"Go back . . ."

I pause for just an instant, but there's no time to waste. Jump out and fight, or listen? Jump out and die, or listen?

I listen.

I pull my leg back into the car.

"Go back . . ."

My left hand pulls the door shut as my right hand goes back to the gear shift.

"Go back to break free."

My left leg pushes the clutch down as my right hand pushes the shift all the way to the left and up. I let out the clutch and push the gas pedal down fast and hard. The Mustang jerks backward and slams hard into the back of the cop car causing both our rear ends to jack-knife a foot into the air and crash back down. I can see out of the corner of my eye Andy Y jump back a step.

I jam the stick into first and let out the clutch as I gas it harder than ever. Andy Y lunges for the door handle. The bumpers release with a snap and immediately we lurch forward. Andy Y's hand rips off the door handle and I hear him swear as we pull away.

A shot rings out and a bullet pierces through the back window, through the passenger seat and into the front dash. Candy's still crouched over Sunny, so the bullet misses her.

I get it into second, third, then forth as fast as I've ever done, racing or not. Another bullet shatters the passenger side mirror. We make the bend out of town almost on two wheels, and once on the straightaway again, I put 'er into overdrive. We're going 90 in the blink of an eye.

"What are you *doing?*" Candy gasps. *"What are you doing?"*

"Whatever I can," I reply.

"What's going on?" she cries. "Oh God, *what's going on?*"

I don't say nothin'.

At first I think the cop car got disabled. But after a minute I see it behind us again, it's flashing lights off now, but still keeping pace. Think ahead! Think ahead! What can I do? Candy's sobbing and moaning, but I pay her no mind. I stay focused. I *have* to stay focused. A minute goes by. My mind is searching and thinking of the highway in both directions trying to remember if there's a stretch that would give me a chance to shake 'em or hide on 'em again or run 'em off the road.

Run them off the road! That's it! I'll force them into a game of chicken: running straight at 'em and hoping they turn away at the last second into the ditch. At least that gives us a chance. This Mustang can handle better than the cop car, so if I have to, I'll be the one to turn away at the last second. But even if we hit 'em head on and die, at least we'll be taking those bastards with us.

I hit the brakes hard. When I'm down to 30, I turn the wheel and spin the car around in a 180, skidding and leaving rubber on the road as I do. Those bastards, I think.

"Agghh . . ." Candy screams. "*What are you doing?*"

Nothing's gonna stop me, I think. I'll kill you sons of bitches first.

I hit the gas and get it into fourth gear and move over into the oncoming lane, pointing the hood of this candy-apple red Mustang right between their headlights. The cop car is only a hundred yards away now and it's slowed down, almost to a stop. It hasn't turned away or swerved off the road, and my body instinctively braces for the impact that's just a few seconds away. But then—

I see something poke out the passenger's side window.

What are you thinking, you idiot? They have guns! They already shot at you! "Get down!" I yell. "Get your head down!"

I turn the wheel—more to try and avoid the bullet than their car— and just before the bullet pierces through the windshield and then into the rear seat, Candy ducks. And it saves her life. In another second, we're past them, doing 60. The windshield cracked but not shattered—with a clean hole just below the rearview mirror.

How dumb can I be? I was so consumed with revenge, I completely forgot they'd shoot! You fucking moron! You can't do nothin' right!

Another shot rings out and hits the back tail light. It must be Jackson in the passenger seat shooting. Pretty lucky for being so wasted. I stay crouched down and drive as fast as I can. It's quiet as death in the back seat; Candy's not even whimpering.

Back into Greenpond, through the street light that's now turned to green, out of town, doing 90 again, with the cop car still behind us. "Candy," I call back to her.

I don't hear nothin'.

"Candy! Are you okay?"

Finally, she picks up her head and says weakly, "Wha . . . ?

"Are you okay? *Are you okay?*"

"Uhhhh . . . I . . . I . . . guess so."

"How about Sunny?"

"I . . . I . . . guess so."

We're on a straight-away and we're going 90 and the wind is whistling through the holes in the windshield and back window and the cop car is still behind us and there's sweat rolling down my forehead and Candy's huddled over Sunny who's still passed out on the back seat and Kaitlin's perfume is still itching in my nostrils and every one of my muscles is tight as a drum and every corner of my mind is as twisted as messed-up flypaper.

"Can . . . Candy," I say in a panicked voice. "I'm not sure what to do. *I don't know what to do!*"

I feel a tear well up in my eye and I have to fight it back and I think that my failure now is gonna kill me and Candy and Sunny and how it wasn't supposed to end this way or even be this way to begin with and now it's not just my mother's fault and my grandmother's fault and my great grandfather's fault, but my fault too!

It's my fault too!

"I don't know what to do!" I scream.

No response. There's silence for what seems like a year. I glance back thinking Candy must have fainted, but I can't see nothin'. My thinking is muddled and I see a Y in the road coming up and I don't even know where I am anymore as I slow down and take the turn.

Then finally, I hear her voice, soft with comfort, come out of the darkness of the back seat. "You're good, Sam. I trust you."

Those words—so foreign and unfamiliar—don't register in my brain at first. But they reverberate in my head as if there's an echo . . .

"You're good, Sam. I trust you."

Just a few common words. A few ordinary words strung together into two simple sentences. But those ordinary words in those simple sentences prove to be the most important words of my life.

"You're good, Sam. I trust you."

And those words . . .

Those words go into my ears and into my brain and get sucked down right into the middle of my thirsty soul as if it were a black hole or somethin'. And as that vacuum of my soul, with its immense gravity, its immense need, is sucking up those words and their meaning, it feels like the hard crusty shell of a false weathered skin cracks open and falls away.

And suddenly, I'm free.

"You're good, Sam. I trust you."

I rise up in the seat—my back straightens, my head perks up, my mind settles—the panic gone.

"You're good, Sam. *I trust you,*" she said!

My senses wake up. The air is thick and heavy with the smell of stale beer, rotten eggs, and piss. And out of the corner of my eye I can see the cattails and tall grass whiz by us in the scatter from the headlights. I tighten my grip on the steering wheel. I remember where we are . . .

Then it hits me! That's it! Yeah! That might just work! We've only got a couple miles to go before I'll be able to do it, so I've got to figure out how. Gotta keep them in the right hand lane going just the right speed.

Speed's not the problem. Anything faster than 45 will do. But how to keep them on the right? I can't slow down and force them there, they'd put holes in us like Swiss cheese. How do I keep them on the right? How? *How?*

The pretzels and celery! Maybe they'll think I'm throwing nails or something out the window at them. It's my only thought, my only hope. I grab the bag from the passenger's seat, put it on my lap, and roll down the window. I straddle the centerline so when my left hand is outside the window, it's directly over the middle of the left hand lane. I slow down to 70, then 60, then 50. They've closed the gap and are in the left hand lane now. Easier to get a better shot, I'm sure they're thinking.

"Get down!" I yell back to Candy. "Get down!"

I see them gaining on me fast and then they slow down too. But they're still in the left hand lane! Damn!

Okay. Here goes. I grab a handful of pretzels and toss them out the window. Maybe the salt on the pretzels will sparkle in their headlights and look like nails. Now a few celery sticks—maybe they'll look like railroad spikes or something. I throw another handful of pretzels and celery out the window. A couple shots ring out and a bullet hits the trunk. Another handful out the window . . .

They're still gaining on us—but there! They swerve first left and almost off the road and then right, into the right hand lane. Candy is spread over Sunny and covering her own head with her hands.

The yellow warning sign *Dangerous Curve Ahead, 25 MPH* whizzes by us.

Just a second or two more! We need just a second more!

They're just thirty yards behind us now. Another shot is fired and the bullet zips right past my shoulder and shatters the dashboard, killing the dash lights. Now I can't see how fast we're going!

Play it by feel, Sam. Play it by *feel* . . .

I take my eye off the rearview mirror and look straight ahead and there it is, right in front of me—*Wetman's Curve!* I take my foot off the accelerator and lean into the curve staying in the left hand lane. All I can do is hope there's no oncoming car. Please, God. Just one more time!

Tap the brake. Tap it once.

I feel the G forces push me towards the stick as we bank into the curve just a little too fast. I tap the brake once and tighten my grip on the steering wheel and use all my strength to keep the wheel turned so the car keeps banking into the turn.

Gotta keep the flaps down and hold it into the turn. "Hold it, Steve! You've got to hold it!"

"I can hold it!" he screams. "I can hold it!"

The outside wheels leave the pavement and it feels like we're going over . . .

"Stevie! We've got to hold it!"

"We can hold it, Stick! We can . . . hold . . ."

I put my hand on the passenger seat and push against it as hard as I can to push the side of my body against the door and the G forces, trying like hell to keep us balanced.

"We can hold it! Damn it! *We've got to hold it!"*

The wheel slips a fraction in my hand because of the sweat pouring off them and I squeeze the wheel as tight as I can and don't let go and keep pushing against the seat and looking straight ahead and then I see the road straighten and I feel the flap break free.

The wheels bang down to earth and my head bumps up into the

convertible roof. The moment all four tires are on the pavement, I let the wheel slip through my fingers to return to center and the car straightens and tears headlong into the night.

I can't tell by looking since I'm concentrating on the road and trying to stop shaking, and I can't tell by listening since the wind is rushing through the window and all the bullet holes. But I can tell by feeling it deep in my gut. Or maybe it's just a strong hope that finally comes true, I don't know. But whatever it is, suddenly, I know.

They skid off that wrong-sloped crown on the right side of the road and dump themselves smack-dab into the swamp. Just like a hundred racing teenagers before them. But this time, it matters. I look in the rearview mirror, and there's nothing. I get back in the right hand lane and no longer feel the need to speed. "Thanks, buddy," I mumble under my breath.

Candy picks her head up and turns and looks back. "Oh, God," she says between breaths. "Oh my freakin' God!"

She turns towards me and inches forward in her seat. "What just happened? Did we shake 'em? Are you okay? Oh my God! Are they gone? Are you okay?"

"Just barely," I say as I exhale. "We did it."

"We did. We sure as hell did." She looks back over her shoulder again. "Good . . . good job," she says.

"Yeah," I say, my hands still trembling like a son of a gun. "Not bad. Not bad at all."

After a couple miles, I turn the radio on and catch the end of the top-of-the-hour news. It's 2:07 a.m.

Chapter Sixteen

A few more miles down the road and there on the left are the ruins of the old church. We turn onto the sandy dirt road just before it and pass by the backyard where Martha Chimes rose from the dead and floated down to the river. I wonder how she's doing and if she liked the flowers Kaitlin left her.

I turn off the headlights. It's early, I know, but I don't know when or how the drug runners are coming or if the judge might be here early, so there's no need to risk anything. The second I turn the headlights off, before my eyes can adjust, all I see is black. So I stop the car. But my mind keeps racing, right here, in the black. In the black of night. Like the black when you close your eyes. *That* black. That's the black that's the closest thing to you that will ever be—the closest you're ever going to come to the now, to the present, to reality.

And when you're close to the other and you look into her eyes and see the black in them, then, that too, is the closest you'll ever come to the now in her—the reality in her. All her thoughts, all her hopes and dreams, all her fears, harbored in those two circles of blackness. And when that black and your black linger on each other and touch each other and meld together, like two sides of an Oreo cookie, it's like two partial realities finally come together to form a new completion—a completely new reality. Another can not only unlock you so you become complete unto yourself, but unlocks the universe so it can complete those blacknesses into something new and extraordinary: The light, creamy filling that satisfies the best.

I ask Candy for the water bottle and take a few sips. Now, I can see. I put the car in gear and drive cautiously but quickly on the two white sandy ribbons of tire tracks that melt into the darkness ahead of me. Even though it's dark and there's only a crescent of moon coming up behind the trees, I have a feeling for how far we need to go and I remember there's a hard left turn just before the road gets to the river near the rope swing and pier.

As we drive, every now and then there are other less traveled secondary roads that go off into the trees and swamps that hunters and dirt bikers use. And luckily, there's one just before the turn to the river. I turn onto it and drive up a hundred yards and then swing the car around and pull off into the brush. The car is well hidden and far enough away from the river that Candy and Sunny will be safe. I turn off the car and take the silver locket off the keychain and put it in my pocket—not that I'm superstitious or anything.

I go back to the trunk and survey the damages. Not too bad. The trunk door opens after just one bang of my fist, and I take out the flashlight and baseball bat. I see only a dent where a bullet hit the fender. They don't build 'em like that anymore, I think. But there's a bullet hole in the trunk and the right tail light is shattered.

I go around the side of the car to Candy and she rolls down the window. I say, "I think you're safe here. But just in case, get into the front seat and be ready to high-tail it out of here. When I come back, I'll blink the flashlight four times so you know it's me. If I don't get back here in a couple hours, take off and go find Kaitlin at the Holiday Inn in Charleston. The round one, right before Ashley River on Highway 17. You know which one I'm talkin' about?"

"Yeah."

"She checked in under the name Sarah Wilson. Have the desk clerk ring her and tell her you have your Sunday bonnet on."

"What?"

"Yeah, I know. But you won't forget that. She has money. You'll be able to last a while. If Sunny doesn't wake up by mornin', take her to the hospital in Myrtle Beach. Just follow Route 17. I doubt they'll look for y'all that far for a while. All the doctors will do is give her the IV anyway, so there's no harm in waiting a day or so."

Candy doesn't say anything, but just looks up at me with longing and concern.

"Got all that?" I ask.

She looks down at my hand that's resting on the door. "Wha . . . What are you going to do?"

"Not sure. Hide in the bushes and spy on them, I guess. Maybe I can get something to blackmail them with or get some evidence or something." I can tell she's listening, but just barely, and she keeps looking at my hand.

"Okay? So get up front and don't fall asleep. And if anyone comes around but me, get out of here. Get out of here fast."

Slowly, almost painfully, as if doing so is a concession the magnitude of the surrender at Appomattox, her hand creeps up and falls softly on top of mine. She leaves it there for a moment, and then she raises it to my neck, pulls me into the window, and kisses me on the cheek. "Be careful," she mumbles into my shirt, and then looks up at me through the dark. I squeeze her hand, smile a brave and tight smile, turn, and walk away down the sandy dirt road towards the river.

I notice the bullfrogs are quiet. I don't hear any cars on the highway. And the night sky wraps around me just like it does when I'm sitting in my lawn chair—with the same stars shining above me, just like they always have.

My lawn chair and trailer and Candy pulling weeds and Sunny running around bugging me suddenly feel very strange—surreal. Unfocused, choppy memories from a bygone era of ignorance and innocence. They're like watching old movie reels of people in the early 1900s with ladies in long fancy dresses holding parasols and men with handlebar mustaches wearing top hats. They're all so happy, all so perky, all so one dimensional. And if these people ever saw themselves as they really were—so young, so naive, so eager—they would have a hard time believing it was really them

We forget so much. But maybe sometimes that's a good thing. If I forget about how in the past two days my life has changed and how much higher the risks and responsibilities are and how a kind of fairy tale has ended; if I forget all that and everything else—forget the story that is my life—not only are the stars above me still the same, but I am too. Deep, deep down, in the depths of my soul where light cannot reach, I am the same. As I always have been.

Yes, my world has changed. But the indefinable *un*-me-ness, has not. You see, *I am* is nothing but a bunch of memories. When those memories are released and forgotten, *I am* no longer. 'I am' becomes just 'I.' And that 'I' never goes away and never really changes. It's something I've always been and always will be—backwards or forwards in time.

All the pains, all the sufferings, all the *thats* in my life, are just layers on top of that indefinable I. They haven't changed the stars in the sky, and they haven't changed I.

We're all the same in that respect. Once we take away all the old stories of the past and forget ourselves, you and me are of the same stuff. We are that undefinable un-me-ness that never changes: We are 'I.'

And just as you'll always wonder at the night sky with its stars and never be able to grasp the sheer enormity and sublime continuity of it all, you'll always look down into yourself, when it's quiet and dark and clear, and wonder the same way. Sometimes you might be able to sense it. Sometimes you may smell it. Sometimes you might even feel it. But you can never seem to taste it. Maybe that's what keeps us coming back. "*Next* time, I'm gonna taste it!" we think. "For sure, I'm gonna get it *next* time! And when I do, oh, how sweet it will be!"

After walking a hundred yards or so, something darts out of the underbrush and onto the dirt road. I stop in my tracks as my stomach jumps and blood rushes to my head. The figure is about fifty feet in front of me, and all I can make out is its outline since the sliver of moon is now behind a cloud. I bend down and put the flashlight quietly on the ground, grip the bat and assume a stance like I'm ready to take a rip at a fastball. Then I wait. Is it Jackson? Andy Y? They're stuck in the swamp. How could they be here already? The judge? The drug runners? Do they see me?

I think to run back to Sunny and Candy 'cuz my heart is beating through my chest and I'm tired and scared and worried and really don't need to hold my ground. It would be so much easier just to turn and run. But running isn't just running; it's like stepping aside and letting them pass. As if you're not even there. As if you didn't exist. So much easier to make like you're not even there to avoid any friction, any confrontation, any criticism, any animosity. It's so much easier to melt into the background and stay in a chair in the corner because that's where she forgot you and what she must have really wanted. So much easier to live in a trailer away from everybody and loose yourself in books and music and philosophy and daydreams and stars and pain to make yourself an SOB when you're really not so nobody can get close because you're so afraid of being forgotten and ignored and left in a chair or the closet again. It would be so much easier to drop the bat and run into the bushes and step aside. But . . .

But no.

But *hell* no.

Because eventually it gets to the point in every man's life that no matter what the risks, no matter what the dangers, no matter what the consequences, he has to make a stand. He has to hold his ground. He has to make himself visible and make some noise. Even if it costs him his fortune. Even if it costs him his freedom. Even if it costs him his woman. Even if it costs him his life. And if a man doesn't do it when he has to, and even sometimes when he doesn't, I hate to say it, but he's simply not a man. It's not so much that he's trying to beat someone or get something. It's just that he's sick and tired of being run over—being taken advantage of or being ignored. There are two kinds of people: the ones who will run you over for fun or fortune, and the ones who want to jump aside when they see one coming. Each of them has to learn to do more of what the other one is good at.

The figure moves—more like twitches—to the right, across the middle strip of weeds of the dirt road. As it moves, it seems to widen to almost twice its width, and the moonlight that's now making it around the cloud, shows two points close together glimmering about five feet off the ground. I strain to see and hold my breath and listen. And mindlessly, abruptly, I find myself gritting my teeth and hissing at it. Like an animal I hiss as I take a stride forward and swing the bat like I'm hitting for the fences. Immediately, the figure breaks its silence with a powerful crack, like a limb snapping off a tree, Ccccchhhaaaccccchhh. Ccccchhhaaaccccchhhh.

I swing the bat again and hiss in return. "Ccccchhhaaaccccchhh." Then another figure jumps onto the road, like its falling out of the sky. Both images widen and bounce once, twice, as I swing and hiss at them again. They bounce once more over the underbrush and disappear into the trees. Deer. Two deer.

I let out a sigh and steady myself. I lower the bat. Take that! I think. Go ahead and run! After all, fortune favors the bold, does it not? And I am the bold one tonight! I am . . . a man!

I notice I have to piss. The thought crosses my mind to wait, but I turn to the side of the dirt road, unzip my shorts, and give the bushes a good hearty drink.

I can smell the river and the swamps stronger now as I walk along an animal path, trying to avoid the underbrush. The welts from my beating and the gash on my hip with the stitches are burning and throbbing, and if I was lying in bed they would be very hard to take. But my mind is on other things now, so I don't notice the pain all that much. I know, however, that if I'm forced into hand-to-hand combat again, I doubt I'll be the winner this time. The bat may make the difference. But I resolve to avoid being seen or getting carried away with the need for revenge. Just not for my sake, but because if I lose, they'll definitely go looking for the car I came in, and would likely find Candy and Sunny. If they attack me, I fight. If not, I sit and watch. Being a man is one thing. Asking for trouble is another.

I come to a bank of the river, right near the pier the Ditto Amigos and me played on just a couple days ago. I find a place behind a sumac bush that will give me cover, and sit on the dirt. I decide to take my own philosophizing to heart and try and think ahead, to the future.

Where is the rendezvous gonna be? At this small pier downstream of the rope swing. Who's gonna be there? Drug dealers and Jackson and the gang. When? It's supposed to be at 2:30, but it might take them a while to get out of the swamp. I'm sure they've radioed for help and will be here eventually. What's gonna happen? They're gonna get drugs and equipment and supplies for some kind of new drug lab. I forgot the name. Begins with an 'm' I thing. Why? Money, greed, pride, power. How's it gonna take place? Well, the drug guys will likely come up the river in their boat, tie up to the pier, unload the drugs and supplies to the boys, get their money, and go back down the river. The boys will load up their car and take it all back to their hiding place—wherever that is.

So what will I be able to do, rush down and knock them all out with my bat? Hardly. Where there's drugs, there's guns. Slit the tires to their vehicles? Maybe, but I don't have a knife, and what good would it do anyway? Abduct one of them, the judge maybe, and hold him until they agree to drop the charges and let me go? Maybe . . . maybe. But would Jackson and Andy Y care enough about the judge to make that trade? If he's still got the 25 Gs they would.

Think ahead. Think ahead. I could spring on the judge when they first get here, and then what? Hold my Louisville slugger to his head and yell, "Drop your guns, fellas, or I'll knock the judges noggin' into the center field bleachers?"

Just then I hear the sound of a motor coming from down the river. I get up and crouch behind the sumac branches and stare towards the sound. The moon is higher above the tree line now and casts a faint milky glow onto the river, which, with the reflection of the light off the water, illuminates the area so I can just barely see. It takes a minute or so for the boat to get to the final bend of the meander loop that is River-hole. And from my vantage point, I see the tip of the bow come from beyond the weeds covering the bank and slice sharply through the water.

As the boat comes slowly into view, it seems to stretch out longer and longer and the sound of the motor becomes more defined until I can tell that this is not some simple John-boat or hobby craft. This is a boat built for speed, with a large two-prop inboard and a sleek, sharp, slender hull. A modified, really long, cigarette boat with an open cargo bay behind the cockpit chairs.

I see two figures behind the windshield and a couple drums and boxes stacked up behind them. As the boat makes it around the bend, I hear the engine slow, and the bow of the boat sinks further into the water. When the boat's about a hundred feet from the pier, the engine cuts out completely, and the sleek and now silent craft glides seamlessly to the pier and settles besides it. It's obvious whoever the pilot is has done this before.

Without a word, the two men, a tall slender one and a short stubby one, climb out of the boat onto the pier and tether the boat to the pylons with ropes. Then, to my amazement, they reach into the boat and pull out two folding lawn chairs and what I guess to be, the way the short, stubby one carries it, a six pack of beer. Without a word, they walk up the pier onto the narrow gritty beach, set up the chairs, sit down, and pop open cans of beer. Right after their first sips, they each light cigarettes. The faint breeze blowing off the river brings the smoke up the bank so I can smell it.

"Yeah," the tall one says in a high pitched, almost squeaky voice. "Might as well get comfortable. These bastards are always late anyways."

"You got that right, JL," the short, stubby one replies. "What do you expect? They work for the government!" They both laugh.

"Here's to your wealth, partner," JL, the tall one says. "Another hundred Gs richer ain't bad for one night's work, wouldn't you say, JD?" They click their cans of beer together.

"Yeah, buddy. I like the sound of that!" JD, the short, stubby one replies.

"Nice night, too. Not bad being out on the river on a night like this," JL says.

"You can say that again," JD replies. "Nice."

"It's a tough job, JD, but someone's gotta do it." They both chuckle.

"Remember," JL continues, "what it used to be like to actually *work* for a living? Man, I hated it! Couldn't stand getting up every morning and going in to the same office with all those dumb-ass clients."

"Yeah," JD agrees.

"But I can't say it was all bad. Had its good moments, you know? Like when you'd get to milk some sucker for all he's worth."

"Shit yeah."

"Yeah," JL continues. "I remember one time, you know," he takes another sip and chuckles to himself, "I had this one client. He was out in the waiting room, pacing back and forth. I could see his blurry image through the frosted glass of my office door, you know. So he was pacing back and forth for almost an hour while I finished up a brief for another schmuck." He pauses again for another sip, which was more like a gulp this time, and a drag off his cigarette. "And then, when I finished the brief, you know, I had Melissa come in and get under the desk."

"Ha!" JD snorts. "You're kidding!"

"Hell no! I was so tense from straining the brain in my big head, I needed to blow off some steam with the little head!" They both erupt in laughter. "By the time Melissa let the guy in, you know, he'd been waiting over an hour and was so tired from pacing that he never even complained! He just looked at Melissa like a dumb sucker, you know, when he noticed somethin' funny on her chin!" They laugh even harder.

"The guy was so dumb-founded, I don't think he ever let himself believe what he actually saw! His eyes just kinda glazed over, you know, you know, like they were saying, 'does not compute . . . does not compute'!"

They keep laughing for a minute or two like it's the funniest thing they ever heard. Then each of them pop open another beer and settle back in their chairs.

"But that's not all," JL continues. "The poor bastard was up for tax evasion, and he wanted to pay them. He wanted to pay the, you know, all $300,000 of it, so he thought they wouldn't indict him, you know. But I told him, hell no! Don't pay! It's the worst thing you could do!"

"Dumb sucker," JD says under his breath.

"So the idiot listens to me! He never got a second opinion, never asked the DA or the IRS—nothin'! He actually trusted an attorney to do a good and honest job!"

"Dumb sucker."

"And six months later, the dumb sucker catches the case and has to plead to three years! Three fucking years!"

"Dumb sucker."

"And you know how much time I spent on that case? You know

how much?"

"No, how much?"

"Oh, I'd say about fifteen hours. All I ever did was talk to the guy. Never filed a motion, never wrote up a brief, never tried to overturn the search warrant, never talked to the DA or the IRS. The dumb sucker paid me, I figured, $6,666 an hour! And he ended up paying the taxes and getting three years in the pen anyway!"

"Oh man, JL! You got him good. You got him real goooood!"

"Yep! Sure did!" JL slaps his thigh. "You know, I sure did! So now I make money an *honest* way, JD. I'm a *distributor!*"

They both laugh again, this time it's just a chuckle though, since it's probably a worn out joke by now. "And the dumb sucker actually had the nerve to get angry at me. He said, 'I paid you a hundred thousand dollars for what? To get indicted?' It really pissed me off, I tell you. But who cares, right? I got paid and that's all that matters."

"You got that right, JL," JD says. "Who cares about them? For me, I was sick and tired of seeing those drug kingpins make a hundred times what I was making at the PO. And how else can you make so much money doing so little work selling something people need so much they become slaves to it and will turn on their own family and friends to get more?" They click their cans together again.

"Amen to that, brother," JD chimes in. "Hey! Did I tell you about the time . . ."

There's a rustling in the bushes up on the bank and JL reaches down to his belt and pulls out a pistol as they turn in their chairs to the sound. A breeze blows across my face. They sit there a half minute or so, and then hear it again.

"You see anything?" JD asks.

"Not really," JL whispers. "Wait. There's something . . . Something gray . . . or . . . white . . . just barely in the bushes."

"Hey, you!" JD calls out. "Come on out, or we'll shoot!"

Nothing moves. JL gets out of his chair and sprints sideways at an angle to the edge of the bushes. Then he stands up and walks leisurely along the brush line, reaches over some weeds, and pulls out a tattered piece of cloth. He walks back to JD and shows it to him, "An old white rag or something. It's so old, it's fallin' apart. Just a piece of trash rustling in the wind." He throws it over his shoulder as he sits back down. "You were saying?"

"Oh, yeah. You screwing that guy reminds me of how I put the screws to this other bozo even better. Was about six years ago, just before I left the PO. This guy—a smart guy too, found out later he was borderline genius and had a PhD, you know, but man, was he gullible! A real sap!" JL snorts into his beer with laughter.

"He was selling this thing that was supposed to turn water into wine—that's what I called it anyway. It was supposed to clean the water and put some kind of charge on it or something, that made it better for you, you know. I forget exactly . . . never really understood it and never even tried it. I never had it tested, either.

"Anyway, I drummed up a bogus search warrant and raided his office, which was in his house, you know. Brought in the FBI and SWAT team and everything. His wife and kid were so scared, I swear, the little boy shit in his pants. For real! There they were, face down on the floor with guns pointed at 'em. And so fucking scared! Oooooeeeee! So damn scared their eyes were, I swear, bulging out so hard I thought they were gonna pop out and roll under the refrigerator or something! I'll never forget it! Mummmummmm!"

He pauses for a long time, like he's savoring the taste of a fine wine. JL can't stand the wait. "Come out with it, JD. I hate it when you do that! Just come out with it!"

"Aw right. Aw right! So we cuff him and his wife and ransack the place, you know. Turn everything over and really trash the place, 'cuz we tell him we suspect him of having guns or drugs. We take all his equipment and records—twenty-two big-ass boxes of them. All his fucking ledgers and tax returns and documents. Everything. The SOB was just making too much money, like half a mill a year, you know. Too much money and too successful. I couldn't stand it, you know. Didn't matter he was spending a hundred Gs a year on postage. We had to take him down.

"Turns out he really believed in what he was selling and customers said it really helped them feel better so we couldn't get him for fraud. And all his customers loved him, so no one gave him up. So we had to cook-up a charge for money laundering. Totally bogus, of course."

"Of course," JL chimes in. "Wouldn't have it any other way!"

"Hey!" JD continues, "I spent all that money on the investigation, you know, so I had to come away with something! Had to get a conviction. It didn't matter he was totally innocent, right? What would my boss say if I didn't get something out of it? After all, we get paid to convict, don't we?"

"Damn straight you do!"

"So we lied to him saying we had witnesses and enough evidence to put him away for 15 years. Scared the piss out of him, you know. Dumb sucker plead to five years and paid the whole $50,000 fine too."

"Hey. That's not bad, JD. Not bad at all."

"And of course, his business went down the toilet, lost his house, even his freakin' watch because we got to impound all his valuables. His wife left him, and the kid grew up and ended up on heroine I hear 'cuz his daddy was gone to prison!" They both snicker.

"You got them goooood!" JL says. "Nice work, JD. I'm right proud of ya!" He slaps JD on the back. "He never challenged the warrant?"

"Oh yeah, he did. But the judge came through for us, as he always did, you know. Just said it was a good faith exception on my part, you know, when I filed for the warrant. You know how it works—we can lie and then claim it's just an honest mistake and get away with it, but if one of them makes an honest mistake, we tell them there's no excuse for not knowing the letter of the law."

"Of course. Wouldn't have it any other way." JL pops open another beer, and says, "That's a good one, JD. Good one. But I got an even better one! This bitch . . . a real piece she was, came to me with . . ."

Just then the beams of two sets of headlights swing across the pier and the two guys sitting there like a beacon on top of a watchtower sweeping the yard. The guys get up and scramble down the pier like cockroaches scurrying out of the light and put the chairs and beer back in the boat. The vehicles—a cop car and a brown van—drive down the sandy dirt road just ten yards in front of me. I duck down behind the sumac and listen until they're past me. Then I slowly rise up, just above the top of the branches, and see both the car and the van stop even with the pier.

I have a pretty good view of the festivities. In front to my left are the cop car and van, parked just on the down slope of a not too high and somewhat rounded ridge that slopes down to the underbrush back away and downstream. Below the other side of the ridge, further away from me and beyond the car and van is the pier that juts out perpendicular to the shoreline of the bend in the river. The shoreline curves right, in an backwards 'C', back up around and then upstream again. In the armpit of the inverted 'C' is the hundred-year-old oak tree with the rope swing, and I notice the end of the rope is still wedged in the crook of the branch where Kaitlin left it the other day. Past the tree, further along the shoreline, are a number of jagged boulders and rock outcroppings.

So if I look forward left, I see the car, van and pier. If I look straight, I'm looking at the river upstream, and if I look forward right, I see the tree and bank where we laid on the blanket, and then past that the rocks that jut out into the water. Over my right shoulder is the moon, the crescent of which is above the tree line now so the light it casts extends over the dirt road all the way to the water.

Someone comes out of the cop car, and someone else from the van, and I hear the doors slam. It's show-time, I think. I exhale, then hold it for a few seconds and force myself to think. Now pay attention and try to think one step ahead of 'em.

"JL!" I hear Andy Y call out. "What's up, brother?"

"Hey Andy! What'cha know good?" JL calls back.

"Not much. Not much. Is that you, JD? How you doing?"

They meet at the foot of the pier and shake hands.

"Hey, Andy," JD says. "What's that on your hand?"

"Oh nothin'." Andy replies. "Scraped it on the door handle this evening. Just a small cut. Nothin' to worry about. I got a buddy I want you to meet,"

"Hey, Andy!" JL snaps. "What you talkin' about? That's not Jackson?"

"Now hold your horses . . ."

"We had a deal. No one else . . ."

"Calm down," Andy Y interrupts. "This here is our bank-roll. I told you about him, you know, Judge Mooney. The judge who's fronted us all the money that got us started with you guys. He's cool."

JL clears his throat. "Err . . . Judge Mooney? Yeah . . . you mentioned him." JL holds out his hand. "Yeah . . . okay . . . judge . . . yeah . . . nice to meet you, Your Honor."

"The pleasure is mine," JM replies in his deep, resonant voice. He turns to the other drug runner and says, "And you must be JD."

"Yes, sir," JD says like a little boy. "Pleased to meet you, sir."

"Oh, enough with the formalities. We're all friends here. Just call me JM, and JD, your reputation precedes you. Didn't you used to head the Western District of . . ."

"Wow!" JD jumps in excitedly. "Yeah, I sure did!"

"I've heard of your work. Nice to meet you." JD shakes JM's hand a long time and even from where I'm standing I can see JD's shit eating grin.

"Yeah," JL cuts in. "Well, we got everything you guys want. Hey, where's Jack?"

Jackson gets out of the passenger side of the cop car and walks, or more like wobbles, down the bank with a bottle in his hand. "That's him," Andy sneers. "His fiancé paid him a visit and got his ass drunk as a skunk."

"Ahhh, shat up!" Jackson mumbles. "I'm doing jus fine, thaaank yooouuu! A-okaaaayyyyy. Peachy keeeen. Fine and daaandyyyy. Couldn't beee bett . . . ."

"Yeah," the judge slaps him on the shoulder. "Gonna have to take his badge and sever his pension for drinkin' on the job!"

Everyone laughs, but Jackson keeps blubbering, "An who put alll thossse buuuullets into that Stick . . . er's car?"

"That's right, Jack," Andy Y says. "You shoot better drunk than sober. But that was your fiancé's car you hit."

"Oh, yeahhh. May . . . be, but who drove usshs into the swammmp?" Jackson counters.

"Well, if your girlfriend hadn't let that SOB out of jail . . ."

"Don you dare talk 'bout her . . . my fiiiaaaaannncaaayyyy . . . I looove her an . . ."

"What're you talkin' about?" JL interrupts.

"Oh," the judge says, "these two had a little adventure getting over here. No big deal, no big deal. We'll deal with Jack's little girlfriend later. So what you fellas got?"

"Like I was saying," JL continues, "we got everything you guys want: the blow, the lab and all the chemicals you need to make meth until the cow jumps over the moon."

They all chuckle, and Jackson says, "Yeah, till the cow jumpsshs over da moooooon."

Then the judge says, "And how about the instructions? You got all the instructions and the MSDS's?"

"Yeah, inssttrruuctionnsshhhnsss," Jackson mumbles. Everyone ignores him.

"Yeah, of course," JD answers. "Got them straight from the pharmaceutical rep, you know. Right out of their lab manuals."

"Righ ou of da manualssshs . . ." Jackson slurs again.

"You sure?" the judge asks.

"Just a minute," JD says and walks down the pier to the boat, ducks down into it for a second, and comes back with a three-ring notebook.

"Here," he says and opens the notebook as JL shines a flashlight on the pages. "The sheets have the company name and logo right on 'em. You'll be making meth exactly like they do—except your customers won't need a prescription!"

Everybody laughs, Jackson included, who topples over onto the ground. They all ignore him as the judge flips through the sheets.

"It's easy as pie," JL continues. "A high school chemistry kid could do it. Easy as pie."

"Sure is," JD says. "All you gotta do is make sure you don't mix the ________ and ________, and make sure the anhydrous doesn't get too hot. If it does, you're gonna think it was the 4th of July."

"That's why I want the MSDSs," the judge says.

"Right here," JL flips a few pages and points with the flashlight. "Here."

Oh shit, I think. I left the flashlight on the ground back there! But I can't go back now. Just keep paying attention! "Don't mix the _________ and the _________," I repeat in my head.

"And don't light any matches or make sparks or anything. Don't even turn on a light bulb around that anhydrous when the valve's open. And the acetone, that'll go up too." JL continues.

"Okay, okay," the judge nods. "Looks easy enough. Just need to be careful."

"And hey!" JD chimes in. "If you have any questions, you just give us a call, 24/7. We're your full service drugstore and we're always at your service!" He sings it in a jingle I never heard before. Nobody laughs.

Jackson gets up to his feet, slaps his thigh, and says, "Full servish drugggsschtooore." He brings his hand up to his forehead and swoons, "Oooohhhh. . . ."

"Go back and sit in the car, you jackass," the judge sneers.

Jackson takes a couple steps towards the car and then falls flat on his face again.

"Hopeless," the judge mumbles.

"Hey," Andy Y says hurriedly. "Don't worry about him. He's used to it. Just let him sleep. We'll scrape him up before we leave."

"Okay," JL says. "You guys come prepared?"

"Sure thing," Andy Y chirps. "But let's see the blow first."

"No problem," JL says. "Come on down." He waves his hand as he walks down the pier to the boat.

They all go to the boat and JD climbs in and points, "Here's all the lab stuff—beakers, jars, tubes, burners. Of course, these drums here have the chemicals and the pressure tanks here has the anhydrous. You've got enough of everything to make at least a couple million worth of meth. And here," he reaches under the front seat and pulls out a duffle bag wrapped in a plastic trash bag, "is the blow."

He pulls a white plastic bag out of the duffle bag and opens it carefully. Andy Y and the judge stick their fingers in, pull them out, and put them to their lips. "Mmmmm, mmmm good," Andy Y says sounding like he's tasting a bowl of soup. "Ain't that right, judge?" he asks.

"Yeah," JM replies. "That'll do."

"Best stuff yet," JD says. "Best stuff in three fucking years it is! You guys are getting a real bargain this time. Some might even mistake it for China White."

"We don't mind that!" Andy Y calls out over his shoulder as he walks away from them down the pier. "I just hope we don't sniff up all the profits!"

He goes to the cop car and opens the back door and pulls out a briefcase. He walks back up the pier and holds it up and opens it for inspection. "Here you go," he says proudly. "There's 25 Gs for the lab and the usual 75 Gs for the blow. You wanna count it?"

"Nah," JL says as he takes the briefcase and puts it under the boat seat, along with his pistol. "We trust you guys. Besides, we know where you live." JL and JD laugh, but Andy Y and the judge don't.

"All right," the judge says. "We don't have all night. We need to load all this up in the van and get out of here. I've got court in the mornin'. We'll get the equipment boxes first, and then the drums and tanks."

All of them get busy scurrying and carrying stuff from the boat, up the pier, up the ridge to the top of it, into the van from which an overhead light shines from its ceiling; then empty handed, out of the van, down the mound, and back to the boat for another load.

The light in the van makes it possible for me to see inside of it, and it's only about twenty yards from where I'm standing. Maybe I can hijack the van, I think. But I wouldn't be able to turn it around with the car right in front of it. And I couldn't just back it up all the way to the highway—they'd fill me with bullets before I got 50 yards. How about taking my bat and smashing up all the equipment? Might be fun, but what good would that do? Slit the tires? Don't have a knife. Deflate 'em holding the valve in? That'd take too long.

After all the equipment boxes are in the van, they get to the tanks and drums. It takes three of them to carry each one of them: one at the front, one in the middle, and one at the end. One round tank held horizontal, with six legs carrying it up the mound and into the van.

"Watch that valve there," JL cautions. "Don't knock it off or let it open or we'll have a real mess on our hands."

They finally get the pressure tanks up into the van and secure them with straps to the walls. Andy Y pulls the short string hanging from the light to turn it off, pushes the double doors shut, and turns the handle, but doesn't lock it.

Well, that's it, I think. Now they're all just going to leave and I didn't do a Goddamn thing. And I'm sure they've already put out an APB on me and Candy and Sunny and every cop on the East coast will be looking for us. I can see the posters already: "Wanted. For murder and drug trafficking. Sam Othello Barlow. Considered dangerous and probably armed. Probably traveling with two female accomplices . . ."

Yeah, armed with a 35 inch Louisville slugger and carting around a nine-year-old in a coma. And even though I know the truth of my innocence and character, the thought of being known that way brings a flush of shame to my cheeks. But I have to stay focused, so I force myself to think. Now I have to figure out a way to keep Candy and Sunny safe and away from these guys, and get Sunny to some medical help. As for me, it's either turn myself in, run, or keep trying to turn the tables on them. But how?

The boys gather around the car, and Andy Y puts his hand on the door handle to open it, but before he does, JD says, "Hey fellas. We deserve a break, don't ya think? And I want to make a toast to your future success!"

"We really need to be going," the judge says.

"Awww," JL replies. "One beer ain't gonna slow you down, judge. You need to unwind. It'll help you sleep."

"Yeah," JD agrees. "If you ain't gonna reward yourself for this deal of the century you just made, you never will. Here . . ." He puts his arm around the judge's shoulder and leads him to the pier. "Come on, JM. You got a couple new drinkin' buddies here who want to treat you to a brew."

Andy Y takes his hand off the door handle and walks around the front of the car.

"Besides," JD says as he and the judge walk past Jackson, who's still passed out on the ground, "you don't want to forget your buddy here, do you?"

They laugh as they pass him, and Andy Y says, "Yeah, I'd love to see his face waking up in the mornin' if we left him here."

They walk down the pier to the boat, and JL hands the judge a beer. "Here you go, chief." I hear the pop-top open. Here's my chance! For what, I'm not sure. It's like I read in a book once about a king and all his men: I've gotta try to turn nothing into something, 'cuz nothing is all I've got. I'll just get in the van and see what I can see. Maybe I'll figure something out.

I duck down and while holding the bat, go around the sumac down to below the van. Now the van is blocking their view, so I stand up and sprint up the small embankment to the dirt road and get to the van. I stop and listen. My ears are thumping again, but I can hear them talking and laughing still out on the pier. I grab the cold chrome door handle and turn it. It's sticky, but it turns all the way open. I pull the door just a couple of feet open and slither like a snake into the van. It's dark and musty and I can't see a thing. I grope around where I think the ceiling light would be, but can't find it. I curse myself for leaving the flashlight behind and then I remember they said something about not even turning on a light around some of the stuff, so not having the flashlight might be a good thing. The thought comes to me to just stay here and ride in the back with them to where they're going. Then I can jump out and knock them silly with my bat. Yeah. Yeah, that sounds good. That's what I'll do!

I squat down and sit on the floor, put the bat down, and lean back against one of the drums. My back digs into something pointy, protruding from the bottom of the drum. I feel around with my hand. It's the valve JL warned them about. And just as I touch the valve, I remember Candy and Sunny back at the car. I can't stay in the van and go with these guys—what will the girls do without me? Candy would probably freak out. My hand grasps the valve and turns it. At least this will stop them from making the drugs. I stand up as the liquid starts gushing out of the drum near my feet and onto the van floor.

I push the van door open about a foot as my other hand braces against the top of one of the pressure tanks. I look down to see, just barely in the moonlight, the word 'ANHYDROUS' stenciled on it in red paint. The gas valve handle, just like a handle of an outside water spigot, juts out from the pipe coming out of the top of the tank. I turn it too, and it starts to hiss as the gas escapes. They'll be madder than firecrackers when they discover they've run out of gas, I think.

I slither out the door and close it quietly behind me. I step off the van and onto the ground and I notice the liquid dripping out from under the doors and onto the ground. I sprint back to my hiding place behind the sumac bushes and wait. Maybe I'll hear more about the drug runners and where they're from. Maybe I can take that to the police in Charleston or Savannah. Maybe a city cop would believe me. Maybe they're all not corrupt.

The boys are still down on the pier, drinking, smoking, and laughing up a storm. The judge has loosened up and I can hear the deep resonant bellow of his laughter echo off the trees. They sure aren't worried about being heard. Another five minutes go by and nothing I can use has been said. I can smell their cigarette smoke come wafting up the incline on the gentle but steady breeze. I can also smell a faint and pungent aroma I've never smelled before coming from the van—the anhydrous and chemicals.

More cans of beer pop open, and I notice movement out of the corner of my eye. It's Jackson picking himself up off the ground. He pauses when he pulls himself up to his full height and then looks down at everyone at the end of the pier. I expect him to go to them, but instead, he stumbles around the cop car to the driver's side and opens the door. The interior light goes on, but none of the boys seem to notice.

"Gotta get ta my girrrlll," he mumbles. "Gotta go see my woooman." He climbs into the seat and pulls the door shut. "An keeep her saaafe." The party down on the pier stops.

Jackson starts the car and races the engine a few times like a dragster getting ready to peel out. When the engine calms down, he puts it in gear, and with a jerk, moves the car forward. JL, Andy Y, and the judge start up the pier towards the car.

"Oh, Jesus," Andy Y says. "What the hell is that jackass doing now?"

"You'd better stop him before he hurts himself," the judge says. "We don't need another car getting messed up tonight."

Jackson drives about a hundred feet straight forward and then swerves to the right, finding a flat and open area that almost looks like a cul-de-sac, to turn around in. He cranks the wheel hard left, and comes about in a tight circle until he's turned the car completely around, and is now pointing straight at the van. As the tires spin out, the car stops.

The engine roars again a few times, the car's headlights shining directly at the dark headlights of the van. Like a bull starring down the matador and pawing the dirt, it gathers its strength and resolve to make a charge. Then, with another roar and its rear tires spinning, it puts its head down and runs straight ahead.

Andy Y dashes up the slope, waving his arms wildly and yelling at the top of his lungs, "Stop the car Jack! Stop the car!" He gets to the edge of the dirt road, right near where the cop car had been parked, "Stop! STOP!" he yells. JL and the judge are yelling now too.

Jackson must have floored it, wanting so desperately to get back to a warm and comforting bosom he thought waited for him with open arms. When the tires get a firm grip on the slippery dirt, the car starts speeding right at the front of the van. Andy Y takes a leap of faith, a huge leap of faith considering who's driving; that, or he's so concerned about saving what's in the van he's willing to risk his life for it. He jumps out in front of the van, still waving and shouting. The headlights hit him like spotlights and light him up with his arms waving like a marooned sailor waving down a rescue boat.

Jackson keeps coming straight at Andy Y for a second . . . two seconds, and I brace myself, expecting to watch the car plow right into Andy Y and pin him against the front of the van. Either that, or slice him right in half.

But Jackson finally sees him and pulls the wheel hard and swerves right—just missing Andy Y and the van—as Andy Y dives in the opposite direction, tripping as he does. The car angles down off the side of the dirt road and goes right along the side of the van, bouncing up and down over the rugged ground with Jackson bouncing up and down inside looking just like a jack-in-the-box. The front wheels fall into a pothole stopping the car completely. After a few guns of the engine, which cause the wheels to spin and smoke, Jackson gives up and drops his head dejectedly onto the steering wheel.

JL and the judge rush to Andy Y, reach down, and pick him up.

"Oh Jesus," the judge mumbles.

"Are you okay?" JL asks.

"Oh shit!" Andy moans. "I don't know. I landed on it funny. It think I broke my ankle. Owwww! Shit!"

Meanwhile, Jackson picks his head off the steering wheel and opens the door of the car, which is just about even with the back step of the van. He pauses and sniffs, and sees the liquid dripping out from under the back door of the van. "Hey you guysshss . . ." he mumbles, more to himself than anyone, and takes a step towards the van.

"Sit tight," the judge calls out as he and JL help Andy Y to his feet. Andy Y drapes his arm over each of their shoulders and hops on his good leg a couple times, swearing up a storm.

Jackson keeps looking at the liquid dripping down the van steps and mumbles to himself, "Wha the ell is at?" He steps up onto the van's back step, "I wonder wha at is," and grabs the handle to the double doors.

JL, Andy Y, and the judge, move slowly past the hood of the van on the passenger side. "Just hang on there Jack!" the judge booms out. "We'll be there in just a second. Just stay put."

JL and the judge help Andy Y hop along the side of the van, out of my view since the van is between me and them. They're still upwind too, since they apparently haven't smelled anything out of the ordinary. Jackson pulls the van door open all the way and steps up into the van, looking in curiously as he does. The faint moonlight is enough for him to see by.

"Wha the ell," he mumbles again. Then louder, he calls out, "Hey guysss! There's suffff in the van! Where'd all this sufffff come ffffrom?"

The boys finally make it to the back of the van, just as Jackson notices the string for the overhead light. The boys are looking down at the ground, picking their way gingerly as they come around to behind the back bumper. Finally, JL notices the liquid on the ground beneath the bumper.

"Hey," JL says. "What the . . ."

"Somethiiiing smellllls realllly weird in ere," Jackson mumbles, oblivious to anyone else, as he reaches for the light. His fingers grasp the string.

The light! The gas! And just as I realize the danger of the situation, a bell begins to ring . . .

Clang, ding-dong, clang.

The sound is eerie—like it's faint and far off but at the same time loud and right next to my ear.

Clang, ding-dong, clang.

A ringing that's irregular and fast—not the slow bonging of a church bell summoning its parishioners, but a sprightly, joyous cadence that beckons you to dance. And it's more than just a ringing. It's a harmonious, musical sound. Not just ringing, but a chiming.

The judge, JL, and Andy Y pause just a moment, bewildered. I jump out from behind the sumac with my arms raised as words form in my mouth. Andy Y sees me and grabs his gun. Jackson turns his head to look for the sound, and with it comes his shoulder and then arm and then hand and then fingers.

"NOOOO!" I yell at the top of my lungs!

And simultaneously to my voice, the judge yells "GAAASSSS!" and Andy Y raises his gun and points it at me.

But Jackson's fingers are still holding the string, and as his shoulder turns, they pull the string one eight of an inch too far and the light-switch closes. Electricity flows at the speed of light from the battery near the engine through the switch, through the filament of the bulb and then back out the other wire as the filament heats up. And the smallest of sparks— one that would barely be visible to the naked eye—jumps from one rusty corroded light receptacle contact to the other.

Andy Y pulls the trigger as I dive sideways.

As the spark arcs across the gap, the gas that's accumulated in the van that was supposed to be used to make a chemical that would give confused and mislead souls a false sense of power and enlightenment, ignites with its own power in a flash of blinding brilliance. From one molecule to the next, effectively instantly, the gas is raised to a higher level, a higher orbit, a higher rank, and shows itself as a flaming ball and geyser of white-hot fury. That white-hot fury engulfs the liquid on the floor of the van and ground and drums filled with more liquid and the other tank of gas, and as if all of it wants to be spent right then and there instead of being used as intended, it becomes the first explosion at the same instant as Andy Y's gunshot. An explosion that pounds the ground like a meteor pounding into the earth. An explosion that shoots flames four stories high and a hundred feet around.

I'm still looking at them as I'm falling through the air and I see the look on all their faces is the same: eyebrows raised, eyes wide open, jaws dropping. But their jaws didn't have time to drop all the way open because that flaming ball of white-hot fury exploded into them and then through them and pushed them so hard and so violently and with such searing heat that every molecule in them became part of that white-hot fury too and ignited them and burned them up instantly right along with the gas.

As I hit the ground, I'm simultaneously pushed away by the concussion and I land face down in a small depression. I feel the flames shoot over my back, see the light through my closed eyelids, and hear in my ears and feel in my chest the concussion as the air pushes away from the center of the blast at the speed of sound. If I hadn't dove when I saw Andy Y raise his gun to shoot at me, I would have been incinerated too.

A split second later, there's another explosion as the gas tanks of the car and van explode. Glass and metal and bits of debris—some on fire and some that isn't—fly up and out and rain down on the land and water. I cover my head with my hands, and feel some of the hairs on my forearms burn and feel some debris fall on me. A piece of metal the size of a hubcap bangs onto the ground a couple feet from my head.

Five seconds go by. Ten seconds.

Finally I take my hands off my head and look back as I rise to my knees. The van is gone—a shallow, charred crater in its place—with bits of debris burning and smoldering scattered in and around it. The car looks like a mortar shell hit it, with the rear half of it totally gone and the cab and engine mostly gone too and what's left just a mess of tangled and burning junk. I see nothing of JL, the judge, Andy Y, or Jackson. They simply disappeared. The ground is scorched and bare in a twenty-yard radius around where the vehicles used to be and the air is thick with smoke and dust.

The demolition experts who later examined the site remarked that the explosive force generated was about ten times more than what would be expected considering the amount of chemicals and gas in the van. They attributed it to an atmospheric abnormality.

Finally I stand up and take a couple steps up the incline of the mound towards the crater and remains of the car. The burnt smell stings my nostrils. Apart from the almost imperceptible sound of the small flames licking the vehicles' remains, all is quiet. No crickets or owls or frogs, no breeze. No nothin'. Like everything is waiting to see if the world is gonna return to normal. I look at the flames dumb-founded, as if I too am wondering if the world is ever gonna return to normal.

I look at the crater, and floating down right into the middle of it is that ragged piece of cloth JL tossed away earlier. As it floats down to the scarred earth of the crater, it ignites itself and flames for several seconds until it burns out completely, leaving nothing behind. As I gaze at it, my attention is drawn through the dying flames to a solitary figure standing on the shore a step off the pier. Before it registers in my mind that one of the boys was not in the blast, he sees me, turns, and runs down the pier towards the boat.

"Hey!" I yell. "Hey you!"

He's running away from me, so I figure I'd better chase him. I pick my way around the wreckage, scamper down the mound, and get to the pier. Then it dawns on me. It's JD, the other drug runner! I sprint down the pier as he pulls the ropes off the pylons and jumps into the boat. I have to stop him, don't I? Doesn't my safety and that of Candy and Sunny depend on it? I can't answer yes to that. If I let him go, he'd probably never come back looking for me. He doesn't even know about Candy and Sunny. So why am I chasing him? Why am I jumping in the boat just as it pulls away and diving into the cargo hold behind the pilot's seat?

I want to get him. Not because I want to do the right thing. Not because I have to save myself or others from some future crimes he might commit. I want to get him because the taste of the fight is still fresh on my tongue and that taste is sweet and has me wanting more. I want to get him for the suspense of the hunt and the thrill of the kill. I want to get him because the rush of domination comes over me. And mostly, I want to get him simply to see if I can.

And maybe that's why all wars are waged.

It's prideful, I know, and I'm sorry. But that's what it is.

I land in the boat on my hands and knees and slide along the slick, wet floor. As the boat accelerates, I get thrown back against the back wall of the empty hold. Then the boat turns sharply left, and I'm still off balance and can hardly move due to the G forces, but I manage to start crawling forward. JD is holding onto the steering wheel with his left hand and reaching under his seat with his right, and I know he ain't reaching for another beer. I scramble forward on my hands and knees as the boat keeps turning past the old oak tree and rocks, close to the bank, and towards the main channel of the river. When I make it up to the front of the cargo hold just behind the front seats, I reach up and grab the top of the passenger seat just as JD's right hand swings over it holding the gun. Oh my God! It's pointing right at my head!

I chop his wrist just as he's pulling the trigger. Pow! Pow! Two bullets slam into the side of the boat and kick out splinters of wood. I grab his arm with both hands and push it skyward. JD's still holding onto the steering wheel with his left hand trying to keep the boat from slamming into shore, and his head is turning back and forth from me to the river, from the river to me, from me to the river. I see the open channel ahead as the boat keeps turning in an arc. I take my left hand, put it over his face, and yank his head back around. His left hand stays on the wheel as we struggle, and the boat keeps turning through the channel, close to the opposite shore as we're now heading downstream.

And the boat keeps skipping on the water and turning, back towards the bend and the pier. JD finally lets go of the steering wheel and tries to pull my hand off his face. He pushes the gun down close to my head and pulls the trigger again. Bang! Bang! The bullets scream past my ear and splash into the water. It feels like my eardrum just burst. I move my other hand off his face to his hand that's holding the gun and he does the same, so all four of our hands are pulling on the weapon, trying to get control.

Now the boat's swinging around past the pier and is pointing at the shore to the left of it. We both rise to our feet, and the boat skips on the water and keeps turning. I push him hard, and his hip bumps into the steering wheel and pushes it down so it turns and straightens out the boat's course.

Now we're headed straight for the rocks beyond the old oak tree, and if we don't turn soon, we're gonna plow right into them. Then I feel something pull my eyes . . . something . . . a force . . . a presence . . . and it happens so quickly, since everything is happening so quickly. I see a figure—a silhouette in the moon light—and without being able to tell with my eyes alone, I know who it is, standing up on the bank, next to the oak, and holding onto the rope.

Another second goes by. JD and I, both standing now, him in front, me behind him in the cargo hold. Both of our arms are raised, struggling with the gun. And in a blink—just a flash—I'm not in the boat struggling with a gun, but I'm in the back of a canoe on a tropical river, hundreds if not thousands of years ago, being tossed downstream by rapids and struggling over a knife with a bronze-skinned savage with war paint on his face.

Later I would think about it a lot—while I gazed at the stars at night. I figure it was a flashback of some kind to a previous life. Not that I believe in that kinda stuff. But it comes out showing me what might have happened to someone, somewhere, a long time ago. Maybe it was me—or part of me. And maybe that makes no difference. But it felt real for just an instant—more real than what was happening at the time. I suddenly smelled the jungle and felt the water spray from the rapids and saw the savage in front of me with red and black war paint running down his face with his sweat who I knew was the tribe's medicine man. And I had a bad feeling in my gut that I was about to die.

I shift my eyes to the gun. I grit my teeth and exert all my strength to wrestle the gun away. As I do, out of the corner of my eye, I see something swoop out of the night sky right at me. Immediately it hits me—right in the gut, right in the solar plexus. In the perfect spot to knock all the wind right out of me. And it does. "Huuuuugggghhh . . ."

My backside slams into the rail of the boat and I fall backwards, with two feet in white running shoes pressed into my stomach. The gun goes off again, but the bullet slams into the hull. I fall and flip backwards hard into the water. My head plunges underwater first and my feet come up over me and her legs and butt bump into me and follow me over the side and down into the water.

Involuntarily I gasp for breath and several drops of the river go down my throat and into my lungs. I stop my inhale, and try to hold my breath, but there's no breath inside of me to hold. I want to get to the surface, but I'm so dizzy and disoriented I can't tell which way is up. The moonlight isn't penetrating far enough into the water to show itself and all I can see is black. I start to panic—my arms waving in front of me and my legs kicking wildly. My abdominal muscles finally relax, and I know I won't be able to stop the reflex that's starting—a reflex that will pull my diaphragm down towards my navel and create a vacuum in my lungs that will suck in the water that will drown me. And just as it starts, just as I feel the cool water hit the back of my throat and start down my windpipe, I feel a hand grab the back of my shirt collar and yank.

Water rushes into me. Cool and smooth and penetrating. I can't stop it, and surprisingly, I find I don't want to. A sense of euphoria floods into my chest and my arms and legs and finally my brain. Then an arm wraps around my throat, and my body feels nothing more . . .

I was running up a hallway with doors alternating on both sides. Running—my head turned, looking back at the tidal wave of darkness thundering up the hallway nipping at my heals. Closer it came. Closer. All those doors. All those choices. "Which one?" I yelled to no one there. "Which one?"

I tripped and fell into an ocean of cool but welcoming water. I took a deep breath . . .

Floating. Floating in water. Floating on a cloud. Or floating up to heaven. It would all feel the same. And it would all feel good. There would be no more holes. You would realize that all the *thats* were just things to break the boredom and laugh at. You would know that all the injustices would bounce off mirrors and back to their makers.

And during the peace and serenity and emptiness that flooded into me soon after the water did, I became no longer a body, but a piece of light. I did not see the light as much as became it. I was suddenly a wave and a particle at the same time, and it wasn't so much that I was traveling forwards, to the new, but backwards, to the familiar. I was free and streaking up away from earth through the silent and black void and it felt totally normal and all the stars had condensed together into one large, excruciatingly bright and pleasant figure and I was going to turn my head to watch the earth get smaller but I didn't have to because suddenly I could see in every direction all at once and I looked and saw the boat crash into the rocky shore just past the old oak tree. I saw the chemicals in the front compartment behind the bow—chemicals that should have been part of the payload in the van but were held back by JD to cheat the judge and Jackson and Andy Y—get squeezed out of their cheep tin containers and mix and create an exothermic reaction that exploded and tore through the bow and bulkhead and windshield and JD. And I saw Candy, barefoot now as she kicked and swam towards shore with all her might, with her arm clamped tight under my chin and around my throat as she pulled my limp body to shore. I looked down at it all and just saw it all and nodded and smiled my own Mona Lisa smile and kept streaking up to the stars, knowing that life as I knew it was now over for good.

I could hear and feel and taste and smell and know in every direction and every dimension all at once and my life started replaying itself backwards, in reverse, like it was unwinding a tangled up clump of fishing line, not just before my eyes, but before all those other senses as well. I, as light, kept streaking back towards that ultimately large and familiar and luminous light from which I came, and the farther away I got from earth, the less my life's unwinding-reenactment phased me; and instead, I started replaying, or really, unwinding, the lives of other people I knew—my mom, dad, sister, Sunny, Candy, Kaitlin, Steve, Tom.

I saw their lives too and sensed what they had sensed as if they were me or I was them and I felt fear and hatred and jealousy and anger and sorrow and happiness and joy and friendship and sympathy and empathy and love and then trust and forgiveness and gratitude. Then the same thing happened with people I knew even less—like Tony and Andy Y and Jackson and Kathy and Kaitlin's dad and JM and JD and JL and even the girl behind the counter at the Dairy-Barn and Martha Chimes.

All of this flashed before my senses in reverse, without any effort, like it was being done to me. Like I was sitting on the roller coaster and it was doing all the work as I sped along backwards, back to the starting platform. I was just an innocent, actionless, spectator . . . sensorator.

Then the scope expanded even more—to people in town and the county and Lowcountry and state. All of their lives and experiences were registered and sensed in the wave and particle of light I had become. There was plenty of time for all this to happen because I was traveling so fast, time slowed down to a crawl. And I saw earth was getting very small. Then an explosion as I whizzed past the moon—into the real black, the real void—of all the people and animals and insects and plants and life that played through me so fast and so hard it was like the most powerful explosion imaginable went off in every part of my new being.

You see, dying is not a death. Yes, it is a closing of the eyes, but it is an opening of the void into time and therefore everything else. My consciousness expanded super-exponentially, but as it did, it became less and less concerned with itself. It was like I was being diluted. Like if you were to drop a drop of iodine into a washbasin filled with water—that iodine spreads out into the whole volume and touches it all, and yet, becomes less and less itself as it does. My drop of conscious self—my ego—was spreading out into the whole of the universe, and as it did, it became less and less distinct. I experienced more and more, and cared less and less. And I felt an emotion that is impossible to describe. The closest I can come is that I felt every conceivable emotion all at once, times infinity.

—All the babies' cries and all the innocent smiles; all the cripples' struggles and all the warriors' triumphs; all the old maids' sorrow and all the brides' joy; all the labors and all the slumbers; all the broken promises and all the kept commitments; all the premature deaths and all the extended lives; all the starvation and all the gluttony; all the doubt and all the confidence; all the despair and all the elation; all the abuse and all the nurturing; all the guilt and all the innocence; all the shame and all the pride; all the loneliness and all the friendship; all the lies and all the truths; all the fear and all the courage; all the pain and all the pleasure; all the hatred and all the love; all the war and all the peace; all the condemnation and all the gratitude; all the good and all the evil; all the noise and all the silence; all the darkness and all the light—

It was like I had become more. Like I had become more life. When I did, all I wanted to do was focus on the light, because it was there I knew even more waited.

And I sensed that once I got there, I would see how it all got started. I would see that before the beginning, everything, everywhere was life. Pulsating, throbbing, boundless life. Every piece of matter, every ray of light, every star, planet, black hole and speck of dust, every magnetic and electromagnetic charge, had started out as one—one unbounded mass of concentrated life.

Life—pushing back with more force than the forces against it.

Life—super density, super energy, super order, super consciousness all rolled into one.

Life—playing within itself, fighting against itself, being everything all at once.

And the Big Bang was not just an explosion of energy, but an implosion of entropy. Disorder and chaos born for the first time in this boundless mass of everything called life. Disorder and chaos that spread as fast as the explosion itself.

You see, the Big Bang wasn't just the birth of the universe. It was indeed, the birth of something else. Something other than life—the flip-side of life. It was essentially and quintessentially, the birth of . . . death! For life as we know it—the evolution of life, or should I say, the devolution of it—could not exist were it not for death.

And through the ages, as the disorder and chaos of energy falling to its next lower level kept occurring and gaining momentum, life became less and less dominant. It became scarce. It became abnormal instead of common. And what life did remain found it harder to stay charged—to stay up out of the chaos.

And so it goes with us. As much as we fight that disorder, there's no escaping it. That is, until we pass into the flip-side dimension where it no longer dominates.

For as disorder and death is gaining in this dimension, in the flip-side dimension, order and life is. So as this dimension will eventually become totally lifeless, the other will become totally life.

Total and ubiquitous life. Pulsating, throbbing, boundless life.

As it once was before. And the cycle starts anew.

But throughout all of this—all the mind-numbing realizations and all the trillions of lifetimes I experienced in the one and a half seconds on the way to eternity—there was something missing. Something I forgot. Something left to do . . .

Like when you leave your house and then think you forgot to turn off the stove after making tea. And as that quandary grew to an unquenchable obsession, the luminous bright light went out. It was suffocatingly dark for a moment . . . no light, no sound, no feeling . . .

And then . . . I'm coughing. I cough and spit out what seems like a gallon of water, up onto my face and down my cheeks and neck. I gasp for breath and open my eyes and see her wet hair dangling down, her face in shadow, with the moon and the branches of the old oak tree above her. After several long, uncomfortable spasms, I try to talk as Candy hovers there above me, watching me.

"Umhhgmh," I cough.

She holds my head in her hands. "Yes. . . ?" she says.

"Uhhh . . . Ca . . . Can . . ." I sputter.

"Uh-huh?" she says softly as she strokes my hair.

"Ca . . . Can . . . dy," I finally croak out.

"Yes?" she says again.

"Candy . . . Uh . . . Candy . . ."

She remains silent.

"Candy," I say, "this is one hell of a way to finish our first kiss."

Part Three

"And I felt something tickling my stomach.
You know, Stick, like butterflies.
And the butterflies . . . the butterflies
were my friends and they wanted . . ."

Chapter Seventeen

She blurts out a sigh and laugh of relief and lowers her face to my neck and hugs me and I feel her breath against my shoulder. Then she pulls me up a little, closer to her, and puts her lips to mine and kisses me for real.

I wrap my arms around her and pull her body down on me, and we lie there together, under the moon and the stars and the old oak tree with its rope still quivering over the water. I hear the crickets and an owl way off in the distance, and every part of me hurts like hell. And I realize I never felt better.

On our way back to the car, Candy tells me that Sunny is still sleeping and that after the explosion, her woman's intuition forced her to come and see what had happened.

"I had a feeling I had to do *something*," she says. "I couldn't sit there any longer and just do nothing! I just had a feeling. It was like a bell went off in my head. I actually thought I heard a bell! I just had to do *something!*"

"Well, it's a darn good thing, too," I say, wrapping my arm around her waist and pulling her closer as we walk. "And I never realized you were a superhero."

"Huh!" she scoughs. "I had a good teacher. I saw you jump into the boat."

"Yeah, well we both got lucky. But next time could you please hit the other guy? You pack a powerful punch, you know."

"Well, you needed to be knocked down a notch," she says. "I could tell you were getting all cocky, thinking you could pull a James Bond, fighting off the bad guy on a boat speeding up river about to explode on the rocks. Some people! I swear!" she says teasingly. I pat her on her fanny and laugh.

"No more of that, you hear me?" she says in a voice still playful, but with a hint of serious.

I don't say anything.

"You hear me?" she asks again as she reaches around my waist and grabs one of the belt rings on my shorts.

"Yes 'm." I say teasingly, with a hint of serious. "Yes 'm."

We drive straight to the Holiday Inn in Charleston and have the night clerk buzz Sarah Wilson and tell her I'm in the lobby with my Sunday bonnet on. We take Sunny into Kaitlin's room and lay her on the still-made queen-size bed. I want to call an ambulance or take her to the hospital, but Candy's convinced she'll be all right. It's her woman's intuition again, I reckon.

"I just know she'll be okay," she says. "I just know it."

We clean ourselves up and Kaitlin helps and is happy to see us and concerned about Sunny and sad about Jackson and Andy Y and the judge, but accepts their fate as part of them doing the wrong thing. She hugs me and we look at each other deeply, but she can tell by her woman's intuition that something has changed between Candy and me.

Kaitlin and I are standing near the window and we look down into the parking lot. "Sorry about your car," I say. "We had a few problems."

Her jaw drops and her face turns a little pale. But after a few seconds, she gathers herself and says, "Oh, that old thing? I wanted a newer one anyway. Just gives me an excuse."

I hand her the key on the keychain, but she says, "You'll be needing that to get home."

"Uh," I say, a little embarrassed. "I guess so." I take back the key.

"I'll just take Kathy's car," she says softly. "You know, the one I came here in?"

"Got it," I reply. I pull the silver locket out of my pocket and hold it in front of me in my open palm. I look at her with raised eyebrows.

"Of course," she whispers as she pushes my fingers closed around the locket. "It's always been yours anyway."

Our eyes meet again and it takes all my will-power to stop myself from pulling her into my arms.

"But now," her eyes sparkle, "I've got a story to report, so I'm gonna get going."

We say our goodbyes with long hugs and short pecks on the cheek, and as we do, we each realize that we three are now bonded together forever in a way few people ever are. Bonded by a respect from knowing that each of us did something extraordinary. And it's not just the acts that were extraordinary, but the character that the actions sprang from:

Character that can perceive the truth, understand the truth, and act on the truth.

And a character that dares for more. A character that sees beyond, into the future, a step ahead of its own truth, to the next generation of truth. A generation of greater truth.

And at 6:12 a.m., Susan Abigail Talbert opens her eyes.

Candy strokes her forehead and we ask her how she feels and we hug her and I bring her some water that she sips slowly. I order room service and we get bacon and eggs and sausage and hash browns and grits. Candy and I gulp the food down ignoring our manners and Sunny takes a few nibbles of hash browns and then says she isn't hungry. She looks tired and pale, but Candy says, "It's nothin' that my good old chicken soup can't fix."

On the way home, Sunny falls back asleep with her head on Candy's lap and Candy nods off too. I listen to the radio and keep my window open and feel the wind toss my hair around. I drive and don't think. I just drive.

I pull into my driveway, not Candy's, and we get out and I carry Sunny into my trailer and Candy pulls back the sheets and I lay Sunny down on my bed. Candy doesn't have to tell me she'll never step foot in her house again. Call that male intuition.

"Oh, my God!" Candy says when she first steps in. "This place is a mess."

"Aw, it's not so bad. A little cluttered, but it's pretty clean."

"Clean my ass!" she says running her finger across the stovetop and showing me a glob of grease on the end of it.

"Well," I say, "maybe not the stove, but the bed sheets are clean."

"Good thing, too," she replies.

After we get Sunny in bed, Candy starts making her world famous chicken soup from a recipe handed down from McCall's Magazine, using a whole chicken with all its innards I had in the refrigerator. When Sunny wakes again in the afternoon, she eats a bowl of it, but she still looks pale and her speech is slurred and she's generally lethargic and hardly says a word. I'm concerned she's got some brain damage and I tell Candy we should take her to a doctor or hospital to have her checked out. Candy insists she's going to be okay. "All those doctors do is give you drugs anyway," she says in her simple wisdom. "And isn't that what she's recoverin' from?"

"Well, if she doesn't show more life by tomorrow mornin', we've got to do something."

"Stop buggin' me," Candy says, almost sounding like her old self. "She's gonna be all right, so just stop talking about it."

"All right. All right," I say, and I leave it alone. I get out the phone book and my personal list of numbers and start making calls. Between the phone calls I make, a bunch of people call me: the local TV station in Beaufort and the Charleston newspapers; two national TV networks; the FBI. I figure Kaitlin must be doing her job. I find out who Tom's attorney is and call him, and he tells me that Tom had put the house and land in Candy's name when they were married, even though he had advised against it. He said that Tom insisted on it so he'd save on taxes and liability or some such. He never changed it after the divorce, even though Tom said he was going to. He just never got around to it. So the land and house are all Candy's now, free and clear, and actually, always were.

Then around three, Carl, Candy's insurance agent who always had a crush on her (who hasn't?), comes by and inspects the house. He says that, in his professional opinion, the house had suffered irreparable damage due to an act of God and that Candy would be receiving a check for the replacement value of the dwelling and everything in it.

"I guess you'll be getting that new carpeting now," I tell her.

I call a guy I know who owns a construction company and all sorts of heavy equipment and he says he'll come on by tomorrow morning with his dozer and dump truck. At six, Al, the local 'I do everything and anything' guy, comes by with a moving van and loads up all the furniture and everything else to sell at his flea market in Beaufort. Candy's been walking around barefoot ever since her Tarzan impersonation last night and I tell her, "Well, you've got the barefoot part down pat. Now all you need is the pregnant."

"That'll be the day," she replies a little sarcastic, but with a smile and a glimmer of baby in her eye; a look that always seems to surface whenever a woman thinks of one.

"So do you want me to get a pair of shoes or something before Al takes it all away? Clothes, dishes, pots and pans?" I ask her.

"No. Don't bother. Just save my pictures and scrapbooks and Sunny's toys and stuffed animals. The rest of the stuff he can take away. We don't need it. But oh, get Guppy. Don't forget Guppy the Goldfish."

In the evening when it's almost dark and all the calls have been made and all of Candy's and Sunny's things are out of the house and on their way to the flea market and Guppy the Goldfish is swimming happily in his bowl that's now sitting on the tiny coffee table in my living space (you really can't call it a room, since after all, it's still a trailer), Candy and I go outside and sit in my lawn chairs under the overhang and sip lemonade Candy made earlier in the day.

"Just the way I like it," I say.

"Yeah," she replies, looking at her house. She glances up at the *Super-Duper, Super-Sticky, Super-Large, Super-Flypaper* hanging from the nail in the middle of the overhang. It has seven black flies stuck on it now. "Do we have to have that hideous monstrosity hanging there?" she asks.

"All right," I reply. "I'll get to it later." I look down at the ground and notice the anthill that had begun to form yesterday is a little bigger. "Come on," I say. "Let's go for a walk."

"No, I don't want to. Not right now."

I get up and leave Candy outside, go into the trailer and back to the bedroom. Sunny's lying on her back with her eyes closed. She's kicked the corner of the cotton sheet that's covering her off her feet, and her feet still have the little white socks on them. I sit on the side of the bed and take off her socks, take one of her feet in my hands, and rub it gently. I see a faint smile come to her lips, and her eyes creak open lazily. "Does that tickle?" I ask.

"Kinda," she smiles again, but in a way I'd never noticed her smile before. It's not a big, open-mouthed smile she might have given had she been tickled for real. And it's not a joy-filled smile like she had just gotten her favorite treat. It's a Mona Lisa smile plus. A Mona Lisa smile squared. And it wraps around my heart and makes me forget the day, my life, and how much my body still hurts. And it suddenly makes everything worthwhile and everything make sense.

"Stick?" she asks softly.

"Yes?"

"I had a dream."

"You did? What kind of dream?" I ask as I gently rub her toes.

"I had a dream I was flying . . . like a bird . . . up to the sun. I just flapped my arms and started to fly."

My hands stop moving. I look over her feet at her little head lying on the pillow, her eyes looking up at the ceiling.

"Is that so?"

"Yeah. It was fun. It was fun, Stick. I just flapped my arms and flew away."

I start rubbing her toes again. "And then what happened?"

"Well," she pauses, "I looked down, and I saw you . . . and Mama. Stick, you were on your knees, and Mama was by your side sleeping."

"Really?"

"Yeah, Stick. But you were yelling . . . yelling up at me. Not angry-like, but just worried. You know, Stick, you looked real worried."

"That's because . . . because . . ." my voice trails off.

"Because what?" Sunny asks softly. "Because what, Stick?"

"Because . . . I like you."

"Yeah, Stick," she smiles. "I know." She turns her head a little and then looks down at me for a second. Then she says, "Then all of a sudden, Stick, it got real cold."

Again, my hands stop moving. I can't believe what I'm hearing.

"And I felt something tickling my stomach. You know, Stick, like butterflies. And the butterflies . . . the butterflies were my friends and they wanted me to come home . . . to fly back home. And it was still real cold. It was so cold, Stick, I started to shiver. And I looked down and saw Momma and you still worried, so I thought I should go home and get a jacket or somethin'. So that's what I did."

I fight back a tear. I came back for her; she came back because of me. Finally, I say, "Yes, little one. I have a jacket for you. If you ever get cold, I have a jacket for you."

She looks at me and smiles again. "Thanks, Stick," she says softly as her eyelids droop. "That's nice."

I get up and go to her side and take my hand and gently stroke her forehead a couple times. Within seconds, she's fast asleep. I leave her socks off and cover her feet with the cotton sheet. You won't be needing these anymore, I think. We'll get you some new ones tomorrow. Maybe we'll buy you a jacket too, just in case. On my way out, I toss the socks into the garbage can in the bathroom.

I go outside and stand on the ground in my bare feet just in front of the steps. Candy's walking across the back lawn, behind the pool and towards her driveway. She goes around to the front of the house and I hear her car door slam. She drives the car across the side lawn, onto my grass driveway, past Kaitlin's banged-up Mustang, and up besides my pickup. She gets out and comes over to me and says, "Might as well get it out of the way now." She passes me as she climbs the steps, opens the trailer door, and takes a step inside.

"Would you please make some room in here?" she asks. "It looks like we're gonna be here a while."

"Yeah. I'll clear out my books and some other stuff tomorrow."

"Okay," she says as she reaches down and pats me on the head. "I'm soooo tired. I'm going to bed."

"Okay. Sleep tight." I say as she heads for the bedroom. "Oh, Candy," I call after her.

"What?"

"If you hear something crawling around in the middle of the night, don't pay it any mind. It's just my pet dung-beetle Greg movin' out."

"What?" she gasps. "What the heck are you talkin' about?"

"Just kiddin'. Just kiddin'. Don't worry about it. I'll explain some other time."

"Well, tomorrow we clean. I'm not gonna have any dung-beetles or whatever they are livin' in my house!" She shakes her head, "You're still very weird, you know." She goes in the bedroom and closes the door.

I come inside and go into the living area and turn on the TV. The national news is on, so I sit on the couch and put my bare feet up on the coffee table. Guppy looks at me through his glass bowl and gulps at me as gold fish will do. The TV announcer says, "Earlier today we reported about the massive explosion that rocked this quiet, Lowcountry county. Here again, with an update, is local news correspondent Kaitlin Carlisle. Kaitlin, tell us again what happened, and are there any new developments?"

Kaitlin appears on the screen, holding a microphone to her lips. Her eyes are serious and focused, but her lips are, of course, smiling a little. She says in a professional, serious voice, "Thank you, Dan. Less than twenty-four hours ago, at three in the morning, a drug deal turned deadly. A simple little light bulb touched off an explosion that was heard and felt fifteen miles away . . ."

I watch her fascinated and proud as she reports what happened. The TV shows taped coverage from earlier, panning across the pier and river and oak tree, showing close ups of the crater and junk and remains of the boat. It turns out a major producer who saw the broadcast was fascinated by Kaitlin too and flew her up to New York for an interview. She ended up becoming one of the first women TV news anchors in the country. But after just over a year, she quit and came home with her new fiancé saying she soon realized something her daddy always told her was true:

You can take the girl out of the Lowcountry, but you can't take the Lowcountry out of the girl. She and her fiancé, Aaron, bought a farm out halfway to Charleston. They never did get married. But that's another story.

I turn off the TV and lay on the couch. My stitches are tight and stinging, and my body still aches all over. But I've gotten kinda used to it. I close my eyes and quickly fall into a deep, dreamless sleep.

Chapter Eighteen

My eyes open and it's still dark. I look at the clock on the stove: 2:46. I poke my head into the bedroom and the moonlight coming through the single window reveals Sunny and Candy nestled together sleeping peacefully.

I go outside in my bare feet, yawn, and stretch. Something crawls across my big toe, so I jerk my foot up and swat it away. The anthill. I go behind the trailer to the shed and get the can of gasoline I use for the lawnmower and bring it back and pour some on the small mound that's formed overnight. I step out from under the overhang and look at the waning moon, just killing time waiting for the fluid to soak in. I find some matches in the kitchen and come outside and light one and toss it on the anthill. The fluid explodes up and out, and the flames shoot up all the way to the overhang. I watch as the flypaper that's still hanging there with seven dead flies on it catches on fire and slowly and harmlessly burns itself up, twisting and turning with muffled, agonizing sighs.

As flaming and glowing embers drop off the flypaper, Candy opens the door, and from still inside the trailer, watches them fall into the dying flames of the anthill. Like the embers of fireworks flaming out as they fall to earth on the 4th of July, we watch them—as if it was the first time we'd ever seen them. Like we're mesmerized kids. And Candy doesn't say a thing. But I see her face, and it's not sad, and you could even say it's peaceful. After a few seconds, she just closes the door.

The dying flames of the falling flypaper remind me of the white, tattered cloth burning itself out over the crater last night. And I whisper to myself, "You done good, Miss Chimes. You done real good. You may not have saved yourself from slavery, but you saved a lot of people from becoming slaves in a different way. And you helped save a little girl, a daughter, and a son. You just had to wait a century or so to leave your mark. But what's a little time amongst friends? So you done real good, Martha, and we thank you."

The next year on the anniversary, on the morning after the summer solstice, I snuck out to River-hole. I took a watch. At three a.m., I listened for the bell. I didn't hear a thing.

I take my lawn chair and then the other one and fold them up and take them to the trash besides Candy's house and leave them on the heap. Then I go back in front of my trailer, out from under the overhang on the lawn where I used to sit in my lawn chair, and lay down on the ground. I stretch out my arms and legs and look up to the night. I wonder what, if any, dreams I'll have tonight. Then I think back to the dreams I had a few nights ago.

I see a star shoot across the sky.

I think about the filthy man in the barn and how he started that chain of sin that was passed to his daughter and then her daughter and then me. And I realize that with each passing of that baton, the sin was less and less severe, until now, it's finally burned itself out.

And I realize that my mom and my mom's mom must not have *not* tried very hard like I had so bitterly thought. They must have held fast in their own ways, because although their efforts or consciousnesses weren't up to putting an end to the abuse completely—the abuse that may have started even before my great grandfather—they slowed it down, and even reversed it. They didn't even know what they were doing or why. But something made them do it. Something made them try.

And Candy and me, we didn't know what we were doing either. But somehow we found a way to handle the curves on the road through the swamps and save ourselves from drowning in the river that sweeps so many souls away. Now, at least in our little corner the world, there's some sanity and some peace. And a little blond-haired girl who wants to marry Donny Osmond and who runs around barefoot pretending to be an airplane and who thinks dandelions are the most beautiful things, will be able to live a life that every little girl—and the woman she will become—deserves.

And don't we all. And let's hope that *that* kind of baton starts getting passed along.

The bull frogs are quiet and there's no cars on the highway, and I feel almost satisfied and keep looking at the stars. Another one streaks across the black sky, and as I follow it, I realize that the past—my past—is okay now. I no longer need or want to change it.

I realize that all those things that kept getting in my way—all those things I made happen because of the stress and strain of being so twisted up—happened because I was punishing myself. The weird thing is, I was punishing myself for things that *I* didn't do.

Then it's like a giant boulder rolls off my chest when it dawns on me that because I no longer need to change the past, I no longer want to try and control the future. They very well may be—when it's all said and done—one and the same thing anyway.

I see the crescent moon above me and with the way I tilt my head to look at it, its corners are both turned up, such that, with a couple twinkling stars imagined as eyes, it looks like the universe is smiling. So I smile too. Life can be good, I think. I don't remember closing my eyes.

I wake up to somebody pulling my arm.

"Sticker! Sticker! Wake up!"

I hear a voice I've been anxiously waiting to hear.

"You fell asleep on the ground! That's so dumb, Sticker! Why'd you fall asleep on the ground?"

"Huh?"

"I said wake up!"

"Five more minutes," I mumble and turn over, pretending to go back to sleep.

"Get up, Sticker! Mama's getting breakfast ready!"

"The sun's not even up yet. What's the hurry?"

"Come onnn! Stick!" She tugs on my arm again. "Come onnnn!"

"Okay. Okay. I'm awake," I say, trying to sound testy. "Thanks to you!" I let her pull me up and I brush the sand off me and give her a hug and she hugs me back and we go inside and stand at the table.

"Here," Candy says to Sunny. "One more bowl of chicken soup and then you can start eating normal food again."

"Aww, Mom! Not more soup!"

"Don't 'Aw Mom' me," Candy says matter-of-factly. "Now sit down and eat and no more complaining." Sunny sits down with the faintest little smile on her lips and starts slurping soup up off the spoon.

"Soft boiled eggs for me?" I ask with a raised eyebrow as she puts one in front of me.

"Yes."

"But I'd rather have them fried . . . or even raw."

"And I'd rather drive a Mercedes. Eat!"

We finish breakfast and hear rumbling outside. We all go outside into the fresh morning air in our bare feet and see the dump truck and trailer with a bulldozer on it pull into Candy's driveway and then around up besides the swimming pool. Sunny starts flitting around, following a butterfly, as Candy and I stand in front of the trailer out from under the overhang with the burned-out remnants of the flypaper. The bulldozer's engine roars to life and we watch the big machine come down the ramp and into the yard. It creeps around the pool, over the deck, over the back porch, and slams into the house right near the back door. We hear the wood crack and crumble as the roof falls in. Sunny pauses in her play and watches in a sort of detached wonder. But she turns to us and smiles, and skips over and holds up to her mother a fistful of fresh, yellow dandelions.

"Momma! Momma! Here! These are for you!" she chimes.

Candy reaches down and takes the flowers and says, "Thank you sweetheart. They're very pretty."

"You see," Sunny insists, "yellow is their favorite color and they love you *so much* they want you to have it!" Then she skips away again and after a couple steps, reaches down and plucks another dandelion, but one that had gone to seed. "Here, Sticker," she skips back and holds it out to me. "And this one's for you!" she giggles.

I take the stem. "Thanks a lot!" I moan and roll my eyes and hold it in front of me with a tight-lipped smile. Candy pulls my hand and playfully blows on the puffball. The seeds spray up and out into the fresh morning air that's heavy with dew, and they hang there, almost twinkling in the early morning light. We laugh quietly, and then watch them for several moments without speaking, as eventually, they fall towards earth.

Then Candy shifts her gaze to the house that's slowly being leveled and her voice becomes somber. "It's scary," she says softly.

"I know," I reply.

"Can we do it, Sam?" she asks longingly, pleadingly, looking up to me until our eyes meet.

"Only time will tell," I reply, gazing into her eyes. "But I have a feeling, that somehow, we'll find a way."

Together we watch that old double-wide fall as the sun slowly rises beyond the house, over the cypress trees dripping with Spanish moss. Candy leans her head on my shoulder and wraps her arm around my waist, and surprisingly, I feel a subtle, yet perceptible, rising of my own.

And I realize I've spent a long time in the dark, having been abandoned in the void. Forced down. To the bottom. To the bottom of the bottom where you can never fall again. Where you can never fall any lower, because you were left there . . . alone.

Then the decision. The decision to not forget and to not forgive and to not give up. To not give up but to fight like hell. To fight like hell to get up out of that darkness. That darkness that was injected into you—by somebody *else*.

Then the question. There has to be the question. Or rather, a multitude of questions that become just one that you need two to answer. For in the end, the answer comes by not just looking into your own blackness, but by looking out from that blackness into the blackness of another—letting them touch . . . letting them mingle . . . letting them complete each other's darkness . . . into light.

The child.

And to know that with that light, with that child, you are trying harder. Now, you can forget. Now, you can forgive. Now, you can get past your past. Now, you can get past . . . *that*.

You see, the past doesn't matter all that much. It's over. Done. What's more important is what you do for the future. Because part of that future is really the present and what we think is the present is really the past. And as I said, the past is over.

As the sun climbs into the sky and warms the land and dissipates the early morning mist, I feel a warm, tender hand nestle softly into mine. And I hear the sound of laughter very close by. I stand here, feeling strong, supported. I look towards the rising sun.

My name is Sam.

And I think . . .

I found . . .

About the Author

Samuel Othello Barlow was born in the mountains of South Carolina in 1966. He endured a tumultuous childhood and adolescence there, but found the courage to leave just before his 20th birthday. After an eventful several years of "living on the edge in just about every way imaginable," he finally ended up in a place the total antithesis of the mountains—the Lowcountry of South Carolina.

Although he never attended college, he's studied a myriad of subjects such as calculus, physics, astronomy, athletics, music, survival, anatomy, physiology, microbiology, psychology, nutrition, yoga, karate, and economics. Among other ways of earning a living, he's worked as a painter, construction worker, lab assistant, office manager, printer, and pizza delivery boy. He's worked on fishing boats in the Gulf of Mexico and dug his own outhouse while living in a shack in the mountains. His eclectic experiences give him unique and thought provoking opinions on history, humanity, science, and life in general.

He wrote Lowcountry Rising over the course of a year and a half while working as a prison guard in a Federal prison. He commented, "You learn that there are criminals who deserve to be there, men who are innocent but were set up to be there, and that turning a profit is more important than serving justice."

Lowcountry Rising is Mr. Barlow's debut novel, and he's currently working on the next book in the upcoming trilogy titled Upcountry Crossing. Its date of release is scheduled for the fall of 2015, but that is uncertain because Mr. Barlow says he'll finish it, "When I darn well feel like it." Please check the website for updates.

The secrets in the swamps are calling . . .

Down in the Lowcountry

www.LowcountryRising.com

www.ingramcontent.com/pod-product-compliance
Lightning Source LLC
Chambersburg PA
CBHW070000120726
47909CB00003B/756